W9-BXL-942

"The Wonderland Trials is everything I want in an *Alice* retelling: magic and family and infuriatingly adorable romance, all bound together in a story that rejects—and even redefines—the impossible. Sara Ella has written an addicting concoction of courage, clues, and mysterious white-rabbit trails that will keep you guessing, keep you gulping your if-only-it-was-magical tea, and keep you turning pages through all topsy-turvy hours of the night."

— NADINE BRANDES, award-winning author of *Romanov, Fawkes,* and the
Out of Time series

"The Wonderland Trials' fresh, modern take on a classic beckoned me down the rabbit hole—and I never want to leave! With plenty of nods to the original story, Sara Ella has crafted a world where fantasy bleeds into reality, and one never knows where the game stops and real life begins. This is *Alice* reimagined, and I'm all in."

— LINDSAY A. FRANKLIN, award-winning author of *The Story Peddler*

THE CURIOUS REALITIES BOOK 1

THE
WONDERLAND
TRIALS

Books by Sara Ella

The Unblemished Trilogy
Unblemished
Unraveling
Unbreakable

Coral

The Curious Realities series
The Wonderland Trials

THE CURIOUS REALITIES BOOK 1

THE WONDERLAND TRIALS

SARA ELLA

For the Daddy who raised me—
You have always believed I was capable of anything.
Thank you for showing me that nothing is impossible.

And in loving memory of the Man who brought me into this world—
You showed me love comes in many forms.
Thank you for loving me enough to let me go.

And, finally, for the Father who gave me life—
You are the King of Hearts.
Thank you for saving mine.

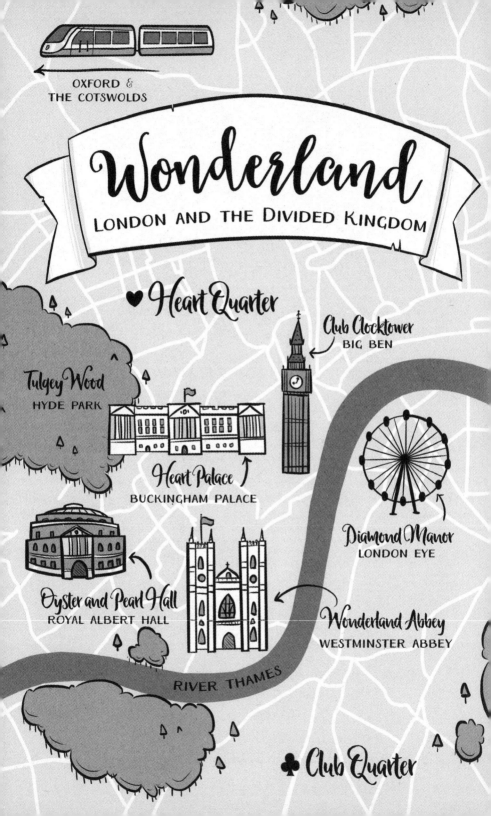

Croquet Stadium
LONDON STADIUM &
QUEEN ELIZABETH
OLYMPIC PARK

◆ Diamond Quarter

Wonderland Children's Hospital
ROYAL LONDON HOSPITAL

Spade Castle
TOWER OF LONDON

WHITECHAPEL &
EAST END

River Tuny

Topsy Bridge
TOWER BRIDGE

Pool of Tears
POOL OF LONDON

N
W   E
S

♠ Spade Quarter

THE TULGEY WOOD

Only someone as mad as a hatter—as the saying goes—would risk her life to win a game.

But this isn't a game. Not anymore.

Any Wonder who's entered my life has managed to turn everything topsy-turvy, upside down, and backwards. I'm the girl in the looking glass. Mirrored. Off balance. Flipped.

I inhale a clipped breath. Pain stabs my heart which *beats, beats, beats* in time with the second hand of the locket watch around my neck.

Beat, beat, beat. Tick, tock, tick.

My eyes close, and the dread kicks in. The same fear that always overtakes me when I'm about to enter a nightmare. The only difference is, this time, it's real.

I have to finish what I started.

When I open my eyes, I step through.

No, this isn't a game anymore.

This is my *life*.

And if I don't risk it?

Then mine won't be the only heart we lose tonight.

SOLITAIRE

"Who in the world am I?
Ah, that's the great puzzle."

— Lewis Carroll, *Alice's Adventures in Wonderland*

CURIOUS

"And thus the United Kingdom was no more, ushering in a kingdom quite divided indeed, following the conquest of the late—"

I groan at the advert droning on through my soundbuds—an unusual find, courtesy of the most intolerable human I've ever had the displeasure of meeting. The advert's not his fault, though. I've heard the historical propaganda more times than I care to count. Let's just say history is not my cup of tea.

The sound glitches in and out, and I flick the side of the right earpiece, which emits static in return. I mute the ad, unplug my soundbuds, then plug them back in. After thirty seconds pass, I tap the volume icon on my cracked, three-decades-old pocketscreen, changing the colour from red to green. Any second now. Wait for it . . .

A rush of orchestral intro music swells and fades. Finally. The sound isn't high quality, but the episode I downloaded the moment I stepped foot off campus flows clearly through both earpieces now. I turn the volume up a little more as the podcast host begins.

"How do you do, and welcome to episode one hundred and seventeen of *Common Nonsense*. I'm your hostess, Madi Hatter, and I'll be interrupting your regular daily dose of sensibility to discuss the predictable topic out of the hat, otherwise referred to as this year's annual Wonderland Trials."

Her American accent never fails to fascinate me. Not because it's anything special, but because it's rare. After the Divide, the queen closed all of England's borders and forbade international travel, cutting all ties with the United Kingdom and severing former peace treaties with neighbouring nations. Most foreigners were immediately sent back to their respective homes. But foreign Wonders? Denied passports if they refused to Register. It was either conform or go into hiding.

There's no question as to which route Madi's parents chose. If I had to make such a decision, would I be as fearless?

My pulse quickens. Rather than ponder the disappointing answer, I slide my thumb across the palm-sized screen, cranking up the volume as I make my trek to the Oxford railway station, checking over my shoulder every so often. I keep the hood of my pullover up, careful to conceal my rare form of mobile tech as I walk west down Park End Street, stealing a glance at the ditch that was once Castle Mill Stream. Most people only have ancient antenna radios at home, just good enough for boring old news. At school, they block most signals entirely. One must have an approved permit stamped with the queen's seal to use authorised tech. If the wrong person were to catch me with an unsanctioned pocketscreen and soundbuds?

They wouldn't think twice before turning me over to the authorities.

Either that or they'd slit my throat to get their grubby hands on what I possess.

I don't know whether I ought to thank Chess or curse him for the inevitable sentence he's bestowed upon my head.

After I cross Pacey's Bridge, I make a sharp right to go north on Upper Fisher Row, following the familiar footpath along the dry bank. Funny how they kept some of the old names from before the Divide—our city, our streets—but did away with most everything else.

"For those of you listeners who might be joining our little party for the first time, welcome! I'd shake hands with you if I could, but alas, we are restricted to this form of archaic—and rather illegal, depending on who you are—connection."

I laugh out loud at that. Tech wouldn't have to be archaic or illegal for most if our monarch wasn't so afraid of the Wonders who invented it.

"And to my faithful followers who are mad enough to return," Madi continues, "grab a clean cup of your favourite drink. Settle in. Because today's episode is sure to be our best yet!"

For two years I've listened to this snarky American girl ramble on about everything from Wonder fashion to why treacle ought to be used to sweeten practically everything. I almost feel as if I know her. And if we met . . . perhaps we might become friends. I'm not supposed to have access to her podcast, but there's always a way into restricted and off-limits places. If one knows where to look.

Or whom to ask.

"It's been a while since we've brought up last year's results, so let's have a quick review." A drumroll sound bite ensues. "First runner-up was Team Spade, led by the elusive Chess Shire, losing by a mere point."

A sour taste fills my mouth. *Chess Shire.* Wonderland's poster boy. Infamous for frequenting the underground—a.k.a. *Wonder*ground—card tournaments I attend. Dependable as ever when it comes to pestering me at said card tournaments.

If he didn't peddle the most hard-to-come-by items, I'd ignore him entirely. Born into an established Wonder family, Chess has had everything handed to him on a silver platter, plus some pudding on the side. Girls swoon. Lads line up for his autograph—or so he's told me countless times. He's perfect, his skills matched by none.

Except by the one who beat him.

I smirk as Madi adds, "Of course you all remember that it was my very own big brother and Team Diamond King—Stark—who took the lead in the end." A round of applause fills my ears. "We Hatters are no strangers to the Trials, of course. Ten years ago, at the ripe age of sixteen, my oldest brother Raving played for Team Club as an Ace. Raving now works as a Trial consultant in the Club Quarter, where he happily advises the Lord of Clubs himself on Wonderland Trial matters."

Team King. Ace. Game consultant. Madi's family history alone makes her a shoo-in for the Trials this year. She's sixteen. I'm actually shocked she hasn't been invited yet. While it's rumoured players much younger were once permitted to compete, a tragic accident many years ago drove Trial officials to raise the age requirement to thirteen.

"As for Stark," Madi goes on, "he's been so busy with his new internship at Diamond Manor, I haven't seen him in months. The Wonderland Trials are about more than fame and fortune, people—although there is a hefty sum involved for the winners—they're about opportunity for the next generation. And finding where you're truly meant to be. Why, Stark has been offered a position as Team Diamond Trainer this year." Madi squeals, and another sound bite of applause carries through my headphones.

Though I've never seen a photo of Madi, when I close my eyes, I imagine what she looks like when she speaks of her brother. Smug expression. Immeasurably proud. And, of course, determined to one-up him when her time comes.

The idea of sibling rivalry is not foreign to me. Charlotte and I have had our fair share of spats. She thinks because she's a decade older she can boss me around whenever she pleases. Always saying, "Mind your manners, Alice," or "That is quite enough, Alice," with not even a hint of a smile drawing the dimpled corner of her lips. So serious. Forever a pain in my neck.

Another advert commences as I approach the train station—this one a reminder that curfew-breakers will face dire consequences. A Wonder podcast shouldn't have adverts. But for all the tech hacks and ways around the rules, the insufferable messages remain.

I lower the volume again, concealing my pocketscreen, double-checking that my soundbuds and nuisance cord are hidden by my pullover, and aim for the walk-up eatery window, which sits nestled between two pillars on the platform. A vintage sign that reads "Mary Ann's" arches over the quick-serve restaurant in bold iron letters. The scent of fish and chips wafts towards me.

Instead, I order the least expensive option—a half ham sandwich and a bag of crisps. Who needs fish and chips? Someday, full buffets with all-I-can-eat everything will be on the daily menu.

The advert ends, and Madi returns, finally getting to the part of this episode I've been waiting for. She released it days ago and, as usual, I'm behind.

"If you happen to be one of many hopefuls itching to enter the Trials this year," she says, "a few reminders. First, all entrants must be at least thirteen years of age and no older than nineteen. Rules are rules, and this one's unbreakable."

Check. I'm well over the minimum age requirement. I recently turned sixteen. I think. Since I only know the general time of year I was born, and not the actual date, Charlotte had to guess one for my legal papers. Seventeen March. An Irish holiday from the previous era, now a day that marks another year passing. Another year I'm stuck here. Either way, I'm over thirteen. And each year, I get closer to aging out. If I'm not invited this year, I only have three chances left.

"Second, the Trials are by invitation only. Each season's curious invites are a bit different. And each quarter likes to put their own spin on it. Last year, several Wildflower contestants invited by the Club Quarter were given a password which they had to decode before the entry window closed. The previous year saw a number of forfeited entries, due to a particularly difficult task set forth by the Spades that involved pepper and a teacup pig."

I tap "pause." Ah, yes. Fans discussed the incident for months inside incognito chat rooms and encrypted groups on the internet's clandestine social network. Another rule of the many I've broken. One post claimed the contestant ended up in the hospital after a severe allergy caused her to sneeze nonstop for two weeks straight.

When my order is ready, I take the brown paper sack and find a vacant bench. I've only eaten a few crisps when the unmistakable sound of a train approaching has me shoving my dinner out of sight.

A rush of air sends my hood backwards. I yank it back up, whipping my head left and right. My pulse hastens as a security guard marches straight towards me.

He saw my soundbuds. He must have. This is not good. I have to get out of here. I have to—

But he strides past me, not bothering to pay me a second glance.

To say my sigh of relief affects my entire body would be an understatement. Even my toes, which were clenched tight inside my Mary Jane shoes, relax.

When the train comes to a complete stop and the conductor steps down onto the yellow-lined platform, I rise and take a step forwards. Close my eyes to shield them from the wind.

When I open them again, my vision blurs. The all-too-familiar sensation of vertigo makes me feel as if I'm shifting on an invisible wave to my right. Music swells. The same haunting melody that accompanies my nightmares.

"'Ey, kid, you okay?" the conductor asks.

I rub at my left temple with two fingers. Blink. The moment my sight clears, I shudder. Clutch the concealed device in my pocket. No noise passes through my soundbuds. Where was that music coming from? No matter how often I try to place its source, to help myself feel a bit less mad, nothing comes of it.

"Kid," the man says again. "You'd better board if that's what you're after. Otherwise, step behind the yellow line." His particular dialect tells me he's from up north, but there's a bit of Londoner in there too.

And, as if it never happened, the sensation is gone. The melody dissolves. I blink again. Adjust my square-framed glasses. And nod. "Fine," I say to the conductor, focusing on my target. My arm brushes his as I pass by.

He startles.

I stumble. This, however, is not a result of my momentary lack of balance—or sanity.

"Wotcher!" he says, a nasty look wrinkling the already prominent lines on his forehead and around his mouth.

"Pardon, sir." I offer my apology, distracting him with eye contact and my schoolgirl clumsiness.

He sniffs, turns a cold shoulder, and proceeds ignoring me.

When I board, out of his sight and mind, I open the billfold I swiped from his back pocket and remove a few fivers and a tenner. A smart thief never takes everything. They snatch enough to make the con worth it, but not so much it's obvious something was stolen. Not right away, at least.

Placing the billfold on the top step, I move deeper into the train. When the conductor finds his belonging, he'll assume he dropped it. If he notices some notes missing, he might question it. But suspect a thief? Most likely not.

After all, what sort of thief leaves fifty quid untouched?

I wrinkle my nose at the unpleasant fragrance of sweat and stale air freshener. I trek down the aisle to the next car, hunkering down in an empty seat beside an open window where I can breathe in some fresh air. Finally able to relax, I unzip my pullover and unbutton the collar of my cornflower-blue shirt. My Bedford check skirt rides up too high when I shift. I tug it towards my knees, wishing I'd had time to change into something more comfortable.

At least I have my black-and-white-striped tights, the one semblance of personality we're allowed at Great Expectations Preparatory Academy. Once upon a time, year-twelve girls weren't required to wear uniforms, an opportunity to discover their own creative expression. Since I'm one year ahead of my age, that would've been me this year. The Divide changed everything, though.

Creativity, personality, talent?

Nonexistent.

Reform, conform, uniform?

These mean everything in a world where standing out too much is an unspoken crime of its own.

And tech? What a joke. I'm grateful I have my soundbuds and a pocketscreen that will actually turn on. They say advanced technology is what led to the Divide in the first place. It's why the Modern Monarchy aimed to return to what Her Majesty refers to as "simpler times" and declared only "necessary and acceptable use" of tech would be allowed. And monitored. Centuries before, there was a democracy, a Prime Minister, Parliament. Now you're fortunate if you can find a decent device to play music on—and a signal with which to download it from pirated sites. And if you can? You're one of the lucky ones if it's not confiscated and destroyed—or stolen—before you've had a chance to use it.

I hug my rucksack to my chest and check my reflection in the window to ensure my soundbuds remain hidden. Then I lean my head against the window frame and press "play." Enough interruptions. I've been looking forward to this all week.

"Third," Madi continues in my ear, "and this is perhaps the most vital requirement of them all. All entrants must have tested positive for the Wonder Gene at birth. An original copy of your birth certificate is mandatory. Contestants must also provide a signed permission slip from their parent or legal guardian."

I slump lower in my seat. There's the clincher. I don't have a copy of my original birth certificate. If by slim chance I did have the Gene, the vital record is, well, vital. Besides, Charlotte would never allow me to participate.

"You are Normal, like me," she'd say. *"And if you did have the Gene, we'd simply Register you, and that would be that."*

Register? She might as well issue my death decree. Everyone knows Registered Wonders are treated worse than dossers or street workers. It's why most Wonders have retreated underground, gone Rogue, escaped to the hidden safe haven known as Wonderland. Not even Her Majesty the Queen knows its location.

The train lurches. I bump my head hard against the window—*ouch!*—and my rucksack falls to my feet. I press "pause" and reach for my things, gathering a few loose items that have scattered. A worn pack of cards. My locket watch. A tiny corked vial containing a few drops of reddish tea. I've carried the thing since I can remember. Ironic really. I'm deathly allergic to the stuff, same as my sister. Yet Charlotte—who doesn't like me crossing the street on my own—insists I always keep it on me.

"Follow my advice," Charlotte said when she gave me the morbid token years ago. "Never take risks. Even the smallest ones can kill you."

I stare at the vial, at the single word printed across one side. *Poison.*

Like so many times before, I consider tossing the thing. Who in their right mind carries around a bottle of poison? Unless, of course, they intend to use it? What if I'm not actually allergic to tea? After all, I've only ever taken Charlotte's word for it. Perhaps just a drop, to see what might transpire?

Twisting the cork this way and that, I loosen it a smidge. Smelling it won't kill me, right?

I shake my head. What am I doing? Have I gone mental?

I tighten the cork. Store the vial in my sack, removing the temptation.

No one is that curious.

VANISHED

Yawning is dangerous.

I'd better set my alarm. Just in case.

The silver locket watch is my least valuable possession. I couldn't pawn the thing if I tried. The metal encasing the timepiece isn't true silver but a cheap knockoff. The glass inside is cracked. Besides, I have my pocketscreen, which tells the time just fine.

Except, the nuisance alarm on my pocketscreen can't save me. I've tried. In contrast, the locket watch might as well be my knight in tarnished armour. I open it slowly, careful not to disturb the fragile hinge too much. The colourful scene on the clock's face never fails to mesmerise me—a watercolour image featuring a bed of bright flowers blossoming along a lush riverbank. At the scene's centre is a small window, revealing the real gem hidden underneath.

I turn the tiny key-shaped knob on one side, moving the fourth and fifth hands until they're set. If I do fall asleep—which is likely—the tiny music box within the watch will wake me before we arrive at our destination. Once it's around my neck, the watch rests over my heart. I tuck it safely under my shirt, the metal cooling my skin.

It may not be worth ten pence, but the heirloom is everything to me.

The sole item left behind by my parents.

A few passengers make their way down the car's aisle, the same tired nine-to-fivers one might expect to board the six o'clock train.

"Vait!" a distinguished voice calls from the platform below.

I sit straighter, craning to see.

A slender woman wearing a fascinator atop her primped head waves her arms frantically.

She'll never make it. The train's already started moving. There's not enough—

And then she's gone. Vanished. One moment there and the next, poof. Nothing.

I sit back. Blink. What on earth? Have I already fallen asleep?

"Oh, dear. I do beg your pardon, *monsieur*," a female voice says.

I slide to the aisle seat, twisting towards the speaker's direction.

It's *her*. But . . . how can that be?

She brushes off her pleated, cream-coloured trousers, then tugs on a pair of lacy fingerless gloves while holding a small fan between her teeth. Once finished, she flourishes the fan and flips it open, withdrawing a pocket watch on a chain with her free hand. "I am alvays terribly late, you zee," she tells the conductor. "I am told my clock eez two days slow."

Her voice. That accent. White hair pulled into a flawless bun. Why is she so familiar and foreign at the same time?

"Move down. Move down." The conductor waves on a pair of passengers lingering between the cars.

Is he really so dense? He must have noticed her vanishing act.

Then again, the notes in my pocket relay he is, in fact, very dense indeed.

The woman *click clacks* towards me in a pair of pompadour heels, fanning her face as she nears.

I face forwards, slowing the breaths that somehow had picked up speed.

When she reaches me, she pauses. Lowers the fan. Pockets the watch inside her fitted white waistcoat.

My own watch ticks in time with my pulse.

"Eez zis seat accounted for?"

I glance up at her and take in a sharp breath. How did I miss it? She's as recognisable as the Wonder Queen—known to most as Lady Scarlet—herself.

Blanche de Lapin. Rogue Wonder. Wanted outlaw. Unregistered foreigner. The reward for turning her in alone could set one up in a high-rise London flat for a year.

I scoot towards the window.

Seemingly satisfied, Blanche sits beside me.

Lady Scarlet's most trusted advisor is *here*? Why? And how did she slip past the conductor unnoticed? If I don't turn her in, he most certainly will. Wonders don't usually ride the train, or travel in broad daylight, for that matter. Yet here she is, Blanche de Lapin, in the flesh.

I shift uncomfortably, pressing myself against the window and drawing my rucksack onto my lap. An inked daisy chain trails along the plain canvas of my bag. I trace the petals with my fingers, calming my nerves with each pass over the black drawing.

"You can learn a lot ov zings from zee flowers," Blanche says.

My curious expression does nothing to alter her amused one.

"Train pass?" the conductor asks.

Startled, I fumble to find the little plastic card with a barcode and my photo. Once he scans my pass and I'm cleared, he ambles away, trousers drooping at his hips.

He never asked Blanche for her pass.

Shock doesn't begin to cover what I'm experiencing. Doesn't he notice there's a wanted Wonder travelling with us? He must be one of the few Wonder sympathisers. There's no other explanation. That, or he didn't see her.

How could he not *see* her?

My gaze follows the conductor until he's out of sight. All I would have to do is feign a need to use the facilities, then find the emergency mobile. I could alert the authorities. They'd meet us at the next station. I'd be considered a law-abiding citizen by the crown. The reward would be in my hands within days. I could move out of my dormitory, start my new life in London before the season changes, and—

Movement catches my attention. I watch from the corner of my eye as Blanche opens her handbag and places the fan inside. Next she withdraws a . . . book?

My eyes widen. I stare at the seat back in front of me.

Charlotte would forget all propriety and ask to hold the tome if she were here. Books are my sister's Holy Grail. And while tech is outdated and hard to come by, books in their original sewn bindings are all the rarer. And the one Blanche holds, covered in a dust jacket?

That's unheard of.

Most reading material available now is mass-produced. Printed on the thinnest, cheapest paper with nothing but a plain white cover featuring the title and author in basic font.

No pictures.

No cover illustrations.

I shift, hoping Blanche won't notice my wandering gaze. Perhaps I might catch a glimpse of something I can tell Charlotte about.

Then again, Charlotte doesn't know I'm on a train.

Blanche moves her elbow a few inches forwards on the armrest, blocking my view.

Disappointed, I feel for my pocketscreen inside my pullover and press "play" once more. I'm not too worried about Blanche noticing. Her very existence is illegal. I doubt she'd report me for a bit of measly tech.

Madi prattles off a few statistics, sharing how, more often than not, all-boy teams tend to take the lead in the Trials year after year. "But not this time," she says. "As you know, I also have the Wonder Gene. Now I'm pleased to announce that, like my brothers before me, I've been invited to play in the Trials."

Bravo! Well done, Madi!

"While the official rules state I cannot reveal the contents of my invitation or the details of my position or team, I *can* say that something tells me this year's Trials will be the most challenging yet! To all you Wildflowers outside of Wonderland who face the extra test of finding your way in to our humble home, cheers! It is to you I raise my teacup."

Wildflowers. Those in our Normal world who've been handpicked, given a chance to escape this mundane life and join the Wonders in their hidden haven. There's at least one each year. No Wildflower has ever played on a winning team, of course, so it's a mystery as to why they keep showing up in the Trials. Their chances are slim to none of reaching a high score. But the tradeoff is Wonderland. Who cares if they lose? The life upgrade is a prize of its own.

"Let the Trials begin!" With another squeal and swell of music, my favourite podcaster transitions into the history behind the Wonderland Trials, along with her predictions about what this season might hold.

"The four Trials are different every year, but we do know . . ."

I take the opportunity to close my eyes. Settle in after a

long day of dull lessons and card practice under my desk at school. The four suits or quarters of Wonderland make up four competing teams.

Diamonds.

Spades.

Clubs.

And Hearts, the Wonder Queen's very own.

Most players consist of Wonder-borns like Madi—those who grew up in Wonderland with a Wonder family. They receive special training and preparation in their chosen Mastery—a unique skillset that makes them invaluable to their team.

And then there are those who grew up outside of it all. Some call us Wonder-less. Others are a bit harsher and say we are Unders. Those who believe the Wonders to be dangerous, unnatural, abominations—ahem, like my sister—simply call us Normals.

Is there such a thing?

What would it be like to be a Wildflower? To receive an invitation to join the Wonderland Trials?

I guess I'll never know. No birth certificate. No test. No Gene.

I drift in and out of consciousness. Every bump and sway rocks me deeper into a daydream. If I'm fortunate, a daydream is all it will be.

My eyelids fight the fatigue weighing them down.

Madi's words swirl on a colourful carousel through my thoughts. I've heard it all before. I catch bits and pieces but know I'll have to replay the entire episode when I'm not so knackered.

"Not everyone with the Gene has what it takes to face the challenges of the Trials. Thus the need for invitations."

Nod.

"The entrance to Wonderland is hidden. Wildflowers who are invited must find their way in. A pretest, if you will."

Inhale.

"Once you've entered Wonderland, you will never see things the same way again. Wildflowers, come prepared to give up Normalcy in every sense of the idea. And if you do return to the life of a Normal, you'll most likely end up Registered. And alone."

Hmmm . . . Yawn.

"Of course, my listeners know I'm ever the optimist! I like to believe there's always a way home, if you wish to find it."

Stretch. Shift.

"The risk for any Wildflower is always higher. Wonderborns know the ins and outs of life in the Wonderground. We come and go from Wonderland as we please, slithy as a tove at brillig. Since I don't believe in luck, let me offer another 'Cheers!' and give you my best. You're going to need it."

Sigh.

"I'll keep you updated as much as I can during the Trials. Until then, remember," Madi says, ending with her signature line, "nonsense is as common as nonsense ought to be, so let's all congratulate us with another cup of tea!"

"End of line!" the conductor calls.

I sit up and push the hair away from my face, wiping a bit of drool from my chin. Lovely. We're here already? When did day turn to nightfall?

The bright melody I know inside and out plays from my locket watch. The inscription on the back notes the title—"All in the Golden Afternoon." I have never heard the lyrics, but I imagine they speak of a place better than here.

A glance at the time reveals over an hour has passed, taking us well beyond the quiet streets of Oxford and into the countryside.

The Cotswolds.

Graffiti covers the walls of every cottage and corner. Lamppost lanterns flicker. A staggering man who is clearly sloshed wanders aimlessly down cobblestoned streets. This is a place for the shady, the lowly, and everyone in between.

Including a thief like me.

The risks Madi mentioned wouldn't be a problem. Who would ever want to leave Wonderland? And why? Anywhere is better than here.

Being Normal is overrated.

My morning conversation with Charlotte replays in my mind as I gather my things.

"We need to talk," she had said, blocking my path as I headed to class. "Your math professor told me you received low marks on your last exam. He's out for you, Alice. I don't think you'll be able to swindle your way out of this one."

My chest had tightened. I'd tried to go around her. Failed.

"This is serious, young lady."

Ugh. I'd rolled my eyes at that. With Charlotte, everything is serious.

"You could lose your scholarship. How do you think that reflects on my position?"

"As if I care," I'd grumbled. But silent guilt twisted my insides.

I may not worry about graduating or living the mundane, planned-out-for-me life I'm expected to lead. But Charlotte adores her job and her little flat above the library. Oxford is her home. At only twenty-six, she's a spinster at her core and a cat-lady too. As opposite as we are, I can't let the only family I have lose everything she loves.

"Sorry," I'd said, surrendering. "I'll study harder."

She let me go to class. But only after reminding me to feed Dinah on my lunch break. Of course I forgot about her bothersome cat, which only adds to my guilt. If Charlotte knew where I really spend most of my evenings, she'd be mortified. I'd probably be expelled, and she would lose her position by association. Headmistress does not tolerate anyone who steps out of line.

I rise and shoulder my rucksack, determination fuelling my resolve. Tonight has to be worth it. If I can't win at the tables, there are other ways to make up for the loss. The more I save, the sooner I can be independent, get my own place in London rather than relying on Charlotte's benefits to pay for room and board. She doesn't need my poor marks and bad reputation hanging over her head any longer than necessary.

Blanche rushes down the aisle before I have a chance to say, "Excuse me." I'm about to follow her lead when something on her seat catches my eye. The book. I snatch it and jog after her.

But when I step off the train, the evening breeze meeting me where I land, Blanche is nowhere to be seen.

She just . . . vanished.

Again.

THIEF

CHARLBURY VILLAGE. NO TRESPASSING, BY ORDER OF HER MAJESTY, CORDELIA REGINA. VIOLATORS SHALL BE PROSECUTED TO THE FULLEST EXTENT PERMITTED BY LAW.

The red letters taunt and tease.

Prosecuted, indeed. Officers never come around Oxfordshire and the surrounding villages. If they do, they're as guilty as I am. This is part of the Wonderground Network. Where Unregistered Wonders mingle with the Normals who wish they were anything *but* normal. While raids are not unheard of, they usually take place in the more populated cities, such as Birmingham or Liverpool.

Or where I'm headed, when I can manage it—London. I'll have Scotland Yard to deal with then.

The greater the risk, the more plentiful the reward, right?

Beyond the village, Wychwood Forest slumbers. Leaves slump beneath drooping branches, and paths overgrown with thorny vines warn intruders not to enter. I shove the abandoned book into my rucksack, glancing back at the few homes and businesses this side of the sign that remain occupied. All curtains are drawn, the lights long since dimmed.

It appears I have my chance.

Setting all thoughts of Blanche aside, I stick out my tongue at the hand-painted sign, which hangs crooked on the chain-link fence standing between me and my destination. The barrier looks like a juxtaposition around what was once a quaint countryside tourist attraction. The ill-fated present contradicting its fairy-tale past.

I toss my rucksack over. It lands on the opposite side with a *clunk*. The climb is awkward, and I'm grateful for the extra coverage my leggings provide. This is the routine.

Get in. Get my share of winnings. Get out.

On the ground once more, I smooth my skirt and adjust my pullover. Then I shoulder my rucksack. A small window pops up on my pocketscreen, offering a list of new WiFi networks to choose from. Some are sanctioned and begin with "Crown," followed by a string of numbers. Others are hack jobs that will be shut down as quickly as they were connected.

The Wonderground Network WiFi is more advanced, requiring device verification and encryption. I lost signal on the train and need to reconnect—again. It's part of the added security. Connection is never automatic and doesn't appear as an option on my screen. Instead, I search for it manually in my settings, typing in the network name, followed by the nonsensical password.

Network name: WondergrOuNDEntRance

Password: FrabjousDayCalloohCallay!

Access cost me more than I wanted to pay, but it was worth it. When three curved bars appear in the top corner of my screen, I know I'm in. I enter my desired destination into the dinosaur GPS application, in case I need it. Night has a way of making everything look the same, and I'm already running behind as it is.

Once I have the address in, a notification lights the top of the screen.

Running a tad late, aren't we?

I scowl at the message. Type, *Wouldn't you like to know?*

Would I? he replies almost instantly. *Or is it you who would like to know that I know you are running late?*

His unending nonsense only makes me pick up my pace. The last thing I need is him tormenting me for my inability to arrive on time.

Or reminding me that he's the sole reason I have access to a GPS in the first place.

When I take a moment to catch my breath and survey my surroundings, I'm reminded that each village of the Cotswolds is strikingly similar. Picturesque, honey-coloured stone buildings. Roads winding in and out of forsaken homes, inns, cafés, and white-fenced pastures. The grass has long overgrown and died and regrown again. What must once have been properly tended gardens now live out their days as weed-infested plots of dirt. A forsaken parish church with broken windows and chunks of bricks missing from its corners appears to have taken a good beating. Each village is distinguishable only by those who've learned to recognise the subtle differences. A cracked lamppost here, an abandoned schoolyard there.

I make my trek through the tourist trap turned ghost town, accelerating my steps with nightfall as my cloak. I'm not supposed to be here. The knowledge thrills and terrifies. There's something about the risk that keeps me returning and pushes me to lie to my sister about what I'm really doing each night.

"Your Occupational Exams are coming up. Have you thought about what you'd like to do?"

Always the same loaded question. As if I have a choice in the matter. As if my career, my life, won't be chosen for me.

"Your assigned occupation will make or break you, Alice. It's everything. It's who you are."

Who I am. And what genius decided that the results from an exam ought to determine what we become? Where we work? To whom we answer? Did Charlotte think to ask if I want to be anything here? Did she bother to inquire as to whether anything *here* feels like nothing because the something I really want to be isn't here?

Of course not. Why would she? Charlotte is content with the predictable and the plain. I'm just the charge she was burdened to care for after our parents left.

A cat screeches from a nearby alleyway, making me think of Dinah in her cosy setup back in Oxford. Few people keep pets these days. They're a nuisance. An extra mouth to feed. Leave it to Charlotte and her unrelenting soft spot for anything with fur to treat a cat better than she does her own sister.

Another block north and I'm checking my GPS again. As expected, it's glitching. I could afford to upgrade my device. Surely Chess has a few options he could come by. He'd give me a loyal customer discount too.

No. My savings are better kept for other things. Things that start with "L" and end in "ondon." Besides, I don't need to give Chess yet another excuse to pester me. Honestly. He's worse than a cat.

At least I don't receive any more messages from him. I sigh my relief, which turns to fog when it touches the night air. Glass breaks, and the distant laughs of questionable individuals move my feet faster. After the Wonder Gene was first discovered by genome researcher Catherine R. Pillar three decades ago, most residents without the unique DNA anomaly traded the quiet country life for the safety of well-guarded cities. And those who tested positive for the Gene?

Forced into hiding if they didn't want to Register.

"For the first time on record," Pillar said during her infamous talk at what was once the revered institution known as Oxford University, *"we are finding that those genes which lie dormant within the darker parts of particular DNA strands are precisely the very fibres that pushed many of our long-ago ancestors to greatness."*

I exhale, recalling one of the only school lessons I've ever bothered to pay attention to.

"Sir Winston Churchill. Alfred the Great. William Shakespeare. Why, I speculate that our very own Queen Elizabeth II—may God rest her soul—discovered that by simply employing this hidden code within her DNA, she could, in theory, accomplish what was once believed to be impossible."

And that's how it began. A theory. An idea. A speculation. Fear makes people do senseless things. Innocent lives were taken. Good people murdered. Many unborns were eliminated if they tested positive in the womb. Young children were drowned in the River Thames if their behaviour led their parents to believe they might grow out of control. Anyone who tested positive at birth was Registered and branded with a red *W* above their right collarbone. Those left alive, anyway.

I reach three fingertips under my collar, touch the blank space of skin beneath my shoulder. I don't need a looking glass to know nothing's there. Charlotte is a rule follower to her core. If I were Wonder, she would have Registered me in a heartbeat.

And Pillar? She didn't have the Gene. Still, she lost everything. Various reports and conjectures blossomed into grand rumours. Most accounts say someone broke into her lab, set the place on fire, and destroyed her research.

No one heard from her again.

Some say she died. Others believe she went into hiding with the very Wonders she'd exposed. Either way, she disappeared like smoke in the night. I don't consider it a coincidence that according to public record, it was only a week prior to Pillar's disappearance when Queen Cordelia received her own results back.

Negative. Not a Wonder. But her fraternal twin sister, younger by a mere fraction of a minute?

Lady Scarlet. Positive. A Wonder. A threat to the throne. And so exiled. Many argued Scarlet was the rightful heir. The Prime Minister took her side, and much of Parliament voted in her favour.

But there are some wars democracy cannot win. Cordelia used fear of the Wonder Gene to divide the people. To separate from the bordering nations of Northern Ireland, Scotland, and Wales. She swayed the House of Lords, who in turn convinced most of the House of Commons that a Wonder on the throne was a threat to society.

Thus began the Great Divide. Queen Cordelia was furious, naturally, that so many had turned against her. New laws were passed. An emergency decree was set in place that gave all authority to what Cordelia called the Modern Monarchy. So long, checks and balances. Farewell, Prime Minister. A select few were appointed as Ministers of the Monarchy—more commonly known as Queen Cordelia's lap dogs.

Over time, technology was limited, and, eventually, forms of it were banned. Dozens of research programs were shut down completely. Fear drove our divided kingdom to make it near impossible for anyone to finish what Pillar started.

Those with the Gene who wished to live among us and remain in the queen's good graces would be Registered and chipped. Tracked like animals on a leash and required to drink a prescribed cordial that would keep any "symptoms" of the Gene subdued. Unless you're invited to participate in the

Trials and find your way in to Wonderland, it's either Register and comply, never allowed to use what you were born for, or—gulp . . .

Be prosecuted.

To the fullest extent permitted by law.

I shake off a shiver and veer left past a boarded-up library. Once full of books like the one in my bag, the places became obsolete after popular literature was banned. The mass-produced publications we have now lack creativity, imagination, and most of all, heart.

And pictures. None of them have pictures.

Restraining my breath, I avoid a dosser who's passed out on the kerb. His right hand grips a paper-bagged bottle of what is most certainly liquor, while his left holds a half-smoked cigarette.

That's another thing each village of the Cotswolds has in common—they all smell exactly the same.

Of knockoff whiskey and cut-rate cigars. Cheap perfume and yesterday's stale coffee. At least no one pays me much mind. Who might guess an undersized teenage girl would be involved in illegal activities such as gambling and cavorting with Rogue Wonders?

A new message appears on my pocketscreen. I decide to ignore it, then curse myself for my own unceasing curiosity.

Tap. Swipe. Groan.

You had better get a move on, Ace. Tables are filling up. But don't you worry. I'll save you a spot next to me. The most talented players ought to sit together. It's more challenging that way. ;)

The most talented. Right. His talents and mine are not the same, and he knows it. My thoughts double back, focusing on what I've always felt but could never be quite certain of, not without a test. The Gene. Some call it a mutation. Others a virus. And then there are those who see it for what it really is. Incredible. Extraordinary. Magic.

And magic—or sleight of hand, at least—happens to be my forte. A skill I've worked to master since Charlotte gave me my first pack of cards on my seventh Christmas, one year after our parents left. Though hand-me-down, the pack became a symbol of all I wanted and everything I never had.

And never will have. Because no matter how skilled I become at my craft, a Wonder will always have the upper hand.

The map on my pocketscreen shows I'm headed straight for my target. I end the GPS and make a beeline for a building that's nearly identical to the ones surrounding it. No sign. Not a single window. Zero light, aside from a few scattered street lanterns.

The limestone walls aren't much to look at. I dig out my pocketscreen to confirm the start time. Right on schedule. Scanning the details on the event page, I search for any other pertinent information I might have missed.

Event Name: Clash of the Cards, Game No. 77
Time: Eight o'clock sharp
Location: The Rabbit Hole, Charlbury Village

I circle the building. The entrance is around here somewhere. The unmistakable reverberation of music pulses from beyond the yellow brick. I've been here before, but each time it's as if the way in shifts. As if the door literally picked up and walked to a different side of the club to keep unwanted riffraff at bay. Is it some sort of optical illusion? A new paint job, perhaps?

Upon a second orbit, I slip into a slender alley. The music grows louder. Closer.

Then there. A lightbulb, caged and flickering above a single side door. Different from a common entrance, this one is squat and circular, like the doors described in those Hobbit novels Charlotte used to tell me about as a child.

I shake the memory from my mind. I can almost smell my opponents' defeat as I approach the door, feel the cards at the tips of my—

"You there. Girl. What is it you think you're doin' 'round these parts?" A night watchman, with lizard-like skin and wide as he is tall, steps from the shadows, blocking my path to the entrance. His girth alone could feed an orphanage for a week.

"Where's The Walrus?" I ask. Though the event's location often bounces from one establishment to another, it's always been the same guard at the door—a burly man with buck teeth and bushy eyebrows who calls himself The Walrus.

This is not that man.

"Took the night off."

"And The Carpenter?" Another watchman, half as intimidating as The Walrus but equally daft.

"On holiday." The new bloke picks at his teeth with his long, pointed thumbnail, pulling something green and slimy free.

It takes every seed of willpower I have not to gag.

When he doesn't budge, I form a plan B. He doesn't know me. No matter. The challenge could work to my advantage. I square my shoulders, take in his overconfident manner, and conjure a glare that says I belong.

"I'm here to play," I say. Casual. Confident. Controlled.

He snorts, takes one look at my Mary Jane shoes and black-and-white-striped tights. At the ribbon holding back my shoulder-length hair that never changed from the straw colour of my childhood. Then he folds his arms over his convex chest and eyes me down the bridge of a nose that I'd wager's been broken a time or two. The scar beneath his left eye. The crooked path of his jawline. The tooth missing from the helm of his grin.

Oh, yes. This man not only invites trouble, he seeks it.

"Over eighteen. Rules. Sorry, kid. You gotta be this tall to play." He lifts a facedown palm and holds it a few inches above my head. "Maybe bring a ladder next time. Or some stilts."

Kid. He might as well call me infantile. Is it my fault my five-foot-nothing stature makes me appear younger than I am?

"Since when has the age requirement ever been enforced?" Besides, ten quid says I'm twice as clever at sixteen as half the middle-aged players beyond the door. I may not be a Wonder—maybe—but I can hold my own.

"Since I says so, that's when. 'Sides, me doubts you could afford tonight's buy-in." The watchman doesn't budge.

And neither do I.

He grunts and digs a finger into his flappy ear. I don't often use the derogatory term associated with those who are Wonder Gene-less, but this fellow is the epitome of all that is an Under. No more extraordinary than the next bloke, but thinks he's something because he reports illegal activity to the authorities.

Time to show my hand. I stow my pocketscreen in my rucksack, withdrawing a clip of folded pounds in its place. It feels like control in a world where I'm far from it. "Oh, really?" I dip my head, ten percent show of respect and ninety percent mockery. "Because this says I can more than afford it. Unless you'd prefer I take my business elsewhere."

His eyes expand, crowding his forehead and cheekbones. "Where'd a kid get so much dough?" He strokes his chin.

I suppress a laugh. So much dough, but not nearly enough to escape the confines of my dormitory. "Does it matter where I got it?" I remove the clip, pluck out a generous amount, and wave the crisp paper notes in the air between us. "I do not believe it is customary to turn down a paying player, *Bill*."

He snatches the buy-in from my fingertips, counting it slowly, as if questioning it's legit. "How'd a fine lil' weed such as yerself come about knowin' my name?"

First I'm a kid, and now a weed? He needs to come up with better insults or pick a different profession. I don't inform him attention to detail is my curse as much as my talent. Instead, "It's a bit telling to have your name tattooed on your neck, wouldn't you agree?"

He grumbles under his breath, stoops to open the small round door, and steps aside, adjusting his newsboy cap and sniffing his new asset. "Pardon, milady. I didn' realise we had a joker in our midst." He snorts, and the action flares his nostrils as he stuffs the note into his stained shirt pocket. The sarcasm is not lost on me.

He doesn't have a clue. I almost feel bad for the fellow.

I move to cross the threshold. *Bump.* "Oops!" I drop my rucksack. *Thump.* As I stoop to grab it, Bill does the same. Our heads knock. How very unfortunate.

For him.

"Are you off yer trolley, girl? Watch it!" He rubs his forehead and blinks three times.

My fingers and wrists work their magic. I hold eye contact the entire time. "Apologies, sir." I steady him with both hands. His heavy cologne makes the undertone of his stink more pronounced. "I tend to be a bit clumsy." When it suits me.

He rubs his head again. "On with ya before oi change me mind."

I nod, seize my rucksack, and enter a black hall. Once concealed, I replace my retrieved currency. The rounded door frame barely clears the top of my head, and if Bill were to follow me, he'd need to hunch and crouch. A glance over one shoulder reveals the clueless bloke hasn't yet realised what he's lost.

By the time he does, I'll have made double what I brought and be out of sight before he knows what hit him.

Poor Bill.

Then again, guilt is a luxury I can't afford.

BETS

Welcome to Clash of the Cards! First game begins promptly at eight o'clock.

Neon words scroll across a digital banner suspended from the high ceiling. A mirrorball twirls in time with the music. Swirling. Sparkling. Sprinkling the club with magic, mystique, and perhaps a bit of romance too.

Not that I know anything about that, thank you.

With every step deeper into the club, I'm reminded of one more reason I risk my time among the Wonderground community. This is my version of romance. The tech down here is nothing short of fascinating.

Strobe lights flash and blink. Up, across, down, diagonally. One could get dizzy from such theatrics. And I do. The halolike glow around every light causes a familiar headache. I look down to give my sensitive eyes a break from the intensity.

Cursed astigmatism. Charlotte came out winning in the

beauty department, but astigmatism is the one trait we share. It is, perhaps, her only flaw.

No, I think smugly. That's not true. Charlotte is afraid of literally everything. All the time. Of a burglar breaking into her flat. Of Dinah falling out a window if it's left open. And, most of all, Charlotte is terrified of Wonders. And this is but a taste of Wonderland. The fact that my sister wouldn't be caught dead or alive here may or may not add to my motivation for taking such risks to attend.

I adjust my glasses. Check the time. Seven fifty on the nose. Ten minutes. And two solid hours before I have to leave to make the last train.

Forcing my attention away from the fanfare, I focus instead on the evening's landscape. This really is a rabbit hole. A hidden escape beneath the ground one might only find if they knew where to look. The club's unique layout features multilevel tiers in spirals, separated by winding stairwells and slides leading down, down, down. Oddly shaped, lopsided paintings in elaborate golden frames decorate the walls, and the dance floor features alternating patterns of checks and stripes and polka dots.

Chairs and tables border the outer edges of the floor on the lowest level, forming a circle around a central space reserved for dancers and partygoers. A DJ on a balcony high above the growing crowd moves to the beat of her choice. Her wild, corkscrew curls bounce with her, their unnatural silvery lavender looking like one of the decorations.

The song transitions, and so does her sway. It's an older tune. An electronic mix between rock and pop. Not approved listening aboveground. The band sings of immortality. Of the inability to live without another. It's about tested faith. About past and future and living forever and losing time.

It's a love song.

A fantasy.

What would that be like? To rely so much on someone else? I love my sister, but most of the time we can't stand one another. Sometimes, I think we'd be better off apart. That *I'd* be better off alone.

As would she.

I slide down a level, my stomach dropping with a whoosh. I've heard places known as amusement parks once existed. Acres upon acres designed for the sole purpose of having fun.

But those were imagined by Wonders, too, and thus completely shut down. One park in Paris was particularly popular, the legacy of a man some say was the most imaginative Wonder of his time, a master of animation and art.

What would he think of the way things are now? Of books without pictures or colours or happy endings?

When I reach the next level, I stand, smooth my hair, and take a stool at the polished bar. A woman wearing high heels and a flashy tank top orders a round of drinks I'm too young to try. The bartender-slash-barista slides over a pitcher filled with bubbly liquid gold topped with foam and a stack of glasses.

"What'll it be?" he asks me, drying a clean glass.

"Triple cappuccino."

His expression reveals he thinks I'm too young to be ordering anything with espresso in it either. Curse my childlike features.

"I'm sixteen." And curse my constant, ingrained need to explain myself.

He stores the glass on a shelf and lifts his white rag in surrender. "I didn't say a word. As long as you pay, I don't care what you order."

Oh, I can pay all right. And tip too. But I don't tell him that. I don't inform him that, despite my girlish exterior, I'm more adult than I'd prefer to be. That's what happens when your parents leave you at the age of six. When you're raised by a sister who was just sixteen herself when it happened.

You grow up.

And you never look back.

I pull out my pack while I wait, sliding off the elastic band holding the faded cards together.

Warm-up time.

Riffle-shuffle. Bridge. Repeat. Shuffle. Tap.

The progression of the cards between my fingers provides a calming cadence. The pack moves in time with my pulse, and I'm lost in its choreography. I count all fifty-two, once, twice, three times.

Riffle-shuffle. Bridge. Repeat. Shuffle. Tap.

Four suits rest between my palms. I pause, take a cautious sip of my drink, the contents burning my tongue and throat, then resume my warm-up. A sense of power and purpose courses through me. Suits, just like that of Wonderland's four quarters.

Yet another reason I listen to Madi's podcast. I set my cards on the bar and, after a few minutes, down my now-cooled cappuccino, the foam at the bottom catching my upper lip. It tastes like vanilla with a hint of cinnamon, a paired luxury rarely found aboveground. When I find the archived episode still downloaded on my pocketscreen, I set the cup down and focus on my audible version of caffeine. True, I've heard this one before, but sometimes a girl needs something familiar to calm her nerves.

Episode Forty-Four: The Origins of Wonderland

Soundbuds in. Volume up. Play.

Once the Normal adverts are over and Madi gets through her introductions, she ventures into her own research and conjectures.

"Known to the Wonders as the self-proclaimed Queen of Wonderland, the younger royal sister has no heirs to speak of. She built her own kingdom from the floor up following her exile underground, gathering followers, proving that banishment might not be so bad after all." Madi's ominous tone can't help but carry a nib of lightheartedness.

I smile to myself. The music thumps so loud I can feel it rattling my ribs. I press my soundbuds deeper and resume my card-shuffling warm-up as Madi continues.

"Rumour has it, Scarlet is always on the lookout for her next successor, and the Trials are her way of auditioning potential heirs. Wonderland has grown to be a marvelous, sparkling metropolis. A rival to London herself. With every season of Wonderland Trials, the rumours abound. But you didn't hear it from me. This is all speculation."

My thumb taps the pause icon. The cards fly between my fingers, and my thoughts soar with them. Is court truly all ballgowns and laughter and eating pastries until dawn? Here they tell us we can be one thing—whatever our exams determine. But in Wonderland, you could be anything.

Perhaps even the heir to the throne.

The guesses and possibilities go on. I used to speak some of them out loud when I was younger. Charlotte would roll her eyes and change the subject. Until the day I asked the one question that shifted her mood from tolerant to tyrant.

"What if our parents are actually Won—?"

"We have no parents," Charlotte had snapped, cutting me off as she pulled my hair a bit too tight in an effort to make a perfect plait. I'd never seen her cheeks so red. "You and me, Alice. That's it. That's all we have."

I never brought up Mum and Dad again. After witnessing the expression on Charlotte's face in the looking glass that day, fear trumped curiosity.

Riffle-shuffle. Bridge. Repeat. Shuffle. Tap.

"Nice trick. I learned zat vun in primary school."

Blanche de Lapin slides onto the stool beside me, sleek accent throwing off my rhythm.

I tap the pack on the bar to match up the edges. Swallow.

"Yes, well." I force myself to hold her scrutinising gaze. Refuse to reveal how starstruck I truly am underneath my composed exterior. "Not everyone has the luxury of cheating their way into winning." Why did I say that? Though most Wonders have a reputation for taking shortcuts with their unique abilities, that doesn't give me the right to assume Blanche does the same. I'm acting like a git. Way to make a second impression, Alice.

It seems she's not offended though. "Good vun. Party tricks and clever quips vill only take you so far, however." She swivels on her stool and rests an elbow on the bar. "You are zee girl from zee train, no? Zee one vith zee vintage tech?"

"Depends on who's asking."

Blanche smiles. "Deed you like my gift?"

Forehead scrunching, I blink, looking around as if understanding will materialise in the air before me. "Gift? I didn't realise it was my birthday."

She waves her fan towards my rucksack.

Ah, okay. That gift. I withdraw her book. The title on the dust jacket catches my eye. *A History of the Modern Monarchy and a Kingdom Divided*.

Odd. Such a title would have been from more recent years. But the dust jacket alone suggests the book is much, much more outdated. I'm suddenly intrigued, curious to peek inside, but I offer it to Blanche anyway.

Fanning her face, Blanche gives a protesting laugh behind the mother-of-pearl and lace. "No, no. Eet eez a gift. I hope eet vill be ov use to you een finding your vay."

My way? I take her in. Every pristine inch. She sticks out like a white bloom in a garden of bleeding red, her perfume the sort of sweet that makes you wonder where the dessert tray is. From the delicate lace headband to the white silk coattails trailing to her ankles, every inch of this woman screams one thing.

Wonder.

She's all I wish I was and more. Elegant. Authentic. Certain. Oh, yes. Blanche knows what she brings to the table, and it's more than riches or card skills. She's different from the usual Wonders who find themselves mingling with Normals at a Rogue event, such as this one. Blanche is an elusive Unregistered not even our queen or her guard have been able to track down. The train conductor didn't stop her. No one here seems to have the notion to report her. Yet her face has been on plenty a wanted poster, underlined by a hefty sum for years. So why doesn't anyone turn her in?

Why don't I?

Loyalty to a principle rather than any one person is a curious thing, indeed.

The song wanes, replaced by the DJ's animated voice. "Players, take your seats. Dealers find your posts. Let the games begin!"

It's her American accent that has me looking up. Squinting through my outdated prescription to see her. I'd know her voice anywhere. It has to be Madi Hatter, in the flesh, who oversees the night's soundtrack. She could very well be a hologram. The way she moves. Shifting, swaying, lip-syncing. It's as if she's in her own world, here and there and all the spaces in between.

Now I really am starstruck, but the moment passes as quickly as it arrived. My attention shifts to the dance floor. Some rush to find an open seat, while others who are here purely for entertainment bump and sway and move to the new beat at the centre of the floor.

"Zat eez my cue." Blanche fans herself, rounded nails manicured to pink and white perfection.

I'd been so mesmerised, I'd forgotten Blanche was here.

And she's clearly a person accustomed to being at the heart of attention. "You had best move eef you vish to play, no? Or do you not like games?" The last word rolls off her tongue, the *s* elongated, an unspoken question within her question stirring between us.

What interest could someone like Blanche de Lapin possibly take in me?

"See you down zere," she adds. "Or vill I?"

I tuck the book—*gift*—away, and hurry into the action. Choosing the table nearest to the stairs, I sit and wait. My legs jitter, unseen beneath the black tablecloth.

Why am I nervous? This isn't like me.

Maybe this is a bad idea.

Or perhaps the triple cappuccino is taking effect.

Each crescent-shaped table hosts three seats on the inside and a single chair on the outside. Every game begins with three players. One dealer. As the rounds continue, the final player standing at each table moves on. In the end, there is one champion, but if you play your cards right you can still make it out with some decent winnings. Clash of the Cards is a tournament of elimination, concentration, and—for those like myself—a total and complete adrenaline rush.

A pair of players I don't recognise joins my table. There's no questioning their status—as Normal as they come. At least the odds aren't against me this time.

Our dealer takes his seat, balding head with a sheen of sweat reflecting the lights above. Him I've seen before. Also Normal.

"I'm Gryph," the dealer says. "Place your bets." He doesn't make eye contact with any of us.

Nobody moves. A full minute passes before I take the lead.

Throat cleared, I say, "What's the game?" Has he had one too many drinks? At this rate we'll end up behind the other tables. I'll never finish a game before the last train.

Gryph glares, beady eyes unblinking. "Place. Your. Bets," he snaps.

"How are we supposed to know what to bet if you don't call the game?" The player beside me—a girl with half a shaved head and a mouth full of gum—leans back and crosses her arms over her chest. Her style screams Wonder-wannabe, but in the light of day? She probably wears a French-twist wig and collared shirt in the name of conformity.

"And you are?" Gryph asks.

"Lory."

"Well, *Lory*, if you don't want to play by my rules, there's the door." He makes a flinging gesture with his arm in the general direction of the exit. "Leave or place your bets. Makes no difference to me."

We do as we're told. What choice do we have? Because Clash of the Cards is technically illegal, all bets are physical forms of payment only. No QR quid. Or wire transfers. Or credits. Exchanges must remain untraceable. I take out a few notes, laying down the minimum requirement to start.

Once we've all put ourselves on the line, the dealer grins. "Scabby Queen."

I scoff.

"You can't be serious." Smacking her gum between each word, Lory shoves away from the table. Her chair legs scrape the checkered floor. "I paid good money for a decent challenge. My grandmother could play that game."

The dealer shrugs. "Tell her to come next time. I have a feeling she's much more pleasant than you and far better looking."

I press my lips together to save myself from inviting a punch to the face. Who needs card games when you have these two for entertainment?

Lory seems to consider her options. The sour look on her face grows more pronounced when she pulls her chair back in.

Our other opponent—a boy with sunken shoulders and a jacket that looks three sizes larger than his small frame—remains quiet as we set up play, using the pack the dealer provides. As inconspicuous as the boy appears, he wins the first round.

Because I let him. I can't reveal I have the upper hand. Not yet.

"Gleek," Gryph says next, shuffling the pack.

We place our bets and play. This time I come out on top, feigning surprise so they don't suspect my mad skills. Best two out of three games is named table champion.

"Whist."

Lory rolls her eyes, the piercings in both of her eyebrows glaring as much as she is. But she keeps her thoughts to herself as we place another round of bets. Hopefully the next table will present games that require more skill and strategy.

Gum girl wins this time just as I'd planned, leaving our table tied. Whoever wins the next game moves on.

That'll be me.

"Black. Hearts," a voice says. But it doesn't belong to our dealer. I do a double take.

Blanche taps Gryph on the shoulder. "I vill take eet from here, sank you."

He obeys her without a word. Without a protest or smart remark. What happened to the fellow who put Lory in her place an hour ago? Does Blanche really have that powerful an effect on—?

Yes. Of course. That must be why the conductor ignored her. Why I've felt little impulse to report her or collect a reward. Though how the Wonder Gene actually works remains a mystery, I have a hunch that Blanche's finesse to elude accountability has something to do with her odd DNA.

My pulse skips as Blanche settles onto the stool. I swallow hard. Is this my chance to see the Gene in action?

"Black Hearts is illegal," Miss Know-It-All informs our new dealer.

"This entire event is illegal, genius." The boy who remains

nameless speaks for the first time. "Or did you think this happens at night in the deepest, darkest corners of the Cotswolds for kicks?"

The girl scowls. "Does anyone here know how to play Black Hearts? That's a *Wonder* game." She eyes Blanche, clearly on to who she is and where she came from. Her mention of "Wonder" carries a negative connotation.

Wonders can't be trusted.

Charlotte's warning resounds at the back of my mind.

Seemingly unfazed, Blanche tilts her head, grace smoothing every feature. Brown eyes rimmed with a tint of pink peer through nearly transparent lashes, focusing on me. Burgundy eyeshadow surrounds her lids, playing in striking contrast against her papery skin.

The way she studies me . . . It's almost as if . . . Can she read my mind?

I shift uncomfortably. "I know how to play." The admission scarcely makes itself known, catching oddly before baring all. I glance up at the DJ's balcony. Madi explained the rules once during a podcast episode last year. So my knowledge is more theory than tangible experience.

I stare at Blanche.

Eyes widening and smile playing, she nods.

I take the encouragement and continue. "The overall goal of the game is twofold. Simple, really." I talk with my hands, as if this will make everything undeniably clear. "Save your queens. Discard your kings. It's similar to chess, in a way. But instead of trapping an opponent's king"—I attempt to grasp thin air—"you want the kings as far away from you as possible. A king is rather unimportant, and taking his side will always count against you." I know I've said too much. Revealing my fascination could land me in a world of trouble if the wrong person were to overhear. Still, I can't help but quote Madi's words. "Play ends when the hourglass sand runs out."

At the mention of an hourglass, Blanche rolls her wrist, flourishing a timekeeper so small she could conceal it in the palm of her hand. She nods in my direction once more.

A new song begins, this one more boisterous than its predecessor.

Raising my voice over the din, I explain the set up. "Four cards in your hand at all times. If you draw a king, you must reveal it and skip two turns. During forfeited turns, your opponents have the opportunity to discard any kings they draw into your hand."

I steal a few glances at Blanche.

But she only grins approvingly, head bobbing, eyes beaming. When I'm finished, I exhale, wait for her to explain the single, most vital rule that makes this game so uniquely Wonder.

"Despite all the rules, there is one wild card that trumps them all." Madi's explanation returns to me, her tone bright . . . ahem . . . with wonder.

"If you want to survive Black Hearts, you have to take risks. Be willing to step off the obvious path. Think outside the box."

What she really means is that, aside from the overall goal of the game, there are no rules for how to reach it.

And where there are no rules, all bets are off the table.

LATE

Taking a risk is one thing. But playing a game without rules?

You might as well cheat to win.

Absolutely, one hundred percent out of the question. I refuse. Not happening.

Steal back a few quid from the doorman? Sure. Pick the pocket of a conductor who makes twice as much wage as Charlotte but works half as hard? No problem. But cheat? At cards?

I've never cheated. Don't need to. I'm that brilliant.

Blanche's eyes level into slits. "Begin," she says with a flick of her fan.

Hands trembling, I lick my thumb. Make my bet.

Lory shrugs but concedes with her bet.

The boy follows her lead.

And play begins.

The feeling of being watched does unpleasant things to my stomach. With Blanche's focus on me at all times, I sense her scrutinising. Sizing me up and down and every which way. What does she expect? That I'll cheat with sleight of hand?

The lively tune from moments ago dissolves, replaced with a new one that's faster, racing to its own rhythm, keeping up tempo with my quickening heartbeat. A glance upwards adds calm to the cacophony. Though I've never met Madi, she feels like a friend. And I could use one right about now.

My palms sweat, breaths grow short. This is my first go at Black Hearts, but the game comes as naturally as anything else does when cards find their way into my hands.

Discard. Draw. Pass. Take two. Discard again. The ebb and flow of it all provides a high I can't describe. I haven't cheated once, and I've already claimed two queens.

"This game makes zero sense," Lory whines, discarding a two of diamonds.

"Agreed." The boy sniffs.

"You may forfeit at any time," Blanche offers. "But zere vill be no refunds ov bets placed."

My opponents don't take action, but their exaggerated huffs and unsweetened-lemonade expressions say more than their words.

With my next turn, I discard a king, draw an ace. Since aces are wild, I can use it to my advantage if I play my cards right.

The slightest movement across the table catches my eye. Blanche coughs.

My vision wavers. I shade my eyes in an attempt to put off the pulsing headache creeping its way to my temples and behind my ears.

"You know," Blanche says to Lory, "you might do vell to hold your hand. You discard too often. Not sure zat strategy eez vorking for you."

My tight jaw and stiff neck can't take the stress of what I'm witnessing. She has the attention of the other two, but I'm watching the hand that's not on her fan. Hyper-focusing on how casually she slips the king I discarded moments ago back onto the top of the draw pile.

Cheater.

Lory scoffs at Blanche's suggestion. She discards one card and draws another. My card. The king. When her eyes lock on its face, her countenance falls. She reveals her king, forfeiting two turns.

I open my mouth to speak the truth. To reveal Blanche as the fraud she is. Who cares if she's helping me win? It's shady, and I will not have any part in this.

I'm a walking oxymoron, I know. The thief with a conscience. The con who won't cheat, as easy as it may be.

Yet, no matter how hard I try to play by my own rule, Blanche rigs the pack. Transfixed, I catch a few of her tricks but spend the remainder of the game baffled. It's as if Blanche is changing the cards with a mere thought or glance. They disappear and reappear at every turn. I can usually pinpoint sleight of hand, but she's so quick, I can hardly catch her.

My vision grows hazy again. For some reason, it's only when my eyesight seems unclear that Blanche's dishonesty appears most apparent. Blast this persistent, wretched headache causing me to see things! The throbbing won't relent, and it's all I can do to stay upright. After nearly an hour, with three queens in my hand and not a king to speak of, I'm one turn away from moving on to the next table. But at what cost?

This isn't worth it. Because, magic or illusions aside, winning by cheating isn't really winning at all, now is it?

I'm about to work up the courage to forfeit. To call it a night and pick a few pockets on my way out to make up for what I've lost.

I lay my cards face down. Scoot my stool backwards.

The final grains of sand at the top of the hourglass slip through the crevice.

Another joins our game, pulling up an extra stool beside

Blanche. Shaggy copper hair streaked with neon-pink highlights covers his forehead and eyes. Only a wide, toothy grin remains visible. I'd recognise him anywhere.

Chess Shire. Forever sticking his nose where it doesn't belong.

In a blink, Blanche's confident air turns sour. She shifts, clearing her throat. "Zis table eez taken. Move along, vermin."

"Come now, B, budge up. There is always room for one more. It's a rare thing indeed to see you in this neck of the woods. The palace growing too dull for you?" His voice, smoother than buttercream on a Queen's Day cake, intoxicates. Invites. Intrigues.

I shake my head. He is absolutely not charming. I don't have time for charming.

Blanche seems to agree. "No room. Vut must I do to make myself clear?"

He shoves back playfully, quite nearly knocking her off her stool. "I'd say there's plenty of room. Wouldn't you agree?" Though still concealed, I can feel his eyes on me.

I inch back. No, and thank you. Not falling into his trap this time. Game over.

"Did you follow me here, Shire?" Blanche lets out an exasperated sigh, speaking the words I'm dying to ask.

"You'd like to think that, de Lapin, but no. I'm here for the same reason you are. A little fun. A bit of mix 'n' mingle, you might say."

He's not wrong. Clash of the Cards events are one of the sole places Wonders venture outside their hidden territory. Chess Shire, in particular, likes to make a habit out of showing up where he's not wanted.

"Eet eez time," Blanche announces, apparently only now realising the hourglass has reached its end. "Players, show your hands."

The others lay theirs down one at a time while mine remains

face down. When I cross my arms over my chest, Blanche completes the action for me.

"Aha!" She claps twice. "Ve have our champion!"

The others appear as if they've been struck by a train. Lory's jaw goes slack, and the boy stomps away, spewing profanities as he goes.

"Eet vould appear ve ave a vinner," Blanche says, satisfaction frosting her voice. "Go find your own, Shire. Zis Vildflower eez mine."

Wildflower? My breath hitches on unfamiliar hope. Does she mean what I think she means?

Chess rises, brushing off the lapels of his velveteen dinner jacket. "Don't let me stand in your path." With that, he spins on his heel and steps away, swallowed by the crowd.

No. Not swallowed. Vanished. Into nothing.

I double, triple, quadruple blink. But this isn't my poor, tired eyes or my need for a stronger prescription. He was there, and then he was . . . nothing. For all the times I've seen him. For every second he's spent pestering me at these events, I've never once witnessed him use his Wonder abilities in the open like this.

I stand, knocking over my stool. Rising on my tiptoes, craning for a glimpse of pink hair.

"And vhere do you sink you are going?"

I ignore Blanche's question and run up the stairs two at a time. When I reach the uppermost floor, I lean over the balcony railing. I want—I *need*—to see more. First Blanche and now Chess. How is this happening? And why haven't I noticed before?

"Looking for someone?"

I whirl. "Must you do that every time?"

Chess Shire stands a metre from me. Shoulders squared with sideburns to match, hands tucked into his pleated trouser pockets with thumbs sticking out, and eyes ever concealed behind a curtain of pink and copper locks. "Ah, but you're so jumpy." He chuckles. "I simply can't help myself. You'd think by now you'd be on to my tricks. And yet, you're incredibly easy to startle."

Attempting to stand straighter, as if this will make me seem taller, I tilt my chin. Adjust my glasses. "Enough child's play. And, if you must know, I was looking for the water closet." Scooting past him, I keep my hands to myself, not bothering to try and swipe his wallet. The sooner I can lose him the better. His mere presence—

"Sure you were. That's why you work so hard to find me and pretend you don't like me at the same time. It must be exhausting."

"I *don't* like you."

"You could at least try to sound more convincing. Why don't you say what I mean?"

He's always speaking in riddles, and it's infuriating. Is this part of his Wonder magic? The ability to smooth talk his way into any heart?

Not this heart.

Drawing a breath, I face him. The deep-seated need to correct his error eclipses my own logic. "I think you meant, 'Why don't I say what *I* mean.'"

"Not at all." He takes one step forwards. Two. "What I said the first time is accurate."

"Well, that's nonsense. How can I say what *you* mean?" My hands are on my hips now. "I hardly know you." Aside from his constant obsession with following me and messaging me and making me mad in the process. I wish I'd never sought him out in the first place. Surely there are other, less painful ways to come by tech.

There's that grin again. "Precisely my point. One we should remedy quite quick, if I don't mind."

"The phrase is, 'If *you* don't mind.' Meaning me. If *I* don't mind."

"But it's clear you do mind. So, once again, what I said the first time is not wrong."

Ooh! Why anyone would want his autograph is beyond me. "Fine. I'll say what *you* mean if *you* don't mind. And *you* mean to play games with my head, just like every other night."

"That's your problem, Ace. You use that head of yours too much. It's probably why you're so afraid all the time."

"I beg your pardon?" Is he serious? "I'm not afraid of anything."

"Of course you are."

He says it so matter-of-factly. How long has he been thinking this?

I loathe how much his blunt comment stings. "You're no better than Blanche," I say. "Are you here together?"

"Me? With the White Rabbit? The idea is laughable."

"The what?"

"No. The Who." Another step closer. "Then again, she might be a What. I can't decide."

I cross my arms to match my current mood. "You can't change the subject like that. It's bad manners."

"Watch it," he says, now a decimetre away. "Or you might lose your temper. Seems you've almost found it. And wouldn't it be a pity to lose something you've only just discovered?"

"You are impossible." Why am I still standing here?

"I think you mean impassible," he says, blocking my way. "Nothing's impossible. Including, but not limited to, you. Least of all you, in fact. You are anything but impossible. You are perhaps the most possible girl I have ever had the privilege to encounter."

"And what's that supposed to mean?"

"Everything, Ace." With that, he takes one hand out of his

trouser pocket, flipping something small and shiny into the air between us.

I catch it midair, my quick and practiced hands reacting before my brain has time to think better of it. The golden key in my palm is too small to unlock an ordinary door and would be much better suited as a charm on a chain. "My name isn't Ace. It's Alice, as I've told you at least a dozen times before." Why am I correcting him again?

"Yes and no." He doesn't elaborate.

I attempt to hand the key back to him.

He raises two palms. "Take it," he says. "A gift." A smirk I'd like to smother spreads from accentuated cheekbone to accentuated cheekbone. "One you're welcome to use when the time is right."

"What is it with you Wonders and your gifts? It isn't my birthday."

"If it isn't your birthday, perhaps it is your unbirthday we are celebrating." He shrugs, returning his hand to his pocket. "And when it comes to you, Ace? Celebrating is absolutely what we ought to do. How's your cat, by the way? Dinah, is it?"

I'm about to answer him when something shatters. A glass? A plate? My senses heighten. I peer over one shoulder to pinpoint the source of the commotion.

My chest tightens. Bill barrels through the crowd below. Searching. Turning one girl around and then another, examining their faces before shoving them out of the way. Someone shouts, "Hey," while two men attempt to restrain the fuming doorman.

"Better run along," Chess says from behind me. "You don't want to be late for the last train."

The train! When did I lose track of time? "My sister is going to murder me."

"Certainly not," Chess muses. "I have always believed it is

far better to be late to where you are going than to be early by always staying where you have been."

I let his words sink in. More nonsense. Shoving the key into the front pocket of my pullover, I look back.

But Chess is gone.

Of course he is.

Keeping to the shadows, I move towards the stairs that lead to the exit. Bill is still a level below me, bellowing profanities at every girl he finds who isn't his target.

But then he looks up at exactly the wrong time. When his eyes find mine, he points a grubby finger. "Thief! Swindler! Cheat!"

That's my cue. I make a run for the exit. Knock over a chair. My rucksack slap, slap, slaps my tailbone as if urging me to *move*. Once at the hall, I sprint down the long black corridor. I'm so close to the door I can taste the night air. A few more steps and I'm—

An arm encircles my waist.

A yank backwards.

A flash of lavender hair.

A splitting headache as I smack my head on the wall.

Bursts of coloured light mixed with encroaching darkness.

I'm not just late for the train.

I've missed my escape altogether.

I should be concerned about whatever comes next and about whoever intends to give it to me. Instead, one image blares hot in my mind.

The look on Charlotte's face when I don't come home.

WAIT

Don't cry.

Don't.

When I come to, I swallow a sob that threatens to devour me should I let it loose. Fear holds me in place as my senses fade in one by one, alongside my consciousness.

Hard floor beneath my body.

Chilled air icing my lips.

Something smells of raspberries and roses and Royal English Breakfast tea—which I've never tasted, but the scent is heaven. Water trickles off in the distance. There is breathing. My own deep breathing.

I sit up and punch the heels of my palms into my eyes. *No.* No, no, *no.*

The eerie tune I dread plays softly from somewhere, confirming where I am. So different from the cheery melody of my locket watch.

I groan and hang my head. I didn't set my locket watch to wake me. There's no telling how long I'll be here now.

This dream—this nightmare—has haunted me since the day our parents disappeared ten years ago. When Charlotte was forced to become my guardian at age sixteen—my age now. Somehow, I've always been fully aware I'm not awake. As real as it feels, subtle details stand out, reminding me none of this would be logical in my world.

The endless hall.

Countless locked doors.

The sound of something terrifying beyond those doors. Growling. Hunting. Waiting to devour. I never see whatever it is, but I know it's there.

Perhaps worse than the monster beyond the walls is the tea. Taunting me. Telling me to drink it when I very well can't. It might be a dream, but it feels so real. Too real, and I've always been too afraid to chance it. It's not as if the tea will help me escape. There's never a way out except to wake. And I only wake when my locket watch does.

That or when Charlotte shakes me. Whichever comes first. Except the latter is a method I can't control.

Another sob, louder this time, followed by a painful hiccup. Cursed tears. Awake or asleep, they've been the bane of my existence since I can remember. When I'd lose a game of cards. Ah, or those moments during which Charlotte would be particularly critical following one of many failed exams.

Anger. Frustration. Sorrow. Why must every strong emotion be accompanied by waterworks? It's maddening!

"Crying never solved anything, Alice."

Thanks for the reminder, Charlotte.

"This is nonsense," I say to the dark. My voice ricochets, taking leave and returning unbidden.

"Is it really?"

My breath hitches. "Who's there?" I open my eyes, blinking

away the tears and swirling spots of colour that come from scrunching my lids too long. Never, in all the nights I've found myself in this unfortunate corner of my mind, has another accompanied me. "Hello?"

No one.

The extended hall of doors I've become so familiar with looms ahead, black-and-white checked floor—similar to the floor of The Rabbit Hole—going on as far as I can see. I stand and turn in a small circle. As if anything has changed.

Unlikely.

I chide my own ridiculousness. "There's no use trying to escape when you very well know you're stuck here until someone wakes you."

A scuffle. Clothes swishing.

My hands collapse at my sides. I take a step forwards.

A flash of white appears far down the hall. "Blanche?"

Another scuffle.

"Blanche!" I call, jogging towards the sound.

"She really can't stay, you know. She's always running late, that one."

I whirl. "Chess?"

"At your service," he says from nowhere, his voice sounding as if streaming through an invisible speaker. His sly tone causes warring feelings of unease and excitement. He's a Wonder. Is it possible he has the power to tap into my thoughts? Why won't he leave me be?

Do you want him to?

Where did that come from? Of course I want him to. This is *my* head. And he doesn't belong.

"What are you doing here?"

Chess's reply is as clear as if he were standing beside me. "I think you mean, what are *you* doing here, Ace."

"I most certainly do not."

"Take off the *not* at the end, and you do. Simply needs a bit of editing."

"You're absurd. This is my dream. Of course I am here." Why, even in my dream, do I feel the need to explain myself?

"Dreams are amusing things indeed," Chess says. "Images, projections of the mind conjured from our own versions of reality."

"Precisely my point," I say. Must he be so exasperating, real or fabricated? "This dream—this *nightmare*—isn't reality."

"Your mind is real," he counters. "Is it not?"

"Well, yes, but—"

"Then, enlighten me, Ace. How is the world inside your mind any less real than the one outside it?"

My mouth opens, but no sound emerges. Once again, he's managed to trump me with one of his illogical inquiries.

"He's dangerous," I hear Charlotte scold in my head. Or maybe I'm scolding myself, and it only sounds like Charlotte.

When Chess doesn't speak further, or appear for that matter, I try the nearest door out of sheer habit. Might as well keep myself occupied. I'm going to be here a while.

Locked. Of course it is.

I keep moving, testing every knob I pass. Glass. Brass. Nickel. Doesn't matter what they're made of. Locked, all of them.

And, with each jiggle of a knob, the beast behind them snarls and snaps.

The farther I move, the lower the ceiling slopes, forcing me to crouch. Every door is of a different size and colour. Some are rounded at the top while others form a perfect square or rectangle. Still others form odd shapes like triangles or octagons. Caged lights like the ones at The Rabbit Hole flicker overhead. My footsteps echo, and my stomach rumbles. Never did finish that ham sandwich and crisps I bought.

"You can't go that way," Chess says.

My tears have dried on my cheeks by now. What feels like hours here might be moments in my sleep. No way to tell. I keep crawling.

"I said"—he clears his throat—"you can't go that way."

I pause. Fine. This is my dream. I'll play along. Anything that might help me snap out of it. "Do you mind telling me which way I ought to go?"

"That depends"—a chuckle—"on where you want to get to."

I sit back, my head bumping against the ceiling. Ouch. "Out, of course. So I can wake up. Isn't it obvious?"

"Wake up?" The jest in his words is clear, though he's still hidden. Maybe he's behind one of the doors. Maybe *he's* the monster. "Whatever gave you the idea that you're asleep?"

I lean against the nearest door, a crick in my neck beginning to form. "Never mind."

"If you want to go out, you must first"—another chuckle—"go in."

"I *am* in."

"Are you?"

Ugh. "Do you always speak in riddles?"

"Do you always speak in contradictions?"

"Me?" I scoff. "You're the one who's contradictory. Go out to go in. Dreams are reality. Nonsense. The truth is, because this isn't real, I ought to be able to do or say whatever I please."

"Or," he says, "because this *is* real you ought to be able to do or say whatever you please. It's your choice, Ace. The difference is merely belief."

I straighten. My lips form an *O*. "I ought to be able to do whatever I please."

Chess doesn't comment, but I can almost picture his smile touching his ears.

I shake my head. After ten years of being stuck in this locked box most nights, could it truly be as simple as believing things can change? That it's been my choice all along?

A shiver, followed by goosebumps up and down my arms. I reach up, pressing on the low ceiling with both palms. All at once, with little effort at all, it moves. Up and away. Floating. Flying. Gone.

"You're catching on," Chess whispers. "Well done."

Standing, I smile into my shoulder, hoping the invisible boy won't notice. Something hard in my shirt pocket jabs at my chest, right above my heart. I reach inside.

The key. Feeling incredibly real at the centre of my palm. It shouldn't be possible, but I have a feeling I know precisely which door this key is meant for.

But how could *he* know?

Resolve drives me at a sprint down the hall. My fingertips brush against the doors, and they disappear one after the other. Windows materialise in their places. Glorious arching apertures with a crisscross design but no glass. And beyond, an exquisite flower garden filled with blossoms of pink and yellow and bright, blooming red. The wrought iron fence surrounding the garden acts as a trellis, hosting climbing vines and ivy and morning glory blossoms.

And, best of all, the ominous roar of an unseen monster is gone, along with its overture of death and gloom.

I'm reluctant to leave the stunning view behind but more motivated than ever to reach the hall's finish line. If the final door leads where I think it does, that garden won't simply be a product of my imagination. I'll be there.

And *there* is Wonderland. I know it.

When at last the hall ends at a circular room filled with more doors and a high ceiling, I stop. Catch my breath to slow my heart rate that I'm sure is as quick in real life as it is in my mind. When the burn in my lungs has eased, I focus on the glass-top table with clawed feet in the middle of the room. The table is small, like the kind one might see at a child's tea party. Several items rest at its centre.

A teapot, steam rising from its spout.

A teacup, overturned on a matching saucer with daisies painted around the rim. It reminds me of the inked daisy chain on my rucksack.

Finally, the words "Drink Me" written in black cursive stare up at me from the doily on which they reside.

I've followed the instruction many times. More than any other detail in my nightmare, this one has stood out as one of the most frightening. It might as well be marked "Poison," like the tea vial Charlotte makes me carry around. Or the cordial that keeps Registered Wonders subdued.

I've heard stories about what they've endured. The side effects the Wonder Gene-suppressing cordial causes. Hallucinations, paralysis, chronic pain, hives. The list goes on. Wonders who refuse to drink the prescribed liquid on their own are administered mandatory injections. On more than one occasion, a Wonder has shown up in the news, reported dead. The articles claim the cause is unknown. But it's no coincidence it's the Registered Wonders—and not the Rogues— who wind up in the morgue. If I didn't know any better, I'd say they're allergic to the stuff.

The gasp that erupts is small but enlightening. Could the cordial be some sort of tea? What if all Wonders are allergic to tea? And if that's the case, I might be a—

I can't bring myself to think the word. It's too much to hope for and too alarming at the same time. With shaking hands, I turn the teacup over, then pour the piping hot caramel-coloured liquid into the cup. When I draw the cup towards my lips, I pause.

Well?" Chess's voice again. "Aren't you going to drink it?"

"That's the trouble." I set the cup down and pace the circular room, tapping my chin with the tiny key. "I have always wondered why. Of all the things to turn up in my nightmare, a cup of tea. It's silly, really."

"Why?"

"Because such a small thing shouldn't be able to kill me."

"How do you know it will? If this is just a dream, it oughtn't harm you in the slightest."

"Perhaps. But the fear is real. And every time I get this far, I wake up anyway. So it doesn't usually matter."

"But this time it does?"

"It appears that way."

"Are you not awake now?"

The ridiculous question is one I'd protest on any other night. Of course I'm not awake. But after all that's changed tonight . . .

I march over to the table and take a gulp of tea before I can talk myself out of it. The sweet, yet subtle citrus flavour tastes like nothing I've experienced. My lips curl up at the corners. Then the flavour shifts from sweet to savory, reminding me of roast turkey and hot buttered biscuits. With each new flavour the tea introduces, I'm soaring upwards, growing three times my height.

"Ouch!" My head hits the ceiling. "Now what?"

"Try the other," Chess tells me.

"The other?" I peer down at the minuscule table, at the new teapot that wasn't there moments before. "How did that get there?"

"Don't ask me," Chess says. "You're the one who put it there."

This time I don't argue. Because this is my dream and I'm tired of being afraid of what's inside my own head. Of dreading what could happen but never having the courage to discover what will. So I pour myself a fresh cup from the new pot, downing it in a single swallow.

The tart liquid tastes send me south. Shrinking, almost disappearing. My clothes morph with me—thank goodness— until I'm just the right size for the smallest curtained door.

Shoving the drapery aside, I find myself staring through a keyhole larger than my head. I have to jump to grab hold of the knob. My feet dangle, and one of my shoes falls off. I tumble after it, landing on my bum, staring up at the brass knob designed with such intricate details, it looks like a face.

As I'm about to jump again, I hear voices from the other side of the door. I pause, straining to make out what they're saying.

"You have to bring her back," a girl says. "It's time. If she hasn't figured it out yet, she will."

"She isn't ready," a woman's voice says. Her tone is sharp and undeniably Charlotte's.

"None of us are," the first says. With the door between us, it's hard to make out, but she almost sounds like— "But if you don't bring her, she'll end up Registered, or worse."

Madi! I'd know her anywhere, though she sounds different. With a bit of static filtering her slightly nasal tone.

I jump and grab the knob again, swinging myself *one, two, three* times towards the keyhole. When I land inside the opening, my head meets brass and my vision blurs.

"You were supposed to keep her safe," Madi says. "You promised. You told Raving—"

"I know what I told him," Charlotte snaps. "I have kept her safe. It isn't my fault she's been irresponsible, careless, inconsiderate—" My sister's voice carries on, but the more insults she spews, the less she sounds like herself. Her pitch goes up an octave, a shrillness there that's far too authentic to be in my head.

"Reckless, brash, cheeky . . ."

I tumble forwards, through the keyhole.

"Negligent, ill-advised, foolhardy . . ."

The garden retreats into darkness. The flowers and vines and trellis fence. All vanished. I'm falling away and back and through the grass as it disappears from under me. Down, down, down. Until . . .

Sirens.

"Shh!" Charlotte hisses from the driver's seat of the school's sixteen-passenger van. "Stay down!"

The switch from dream into reality jars my system. Nausea takes over. Head spins. Spots dance before my vision. "Charlotte?" My mouth is dry, my tongue heavy. "How did you find—?"

"Hush." Shoulders hunched, she leans closer to the steering wheel. "We're nearly home." Her eyes catch mine in the rearview mirror, glasses sliding down her nose. Our poor vision is the one thing we have in common. "What were you thinking? Honestly, Alice. This is the most ignorant thing you've ever done."

Does she know this isn't my first offence? What would she say if she knew I'd been sneaking out since I was old enough to read a map?

"Where's Madi?" I manage to say.

When she doesn't respond right away, I know she's coming up with a lie.

"Who?" she says after a full minute. I spy her slip something small and rectangular into her handbag between the driver and passenger seats. A pocketscreen? Charlotte?

I must still be dreaming.

My eyes close against the burning tears I'd hoped were finished for the night.

Charlotte continues further reprimands I'm content to ignore. I roll over on my side, the combination of the warm bench seat along with the batting eyes of street lights peeking in through the windows soothing my storm. Eyes close. Breaths slow. I feign sleep, and soon, Charlotte's voice fades. The only noises that remain are the rumble of the engine, the occasional squeak of the brakes, and tyres turning against asphalt.

No walls.

No locked doors.

No Wonders.

If you want to get out, you must first go in.

All this time I've thought escaping was the answer. Believed if I finally had a way to get out, I might leave the nightmare behind for good. Charlotte says I was afraid of confined spaces as a child, and no gate or crib bars or four walls could contain me. I'd brushed the dream off as some sort of fear manifesting in my subconscious at night. But now?

What if my subconscious is more than a fantasy?

What if that which appears to be a mere dream is a whole new world?

And what if whatever is on the other side of that door is waiting for me to find it?

LOST

"Do you have any idea how much trouble you've caused me tonight? You could've landed us both on the streets or worse!"

Charlotte paces the sitting area of her one-bedroom flat, knocking her shins on the coffee table every other turnabout. Her rich brown curls bounce in a frizzed mess, stray wisps sticking straight out beside her ears. No makeup. Plain grey pyjama bottoms. Coffee-stained, V-neck tee. It's rare to see my sister in her natural, unkempt state. However she found out I wasn't in my dormitory, she came after me straight from an interrupted slumber.

Her insufferable cat, Dinah, rubs against my sister's calves, purring her pleas for attention.

Charlotte reaches down to scratch Her Majesty behind the ears.

"How did you find out where I was?" I say to Charlotte as I glare at the cat.

"Occupational Exams are less than a month away, Alice,"

she says, avoiding my question. She scoops Dinah up and continues to scratch and stroke, scratch and stroke. "You still have a chance to graduate with your Occupational Certificate." Eyes that match the colour of her curls, but a hint darker, drill into me. As if begging me to refute her statement.

"How did you know I was gone?"

"It's my job to know," she says, making it clear she won't elaborate.

I gaze out the window and draw my knees to my chest on the sinking settee cushion, wrapping a throw blanket around my shoulders as I hunker down for what's sure to be a lengthy lecture. More blankets cover the cushions beside me, hiding one of too many stains my own clumsiness has caused.

"If you do well, you might have your pick of more than one employer."

"Ha!" I blurt. "My pick? As if a multiple choice from their list is a choice at all."

Charlotte gawks, nearly dropping her pet.

Dinah meows her annoyance.

"Sorry," my sister says.

Is she worried about me or the cat? "You know I won't score high enough to stay in Oxford, Charlotte. Which means I'll be sent to work in some Outskirt town with poor conditions and no place to go but the grave."

And no hacked tech. No access to Madi's podcast. No connection to anyone outside of my tiny bubble. No Clash of the Cards or run-ins with Chess. Sounds like the worst version of my own nightmare. I'll take Chess's pestering over being sent to the Outskirts any day.

I shove my worries along. The small wooden clock on the side table *tick, tick, ticks*, the seconds seeming to soar as my own thoughts fly.

"I'll be surveilled twenty-four-seven," I continue. "I'll never be able to—" I bite my tongue. She doesn't understand. She can't. Charlotte is brilliant, with a mind far above her pay grade at a puny boarding school library. The sole reason she's not serving in a proper position under the Queen of England herself is to keep an eye on me. She knows it.

And so do I.

"I've seen your scores, Charlotte. You could've had a life. A house. Gowns and fame and the finest foods at your fingertips. I've never understood why you stayed here." Bitterness coats each word. "With me."

She pauses mid-pace. "There's more to life than material possessions and glory," she says, her voice quiet. "I never wanted any of it."

Despite her words, Charlotte's hesitant tone conveys this is not entirely true. What isn't she telling me?

When I look out the window again, the walkway lights flicker on and off, detecting the slightest movement. Was it a squirrel? An owl? Even something as minuscule as a spider sets them off. I've learned to dodge their sensors over the years, perfecting my invisibility down to a science. As elusive as Chess Shire himself.

And there he is again. Invading my mind. *Leave me alone,* I think. Perhaps I have gone mad after all.

"Not everyone cares about money as much as you do," Charlotte adds, taking her turn at the bitterness game.

When I face her, my eyes go wide. I launch off the couch. "Where did you get that?"

She holds my stash of savings well out of my reach. We may be sisters, but we look nothing alike aside from our glasses. While I'm short with straw-coloured hair and soft, childlike features, Charlotte is tall and poised and angled in all the ways I'll never be. Keep-away is one game she always wins.

"How long have you been planning to leave?" she asks.

I lower my arm but don't back away.

"Answer me."

"A while."

She narrows her eyes.

Is she hurt by my admission? How could she be? I'd think it would be a dream come true to finally have her freedom.

"You know what happens to runaways, Alice. You'll be homeless. Lost. As bad off as Rogue Wonders themselves. Is that what you want?"

Ah. There it is. The thought of me leaving doesn't hurt her. Not really. Because I am forever my sister's project. And the idea of me being one of the Lost—those with no papers, no job, no home, no family—looks bad on her sparkling reputation. Her Majesty forbid I end up in the same boat as an Unregistered Wonder. The sheer horror of it would embarrass my sister to death.

I nod towards the notes I've scrimped and saved. "I think I'll be fine, but thanks for your concern."

"A *legal* job." Her emphasis bites. "Without your Occupational Certificate you'll have nothing. I can't help you then."

"I thought you didn't care about material possessions."

"You know what I mean, Alice."

"Please." I fling out a hand. "Enlighten me."

She sighs. "Sometimes I wish I'd never given you those cards. Playing games and picking pockets is not life. It's child's play. You need to grow up and face the truth."

"And what is the truth, exactly? You won't tell me anything about Mum and Dad. Just that they left us. I need more than that. I need to know who I am. Where I came from."

Her small, sad smile fizzles my anger. "You know, when you were young you used to pronounce it 'ex-act-ek-lee.' Do you remember that?"

I shake my head, trying so hard to hold my tart expression but failing miserably. Where is she going with this?

She stares past me. Through me. It's like she's seeing me

as the small and fragile girl who used to climb on her lap for a bedtime story. "I'd correct you," she says. "Tell you the proper way to pronounce it. When you finally said it right, I missed how it was before."

"What's your point?" My words bite more than I want them to. "Why do you always change the subject when I bring up our parents?"

She leans down to place the pile of folded notes on the coffee table between us. "My point is that as much as I wanted you to stay little, you grew. Your parents left, and I corrected you, and all too soon . . . you turned into a young woman. And now it's time to act your age. Leave childish things behind." Her face twists when she says it. But that's not what leaves my jaw hanging.

"Don't you mean *our* parents?"

"What?" Her quick glance up seems surprised, then she breaks eye contact.

Dinah, perfectly timed as ever, weaves her way between my sister's legs.

"You said, '*Your* parents.'"

"You heard me wrong."

"Were they . . . are you . . . are you not my sister?"

A pause. A scratch of Dinah's head. "Don't be silly."

And with the cat at her heels, Charlotte crosses to the kettle in the kitchenette and pours hot water into a mug. Steam rises like smoke, moistening her face. If I didn't know Charlotte to be as unemotional as she is proper, I'd almost believe she had tears in her eyes. She can't drink tea, but her odd ritual of drinking plain hot water before bed still puzzles me.

"You can sleep here tonight." She wraps her fingers around the hot mug, holding it close to her heart. "I have one of your extra uniforms in the wardrobe. In fact, maybe you ought to consider staying here for the remainder of the term. We can move you from your dormitory over the weekend."

"Why? So you can play nanny? Mind my every move?"

"I have done nothing but care for you since the day we left."

And there it is again. The slightest slip in her phrase. "Since the day *they* left. Mum and Dad left us at the Foundling House in London."

"That's right." She sips her hot water. "And if I hadn't worked my tail off to get where we are, you'd still be there. The opportunities you have now are not given to everyone."

"Opportunities for what? Conformity?"

"Normalcy!" She slams her mug down on the countertop, water splashes over the sides, and the handle breaks clean off. The remainder of the cup tips and rolls over onto the floor, landing with a crash as broken pieces scatter.

Dinah lets off a high-pitched meow and makes a break for Charlotte's bedroom.

I swallow, selecting my next words with care. "Maybe I don't want to *be* normal. Maybe I'm already lost."

There's no doubt my last words sting. But schooled as ever, Charlotte steels her composure, allowing me the final blow. Leaving the spilled water and broken glass behind, she passes me and enters her bedroom, closing the door in her wake with a muted *click*.

It's unclear how long I stand there, unmoving, blanket wrapping me like a shawl. I want to storm out, race across campus, and pack what few possessions I own. I have enough for a single ticket to London, no return. The underground games there pay ten times what I can get in the abandoned towns.

Instead, I let the blanket fall. Without a sound I clean Charlotte's mess, taking my time, soaking in what will probably be the first and last time I ever see her lose her temper.

Wouldn't it be a pity to lose something you've only just discovered?

Unbidden, a smile stretches my lips. I shake my head, tossing the swept-up glass in the rubbish bin. Rather than question the constant presence of Chess Shire in my head, I simply whisper, "Indeed."

By the time I find my place on the settee, it's well past one in the morning. And still sleep eludes me. I stare up at the textured ceiling, my eyes following the curves and dives like paths in a never-ending labyrinth.

Charlotte is wrong. I don't need an occupation to find my place in her world. I need to find a place in my own. Maybe once I'm in London, I can visit the Foundling House, do some digging. Charlotte doesn't have my vital records, but that doesn't mean they don't exist. I can find out whatever my sister isn't telling me about our parents and the past.

I turn on my side. Stare at her closed bedroom door.

Not our parents.

Mine.

FOUND

The musical chimes of my locket watch pull me out of a dreamless sleep.

I wake to the blue-grey skies and mist that accompany a typical Oxford spring morning. By afternoon, the mist will burn off, leaving behind bouts of shade and sunshine peeking through puffy white clouds. A glance at the little clock on the sitting room table invites a grumble. Seven thirty on the button. Exactly thirty minutes to shower and get to my first course. Fantastic.

I'd forgo the charade of school altogether, except I know Charlotte will be watching me. The less she suspects, the better. Besides, taking the day to formulate my precise plan isn't the worst idea I've ever had. I deserve a cappuccino for my patience alone.

I rise from the settee and stretch to inhale what I expect to be the alluring scent of caffeine. Instead, I am met with chilled air and the smell of dewy grass. Why is the window open? If my sister sees it, she's going to blame me.

"Charlotte?"

No answer. I cross to the open window and crank it shut. The lock is stubborn, but with enough force I'm able to secure it. Maybe she felt warm last night? No weather—hot or cold—has ever been good enough reason for her to leave a window open.

"A thief could break in, or worse," she told me the first and last time I left a window unattended. We shared a room at the Foundling House. Back when we used to be close.

"What could be worse than a thief?" Sarcasm coated the question.

She'd huffed and scooted me out of the way before slamming and locking the window herself. "Plenty could be worse." The closed window seemed to calm her. She'd straightened and all anxiety had vanished, the lines in her forehead smoothing.

Charlotte never did tell me what plenty was. And as much as I enjoyed giving her a hard time, I never left a window—or door—open and unlocked again.

My thoughts drift back to the present.

And to the time.

Seven thirty-two. I'll skip the shower and opt for some fuel. But what I find in the kitchenette leaves me puzzled.

"Charlotte, did you want me to get the coffee started?" I call out.

Again, she doesn't respond. She should have brewed a pot by this hour. But a peruse of the kitchenette reveals she hasn't touched the space since leaving her mess behind for me to clean last night. I glance at the row of hooks beside the front door where her handbag still hangs.

"Charlotte"—I hesitate—"are you ill?"

Her bedroom door stands slightly ajar. I ought to apologise and tell her I know I'm reckless and careless and all the things she said. If I can reason with her, force her to understand those decisions are mine to make, I'm sure she'll come around.

The instant the thought sends a surge of hope to my chest, the dream dies. Who am I kidding? Charlotte? Come around? Ha! When flamingoes breathe fire, or some other nonsensical thing occurs, I might actually believe it.

A peek inside her room reveals almost nothing out of the ordinary. Tidy bed. The sole piece out of place is her planner, left on the nightstand, with Charlotte nowhere in sight.

My sister is many things, but forgetful isn't one of them. First her handbag and now this?

A rolling purr against my legs makes me jump.

"Dinah." Despite my irritation, I scoop the aging feline into my arms, stroking her coarse orange-and-white fur as I wander towards the wardrobe. "Where's Charlotte, hmm?"

Another meow from the cat we've had since she showed up on the front steps of the library a year ago. A meow that says she, as usual, will give nothing away. In fact, Dinah doesn't care which one of us is around, so long as someone is here to wait on her. As if reading my mind, she dips her head and nuzzles my hand, asking for a scratch.

"Apologies, Your Highness." I set her down and curtsey. "I don't have time today."

Snobbish as ever, Dinah turns and sticks her tail in the air, pretending as if she doesn't care whether I stay or go.

"She's most likely gone downstairs to start her morning shift at the library," I tell the departing Dinah as she slips into Charlotte's room. "I'm sure she'll be back up in a bit to check on you."

I can almost hear the cat's stuck-up *harrumph* when she doesn't respond.

Seven forty-one. Better move it.

My uniform is exactly where my sister said it was. Pressed and ready to wear. I frown at the image before me in the floor-length looking glass. Once I'm dressed, I opt to untuck one corner of my shirt. There. Much better.

Satisfied with the small rebellion, I make a to-go cup of instant coffee. While I'd rather enjoy a fresh brew, this will have to suffice. With my hot drink in hand, I slip out the door, locking it behind me with the spare key, and head down the spiral flight of stairs.

Seven-fifty. Ten minutes until first bell.

A cramped hall waits at the bottom of the stairs, two doors offering leave. One to my right leads directly onto the campus green, while the one to my left opens into the library. A room full of dull material collecting dust. Charlotte's life summed up in pages no one will ever read.

Not by choice, anyway.

A shudder ripples my spine, reminding me of last night's topsy-turvy dream. The turn of events may not have been real, but they've left me uneasy. Will more changes await me in my sleep tonight?

I dismiss all thoughts of restlessness and Chess Shire and hallways and locks as I press my face against the frosted glass window of the library door. I jiggle the handle. Why are the lights off when the library opens in ten minutes? Could Charlotte have gone for a drink at the trolley outside the dining hall? It's on my way to first course. Maybe I'll run into her.

The walk to class is brisk, spring forgetting its place and bringing up lesser memories of winter. I sip my hot, unsweetened beverage, a shiver pimpling my arms despite the two layers of cardigan and long-sleeved blouse that cover them.

"I'm sorry, Charlotte," I say under my breath between sips, practicing my speech, my shoes the audience. "You were right. I need to think of my opportunities. I'll pack up my dormitory after the last bell."

If she believes I'm agreeing to move in with her for the remainder of the term, she'll give me some space today. I'll have just enough time to gather a travel bag and hop on the last train to London.

It's not goodbye. Without me holding her back, Charlotte may very well end up in London herself. We'll see one another again. We have to.

I refuse to let the tears brimming at my lids spill free. I'll save them for the train.

Once I've reached the dining hall, I hurry around the side to the drink trolley. Mrs. Dodgson and her rosy complexion greet me.

"Good morrow, Miss Alice. Will it be a triple cappuccino again today?"

I scan the menu board above her as if I haven't seen the less-than-exciting choices a hundred times. Same as every other day. Wouldn't it be more fun to offer themed drinks with a hint of something sweet or spiced? I could sure use an Ace-My-Exams Latte or an Honor Roll Cappuccino. I've voiced these ideas in the past, only to be met with a patronizing laugh followed by a recommendation that I add more endive to my diet.

Because nothing says life on the edge like something a grandmother would drink.

I hold up my almost empty to-go cup. "No, thank you, Mrs. Dodgson." It's chilly enough this morning that my breath fogs the air when I speak. I toss my cup into a rubbish bin and tug my cardigan sleeves down with my thumbs, shifting from foot to foot to stay warm. "I'm looking for my sister. Has Charlotte come by this morning?"

Mrs. Dodgson shakes her head. "It's been a quiet one, I'm afraid. It'll most likely pick up round the midmorning break. Best be checkin' back then, dear. And grab a brolly when you're able. The weather looks a bit iffy."

I nod, wave my thanks, and make a beeline for the mathematics building just up the walkway. I'm less worried about it raining and more concerned with Charlotte's odd disappearance. Where could she have gone?

First bell rings as I slip into Mr. March's classroom, though my mind studies anything but physics. Who needs quantum theory and fluid dynamics when you can count cards and read facial expressions without a second thought?

"Good morning, ladies. Please flip your textbooks to page seven-hundred-and-fifty-two—*Metaphysics in Conjunction with Reality and Dream States.*"

I do as I'm instructed, holding my head between both hands to keep it from exploding as I stare at a jumble of nonsense I don't understand. A snippet of a poem I once read invades my thoughts instead.

"I have answered three questions and that is enough,
Said the sage, don't give yourself airs.
Do you think I can listen all day to such stuff?
Be off or I'll kick you downstairs!"

I'd like to kick this textbook downstairs. Or at the very least, remind Mr. March of the highly unlikely circumstance in which any of us would need to know about whether or not existence is a physical phenomenon or something more.

"Furthermore, what is quite fascinating is her *Theory of Impossibility* as it relates to relativity and the idea that all . . ."

Blah. Blah. Blah. Who cares about some scientist and her theories? Do they teach this stuff to taunt us with the hope of a brighter future?

When the midmorning break bell rings at last, I've retained nothing new about the universe, but I have practiced my double turnover technique under my desk, a card skill I could master in my sleep.

London, here I come.

A queue is already forming at the trolley when I exit the building. The sun is stubborn today, refusing to appear and doing nothing to brighten my mood. Perhaps Mrs. Dodgson was right about the rain for once.

Charlotte, as expected, is nowhere to be seen. I don't want to interrupt Mrs. Dodgson during the rush, so I pick up my pace towards the library. The next block doesn't begin until half past, plenty of time to swing by my sister's domain again. If, in fact, she really is my sister.

Unless—

She wouldn't.

Would she?

A half pivot on my heels sends me east, in the direction of my dormitory. Girls huddled in groups of twos and threes pass me without acknowledgement, whispering about exams and what occupations they hope to score.

"I adore needlework," one comments. "A high score for Seamstress could put me in the fashion district in Paris."

"Who needs fashion when you can have power?" another remarks. "Secretary to one of the queen's ministers is where I'm headed."

I try not to roll my eyes within their line of vision. Such high hopes are a fool's dreams. It's difficult enough to score above a ninety, let alone achieve a perfect one hundred. The occupations they're wishing for are impossible.

Nothing is impossible.

I ignore Chess's voice in my head as much as I ignore the chattering girls who pay me no mind.

Making friends has never been my talent.

My single is situated on the third floor of the dormitory, so I'm out of breath after sprinting up three flights of stairs. I dig out my key but before I can place it in the lock, then my heart forgets its place.

The door to room 3C is ajar.

"No. No, no, no, no." My teeth grind, and I push the door inwards, only to have a draft from an open window slam it in my face. That would make the second ajar window I've encountered today. I'm not amused.

"Charlotte, this is a complete invasion of privacy." I turn the knob, beginning an entirely different speech than the one I set out to make this morning. "You couldn't give me a chance to collect my things? Instead you made the decision for me. Again. This is exactly why I—"

But the room is empty, though a bit more mussed than I remember leaving it. A fallen lamp. A crooked looking glass. My backup pack of cards scattered across the hardwood floor. At least nothing's missing.

Except Charlotte.

The woman I called my sister is nowhere to be found.

What reason would she have for going through my room? What could she have possibly been looking for?

The answer isn't too difficult to conjure. Charlotte was looking for me last night. That has to be it. But why would she leave the door open? And a window? Now who's the irresponsible one? It's completely out of character for her to be so careless.

The warning bell for second course rings, but I'm heading in the opposite direction of my History of the Modern Monarchy course. When I reach the library, it's dead as expected, with only a few students studying or researching for their Occupation Desired Personal Essay through the archives of previous student examples. A locked cabinet with glass on three sides behind the chest-high front desk houses the scarce volumes of original literature on campus. Clothbound. Leatherbound. Hardcover. Paperback. Titles such as *The Canterbury Tales, Harry Potter, The Chronicles of Narnia,* and *The Lord of the Rings* grace the secured shelves. There are tomes by Dickens, Austen, and Shakespeare. Some of these authors lived and studied right here in Oxford. Still, their writings are preferred seen and not read. A part of our story, yes, but an influence on our minds?

Never.

Unless, of course, you happen to have an older sister who believes in bending the rules for a bit of C.S. Lewis and J.R.R. Tolkien before bed.

Where are you, Charlotte?

No one appears to be tending the front desk at first glance. I peruse the aisles, checking between study nooks and return carts carrying stacks of identical volumes. It's times like this I wish I hadn't kept my pocketscreen a secret from Charlotte. Then I could send her a quick message. She'd reply in moments, and all would be well.

Then again, Charlotte having that kind of direct access would probably do me more harm than good.

When I finally approach the front desk, it's the headmistress herself who pops her head up.

"Oh," I say, hiding my startled state with a nervous tuck of hair behind one ear. My hidden pocketscreen feels ten kilograms heavier in my rucksack. Can she see the guilt written all over my face? "Headmistress O'Hare."

I expect her to scold me for my tardiness to second course. But the frown and worried crease between her brows hold a different meaning altogether.

"Alice." Her frown deepens, revealing parentheses on either side of lips the same pale colour as her aged but unblemished skin. "I have been attempting to track you down all morning. Did you not hear your name called over the com?"

"I must have missed it."

"Oh, well, in any matter, please feel free to take the day off your courses with a full excused absence."

This might be the best news I've had all year—if it wasn't

accompanied by nausea and the feeling as if I'm going to fall over. "Any particular reason why?"

"So unfortunate about your sister. The truth came as a shock to our entire staff."

I grab the counter to keep from teetering. The world tilts, and my vision crosses. Colours blend together, followed by the familiar haze which fades in and out, in and out. When my focus returns, the faintest reflection of my face stares back at me from the glass cabinet behind Headmistress O'Hare. White as Blanche's lace gloves, but far less elegant. My twisted expression seems to claw at my pained word as I manage to choke it out. "Unfortunate?"

Headmistress blinks. "You haven't heard?"

Can't move. Can't think.

Charlotte.

Thin lips underlining her pointed nose, Headmistress withdraws a copy of *The Oxford Gazette* and unfolds it on the surface before me.

A black-and-white photo of my sister stares up at me.

I've found her.

Charlotte is front-page news.

Ņews

GIRLS SCHOOL LIBRARIAN ARRESTED FOR EVASION
—STORY DEVELOPING

I scan the article, hardly able to contain the rapid breaths escaping my chest.

> *Charlotte Liddell, 26, was taken into custody by local authorities early this morning after an anonymous informer reported the young librarian for failing to Register as a confirmed Wonder.*
> *It has been reported that Liddell surrendered without protest.*
> *She awaits a sentencing hearing while in custody at the Newgate Reform Centre.*

This is a prank. It must be. "Did Charlotte put you up to this?" My voice shakes. Words slur. I've heard rumours of the

Newgate Reform Centre in London. Only rumours because no girl who's been sent there has ever returned.

The expression on Headmistress O'Hare's face—all sharp angles and barbed lines—chills my core. I continue reading.

> *The punishment for Rogue Wonders varies from case to case. Some have managed to evade the law, choosing to find sanctuary in the undisclosed haven known as Wonderland, a location that has eluded authorities since the Great Divide and the disappearance of Lady Scarlet.*

This part isn't news. But my eyebrows arch at the mentions of Wonderland and Lady Scarlet, two topics usually avoided by media.

> *Other convicts are given the chance at reform. They are legally Registered, marked, and chipped. Researchers are still fine-tuning the cordial that is used to suppress the Wonder Gene, the overall goal remaining the safety and security of our society.*

And there it is. My stomach rolls, and I think I might lose my coffee. Hypocrites, the lot of them. The entire reason for the tech restrictions among civilians was to keep us safe. Because only leaders and officials and militia have the control and caution to use such power properly. Yet they abuse that power, wield it to keep those who pose a threat under their thumbs.

No faith in their fellow man.

No freedom.

And Charlotte? A Wonder? How is this possible? "There's no way she would have blatantly disobeyed the law like that," I say. "Who reported her? Who—?"

"You're looking pale, dear. Perhaps you'd like to sit down." Headmistress O'Hare's voice comes out poised and practiced.

My vision blurs again. Have the lights always been this bright in here? I bolt out the door beyond the desk and race up the stairs to Charlotte's flat, tripping several times to the detriment of my now-sore shins. Dinah greets me at the door, weaving between my ankles in a figure eight.

"Not now, cat."

Her pitiful meow does nothing to sway me as I take in the details that confirm Charlotte's in trouble.

Her handbag, hanging on a hook beside the front door, exactly where it was when I left this morning.

Her favourite cardigan, folded neatly on the storage bench below the hooks. I gather it into my arms and inhale, noting the familiar scents of fabric softener with a hint of parchment. Charlotte is one of the few allowed to handle original editions when they are collected for transcription. It's always been her most treasured task, one I never found appealing.

Inside her room, Charlotte's bed is made, but the light's been left on. How did I miss that extra detail before? Did the authorities come for her while I slept? They couldn't have. I would have heard her.

Unless . . .

Unless she knew they were coming for her and she tried to dodge arrest? Out the window, maybe? The fire escape?

None of this makes sense.

Now I'm riffling through her drawers. Tossing clothes onto the floor. Turning over her hamper. Dinah pads in, hopping onto the queen-sized bed and curling up at the centre. She purrs and licks her paw, seemingly unfazed that Charlotte's missing.

"A fine day you must be having, Your Majesty." I curtsey as I did this morning. As I do every other time I encounter this elitist cat, for the life of me unable to figure out why Charlotte has kept her around. "Not a care in the world. Satisfied to sit and be waited on paw and tail."

She purrs, her tail flicking this way and that like the hand of a clock.

A *clock*.

A memory surfaces. A question Charlotte always asked whenever I was late to the supper table—which was quite often—comes to mind.

"What use is it to spend time when we can save it?" She'd point at the little clock on the table, winking, a sparkle in her eyes. "You never know when a few extra minutes will get you out of a bind. Or the secrets a new hour might tell you that the previous one concealed."

Her blathering about time as if it were a living, breathing person always caught me off-guard. It isn't like my sister to speak in nonsense and riddles. Besides, time is never our own. Not really. Charlotte joked about saving it. But what use is it to save what is never ours to begin with?

The locket watch around my neck is a testimony to this truth. No matter how much I rely on the thing to save me, it's merely a device. It may wake me from my nightmares, sure, but they occur regardless. It's one thing to *tell* time but another feat entirely to try and *change* it.

My pocketscreen vibrates from my rucksack. Strange. I've never been able to get a signal on campus with all the security measures they have in place. Only professors and select staff have access to the school's limited WiFi.

No. Charlotte would never. She despises technology.

I rush to the sitting room, knocking over the clock on the coffee table when I bump into the useless furniture. It crashes to the floor, and I promptly ignore it. The vibrating is coming from Charlotte's handbag. I know what I'll find inside, but it still comes as a shock to withdraw the shiny, not-cracked pocketscreen.

Fifty-two missed calls. All from M. Hatter. There are dozens of messages from her too. I try a few passcode combinations—each one failing to let me in—so I can read the texts in full. All I can see with limited access are snippets, tiny blips that reveal Madi is as worried about Charlotte as I am.

Call me back . . .

Why won't you . . .

Are you ignoring . . .

I knew I heard them talking last night when Charlotte rescued me. She must have had Madi on speaker. That part, at least, was real.

I'm still attempting to unlock Charlotte's pocketscreen as I walk back towards her bedroom. The fallen clock trips me on the way, forcing me to pay it a moment's mind. I retrieve it, then turn it over in my hands. It's one of the few items we've had since the Foundling House. An old outdated thing that's as irrelevant as a physical book nowadays. There's nothing particularly unique about it at first glance.

"It's just a clock," I say to Dinah, who responds to my statement with a bored meow.

I'm about to put the timepiece back in its place when a seemingly insignificant detail catches my eye. There, on the side, is a tiny keyhole cut out of the wood. How have I never noticed it before?

Picking it up once more, I examine what I missed. How very curious. I don't suppose . . .

No.

It couldn't be.

Forgetting all logic and reason, I pick up my rucksack and search through the contents. Then my memory catches up to my mind, and I snatch my pullover off the floor by the settee where I discarded it last night. Just inside the front pocket is the key Chess gave me.

Before I can question the absurdity of the idea, I place the key into the hole on the side of the clock. Twist it forty-five degrees counterclockwise. The sound of a little click ticks my pulse up to speed.

The back of the clock pops open, swinging on a hinge I swear wasn't there before.

"Charlotte, what sort of secrets have these hours been keeping?"

Part of me doesn't want to know. But my sister's disappearance and the odd way things have fit into place urges me to investigate. When I open the clock's door, four quarter-folded pieces of parchment spill out. I unfold each one, flattening them out on the coffee table.

An old map of London from before the Divide, their landmarks and sights crossed-off with black ink. In their places, new locations have been written in Charlotte's hand. "Heart Palace" and "Tulgey Wood" and "Pool of Tears" are among the list.

"I've never heard of any of these," I say.

Dinah jumps on top of the map, and I shoo her away with a pillow.

Next is an envelope with my name on it, also written in Charlotte's familiar hand.

Alice.

I withdraw what I expect to be a letter inside, only to find a folded, torn-out page from a book. I set it aside and focus on the third mystery.

A birth certificate. Charlotte's birth certificate.

"Charlotte Jean Spade," I read aloud. "Date of Birth: Twenty-Seven December. Place of birth: Spade Quarter, Wonderland. Wonder Gene: Positive. Parents: Quincy

Sable, Minister of Spades, and Brianna Morningside, Lady of Spades."

I fall back on the settee, not bothering to shoo Dinah this time when she crawls onto my lap.

"I cannot believe this."

Not only is Charlotte *not* my sister. She's a Wonder. A Wonder with parents in positions of importance.

I glance at the fourth parchment, the final piece of the puzzle. Or maybe it's only a corner of the framework.

A lost Wonder poster, a photo of sixteen-year-old Charlotte at its centre.

If Charlotte's a Wonder . . .

. . . Then who in the world am I?

There's only so much new information one can take in a golden afternoon.

Sunshine seeks me through the in-between spaces of the covered windows. I stand and draw back the crinkled blue chiffon curtain. Squint. Seems spring decided to show its face. I won't be needing that brolly today after all.

"Would you make up your mind already?" I complain to the sun, feeling rather ridiculous as I close the curtain with more force than is necessary. "Hot or cold? Cold or hot? It's annoying, really."

Dinah shadows my every move as I pace the flat, clutching the lost Wonder poster in one hand, Charlotte's birth certificate in the other.

"Did Charlotte kidnap me?"

Meow.

"Why? What's her motive? Ha! *Motive*? Really? She's not a criminal."

Purr.

"Does this mean I'm from Wonderland too? It's wishful thinking, of course. But it's possible, right?"

Hiss.

"Oh, you're no help at all!"

Meow.

Think. What's the last memory I have with Mum and Dad?

But no matter how hard I try to picture their faces, closed eyes and racked brain and all, I can't. There are blips of images. A woman's closed, red-lipped smile. A man's hands folded in front of him, trousers pleated and pressed. But nothing substantial. Those images could be of anyone. From anywhere.

"If only cats could talk," I say. "Then maybe you'd be of some use after all."

Dinah simply meows again as I sink onto the settee, letting the pieces of parchment fall at my feet. I rest my elbow on the settee's arm, leaning my head against my knuckles. I close my eyes and take a deep breath in.

What else?

There was a garden, like the one from my dream last night when I changed all the doors to windows. It couldn't have been at the Foundling House. Much too extravagant for a place where orphans reside. We have a garden here at school, but compared to the one in my memory it pales in contrast. Besides, flowers are frivolous. Vegetables are a much more practical thing to grow, even if said vegetables include beets and turnips.

The settee seems to enfold me as I sink deeper, tucking my feet beneath me and raising my shoulders to my ears.

Let's not forget those scents, too delightful to be within reach. The roses smelled better than any flower I've encountered in my sixteen years. Not the fake, concentrated aroma that comes from a bottle of perfume. More subtle. Authentic, with a bit of earth mixed in. And of course there was the added bonus of treacle and tea. And sweets.

Mum always liked her sweets. Puddings and jams and cherry tarts.

My lashes flutter wide, and I sit straight up. "That's something!" My exclamation startles Dinah, sending the frazzled cat beneath the coffee table. "I remember sweets. Loads of them. Which means Charlotte had to have brought me from Wonderland. We never had them at the Foundling House, not on Queen's Day nor Christmas. Here, Headmistress is so strict, you're lucky if you get a modest helping of pudding on holidays."

Dinah meows her agreement out of sight, most likely surprised at my praise in place of my usual sarcasm towards her.

As if cats could understand sarcasm.

I gather both papers again, rise, and resume my walk about the flat. The movement helps me think. Soothes me like shuffling cards. Renewed energy surges, and despite the remaining mysteries swirling around in my head, fresh motivations take root.

I've always longed to search for our—my—parents. To ask them why they left. Whatever reason they had for leaving us—me—surely it was because they had no other option. I had to believe that, no matter what Charlotte said.

But now? Now I'm certain they wanted me. If the lost Wonder poster doesn't prove it, Charlotte's evasions do.

Everything I've ever known is a lie.

PLAY

This school.

My past.

My sister.

Lies.

Is my name Alice?

"Maybe Charlotte's not her real name either," I say aloud. "The birth certificate could be a fraud. Perhaps librarian is her cover. I'll bet she doesn't even know how to read."

The moment I say it, regret and empathy take the place of anger and resentment. If nothing else, my fake sister's love for books was—is—absolutely real. It doesn't take a genius to see that.

Finger-combing my matted hair, I gaze around the room again. I'm dizzy and exhausted. Wishing for a nap. My focus lands on my rucksack.

I snatch the bag up and withdraw the gift that seemed

trivial. Now that I've seen what Chess's key can do, I have to believe this means something more as well.

Blanche's book.

"I'd meant to give you to Charlotte," I inform the yellowed pages, my habit of talking to inanimate objects in full swing. "Did Blanche know?"

Making my way back to the settee, I flip through the tome. But rather than finding a textbook relaying dull history lessons as the dust jacket suggests, I'm greeted instead by nonsensical poems, riddles, and entire sections dedicated to histories of different games and their rules and origins. Card games. Board games. Sports games. Brain games. Never mind about Charlotte's Holy Grail.

This one belongs to me. I flip through the pages, my eyes widening with each game title that catches my interest.

Croquet.

Chess.

Black Hearts.

Labyrinth.

Handwritten notes and sketches fill the margins from cover to cover. I'm immediately sucked in. How can I help it? This entire book is about *games*. Why can't we study subjects like this in school? It would make for a much more interesting lesson, in my opinion.

In between the game histories, riddles and poems offer amusement. Several, surprisingly, are familiar. Charlotte would make me recite these as a child. A laugh escapes.

The sound seems to tell the cat it's okay to emerge. She curls up next to me on the cushion. If I didn't know any better, I'd say she was reading the book along with me.

"You know, Dinah, Charlotte always said a good memory is more valuable than the Crown Jewels."

The cat paws the pages.

My fingers trace the titles as I peruse the silly poems.

"The Golden Afternoon."

"The Walrus and the Carpenter."

"You Are Old, Father William."

"Jabberwocky."

I clear my throat, and voice still thick, I begin.

"*'Twas brillig, and the slithy toves*
Did gyre and gimble in the wabe:
All mimsy were the borogoves,
And the mome raths outgrabe."

Dinah claws at the book, hissing at the nightmarish, made-up words.

I blink away the coloured spots that seem to shuffle before my eyes. They fade in and out, moving up and down and every which way imaginable. When I flip the page, the eye tricks vanish.

"Oh, hush," I say to Dinah. "It's not all that bad. It's a story. Mome raths and slithy toves." The odd words flutter off my tongue like butterflies. I can almost picture them swooshing through the air, circling around me. The sensation of falling sideways causes a bout of nausea. I clear my throat again and straighten where I sit, wishing I had some club soda or a tonic to settle my stomach. "Nonsense."

Dinah's flicking tail and turned up whiskers let on she is not amused.

Page after page, such silliness continues. Every time I think I'll stop, I can't. I'm drawn in by the nostalgia of the poems one minute and the explanation of ways to open a Chess game the next. I yawn, nearly closing the book when the best strategies for outsmarting your opponents in a board game called Labryinth catch my attention.

"Sometimes, the best path is not the obvious one," I say.

It's when I read the words aloud that my world tilts once more, bringing on the familiar and unwelcome vertigo, causing me to take off my glasses and rub my eyes. I must need a new prescription. This pair seems to make my vision worse these days.

I forgo the recitation and opt to read quietly to myself. I read until my eyes start to strain from lack of lamplight. Until I miss my fake sister so much my chest aches. Until the late-afternoon sun casts an orange-red hue over everything, and shadows begin to creep and crawl across the floor reaching for my ankles, my knees. Moving me to pull a wool blanket over my lap.

"Charlotte really is the worst," I tell the tome through my tears, hardly believing the admission. When did I begin to cry?

This book, these poems and games, would never be welcome in our society. It's one thing to restrict our use of technology and entirely another to keep us from our own history and literature. From pastimes and fun. In a moment's memory, I'm sitting on Charlotte's lap, asking her to read the stories to me again.

"Come now, Alice. It's time for bed."

"Just one more? Pretty please?"

"Oh, all right. Just one. But it's straight to bed after that."

She'd smile and curl up beside me on the single mattress we shared, an accent lamp on an upturned milk crate our lone light.

"Which one is your favourite?"

Whenever she had asked, I never hesitated. My answer was always the same.

"The Crocodile."

I search for the simple, two-stanza poem. The Table of Contents says that it's there, but the page appears to be missing. Torn right from its place. I wonder . . .

Snatching the envelope from the table, I take out the folded book page, lining it up with the torn edges inside the book. As anticipated, the missing poem matches perfectly. Someone has underlined certain letters. I opt to read the words in silence for fear my eyes will cross. I couldn't speak past the lump in my throat anyway.

<u>H</u>ow doth th<u>e</u> little crocodile
Improve his shining tail,
<u>A</u>nd pou<u>r</u> the wa<u>t</u>er<u>s</u> of the Nile
On every golden sc<u>a</u>le!
How chee<u>r</u>fully he s<u>e</u>ems to grin
Ho<u>w</u> neatly spreads hi<u>s</u> c<u>l</u>aws,
An<u>d</u> welcomes little fishes in,
With gently smiling jaws!

I cough. Swipe at the tears with the back of my wrist. Then I focus on the underlined letters, the ink lines so faint they would be easy to miss.

HeArtsarewild

Hearts are wild? What does that mean? Or maybe . . . could it be scrambled? I scan the page again, attempting to come up with other possibilities that might make more sense.

Nothing does.

I search the other poems and riddles, scrutinising each one. But this seems to be the sole altered entry. A page meant for me, apparently.

What are you trying to tell me, Charlotte?

I let the book fall closed. Remove the dust jacket covering up the book's true identity. I spread my fingers over the blank red-leather cover. The real title is impressed in gold foil lettering, but no author is listed.

The Adventurer's Almanac

My eyes adjust. I hold the book closer to my face, examining a faint detail I'd missed before.

Smudgy fingerprints near the bottom right-hand corner.

These are my fingerprints, I realise. This is Charlotte's book.

I open the cover again, this time focusing on a scrawled inscription in cursive just inside.

"To my darling, Charlee," I read aloud. "Best of luck in the Trials this year. I hope this book will help you find your way."

The *Trials*?

As in *the* Wonderland Trials?

Now I know I must be dreaming.

This is almost verbatim what Blanche said to me.

Dinah paws my arm as if to ground me in this rather upside-down reality.

I retrieve my pocketscreen and soundbuds from my rucksack. Pull up another downloaded podcast.

Winning Wonders: How Those Before Us Took the Crown.

Play.

I skip past the intro music and wait impatiently for an advert to play through. Then Madi's voice greets me like an old friend.

"There's always been a cloud of mystery surrounding the Wonderland Trials. But let us talk about how winners before us came out on top."

She lists famous Wonders. Lady Scarlet, no contest, is the obvious first. "The initial champion of the first-ever annual Trials, her crown was symbolic."

Madi lists year after year until finally she comes to the Trials from ten years ago.

I turn up the volume.

"Charlee Spade—Queen of Team Heart and daughter of the Minister and Lady Spade—and her team became the closest in a decade to passing the Fourth and final Trial. It was rumoured Scarlet had her eye on Charlee in particular, and considered naming her the throne's successor, should she complete the Fourth Trial, of course. But during the Fourth Trial, Charlee went missing, never to be heard from again."

The Fourth Trial is always the most challenging, or so Madi always says. No one since Scarlet herself has ever made it through the fourth and back again.

"For players to never return from the Fourth Trial is not unusual, of course," Madi says. "At least one player goes missing during the Heart Trial every year. The top performing team still comes out winning, but speculation abounds. Will the Queen of Hearts ever deem anyone good enough to become her heir?"

I press pause. Of course I've heard this story before, but I never connected Charlee to *my* Charlotte until now.

Charlotte detests nicknames.

Maybe I never really knew her at all.

Emotions spent, I read the book's inscription again, this time noting the signature.

With all my love, R.S.H.

"R.S.H.? Who is R.S.H.?"

Dinah purrs, pawing at the book again.

"Bugger off. You'll ruin it."

She doesn't stop. Instead, she jumps onto my lap, succeeding in knocking the book to the floor.

It lands open. A few of the pages come loose.

"Now you've done it, you relentless old fur ball."

But as I lean over to scoop the book up, a corner of red catches my eye.

A crimson, notecard-sized sealed envelope lies at my feet. I set the book on the sofa beside me, out of Dinah's reach, and turn the envelope over in my hand. The wax seal is black, stamped with a heart, the letter *Q* to the left and an *H* to the right.

The Royal Seal of Wonderland.

The Queen of Hearts.

My pulse pounds. I've seen this image online. In secret groups and on hidden pages where I'm not meant to look. In virtual spaces our Normal queen would prefer no one venture.

I break the seal and withdraw a single playing card. The back of the card bears the seal image in black and red and gold. In place of a face on the opposite side is a handwritten note. The sight of my own name stops my breath. I read, lips moving silently.

> *Dear Miss Liddell,*
>
> *Please accept this cordial invitation to participate in this year's annual Wonderland Trials as a Wildflower player for Team Heart.*
>
> *You will find enclosed a clue to help you find your way.*
>
> *Please note you must enter Wonderland by midnight on 30 April, or you will be disqualified. Your requirement to provide vital records has been waived.*
>
> *Thank you.*
>
> > *All my best,*
> >
> > > *Blanche de Lapin*
> > > *Royal Advisor to Her Majesty,*
> > > *Queen Scarlet of the House of Heart*

An invitation.

An *official* invitation.

Not just to play in the Trials, but to play for Team Heart. Her Majesty's own house. I read the note on the card again, checking the envelope for the promised clue and instructions.

"I hope eet vill be ov use to you een finding your vay."

The envelope contains one more playing card—an Ace of Hearts with a question scribbled on its face.

Why is a raven like a writing desk?

"How am I supposed to find the entrance with nothing but a riddle to help me?" I scan the invite a third time. The thirtieth of April. I turn to Dinah. "That gives me two days to find Charlotte in London. Then we can make a break for Wonderland together. She must know where the entrance is."

"You cannot possibly be serious, child," Dinah says, sounding rather like the headmistress herself, distinct BBC accent making me feel as if I'm in the presence of a queen.

Lovely. I'm so exhausted I'm imagining my cat is talking to . . .

"Are you quite sure about that?" Chess's voice too? I must have accidentally fallen asleep.

I stand and smack my cheeks, blink a handful of times. Yawn. Stretch. Run in place. Wake up, Alice.

"Chesster, would you like to tell her, or shall I?"

I whirl.

Dinah, who sat curled up on the sofa moments ago, has vanished. In her place sits a woman in her fifties, vibrant orange hair striped with white drawn back in an old-fashioned do, catlike eyes aglow with mischief. She twitches her nose in a feline manner.

My jaw hangs. "Dinah?"

She clears her throat and nods curtly.

But it isn't the fact that my cat has transformed from feline to female that has me tripping backwards over the coffee table.

Beside her, Chess Shire in the flesh greets me with that massive toothy grin.

"Chess," I say, scowling. What is it about this poster boy that irks me so?

"Ace." He brushes pink-streaked hair from his forehead. His striking eyes never fail to stop me where I stand—when he shows them, that is. Turquoise with a dark spot in the bottom corner of his right iris. "So nice to see you again. Might I introduce you to my grandmother, Dinah FeLin?"

I face the woman who was once my cat and take in the subtle similarities. The stark differences.

"*Detective* Dinah FeLin," she corrects, tone stiff. "And it is about time. I thought you would never find White Rabbit's invitation. Then again, you have always been simple, so what can I expect?"

Chess referred to Blanche as White Rabbit too. Strange. But this is the least of my worries. "Simple?" I say. "I beg your pardon?"

"What my grandmother means to convey"—Chess lifts his hands—"is that she is delighted to finally make your acquaintance . . . er . . . in person." He bows, dipping his head and waving his arm in a courtier-like gesture.

Oh, please. Spare me the niceties. But the word is sinking in. "Grandmother?"

"Indeed," she says to me. Then to Chess she adds, "And not at all." Dinah sniffs. If possible, the action only heightens her snobbish air. "I always mean what I say, and you, my boy, ought to mean what I say too."

These two really are related.

"I mean what you should have said," Chess counters. "Or, at the very least, what you should have meant."

This conversation is going nowhere. "Excuse me? Would someone please mind telling me what in the world is going on?"

"Well, we could try." Chess grins. "But you'd need to specify which world you are referring to first. Your world? Or ours?"

"Forgive my grandson." Dinah waves her hand, almost like she's shooing a pesky moth. "He enjoys playing with semantics. Shall we get on with it?"

"Be my guest."

With the slightest tilt of her head, Dinah sighs. She retrieves the lost Wonder poster from the coffee table and examines it. "There are so many of these. But Charlotte is the first one we've recovered."

The sadness in her eyes is all the confirmation I need. "So did she . . . kidnap me?"

"Hard to say, since we don't actually know who you are."

That's what I was afraid of. I sniff and blink hard. I will not cry in front of strangers.

"Don't fret, child. I have been investigating these disappearances for years, since the foundation of the Wonderland Trials. As best I can tell, every player that's gone missing has one thing in common." She eyes the poster, then hands it to Chess.

"The Fourth Trial. The Heart Trial." Darkness shrouds his words. He doesn't elaborate, but the hollow look in his eyes explains more than words can. He was part of the Trials last year. Did he lose someone?

"You're saying a player goes missing during the Trials every year?"

They nod, but it's Dinah who speaks. "At least one. Sometimes it's more."

This lines up with what Madi said in her podcast. I've always considered her my number-one source, however unofficial. I turn to Chess and ask the question. "Did you lose someone close to you?"

His jaw works. His hold tightens on the poster, wrinkling the image. "My younger brother. Kit. He'd be fourteen now. I should never have let him compete last year. Thirteens are allowed, but in my opinion, he was still too young. Too inexperienced."

My expression softens, my annoyance for this "poster boy" not quite as prominent. Did I misjudge him? I want to find my family too. "How can I help?"

Dinah tilts her head, studying me with scrutinising dark eyes. "We have a proposition for you."

My gaze moves between her and Chess. "I'm listening."

Chess's grin returns, the wells in his eyes sparkling.

Dinah rises and crosses to the window. She peeks through the curtains, staring down at the twilight-shaded campus below. Taking great care with her next words, Dinah replies slowly and with the utmost precision.

"The time has come"—she glances over her shoulder, mischief playing in her eyes—"for someone to finish the Fourth Trial."

PAUSE

Three resounding raps on the entry door seize us from conversation.

"Alice?" Headmistress's voice, muffled but astutely recognisable, calls from the stairwell. "Miss Liddell, are you quite all right?"

Dinah lifts a single finger to her lips. Shakes her head.

I clear my throat, but somehow a croak is still all I can muster. "Yes." I swallow and try again, this time managing a more assertive tone. "Yes, of course. Everything's fine."

Everything is *not* fine. My cat is a grumpy old detective woman, and an infuriating yet charming Wonder boy keeps disappearing and reappearing at every turn.

"I thought you might like to join me for supper this evening. We can chat about your future now that . . ." A pause. A cough. Feet shuffle. ". . . your sister is no longer with us."

It's the shuffling feet that set me on high alert. That have me reaching for something to use as a shield or a weapon.

The best I can come up with is a wooden spoon from the kitchenette drawer. Not very encouraging.

Headmistress Marsha O'Hare is not alone.

"Alice?"

"One minute!" Think. Stall her. "The door was jammed this morning. That darn outdated lock." My nervous half laugh is the opposite of convincing. But the excuse isn't too far from the truth. This building is well over a hundred years old. Probably two hundred, at the very least.

The raps on the door escalate to pounds.

Then a jumble of activities take place, one on top of the other. Like a house of cards falling to its doom.

Dinah sidesteps behind the curtain. Upon her return, she's the feline I've always known her to be, furry, white-tipped tail flicking this way and that.

I blink. This is no time for my eyes to play tricks on me. And yet, unreliable as ever, they do.

Chess vanishes piece by piece from his spot on the settee, his grin the last thing I glimpse before he disappears completely.

Well, that's splendid. What am I supposed to do now?

Three more pounds, this time lower, harder. Someone is kicking the door. Two, maybe three voices mumble in low tones. Male? Female? I can't tell.

"Alice," Headmistress calls again. The doorknob jiggles. Hinges rattle. "It is not a good idea for you to be on your own right now, dear." A hint of force rises into her otherwise calm and practised words. The way she says "dear" leaves me unsettled.

I grip the spoon tighter. A single bead of sweat trickles from my hairline to my brow, and I adjust my glasses.

Fondness is not a word I'd use to describe my feelings for the woman. Until today I believed my antipathy for her was simply that she's too strict. And she's like every other person

in a place of power. Controlling. Stifling. Insufferable. But this
is something more. Now my stomach lurches, and I'm certain
it has nothing to do with my wavering vision.

"Be right there." But I'm out of time. To Dinah in cat form
I hiss, "What do I do?"

She meows. As usual, she's no help at all.

"Chess," I whisper, somehow knowing he's still present.
"Please. Help me."

His voice reaches out from some corner of the room. "Do
what you have always done."

"Which is?"

"See what's right in front of your nose, of course. Nothing's
impossible, after all."

The doorknob rattles again. Metal on metal jangles, and I
know Headmistress must be looking for her copy of the key.

I'm so mad I could cry and quite possibly throw this spoon
and hope it knocks Chess in the head. I focus on his words.
It's what he's been saying since we met.

Nothing's impossible.

But right in front of my nose? Half the time I can't
see that far.

"To get out," Chess adds, "you must first go in."

And now I'm certain he's sticking his mind where it doesn't
belong. Chess had to have invaded my dream. I don't know
how he did it, but he was there with his voice floating around
the halls of my nightmare.

Except . . .

It's not a nightmare. Not anymore. Once a trap where
nothing made sense, last night it became a place where I
felt free and bold and brave. Where I didn't feel like Alice—
the Normal girl destined for ordinary things someone else
planned. Instead I held the power to unlock my own destiny.

To see past the locked door that's always held me back.

To believe in something more. Just out of reach.

That's when the entire room seems to turn on its side. Like a cube tumbling around me, but I stand upright, unaffected by my spinning, topsy-turvy world. Music I've heard before comes from nowhere. I hear laughter.

And a smile.

Nonsense, I almost say out loud. *How can one hear a smile?* But the thought dies before I speak it into existence. Because there is one smile as wide as it is loud. And I can hear it before I see it.

When I turn, Chess stands before me. The vision of him now is startling. Striking. Though similar to how I've always seen him, now his handsome features appear all the more pronounced. The turquoise in his liquid eyes seems to swirl. The streaks in his copper hair shimmer, changing from pink to white to grey. His grin grips me, a magnet drawing me in.

And the dark spot in the bottom corner of his right iris? It jumps from one eye to the other. A moving target, animated and unable to remain still. A shooting star soaring across the universe behind his gaze.

"This is unreal."

"It's as real as you or me." Chess offers a hand. An invitation to challenge him? A request to dance?

I don't know, and in this moment I don't care. Letting the tips of my fingers graze the tips of his, I accept his invitation. His touch is warm and unexpectedly tangible. And then it isn't. My hand passes right through his. "Are you doing this?" I ask, eyes wide.

Grabbing hold of my hand, he shakes his head. "No." Chess holds my knuckles near his lips. "You are."

I hold my breath, waiting for him to place a kiss on my hand, wondering why I don't pull away.

Pound. Bang. Slam.

I drop the spoon.

Chess releases my hand. In a flash he's gone again. The

room spins right side up. Colours fade, and whatever world I'd entered into moments ago vanishes.

"Now focus," Chess says from somewhere behind me. I feel firm hands on my arms, grounding me.

His familiarity startles and soothes. His touch feels safe. Welcome, even. As much as I want to push him away, that same part of me wants him closer. To see him through upside-down eyes again.

"Wonderland is what we imagine it to be," he says. "You can become anything. Go anywhere. That's the magic of the Gene."

When did my hands start shaking? "Let's say I was born a Wonder. I still don't know anything about how to—"

Chess stops me. "Heart will always trump knowledge. Do you want to be Wonder?"

"Yes," I breathe. Desperately. I don't add the last part out loud. But I don't have to. He knows it. I know it. Charlotte—wherever she is—knows it. I've listened to every episode of *Common Nonsense*. Studied everything I could get my hands on about Wonderland, its history, and the Trials. I may not know a thing about what it takes to use this ability, but everything inside of me has been leading up to this moment.

Bang, bang, bang! "That is quite enough, young lady." Headmistress sounds too much like Charlotte. "You will open this door at once!"

"Be one, Ace. Be a Wonder." Chess lets go. I sense him back away, his warmth retreating. "Just like in your dream."

The nickname doesn't bother me as much now. It feels on purpose. As if he's chosen it for me. Closing my eyes, I picture myself back in the nightmare I've always dreaded, in the hall with doors and a table with—

Tea.

I bolt for the kitchen, opening cupboards and drawers. Nothing. Of course Charlotte wouldn't have tea.

As soon as the thought crosses my mind, another replaces it. But . . . I do.

"Break it down," I hear Headmistress say. "I can't find the key, and we can't very well wait any longer. The authorities will be here any minute."

I leap over the couch, grab the book, invitation, and papers. Then I snatch up my rucksack and stuff the items away, digging for the vial Charlotte gave me.

"Charlotte," I whisper. Did she know I'd need this? Her desire to keep me safe from harm and shield me from the truth is more confusing than Blanche's riddle. She'd given me this as a reminder of my—our—allergy. Is it an allergy, though?

Only one way to find out.

The door bursts open.

My eyes lock with Headmistress O'Hare's. There's disdain there. But also fear.

And a syringe full of something I don't want anywhere near me in one hand.

Cordial. Must be. Not today, Headmistress.

"Detain her." She points a finger my way at the same moment two security guards who appear to be identical twins flank her on either side. Each wears a name tag bearing the same title and name.

Officer Deedum.

I don't hesitate another minute. I uncork the bottle, down the bitter tea in a single, solitary gulp.

Then I shrink.

And shrink.

And shrink.

I'm shutting up like a telescope until I'm so small I might as well be invisible.

"Search the bedroom," Headmistress O'Hare orders the first guard, voice booming from stories above. "You," she instructs the other, "stand watch at the door. The girl might be able to hide, but she can't go far." As confident as she's always seemed, I detect the slightest waver in her voice. She, like the rest of us, believes what we've all been taught.

Wonders are dangerous.

I don't have time to wait for her to realise I haven't vanished at all and she could squash me if she wished. Instead I run across the rug, the threads a forest of white and burgundy. When I reach the settee, it feels more like entering a dark tunnel that goes on for miles than crawling beneath a piece of furniture. I leap from the rug's edge down to the wood floor, tumbling face-first in the process.

Ouch.

Headmistress O'Hare's heeled pumps pound the floor. They cause an echo so loud, I have to cover my tiny ears. What feels like an earthquake sends me off balance, causing me to topple again.

I surely hope Chess isn't witnessing this.

"The bedroom's empty, madam," one officer says. His enormous shiny brown shoes appear at the other end of the settee.

"Windows are all latched too," the other one says from the front door. "She must be here somewhere."

"Enough," Headmistress says. "This is what I get for asking a pair of idiots to help me." She lets off a frustrated sigh. "Fine, search the campus. Close the gates. I don't care what you do, find her. If her sister was an Unregistered, it's likely she is too. And we can't have Unregistered Wonders running about in the open. It would cause utter and complete chaos."

When the door finally slams, I wait several minutes before emerging from beneath the settee.

"Well." Human Dinah glides towards me. She offers a hint of a smile and three small claps of her hands in lieu of applause. "That was—"

"Extraordinary!" Chess un-vanishes and kicks his heels

together. He bounces into the kitchen, laughing like he's won a card championship. He withdraws his own little bottle of tea. After a bit of rattling around, he places a saucer on the floor before me, then pours his tea onto it. "You're a natural, Ace!"

His large voice hurts my ears. I cover them as he helps me onto the saucer's ledge. A teardrop-sized sip sends me shooting into the air, stepping on the saucer and spilling the rest of the tea, which tasted different from what made me shrink. Sweet. With a zing of lemon.

My right size once again, Chess scoops me into a hug and whirls me around.

I keep my arms stiff at my sides but lean in enough to sneak a small inhale of his hair. Who knew a boy could smell like cocoa and peppermint?

He seems to remember himself and sets me down. Then he backs away, covering a cough with his fist. "I mean . . ."

"I thought one was always supposed to know what they mean?" I tease and am slightly horrified by a blush fighting its way up my neck and cheeks.

Chess laughs. "Right you are, Ace." And there's that grin again.

"You two are insufferable," Dinah says. "Alice has two days to find her way into Wonderland, or she's disqualified, and here you both are making eyes at each other."

"Come on, Grandmother. You saw her. She was in." He hops onto the settee, kicking back and crossing his ankles on the coffee table. "She's a natural. She's going to ace the Trials."

My heart does some leaping of its own. Is that why he calls me Ace? Because he . . . believes in me?

"And true that may be," Dinah says, "but the Trials are not for amateurs. And getting in is not the same as staying in. Finding your Mastery takes heart, but there is still the factor of experience. Of which she has little."

"Then show me," I say, impulsively taking her hands.

She almost recoils but seems to think twice about it. One word is all she gives me. "Indeed."

"Let the Trials begin," Chess repeats that familiar phrase I've heard Madi say on many a podcast episode.

But for once I'm not really thinking of the Trials or what it would be like to win them. It's my turn to smile at Chess, perhaps the first genuine one I've ever given him. All I can think is to pair Chess's statement with Dinah's final word in my head.

Let the Trials begin, indeed.

MOVE

"Think of tea like a carefully concocted potion." Chess's grin expands with the explanation. The more he talks of Wonderland, the brighter his expression shines. "Each particular blend affects the Wonder Gene differently."

Never in a hundred lifetimes did I imagine myself on a train to London with Chess Shire sitting across from me.

And yet, here I am—here *we* are—and my former annoyance has transformed into mild amusement.

"The tea that made you smaller was no doubt Dwindler's Draught, a unique blend of lavender and black currant."

"And the tea that made me taller?"

Chess pulls the vial from earlier out of his waistcoat pocket. There's still some left. He swirls it around. "Flourisher's Fate. Potent stuff. Serves as an antidote for most other blends. Always a good idea to keep some on hand. Made with lemongrass, ginger, and sunflower pollen. Effects of any blend wear off eventually of course, but if the measurements are off, or the wrong ingredients are added? The results can be deadly." He tucks the vial away, then takes a sip of coffee that's hours old. And judging by his face, it's lost any and all appeal.

I suppress a laugh. Welcome to the Normal world. Where we drink coffee without sugar and add cream so thin it might as well be water.

"How did you know to give me the key?" I ask.

"I didn't." He takes another sip and visibly regrets it. "Your sister gave it to me. She said not to give it to you until the time was right."

My mind spins like a saucer twirling on its end. Tea potions? Invisible realities? And Charlotte and Chess working together?

"She's not my real sister," I say.

"Reality is subjective."

I don't know how to respond to that, so I don't. I'm too spent to argue. It's been hours since we dodged Headmistress O'Hare and her cronies. Hours since I entered Wonderland for a few blissful moments.

According to Chess, I've been glitching in and out of the Wonderland Reality all along. During the day and, apparently, in my dreams too. It's how he was able to speak to me inside my nightmare. He wasn't invading my thoughts. On the contrary. I was entering a world I've always been curious about but never thought I'd see.

He sputters a cough after taking another swig of his coffee. "Now, show me again."

I long to lie down on one of the upper berths of our cramped but private train compartment. If I could shut my eyes for a spell, or two or three . . . But, no. I'm expected to solve Blanche's riddle and enter the Wonderland Reality of my own accord for longer than a few seconds. Sleeping doesn't appear to be in the cards tonight. Just my luck.

Or unluck, as it were.

"I've been at this for ages." I lean against the window.

April showers take their toll on the landscape beyond. "We have less than twenty-four hours before my opportunity to fully enter Wonderland closes. And all I can do is glitch. Shouldn't I be at least attempting to solve the clue?"

"You have solved it." Chess lifts an eyebrow.

I think back to the moment at the flat when I knew in my heart of hearts the tea was what I needed. The moment I knew without a doubt that I am a Wonder.

"Why is a raven like a writing desk, Ace? Give me the first answer that comes to mind."

"It's not," I say. "The riddle is impossible."

"Nothing is impossible."

"That doesn't make any sense. Why would Blanche give me a riddle that can't be solved as a clue?"

"Why, indeed?" Chess leans forwards, a knowing smile coaxing me to mirror his expression. "Again," he says.

Dinah meows her approval from her perch on the upper berth. Evidently there's even a tea that turns Wonders into different creatures—Normal and mythical. Beast's Blend, it's called. It's only recommended for the most skilled of Wonders and must be brewed by a Master of Tea, whatever that is.

I think I'll stay away from that particular mixture. "No one asked you." I scowl at Dinah but do as I'm told.

It takes a few seconds for the wavering vision I usually dread to signal what's taking place. Colours come across more vibrant. Sounds become clearer. The way Chess described it, what I always believed to be a side effect of poor eyesight is really my mind moving in between Realities. It's how he always seems to vanish, when in truth he's only passing seamlessly into a reality unseen. He could see me, but I couldn't see him.

"Do you ever hear music?" he'd asked as I packed for our journey. "Or see things you can't explain?"

I'd nodded.

"Ever heard of the term virtual reality?" Our walk to the railway station with Dinah at our heels accompanied our hushed conversation. "It's older tech, but at one time was quite prominent in society."

The term wasn't foreign to me. As someone who's forever been fascinated by what lies out of reach, technology might as well be another game. One I've done all I can to learn about, despite its illegality.

"Think of it like this," Chess had continued. He'd sped up so he could walk backwards while facing me. "If humans have the capability of inventing tech so advanced a pair of goggles could make you believe you're in another world, what's to say our minds can't do the same on their own? Without the fancy equipment?"

He'd posed a curious question, to be sure. But I still couldn't quite grasp it. Tricks, I understand. Sleight of hand? No problem. But another reality created by the mind alone? Relying solely on the belief of those who were born to be Wonder?

Impossible.

My transition ends almost as soon as it's begun.

"That was only thirty seconds," Chess says. "You'll have to do better than that."

"It takes too much energy." My complaint makes me

sound weak, but at this juncture I don't care. "Maybe this *is* impossible."

"You'll never make it if you keep talking like that." He gestures towards the cat who is all hiss and no bite. "Pretty soon you can master the art of existing in both places. Like my grandmother. Or my smile, for example." All of him vanishes aside from his grin. His teeth almost sparkle, but the effect is a bit disturbing. And irritating

"Would you stop that!"

"Don't get all jealous on me now."

I glare at him. "I am not jealous."

"Listen. In the Trials you're not merely dealing with a pack of cards. You *are* the card." With a flourish of his right hand, he reveals a pack. In a smooth move, he fans the cards out. Retracts them. Another flick of his wrist, and all the cards have disappeared, save one, face towards me.

The ace of hearts, holding my single clue from Blanche.

Okay, now I'm a little jealous. How did he do that? I attempt to swipe the clue card and fail.

"This riddle is not impossible. And neither is what I'm asking you to do."

"You're telling me I have to believe in the impossible, no matter how nonsensical it might seem?"

"Precisely. And yet," Chess adds, "you don't believe. Not completely."

"I believe in what I can see. I believe what I've experienced and what I've seen you and Dinah do."

"It's not enough. You have to know it here." He jabs one finger at his chest. "In your heart."

"My grandson is right, for once," Dinah says, licking her paw. "But perhaps we have made a mistake."

"I thought you said Charlotte is the first of the missing you've uncovered, and so you needed me."

"She is." Chess looks up at Dinah. "And we do. It wasn't

a mistake. She's the missing link, Grandmother. If we can learn what happened to Charlotte, and where Ace came from, we might have a clue as to what happened to the others. To Kit. She could be the key to learning how Charlotte was able to escape their fate." He faces me. "Don't you remember anything? Really, anything at all might help."

Sweets. A garden. A man's hands folded before him. I try to picture those hands through the lens of a magnifying glass. "Spades," I breathe.

If I didn't know any better, I'd say Chess's ears visibly perk at the word. "What about them?"

"You played for Team Spade in the Trials last year."

"Right . . ."

"So, that's what I remember. The symbol for Spades." Digging through my rucksack, I withdraw my pack of cards. I find one from the spade suit and pull it free. "This. Tattooed on a man's right hand."

"A tattoo? That's what you remember?"

I nod.

He glances at Dinah. Back at me. "You're saying the Minister of Spades had something to do with Charlotte's disappearance?" From the look of genuine shock on his usually smug face, the idea is unfathomable to him.

"I don't know," I say quickly, not wanting to accuse anyone of a crime they didn't commit. "Images come back to me in shards and broken up bits." The Minister of Spades . . . Why does that sound famil–? A gasp escapes. "Charlotte's father." Digging through my bag once more, I find the birth certificate. Hand it to Chess.

He takes it, more careful than I expect him to be with the fragile document. "It could mean nothing."

"It could mean everything," Dinah chimes in, licking her paw in between words. "We follow every lead, Chesster. Every lead."

Handing the parchment back to me, the boy I'd always thought to be so confident and untouchable slumps in his seat. "The Minister of Spades was one of my Trainers. Kit was on my team. The minister would have had no logical reason to sacrifice one of his own players."

I study him. The sincere gleam of confusion in those turquoise eyes sends a pang through my heart. I ignore the ache blossoming there. There is a chasm that seems to widen a little more whenever Chess Shire shows more of the side of himself I didn't believe could exist. The vulnerable Chess.

Is this the real him? Is it part of his act?

I don't know what to believe.

"Every lead," Dinah emphasizes again.

"Right." He sits straighter, appearing to gather his thoughts. "We'll run it by Madi when we arrive in London. Maybe she can dig up something on him. Find out who he's talked to. Where he's been."

"Madi?" I'd almost forgotten about Charlotte's pocketscreen and the messages left unseen. "What's she have to do with this?"

There's that grin of his again. "Don't worry, Ace. I won't tell her you're her biggest fan."

He wags his eyebrows in a way that makes me want to clock him in the jaw.

"I resent that."

"Oh, come on now. You listen to her podcast constantly."

"How do you know I listen to Madi's podcast?"

Elbows resting on his knees, Chess sips at his coffee again before responding. "I don't think there's been a single Clash of the Cards event where you didn't have your soundbuds in at some point or another." He taps one ear. "It doesn't take a detective to notice these things. It was my job to watch you. To . . . keep you out of trouble."

"You told Charlotte I was there. At The Rabbit Hole." It isn't a question. No answer is required.

He gives one anyway. One shake of his head tells me more than his next words do. "She knew."

"Why didn't she try to stop me?"

"She was afraid you'd run. She thought by keeping an eye on you, secretly, then at least she still held some semblance of control over the situation. That's where Madi and I came in."

I can hardly believe this. Each new reveal hurts more than the last. "Did you know she wasn't my sister?"

"It wasn't my truth to tell."

I rub my neck with one hand, tapping my fingers on the arm of the chair with the other. Beyond the glass, everything blends together in a smear of black. Black trees, black roads, black buildings. It's so strange to think that a little over twenty-four hours ago I was riding a train like this one, headed nowhere fast.

Now I'm full speed ahead, unable to put on the brakes for how quickly everything around me is changing.

I had a sister. Now I don't know my family at all.

One day I can't stand the sight of Chess Shire. The next I'm not sure what I think of him.

For the first time in hours, our compartment falls silent aside from the rattle of the car over the tracks and the soft patter of rain against the window. I glance over at Chess. He's hunched forwards with his head drooping, bobbing up and down like he's trying to stay awake but can't fight it any longer.

Grateful for the reprieve, I sigh, draw my knees into my chest, and rest my cheek against the soft cotton of my black-and-white-striped leggings. A Christmas gift from Charlotte last year because she knew how much I loved my identical tights.

"For winter," she'd said. "They'll keep you warmer."

A tear, hot and furious, slips from my eye and sneaks over the bridge of my nose. Followed by a second. And a third. I swipe them away with the rolled-up sleeve of my long denim collared shirt. Which is now a dress, thanks to the stretch of black ribbon around my waist. Charlotte never did like my sense of fashion. I stood out too much. Would never conform.

And she was a Wonder all this time.

Chess snores softly, drawing me to shift in my seat and turn my head to face him. He's leaning back now, neck craned and mouth hanging open. Has his nose always been that pointed? I guess one never really looks at a person for too long. There are glances. And brief moments of eye contact. But to really *look* at a person? To see them for all their flaws and angles and irregular charms?

That's something out of the ordinary, indeed.

This Chess—who I'd believed to be an arrogant player so full of himself there was no possible room for heart—seems different to me now. In this state of unconsciousness, with no one around to impress, he could almost be anyone else. Dare I say Normal? Perhaps in another world, we would have been instant friends.

I sigh and stare out the window once more. Because we aren't true friends. I know this is temporary. Whatever I feel between us isn't real. He's keeping a promise to Charlotte and wants his brother found.

I check the time and the current spot on our train route. Another thirty minutes before we reach our destination. As possible as Chess thinks everything is, sleep is one task I know won't be happening tonight, no matter how beat I am. My mind is wired, alight with the possibilities of the Trials. At the same time, my heart feels spent, shattered into pieces like that character from the old nursery rhyme.

Humpty Dumpty sat on a wall; Humpty Dumpty had a great fall . . .

I unlock my pocketscreen again and pull up the file Dinah forwarded to me before we left Oxford. When I open the folder, dozens of individual audio clips pop up on the screen in a list. There's one as recent as a couple of days ago all the way down to one from the year I turned six.

"When you get a chance to listen," she'd said, "all of my reports are recorded for you."

Shoving my soundbuds into my ears, I tap the clip from one year prior.

"Twenty-seven March . . ." Dinah's voice almost seems to purr as she begins her report. The date she gives is from just before she showed up on Charlotte's doorstep. Oddly enough, around the same time I first encountered Chess. I'd never connected the two events. Until now.

"For the first time since she went missing from the Wonderland Trials ten years ago, she was spotted inside our Reality."

I lean in, as if this will help me listen more intently. Charlotte returned to Wonderland over a year ago? Why?

"From what I can tell, she has been secretly meeting with Queen Scarlet's advisor."

I hit pause. Charlotte has been meeting up with Blanche? Did she give Blanche the book? Did she know she would be arrested?

Play.

"And now the law of this land has finally caught up with the young woman we've searched for. Her elusiveness makes her suspect, of course, being the only player we know of who has gone missing from the Fourth Trial and returned. However, after spending time with the suspect in her own home, along with her ward, I have concluded that there may be other motives stirring about. And I intend to find out what they are."

The clip ends, leaving static and feedback in its wake for a few seconds. And then silence.

Charlotte's been returning to Wonderland in secret? Dinah

said a year ago was the first time Charlotte had been spotted, but it sounds like the meetings with Blanche weren't new.

"Interesting listen?" Dinah's low, formal tone pulls me out of the hole I've gone down.

I raise my human eyes to her feline ones. "If you knew who Charlotte was, why didn't you take her back to Wonderland yourself? Surely her parents have been missing her."

"Observation is crucial during any investigation." The way she lifts a paw in front of her whiskers, as if she's examining her own claws, reminds me she's human.

"What aren't you telling me?"

Pouncing from the berth onto the bench beside a still-sleeping Chess, Dinah begins to pace. "I cannot be sure my theory is correct."

"Tell me anyway."

She pauses and stretches to peer out the window, almost as if she expects someone to leap out of the darkness and straight through the glass. "I believe Charlotte is hiding something, yes, but I also believe she has a good reason. I imagine you may both be key witnesses to finding out what or who is really behind all the disappearances. Whether or not the Minister of Spades is involved, only time will tell."

I let the information sink in as Dinah nudges Chess to wake him. A few moments later, the train slides into its destination. We gather our bags. I expect Dinah to shift into a woman again, but she doesn't. Instead she hops onto the upper berth once more.

"You're going to find her, aren't you?" I ask. "You're going after Charlotte?"

A curt nod of her head. Is that sadness I see in those jade cat eyes?

I reach up to pet her between the ears. All this time I've found Dinah to be an annoying pest, when she was really just looking out for me.

And for Charlotte.

"I shall do my best, child."

The fondness in her tone tells me she means it.

"In the meantime," she adds, "you take care of yourself. Don't let my grandson fool you." She doesn't explain further or give any clues as to what I'm expected to do next. She only retreats back into the shadows, another nod her silent goodbye.

When I step off the train, Paddington Station greets me like an old friend. A skylight canopy arches several stories above us, held in place by a maze of crisscrossing metal bars. A Roman numeral clock boasts the early-morning hour, and a woman's voice announces something through an intercom. Her words are difficult to decipher over the screeching of train wheels against the tracks.

Despite being inside, a chill curls around me in wisps and tendrils. I shrug into my academy-issued, fleece-lined peacoat and allow myself to look back at Dinah one last time. There, beyond the window of our train compartment, stands human Dinah with her orange-streaked hair. High-necked, old-fashioned blouse with a broach pinned at the lace collar. And a smile.

It's a rare sight, and I latch onto it like a lifeline. I smile in return, but my sentiment isn't for Dinah alone.

It's for Charlotte.

STOP

Some say you can't go back to yesterday. After five minutes in London, I certainly hope that's true.

"Where are we going?" I ask Chess, trying to keep up, my short legs failing me miserably as we exit the station.

Chess reaches back and takes my hand. His fingers wrap mine, a perfect fit, and I don't pull away.

When we pass beneath the clock above the station's archway, we find ourselves standing on the corner of a quiet street. I imagine during the day this part of the city is bustling with vehicles and pedestrians. Sights I want to see, and sounds I want to hear. Right now, though, it's our own private corner, tucked away from the rest of life at the city centre.

I'd like to hit pause on this moment. Record it so I can replay it over and over again. My first time in London since leaving the Foundling House. The moment I've waited years for is finally here.

"This way." Chess picks up his pace. Still holding tight to

my hand and ignoring my question, he moves so fast I trip more than once. "Hurry."

My feet ache. I'm desperate for a sip of water or bite of breakfast. Every closed café we pass taunts me. When at last we stop on a corner near a walkthrough garden, I release Chess's hand and find respite beneath a birch tree. Leaning against its slender white trunk, I loop my thumbs through the straps of my rucksack and tug. My sore back relaxes, thanking me for the break.

Soundless as a cat, Chess creeps up beside me, the swish of his jacket the sole indication he's there. Even his breathing is undetectable. "Here," he says near my ear. "Let me." As he takes the straps from my hands, skin brushes mine. His thumb? The side of his palm? Whatever part of his hand touched me, the unexpected warmth I feel is—

What am I thinking? Once we're in Wonderland, I'm no match for the dozens of adoring Wonder girls awaiting him there. He's quite the ladies' man, or so I've heard. And if I did feel something—which I don't—it could never work. Chess has too much history back home.

Home. A four-letter word that's miles long and infinitely unreachable.

Still, I have to try. I might not be able to go back to yesterday, but my yesterday can find its way back to me.

"Let's go." With practiced care, Chess attempts to slide the weight on my shoulders away.

I stiffen and keep a firm grip on my only possessions. He pauses, and I realise my error almost instantly. I'm a pickpocket, but that doesn't make Chess one. Slowly, I loosen my hold and allow him to finish the kind gesture.

He adds my cargo to his own—a brown leather messenger bag similar to the kind my professors tote about.

I meet his stare as he steps around me. "Thank you."

"Not at all," he says, standing too close. "And in answer

to your question, we are here because A, London is the hub of Wonderland. Opening ceremonies for the Trials begin at sunset today. The First Trial begins tomorrow. The closer we are in this reality to the heart of it all, the closer we'll be in that one." With each mention of "closer," Chess slides nearer still.

I swallow. My voice is thick when I ask, "And B?"

He shrugs, shrugging the moment away with it. Chess either doesn't notice how skittish he makes me, or he completely notices and enjoys making me squirm. "I didn't have a B, but it sounded so much better to make you think I did." A wink. A tug on his lapels.

I can't help but roll my eyes, but then a smile escapes.

His expression mirrors mine. His endless grin expands. "There now, Ace. That wasn't so difficult, was it?"

Precisely my point. I wait as he strides up the street into the approaching morning. A curtain of blue-grey mist overshadows the indigo that preceded it moments before.

Back towards me, Chess waits at the next intersection. Standing there, head turned ever so slightly and hands in his pockets, he looks like a painted silhouette in the oncoming sunrise.

And maybe that's all he is. A shadow destined to disappear. There's a pinch in my chest at the thought. What in the cards is wrong with me?

Chess crosses a road called Bayswater, gesturing for me to follow, and walks straight into an open area of greenery.

Out of breath, I trail him, passing a sign that reads "Hyde Park." It triggers a faint memory from my brief time here. But nothing significant comes to mind as organised urban streets are replaced by mature trees and worn footpaths. Birds bathe in a nearby fountain, singing of morning's glory.

Several minutes stretch on before I ask, "Chess?" My voice feels and sounds awkward.

"Alice?"

My heart skips. It's the first time he's called me by my name. I ought to be pleased he's stopped with the silly sobriquet.

Then why do I find myself wishing he'd said it?

To everyone I am Alice. But I have only ever been Ace to him.

Or maybe that's what he calls all the girls.

Focus. Distractions are not only detrimental, they're dangerous. I place a palm on my heart, as if this will keep my voice from giving me away. "Stop. Please. I need a minute."

He tarries on the bank of a large pond, then turns. Three strides and he's too close. Again. "You don't have a minute. You're late enough as it is."

"I thought you said Wonderland is everywhere." I gesture with my arms wide, recalling his rushed explanation as we fled Oxford last night. "That it's simply another reality layered over our own. If only a true Wonder can see it, maybe I'm not—"

"You are." His nostrils flare. "You have seen it. Think of it like a door that needs unlocking. You've been spying through the keyhole, catching glimpses of what lies beyond. To enjoy it fully, you need only find the right key."

At the word "key" he brandishes the same one he gave me last night—the one that opened up the clock and changed everything.

"You nearly left this behind." He takes my hand, turns my palm skyward, and places the tiny key in the centre. When he folds my fingers over it, he adds, "Stop spying, Ace. Open the door."

His words sound beautiful. Poetic. "But—what if I can't?" My lower lip quivers, my own doubt manifesting in visible emotion.

Chess sighs and runs both hands through his hair. "You can. But it's as if—" He hesitates.

"As if what?"

"It's as if you don't want to open it." His pause is paired with an arch of his brow. "Why fight what you know is true?"

"True?" I kick a small stone, sending it careening into the water. A family of swans dodges the attack, gliding towards the opposite bank. "*This* is true." Stooping, I grab a fistful of grass. "What I can see and touch and hold." The slick green blades flutter to the ground, a few finding their way into the pond.

"Then you have no hope of being a part of the Trials—or finding any of the lost," he adds, "and you are as lost as you were before Dinah found you."

It's my own doing, but his words sting. I turn away, hoping he won't see to what depth he affects me.

Chess sighs. "It doesn't have to be that way, of course."

The response I give is a very impatient, rather exaggerated huff.

Soon, his hand is on my shoulder, squeezing ever so gently. "Walk with me?"

I glance at him. Why does it feel like there's a question behind his question? "Isn't that what I've been doing?" Sniff.

With a shake of his head, he offers the crook of his arm. "You have been walking *near* me." I spy his reflection in the water. Wavering. As if he might vanish.

When I turn fully to face him again, I catch my reflection too. Also wavering, like so many thoughts in my mind. Standing there so close to Chess, yet feeling so far apart from him and his world.

"Please?" he asks.

Why does this feel like the first time we met a year ago? Him, posing a question. Me, hesitant to accept his offer.

I take a step back.

And my heart, for whatever reason I can't explain, breaks.

His mien hardens. Smile levels out into an expression I don't recognise.

"Who discovered the Wonder Gene?" Chess asks, voice hard as the now-sunken stone.

"Genome researcher Catherine R. Pillar." I cringe at the way the answer sounds like a regurgitation of some dull science lesson.

"You know your history, I'll give you that. But do you know what else Pillar discovered?"

I shuffle through memories of past lessons and illegal internet searches for some bit of information I must have missed. But nothing turns up, not even from Madi's podcasts.

"The Wonder Gene discovery was the pinnacle of Pillar's life's work," I say. "She disappeared, and her lab was destroyed. What else was there?"

"Any inkling as to where she might have gone?"

She died. They killed her. Or silenced her. Unless . . . "No, Pillar didn't have the Gene. She tested negative."

"So they want you to believe. Do you truly think a brilliant scientist such as Pillar would spend her life studying something she didn't have? That she didn't believe in with her entire heart and soul?" His question comes out like an accusation.

Am I on trial? "That doesn't make sense." I step towards him.

This time, it's Chess who moves backwards. Away from me. The reaction is deserved.

"If Pillar had been a Wonder," I say slowly, "nothing could have stopped her."

"Or, consider this," he says. "Nothing did."

"I'm not sure I follow."

"Nothing stopped her," Chess explains, beginning to pace as he does. His voice goes up an octave, but holds the same cruel tone. "What if she staged the entire ordeal? What if Pillar's disappearance was nothing more than her own fabricated vanishing act?"

The notion sends me reeling, and I bend forwards, placing

my hands on the tops of my thighs for support. "You're saying—what *are* you saying?"

"I'm saying people have grown so afraid of what they think the Wonder Gene is, they've forgotten what it actually does."

Straightening, I recall everything I've ever heard about the Gene.

It's magic.

Too powerful.

Witchcraft.

Dangerous.

Speechless doesn't begin to describe what I am right now. Adjusting my glasses, I give Chess my full attention.

"Another question, and humour me on this because I do have a point."

I nod.

"Why *is* a raven like a writing desk?"

"We've been over this," I reply. "It isn't. The riddle is impossible to solve."

"And where do I go when I disappear?"

"Again, we've been over this. You enter the Wonderland Reality. Invisible to the Normal eye, but in both places at once."

He laughs at that, but the sound is off, almost mad. "Stop reciting everything you've been told for once, would you, Ace? You're like a brainwashed child."

Ah. There's the Chess I expect to see. Arrogant. Condescending. "I am not a child. And what do you expect me to do with the heaps of information you've given me in less than a day?"

"Your memory is impeccable. There's no arguing that. But reciting another's words will get you nowhere. This is a matter of the heart, not the head. I expect you to investigate the truth for yourself. To hold onto it with every fibre of who you are. When you truly believe in something, nothing will convince you otherwise. Not even your own self-doubt."

Heart will always trump knowledge.

"How exactly am I supposed to do that?" Frustration festers. Not only is Chess standing here before me, reminding me I basically have no heart. But he's in my memory as well. Is there anywhere he is not? "As far as I can tell, I've never been able to enter the Wonderland Reality long enough to actually believe it's real."

"But you have." His voice softens, as do his features. "You find your way there in your sleep. Every single night." His palm touches my cheek. "You need to stop running from truth. Have a little faith, would you?"

For the briefest immeasurable moment, I lean into his touch. But my eyes burn. And tears threaten to spill. I turn my head away. "That's just a dream." One sniff. Two.

Chess exhales and drops his hand. "If you don't start taking this seriously, you'll never find your way. We're running out of time."

"You're the one who never takes anything seriously. And why would you? Everything in your life is fun and games. Hopping back and forth between Realities is so easy for you. Some of us have to work to get what we want."

His demeanor alters in an instant. One second he is sly and arrogant and thinks he knows all, and the next he appears genuinely wounded. Jaw tight. "Is that really what you think of me?"

"Doesn't everyone think that?"

His gaze shifts to his reflection in the water.

"Isn't that what you want them to see?" I continue, "Nothing bothers you. You don't have a care in the world." The moment I say it, I wish I could take it back.

He turns to face the pond.

"Chess, I'm sorry." I touch his arm, but he shrugs it off. "I know Kit is important to you. We'll find your brother. And the others."

"No," he retorts. "I'll find him. You don't know the first thing about family. Your sister has been arrested, and all you care about is entering the Trials and finding the parents who probably didn't want you."

I blink, the unexpected blow flipping my sympathy over. Images of the lost Wonder poster and Charlotte's birth certificate fill my mind. "Charlotte isn't my real sister."

"You don't have the first clue as to what *real* means." The playful sound of his laughter is gone, replaced by something dark and cynical.

"Or perhaps my reality is just different from yours." When he doesn't respond, I press further. "I thought this was the plan? I enter Wonderland, accept my invitation to the Trials, and help investigate the disappearances from the inside? Finish the Fourth Trial. Dinah's gone after Charlotte anyway. She doesn't need me."

"You don't know what Charlotte needs."

A pinprick of jealousy, sharp and quick, hits me in the middle of my heart. "If I didn't know any better, I'd say you have feelings for her."

He removes my rucksack from his shoulder and tosses it to the ground before me. "You don't know anything. But she knew what *you* needed. You're just too blind to see it."

And those are the last words he says to me. As soon as they're out, hanging in the chilled air between us, my only hope at finding Wonderland disappears.

Leaving me in the middle of an empty park.

Alone.

HEARTS

*"It would be so nice if something
made sense for a change."*

– Lewis Carroll, *Alice's Adventures in Wonderland*

START

You know how sometimes you build something up inside your head, but when you finally experience it, that something is not all you'd hoped it would be?

This is one of those times.

I button my peacoat to my neck. It pinches my throat, making it hard to breathe. Pulling my hood up to cover my ears, I snatch my rucksack off the dew-kissed grass. Fine. Who needs Chess Shire anyway? It isn't as if he was going to stick around.

No one does.

As I march down the empty path, the morning sun peeks over a canopy of trees, splashing the sky in blush and lavender watercolours. All too soon, I'm reminded of him. Of his vibrant laugh and beaming grin. I don't want it to, but my mind drifts back to the memory of our first meeting. And the farther I walk on my own, the less I feel like myself. I'm unravelling, and I don't know how to get back to where I began.

For someone who's always been fine to go it alone, the odd sensation growing hot and rampant inside of me seems to war against everything I thought I knew about myself.

And Chess.

Causing me to question our every encounter.

Flashback to my first official Clash of the Cards event one year prior. Game No. 22. Thanks to Madi and her podcast—plus some digging I'd done in a few of the unlisted groups I belong to online—I finally had my chance. My skills could be tested in the wild. And I might be able to cushion my life savings in the process.

Game on.

Though sneaking out of my dormitory was not a new venture, sneaking out to catch a train for a destination over an hour away? Not a play that was part of my book.

Yet.

"Novice?" And there he was. The first person who spoke to me, aside from the doorman—a.k.a. The Walrus—and a bloke named Steve who worked as a carpenter by day and a game judge by night. Though he seemed intimidating at first, Steve eventually warmed up to me.

They all did.

But it was Chess's voice that stopped me. And made me choke on my drink.

I swiveled on my stool, willing the hand holding my cappuccino to cease its ridiculous shaking. Foam and espresso sloshed over the side of my cup, burning my hand. I hissed through my teeth and reached for a serviette.

"Let me," Chess said, brandishing a crisp white handkerchief.

Who carried handkerchiefs anymore?

Before I could refuse him, he was taking my hand in his and wiping the spilled drink away.

I yanked my hand back. I'd heard of boys like him. Charming boys. Smooth-talking boys. Boys that were the very reason all-girls schools were invented. He was a head taller than I, and that smoldering Chess Shire smirk would make any girl's heart second-guess its own existence.

Oh, yes. This boy gave trouble a name.

"I am not, in fact, a novice," I'd said, answering his initial remark. "And it would do you well to keep your hands to yourself, thank you."

"You are most welcome," he'd replied, laying on the charm so thick it could frost a cake. "And, my apologies." He'd dipped his head and bowed. One arm swept across his midsection, while the other hovered outstretched in front of me. "Might I make it up to you?"

An invitation? A trick? "Doesn't that contradict what I only just said?"

"That depends on your perspective."

"I don't fraternize with other players." It was a line I'd practiced the night before. And in between lessons. And on the train. Every player had a trick or two up their sleeves. I wasn't the only one using my sleight of hand skills away from the game tables.

"Nor do I." Moving the slightest bit closer, he swept pink-streaked hair from eyes the most unique shade of turquoise I'd ever seen. "And I find that the best way *not* to fraternize is to dance."

I stared at his open palm. His invitation to place my hand in his would have been flattering had I not already known exactly who he was.

And I told him as much. "No, thank you, *Wonder*." As soon as the word left my mouth, I'd regretted it. At that moment,

I knew Charlotte had rubbed off on me. And I hated that. Because Wonders fascinated me, though I could never admit it.

Chess Shire's scoff bordered on genuine offence, which only egged me on.

"Your first rejection, is it? Chess. Shire." Confidence shooting up like a weed, I worked my expression to hide the satisfaction I felt at putting him in his place.

"Ah, so you know me. I am not surprised, and yet . . ." At the pause he tapped his chin. "I am so surprised that intrigue has given me a new goal."

"Which is?"

"A bet," he said. "We are here to play games, after all. And I'd wager you can't resist, well, a good wager." He winked.

It appeared I wasn't the only one who had the other pegged. "Go on," I said.

"I'll wager you shall dance with me before the clock strikes twelve."

"Tonight?"

"Some night."

"That's absurd. There must be a deadline."

"Who says?"

"Logic. And manners. And well . . . there are rules."

"I see."

"See what?"

"That you are far too serious for your own good, Ace." Wonder was written all over him. In the bold and pretentious way he dressed. In his confident stance and overzealous smile. "You'll never find your way if you go about following rules of logic and manners all the time. Some lines are meant to be crossed. Some doors are meant to be unlocked." At that, he wielded a pocketscreen, dangling it in front of me. It was an older model, but from where I stood it might as well have been pure gold. "Fancy a trade, Ace?"

"It's Alice," I'd corrected, ignoring the rest of his nonsense and cursing myself the moment I realised what I'd done.

Because my name seemed to be all he wanted in exchange for the device. As soon as I gave it up, he'd nodded and handed me the pocketscreen, backing away and gesturing as if tipping a nonexistent hat. From then on, at every underground card event I attended, Chess was there.

Calling me Ace.

Insisting I was too serious.

Helping me with tech in exchange for unimportant details from my favourite colour to how I liked my coffee. Most of what I gave him was rubbish, of course. One can't be too careful these days. Still, he helped me, and with every rendezvous, he'd ask me something new.

But never again did he ask me to dance.

At the edge of the park, I find myself at a crossroads. And not merely the literal crossroads of Piccadilly and Grosvenor Place. I could set myself in reverse. Head back to the train station. Returning to Oxford would be easy enough.

Except . . .

It wouldn't. Not with Headmistress on to what she thinks I am. Once word spreads I'm supposedly a Wonder, I'll never be able to show my face at home.

Except . . .

It isn't my home, is it?

It's in that sole question I know exactly where I need to go. Perhaps it's muscle memory or sheer determination driving me there. Or is there some place within my subconscious that *knows* the way? Whatever it is, I instinctively cross to the next corner, finding myself in another expanse of green.

And then I'm running.

Up the Constitution Hill pavement. Beneath an awning of trees lining the road. Past lampposts and bicyclists and pedestrians who stare at the awkward way I move. So I'm not an athlete. No surprise there. When at last I reach the Victoria Memorial at Buckingham Palace, I stop to catch my breath and gauge my surroundings. Bronze angels guard what remains of the iconic queen who was said to be one of the longest reigning monarchs in our history.

She was also most likely a Wonder.

"We are not interested in the possibilities of defeat. They do not exist."

The quote from an old history lesson on the former monarch comes to me unbidden. It wasn't from my lessons at the academy, but one from when I was younger. When Charlotte took it upon herself to oversee my schooling until she could afford to send me to a proper institution. She brought me here. It's one of the few monuments left intact following the Divide. I guess Queen Cordelia knows deep down we can't wipe away our entire past. Even if Wonders are a part of it.

"You see, Alice," Charlotte had beamed with pride as she looked up at the frozen-in-time Victoria, "our very own queen believed in the impossible, once upon a time. As should you."

She'd tapped me on the nose with her finger, which annoyed me at the time. I twitched and whined that I was hungry. Complained my secondhand shoes were too tight and my threadbare wool jumper too itchy. Looking back, though, I see what I'd missed before.

The glow in Charlotte's eyes as she rambled on about history.

The protective way she kept her arm around me as we crossed the road to go back to the Foundling House.

Leaning down, she whispered in my ear, "Believe in the impossible, Alice."

At the time, I thought Charlotte was referring to the Occupational Exams I would take one day. Or the first-class school I would attend. The well-paid position she would have. Now, the words seem flipped upside down, holding new meaning and truth.

Queen Victoria was a Wonder.

And Charlotte knew.

What else did my sister know that she didn't divulge? What other moments do I recall as her bossing me around or scolding me to tears that might look different through a mirrored, more mature lens?

I'll never know unless I return to where it all began—where *we* began.

Bidding Victoria and the palace she guards goodbye, I continue my trek towards my destination. I reach for my rucksack so I can pull out my pocketscreen to check the GPS, then I remember where I am.

This is London. The capital city. Illegalities will not be overlooked so easily here.

Heading across town, I pass shops and old boarded-up buildings and quaint little cafés. A blue pub with wide windows and hanging planters spilling over with pale pink flowers and jade vines. A building that appears to have once been a courthouse but now serves as an Occupational Training Facility. A stories-high structure that curves around a corner, its yellowed facade a shadow of the white it must have once been.

The Sanctuary House.

Unlike the pretty blossoms at the pub, the planters hanging from this place boast nothing. Grime makes it impossible to see through the windows, and a chain binds the front door handles.

I remember this place. But from what? From when? Maybe I can come back and investigate when I have more time. For now, I need to move on. The deadline to enter the Trials is looming. Now that Charlotte's true identity has been revealed, it's the safest place for her. For us.

You were right about one thing, Chess. I didn't know what Charlotte needed.

But I do now.

Feet sore and brain spent, I try to focus on what I know if only to keep myself from collapsing in the centre of the walk. Shoving the boy who abandoned me from my thoughts—or at the very least, to the back of my mind behind a locked door with no key—I think of Dinah. The final frame of her departure fills my mind, spreading out into the corners, making itself at home.

The old woman said she believed Charlotte was just as much a victim as I was. But a victim of what? Of whom? Why can't I remember anything from before the Foundling House? Why can't I remember home?

"Home isn't here," Charlotte once said. She tapped a finger to my temple, then adjusted my headband so all my loose wisps of hair returned to their proper places. "It's here." With a palm against her own heart, Charlotte's deep brown eyes shone as if she held the best-kept secret of all.

"Home isn't anywhere," I want to tell her now, but I say it to the abbey instead.

The abbey? It can't be.

I blink. Then blink again. That can't be right. I'm imagining things. Removing my glasses, I wipe the lenses with the corner of my coat. I rub my eyes for good measure. When I return my glasses to their perch, the view ahead comes into focus.

A sigh looses. From relief? Disappointment?

An empty lot where Westminster Abbey once stood. Burned to the ground during the Divide by rioters who wanted Wonders sentenced to death without a fair and proper trial. Once a place of sanctuary for Wonders who'd been forced out of their homes, it became nothing more than a pile of rubble and ash.

Off with their heads, they would chant. *Destroy them all.*

The mere thought of ending someone's life based on misunderstood differences gives me chills.

I feel as if I'm on autopilot as I continue my trek towards the Thames. Down a dingy alleyway smelling of rubbish. Across a street with weeds reaching through cracks in the asphalt, wishing they were flowers. But their true place in the world is not in a garden.

Someone ought to let them know their own worth. No one wants a weed. Not in the middle of the street. Not anywhere.

I bend down to pluck a lonesome dandelion, its furry stem tickling my skin. A few seeds are caught by the breeze and whisked away before I can make my wish. When I straighten, half a ball of fluff remains. My vision blurs, focusing first on the hopeless flower and then on the picture beyond.

The Foundling House. Precisely where I left it six years ago.

"Well," I say to the little weed, tossing it into the air without bothering to wish for anything. "I guess the only thing left to do is return to square one."

DISAPPEAR

The garden is smaller than I remember it.

Or perhaps I am bigger than it remembers me.

Walking across the open space of grass outside the Foundling House gives me an odd sense of calm. I used to play here. I'd splash in the fountain or hide behind the trunks of trees, jumping out to scare Charlotte, who only wanted to read.

"Must you do that every time?" she'd roll her eyes and toss her curls over one shoulder.

"You make it so easy," I reply aloud to no one now, tracing my fingers along the edge of the dried-up fountain. Was it always so dirty? What happened to the water? The thought occurs to me that perhaps it never held water at all. That it was simply my own games of pretend that made it seem so. The trees have changed too. They're smaller than I remember them, their clothing of leaves scarce.

Nostalgia is a strange thing indeed. It causes us to romanticise the past, adding details that weren't there to begin with. I circle the fountain now as I once did when I was small. Then I round it again. Why do I remember it taking me ages to complete one turn? Why can't it be like it was before?

I circle it a third time.

One good turn deserves another, right, Charlotte?

I abandon the fountain and weave on and off the path. Between trees. The space is centuries old, at the heart of what used to be Westminster School. Now there's just the Foundling House and a small chapel off to one side that pales in comparison to the glorious abbey that once overshadowed it. From my position down here, I can pick out the very room Charlotte and I occupied on the third floor, fourth window to the left. Memories of this place have haunted me since we moved to Oxford.

Of Mrs. Cook and how she'd scream whenever one of the younger ones would cry.

Or how she'd lock me in a small cabinet if I ever screamed at her for screaming at them.

"I swear on my life you're Wonders, the lot of you! And we ought to throw you into the Thames before you infect us all."

Ha! What an absurd notion. As if the Wonder Gene is a disease to be caught or cured.

The nearer I draw to the front door, the more memories flood my thoughts and pool in the centre of my mind.

The woman who owned this place—who connected Charlotte to her first job in Oxford—must have sold it and moved on. She'd never let it fall into disrepair like this. Unlike Mrs. Cook, the owner was the kind of woman who took pride in everything she touched. The Foundling House was no different.

Turning the knob on the entryway door, I push. Hard. The door sticks, so I have to give it a good shove with my body weight. When the door finally gives, I'm welcomed into a musty foyer with a creak and a groan.

"Hello? Is someone here?"

My words echo back, sending a ripple of cold over me. What's left of the Foundling House isn't much to look at. A bench where one might sit to remove their shoes. A crooked mirror hanging on the peeling papered wall. Black-and-white-checkered floor caked with what must be years of grime and dust.

The checks trigger a memory. I shake off the déjà vu. Nonsense. The floor from my dream and this one cannot possibly be related.

Then again, Chess did say I enter Wonderland whenever I sleep. What if my dream is a mixture of both Realities? And the locked door is the only thing keeping me from exploring beyond what I know?

Nothing's impossible.

"Quiet," I say to the invisible presence of Chess's words.

Every stairstep whines beneath my weight. The banister seems so old and fragile, I don't dare use it to support my trek up the flights. When I finally reach our room, I stand at the threshold, peering into the four corners of my past.

This can't be right.

When you're small, everything seems big. The ceiling. The windows. The doors. And when you're big?

When you're big, you realise that nothing else is. Not really.

All of a sudden, I can't breathe. My throat closes, and I feel like I might suffocate if I stay here in this abandoned corridor for one more minute. Without thinking of what to do or where to go next, I flee the Foundling House, tripping over my steps as I race down the stairs. Gasping when I enter the yard once more, tears brim and burn. I blink away the blur, but when my vision adjusts, spots float, obscuring my focus. Crisscrossing then clearing. As much as I don't want it to, it's Chess's voice that ultimately finds me in my solitude once again.

"Perspective, Ace." We'd been waiting for the train when he said it. I shivered and he offered his jacket. Stubborn as ever, I refused his kindness, opting for my own peacoat. "Makes everything flip right side up. Maybe stand on your head, and you'll see things differently." With a wink, he boarded the train.

It took a good minute to gather my thoughts. Then I followed him. "Stand on my head?" I asked, buttoning my coat and raising the hood. "That's loads helpful, thanks."

"Always happy to lend a helping hand," was his cheerful response.

My own wool peacoat seems to chafe and itch at the memory. I'd insisted on taking nothing from him. Now I wish I had, if only to carry a piece of him with me.

What if I never see him again?

Why do I even care?

Wandering towards the chapel, I find myself peering through stained glass. Just beyond waits a hall that appears as untouched as it is ancient. Sunlight filters in through the coloured panes, bouncing off the rafters and blanketing the seats in a soft yellow haze. Charlotte loved this more than the library.

"A church is its own sort of fairy tale, don't you think?" she'd say. "It's the one place where believing in something unseen isn't a curious notion at all. Quite the contrary. Here, believing is expected. Here, nothing is impossible."

My breath catches.

"Our very own Queen Victoria believed in the impossible, as should you."

Unlike so many other times before when it was Chess's voice reminding me of the same idea over and over again, this time, it's Charlotte urging me to see beyond my own reality.

Perhaps it's been Charlotte all along.

It's this that moves my feet forwards. That has me entering the quiet chapel hall, in awe of how pristine it appears compared to the Foundling House next door and the shadows of the garden outside.

Wooden bench pews line up in neat rows to the left and right. They've collected some dust but appear otherwise untouched. There's a dais, but no pulpit. Arching windows that are flat on the bottom with a small point at the top. Beyond the dais there is more stained glass up high with a paneled half wall below.

I walk the aisle with steady restraint, taking in every detail and committing it to memory, then pairing it with another from my past. Seeing Charlotte and our time here with new eyes. Missing her more every step.

When I finally reach the front pew, I sit on the end and try to relax. I tug my hair free of the ribbon holding it at the nape of my neck, finger-comb the thin, stick-straight locks. I close my eyes as I run through every impossible moment since Charlotte disappeared. Playing sequences over like podcasts in my mind. One sticks out. One I almost missed because I wasn't looking.

Furthermore, what is quite fascinating is her Theory of Impossibility as it relates to relativity and the idea that–

What else was Mr. March going to say? Who was *her*? He couldn't have been referring to . . . ?

Catherine R. Pillar.

Madi spent an entire episode on the topic of the mysterious genome researcher. It's some of the only information I could gather on the woman since the Wonder Gene is a taboo topic as it is without adding more of Pillar's theories into the mix. The

Modern Monarchy wants to portray Pillar as a madwoman or a criminal. And Wonders as if they are dangerous. Diseased.

But Pillar's discovery didn't create the Gene. It's always existed. Whether we could see it or not, it's been there all along.

In those unexplained moments when coincidence could only be a miracle.

In the quiet subtleties of history when someone achieved the unimaginable. Wars ended. Enemies fell.

In churches where rich or poor, young or old, all hold to the same beliefs that something unseen can be really, truly *real*.

"Oh, Chess," I say. "Is this what you were trying to tell me?"

I've been such a fool.

The scientist didn't have to prove the Gene existed. Because anyone who believed in it already knew.

Could it truly be so simple?

"You can't go out unless you first go in."

And there he is again. Invading my thoughts. Entering my mind. I pull the tiny key out of my pocket. Then I retrieve my locket watch from my bag, unclasping the chain. The middle hole at the top of the key is just wide enough for the chain to pass through. Once it rests beside the closed watch, I connect the chain again, then lift it up and over my head. Now both trinkets rest over my heart.

One from my past.

The other from my future.

"I know you're here," I say to what I'm sure must be Chess's invisible self. Except . . .

He *is* here. I open my eyes and place a hand over my chest.

I've invited him. Into my mind and my heart. All those times I accused and assumed and expected he was playing games, coming into spaces he wasn't welcome, it was me inviting him into my reality.

And he was inviting me into his.

I close my eyes again and allow myself to picture him. All the walls I constructed to keep him out tumble and fall. What's left leaves a smile warming my cheeks. Opening my heart. I have no idea if this is what Charlotte meant by *hearts are wild*. But right now mine beats a stampede. Racing. Running towards whatever comes next.

Towards his eternal grin and quick remarks. But this time I change my perspective like he said. See him as genuine instead of juvenile.

"The door from my dream," I say aloud. "It's not a way out."

I can almost see him nod.

"It's the entrance. It's the way in. My dream is . . ."

I cover my mouth. Think the word before I say it.

Real.

"Real," I say.

My dream is real.

Like Chess. He's still real when he disappears.

And I'm still me when I shrink.

And Dinah is fully human, even when she has whiskers and paws and a tail.

We are all Wonders. And if Wonders are real . . .

Then so is Wonderland.

What I see in my mind at night isn't a figment of my own imagination but a memory of another reality. A combination of the here and the there. One I know very well how to find. Because I've been there before. I merely had to believe it was possible.

One breath out. Another in. I release the words about to burst from my mind.

"I believe in Wonderland."

And my world disappears.

WELCOME

Welcome to Wonderland!

The message dances through the air in a magical ribbon of butterflies. Spinning. Twirling. Flitting. Hovering before my uncharacteristically clear vision in winged wisps of golden letters. As if this is completely Normal.

I blink. Take off my glasses, then put them on again.

Is this happening?

A warm sensation passes over me as the butterfly message swoops under one arm, around my back, and over the opposite shoulder. My toes and fingertips tingle. The feeling is new and different and enthralling.

And somehow . . . completely familiar. A welcome home after years long gone.

Unlike the glitching efforts it took to jump in and out of this reality for short spurts, this is something else entirely. Extraordinary.

It's . . . *Wonder*-ful.

Because I'm here. Witnessing the edges of the world around me folding outward like a map unfurled. Painting every dull corner in bright hues. Splashing a plain canvas in auburns and mahoganies and periwinkles. My senses heighten, and I can all at once hear and see and think with greater clarity. The music I once heard in small clips from a distance now plays as a complete track, flowing from invisible speakers in harmonies, melodies, and all the other "-ies" one might imagine. It's no longer the haunting and broken track from my nightmares. In fact, it's rather cheery, full of light and hope.

And though the chapel within my rather Normal version of Westminster is still visible, it now appears beneath a new layer of fantastic, placing me inside the most glorious structure I have ever beheld.

No. Not a chapel.

This is Westminster Abbey reborn.

At the very thought, the butterflies rearrange. The moment I notice them, they take on a new form, creating an entire paragraph of text before me with their tiny, fluttering wings.

Wonderland Abbey. Inspired by the royal church first built in London during the 13th century, this version is the embodiment of multiple Wonder imaginations over an extended period of time. Like most places within the Wonderland Reality, the abbey is ever changing and transforming. You never know which Wonder mind will add to it next.

The butterflies disperse when I'm done reading, somehow perfectly in sync with my mind and thoughts. Almost as if I created them. I glance up towards the ceiling, testing my own imagination and its effects. Sure enough, the ceiling opens up in five parts, like flower petals stretching towards the sun. Puffy pink clouds float high overhead, reminiscent of the candy floss some shops sell on Queen's Day.

"Fascinating," I say.

Someone giggles.

It's then that I finally see past the transparent screen before my eyes and the new world I've found myself in. Not only has the scenery been given an upgrade, it seems the company has as well.

Clusters of Wonders move to and fro, up and down the centre aisle. Mostly adolescents, probably around my age. A few adults who appear to be directing others or answering questions. One mother stands out, clutching a toddling child with one hand while hoisting another onto her hip. She's disheveled, and tears streak her flushed cheeks.

"Go on home now, Viola" an official-looking woman in a crisp black uniform tells her. "You shouldn't be here."

"But you have to warn them," the frantic mother wails. "My Dan has been missing for a year. They have to know. The Trials aren't safe. You have to tell them, Rose."

The uniformed woman nods in consolation, placing a steady hand on the mother's shaking shoulder. "There, there, dear. Everything will be fine. You've got these little ones to look after. Especially this one who's the spitting image of his older brother." That last part sticks oddly in her throat. Her attention darts from Viola's face to the young toddler at her side. Something spoken in so much unsaid.

Viola seems to catch the meaning too. She sniffs once and wipes her cheeks with the back of her wrist. It's the only time she releases the toddler's hand.

The child steps deeper into the jade-green folds of his mother's floor-length Victorian skirt, never once uttering a word. His face is pale, almost sickly. His eyes are wide with curiosity. And perhaps . . . fear?

I'm all at once reminded of what I came here for. Of the greater purpose I have in being a player in the Trials. New determination washes over me. To find my parents. To understand how Charlotte returned from the Fourth Trial.

And to uncover what has happened to the other players too.

"Very well," Viola says. She's a head taller than Rose, and her eyes are full of thorns. "But this isn't the last you'll hear from me. Dan's disappearance will not be for nothing." Before Rose has a chance to respond, Viola rushes out of the abbey, keeping her children so close, it's hard to tell where she ends and they begin.

I watch the mother go, the vision of her raw emotion imprinted on my mind. Did my own mother try to protect me with such ferocity?

If she had, would I have been taken?

Someone bumps my shoulder. Hard.

"Watch it!" A girl with charcoal hair and beads for eyes glares up at me. She's quite a bit shorter than I am, which is apparently possible, though I've never met anyone close to my age who also skipped their growth spurt stage. The way she looks at me, indignant and waiting, makes me wonder if she's expecting some sort of apology.

I open my mouth to give one so she'll be on her way, but then . . . who does she think she is? The queen?

As if speaking my mind, someone from behind me says, "Mind your manners, Mouse." The voice is one I'd recognise anywhere.

When I pivot, I can't help but drop my jaw at the same time my eyes widen. Madi Hatter in the flesh approaches us, wild lavender hair with silver highlights tied into two knots on top of her head. Between them, the tiniest top hat I've ever seen is pinned at an offset angle.

"Would you look who it is," the girl called Mouse says, making up for what she lacks in height with pure arrogance. "The third-rate child of the famous Maddox Hatter himself." Mouse sizes Madi up from her mismatched shoes all the way up to her green and orange eye shadow. "Come to try your hand at the Trials this year, Mad? I didn't know they were handing out pity invites. Did your brothers get you in? Not really fair to the rest of us, giving the likes of you a handout."

Madi, seemingly unfazed, appears as confident as she sounds on her podcast. But, unlike Mouse's rather unattractive pompous air, Madi's self-assurance is magnetic, radiating from the inside out. To my surprise, she slings one arm over my shoulders when she finally replies.

"I was invited, fair and square. Same as you." No jabs, though I can think of more than a few she could have used. It's like Madi doesn't feel the need to defend herself.

I knew I liked her.

"Right." Mouse rolls her beady little eyes. "And it had nothing to do with the fact that your brother Stark led Team Diamond to victory last year? Or that Raving's practically a Wonderland Trials legend? Tell me, what's it like to constantly stand in your big brothers' shadows?"

"Oh, I don't know. Probably about the same as not being tall enough to have a shadow at all?"

I chortle at that, and Madi side-winks at me. Okay, so that was a jab. But the Mouse girl deserved it.

Mouse turns up her nose, and I almost think I see it twitch from side to side. After she storms off down the aisle, her oversized frock flapping like a tail behind her, Madi spins me around.

"Well, it's about time you got here. It only took you like, I don't know, ten years to come back. Where's Charlotte? I've been telling her for ages to hurry up and bring you home already. I told her it was safe. More than safe. But of course she didn't listen."

"Charlotte. Right. You two are . . . friends, I take it?" I try not to let jealousy seep into my words.

She winks again. "I like to think of it as more of a partnership. We have a shared interest."

I stare at her blankly, not quite catching her meaning.

"Let's just say she kept a promise, and now she's delivered," Madi explains. "Where is she, anyway? I'd like to thank her."

I clear my throat in the awkward silence. "Charlotte isn't exactly here yet."

"Very funny. You certainly have her dry sense of humour."

I frown and shake my head.

Madi's expression falls. "Oh. Well, that's okay. I'm sure she'll be along shortly."

I don't have the heart to tell her Charlotte was taken. The last thing I want to be right now is angry. But I'm fuming. Mad at Charlotte for not being more careful. Resentful that she kept Madi a secret all these years. Charlotte of all people knows how hard a time I've had making friends. And now I learn she's been keeping Madi from me? I wish she was here so I could shout at her or storm off or *something*. Her absence makes it worse. Because her not being here makes me feel guilty for being mad at her in the first place.

"Cheer up, Alice," Madi says. "Don't tell me you've forgotten your very best friend in the entirety of all that is Wonderland?" Madi asks, helping put out some of my unspoken fire. "Why, we're thick as thieves, you and me."

Best friend. In all of Wonderland?

"We are?" is all my genius mind can reply at the moment.

"Ah, well," she says, clearly picking up on my confusion. "It'll all come back later or sooner. Hopefully the latter, though my guess is it's the former. If you could be quite quick about the sooner part, that would be most convenient." British phrases and dialect pepper her otherwise American accent. "The more in tune we are, the better our chances are at winning."

"Our chances?" I swallow. "You mean we're on the same team?"

Madi laughs as if that's the most ridiculous question

ever. "You didn't think I'd play for Team Diamond did you? Raving's coaching the Diamonds this year. I intend to make a name for myself without my brother's help, thank you."

I think of Chess and Kit—who both played for Team Spade. Did Kit feel the way Madi does? Did a need to prove himself take things too far?

Madi talks a mile a minute, and I can hardly keep up as she drags me past the queue straight to the table on the dais. A few of the bystanders who've been waiting patiently stare daggers in our direction.

Either Madi doesn't notice or she doesn't care. "Liddell, Alice," Madi says to a woman behind the table who appears to be marking things off on a digital clipboard. "That's pronounced Little but spelled with Ds instead of Ts because tea, as we all know, never comes before the dawn."

I burst a laugh at her nonsensical joke, only to invite more glares from the players still waiting behind us.

The woman—Carol, according to her name tag—adjusts her half-moon spectacles. "Here she is. Almost didn't make it, did we? Congratulations on completing your pretrial. Only you and one other Wildflower made it through. Every year we see fewer and fewer." She *tsks* and shakes her head. "It's to be expected of course. What with your reality being so Normal and all. No room for imagination. No fostering of creativity."

Madi *ahems*, then taps her fingers on the table.

Carol narrows her eyes at Madi. The woman softens her countenance when she focuses on me. "Alias?"

"Um, no." I tuck a stray hair behind my ear. "It's Alice."

She yawns this time and waves towards Madi.

"She means your player name. You know, your handle. Pseudonym. Sobriquet."

"I don't have one."

"Nonsense," Madi says over a groan from more than a

few people in the queue. She shoots a scowl at them over her shoulder.

They don't appear pleased, but they also don't protest.

This girl has more clout than I thought.

"Everyone involved in the Trials has an Alias," she says to me. "Some are a bit more creative than others. Some are a little"—a nod of her head—"strange. Take Mouse for example. Normal name's Mildred. But the girl's obsessed with cheese, and her nose twitches, and she's shorter than the average person her age. People made fun of her for the things that made her different, but she took that and owned it. And now look where she's at! She's an awful pain, but I respect her. Mouse fits her Archetype too."

"Archetype?"

"Sorry, I keep forgetting you're new to all this." She gives me a sympathetic smile. "Archetypes are the form Wonders take upon drinking Beast's Blend—one of many concoctions a Master of Tea, such as myself, can make."

I nod, thinking of Dinah. I've seen her Archetype with my own eyes. I still don't quite comprehend the idea, but I believe it, all the same.

"Alias?" Carol asks again, this time tapping her pencil on the digital clipboard.

"It can be anything," Madi says. "A favourite character from a book. A beloved pet. A special hobby or game—"

"Ace," I blurt. I don't have to see my reflection to know a blush is blossoming.

"Nice." Madi nods her approval. "You always did love cards. And your name starts with 'A.' It fits."

"It certainly does," Carol says, her expression altering from bored to amused. "You're listed here as the Team Heart Ace. Go figure. I've never seen a Wildflower given a leading position. You must be talented."

"Team Ace?" I ask, confusion abounding. "What's that?"

"It's your position," Madi interjects. "We all have one. I play Nine. The Ace is second only to the Team Queen or King."

I don't tell her there's so much more meaning to the name than an initial or hobby or, come to find out, position. Or how the entire time I've been in Wonderland I've kept one eye out for the Wonder who disappeared on me.

"You'll report to Blanche de Lapin, Team Heart Advisor," Carol explains. She retrieves a semi-translucent red-and-black bangle from a box labeled "Team Heart."

I've never seen any material like it. In the light that streams through the stained glass, the bangle almost seems to disappear and reappear. Carol holds it up to her digital clipboard. A faint beep sounds, and four small heart-shaped red lights illuminate. She hands the bangle to me.

The moment it touches my skin, it unclasps, then practically jumps onto my wrist, securing itself there, a perfect fit. A new sensation shoots up my arm and neck, giving me the briefest headache, stinging and subsiding in a blink. With that blink comes a new sight, like a transparent screen over my vision.

"Neat, huh?" Madi shows me her wrist, where an identical bangle snugly sits. "You can hardly feel it. Wonder Vision 8.0—WV for short—is tech designed especially for the Trials. This is the latest version. The original model was designed by Catherine R. Pillar herself, may her soul rest in peace."

I twist my wrist this way and that. Pillar was a genius, that much is certain. And Madi's right. If I didn't know the bangle was there, I wouldn't notice it.

Carol clears her throat, drawing my attention. "Dinner and opening ceremonies begin promptly at five o'clock at Oyster and Pearl Hall." This time when she taps her screen, new information pops up on my WV. Icons expanding and minimizing. Schedules, menus, a map, a notepad. It's like my pocketscreen grew up into what it was meant to be.

And it is sensational.

Carol waves the next person forwards, and we move to the side.

"The bangle keeps track of your progress in the Trials, including golden petals, team points, and, of course, how many hearts a.k.a. Fates you have left." Madi taps hers with one finger, revealing she too has four lit-up hearts. "It learns your habits and patterns. Think of it as your new best friend."

As if listening to Madi's words, new information appears in my WV. In the upper right-hand corner, four hearts appear, red and pulsing to match the lights on the bangle. In the left corner, the number 100 is paired with a spinning golden flower petal, which I assume is related to spending. "Are you seeing this?"

She shakes her head. "I can only see yours if we link. With each player you come into contact with, the WV will suggest adding them as a Card."

Just then a message bubble appears at the centre of my view. *Add @MadTea to your pack?*

Yes, I think before I can speak, but the vocalization is unnecessary. The text immediately vanishes. In the top centre of my vision, a playing card icon appears next to the number one.

"Now we're linked." Her infectious smile makes me curious. Does she really think as highly of me as I do of her? "I can see your vitals, and you can see mine. We can share petals or hearts if need be. Once you get to know the rest of the team, you'll want to give them access as well. When you're ready."

Too many questions to count. This is all happening so fast, I've barely had time to find my bearings much less worry about Charlotte. Coming from a world where tech is scarce and my pitiful pocketscreen does like five things, this is incredible.

When we reach the double exit doors, I have to shield my eyes from the sun as we step out into a stunning courtyard.

It is then I see who I've been secretly looking for since the moment I arrived.

Chess Shire strides towards me. Pink streaks of hair catching the light. His clothes have changed, velveteen dinner jacket replaced with a silken waistcoat that matches the burgundy stripes on his Oxford shoes. He wears a bow tie that seems to smile, drawing attention to the fact that Chess most certainly is not.

I pause, heart ready to burst. This is awkward. It's more than awkward. Excruciating is a better word for what I'm feeling right now.

"Chess, I—"

He scowls, successfully stopping my words. Trapping them in my throat.

"I'm sorry," Chess says, voice ten degrees cooler than when we argued. "Who are you?"

Tears threaten to make an appearance. A new message appears in the centre of my WV.

Add @ChessShireCat to your pack?

My mouth opens. When I neither accept nor reject the suggestion, the message dissolves.

Madi tugs on my hand. "Let's go, Ace," she says at the same time Chess's eyebrow lifts, softening his harsh stare for a scarce second. "We don't consort with the enemy." The way she says it sounds playful, like she's teasing an old friend.

That almost makes it worse.

As she drags me through the courtyard, one more glance back at Chess reveals what I hoped not to see.

The white-and-black bangle on his wrist. Four little lights illuminated at the centre, the shape representing our opposing team.

Of course. He didn't just compete with Team Spade last year.

Chess has been playing for the enemy all along.

BEGINNING

I've never seen a bus like this one.

Madi immediately boards the hovering vehicle, not giving a second thought to the fact that it has no wheels. The mushroom-like shape is unique in its design, slender near the bottom where we board and widening out towards the top.

Remarkable.

Windows wrap the vehicle's circumference. The outside is opalescent, changing colours depending on which way I turn. I gape for another minute before Madi sticks her head through—not out—one of the windows. As if the barrier is merely an illusion.

What else do I expect? I'll probably be seeing stranger things than this from now on.

"Are you coming?" Madi calls, as if riding in a floating toadstool is a perfectly common occurrence. "I promise, it won't bite. Plus, there are so many snack options!"

A bite to eat doesn't sound half bad. I inhale before

stepping inside the *Champignon*, widening my eyes as my WV alerts me that this is precisely what it's called. An information icon blinks at me, then expands. I read through it and board at the same time.

Based upon the late Count Rory Wise's original design, the Champignon Bus—Champ for short—has been a staple mode of transport within Wonderland for some time. Passengers are often delighted by the choices Champ provides. Riding on one side will make you feel as if you are a giant in a miniature city, while riding on the other side will give the illusion that you are an insect within a mammoth metropolis. Choose wisely.

The information window closes, leaving me to choose between one spiral staircase or the other. Neither side is marked, and there doesn't appear to be an operator or driver of whom I can ask directions. I opt to take the left side, following after the choice Madi already made. The moment I step onto the first stair, I'm transported up a moving staircase. When I reach the top, I find that the seats are as wild as *Champ's* shape and paint job, hovering and spinning in place, moving about the cabin as if on some sort of invisible track of chaos.

It takes some effort, but I finally manage to snag the seat beside Madi before it dodges me again, surprised at how solid the chair feels beneath me, despite the fact it doesn't appear to be attached to anything.

"This is incredible." I reach beneath my seat, waving my hand, feeling around for the chair's invisible base. It isn't there.

"This?" Madi grins. "You haven't seen anything yet."

Our seats cease twirling and escort us smoothly towards the wide windows, giving us a chance to admire the scenery. Everything is enlarged, seeming ten times our size, reminding me of how it felt to be an ant in Charlotte's sitting room.

"Check this out," Madi says after a few blocks. She reaches forwards and places her palm against the window, which now appears to be perfectly solid. The action triggers an immediate change, causing the glass to stretch up and over us, replacing the opaque ceiling with a clear dome. A digital, full-colour menu appears on the glass next, offering rows upon rows of delectable treats from cucumber-mint finger sandwiches and popovers, to chocolate goose eggs and tongue twister licorice.

"Careful with those," Madi says. "Anything you say will come out backwards for hours."

I heed her warning, scroll a bit further, and choose a delightful-looking petit four with a red candy rose on top and raspberry cream cheese filling. I pay for it with a mere thought, taking my golden petals down from one hundred to ninety-six. The miniature cake seems to jump straight off the menu and materialise in the air before me. I take it between my thumb and forefinger, consuming it in a single bite.

"This is absolutely divine," I say, taste buds happier than they've been in ages.

But more than the perfect blend of sweet and fruit and cream is the view of London. My favourite city layered in Wonderland leaves me breathless.

Familiar. Foreign. Wildly Wonder and curiously common all at once.

Madi links her arm through mine and lays her head on my shoulder. It reminds me of the way I used to lean on Charlotte when I was small. The gesture of a sister or a close friend. Though I've just met Madi, the feeling I've always known her lingers, and I'm reminded of what she said earlier.

"You said we were best friends?"

"*Were*?" she says, popping her head up. "We *are*. Your extended absence doesn't mean our friendship ended."

I nod, letting the idea sink in. I realise she isn't just my oldest friend, but also my only.

What about Chess? a small voice asks in my head.

Ha. My cynical side bristles. If anyone fits into the *were* category, it is most notably him.

"We will reach our next stop in approximately three minutes," a satin-smooth female voice says through a hidden speaker. "If this is where you will be leaving us, please gather your belongings, bid your farewells, and prepare to disembark."

Our seats move again, shifting around until an aisle forms that leads directly to the stairwell. A few passengers wearing green-and-black bangles marked with four lights in the shape of a club stand and move towards the escalator. Mouse is one of them and pretends not to notice us. When Champ stops before a grander version of Big Ben that's three times as high and noticeably more filled out, I stand on my seat to get a better view.

This isn't the Big Ben I remember visiting when I was nine. It looks more like a grand hotel fit for royalty, with stories of windows all aglow and an emerald carpet rolled out on the pavement leading to the revolving glass door. The neutral-coloured architecture has been exchanged for some sort of black stone, which reflects the sunlight in a way that moves me to shade my eyes. The Houses of Parliament to the south appear to be an extension of the towering hotel, an arching bridge passing between them, their more muted shade of limestone walls paling in comparison to the iconic timepiece that has me wishing this was our stop too.

"Club Clocktower," Madi explains. "Headquarters for Team Club and Minister Mocktur Telle. He's trained the Clubs for three years, each year running them harder than the last. Rumour has it old Mocktur makes the toughest of tough lads cry."

The Clubs disembark, and moments later we're moving again, hovering across Westminster Bridge. When we reach the opposite side and head north, my WV alerts me we've left Club Quarter and entered Diamond Quarter. The farther we move, the less this feels like the London I remember.

"Use your map anytime you feel lost," Madi explains as if reading my mind.

Sure enough, a map-marker icon sits beside the others in my WV menu.

"But I'm a visual person," she adds, "so landmarks are all I need to turn back around when I get . . . well . . . turned around." She laughs, and the sound pings an emotion that feels close to déjà vu.

I've heard her laugh on her podcast, but this one is different. Real.

Our next stop is the London Eye, or what I assume must be the famous big wheel that once attracted tourists from across the globe. After the Divide, Queen Cordelia shut it down. Yet another frivolous form of entertainment only the likes of Wonders would find themselves indulging in.

"Transportation ought to be practical," Charlotte said once, lifting her head out of a book long enough to quote the queen's autobiography. "Amusement for amusement's sake is pure poppycock."

I look at the oversized glass cars of the big wheel now. They glisten like the Crown Jewels in the white sunlight. Nothing about them boasts poppycock of any sort. I don't need my WV to tell me who resides here.

"Diamond Manor." Madi points to a period home at the base of the wheel that I'm certain doesn't exist in the Normal world. "Team trained by Madame Sevine. Not as hard on her team in the sense of gameplay or strategy. But have a single hair out of place or a chipped manicure, and you'd be packing your bags. Team Diamond is expected to be pristine at all times. The cars are actually hanging dormitories that rotate depending on where the sun is for just the right healthy glow." She rolls her eyes. "In other words, Diamonds are a bunch of divas."

I watch several more players disembark, catching the

dazzling silver-and-black bangles they wear, the white diamond-shaped lights looking like real jewels. Everything from their flashy clothing to their athletic builds screams "dream team."

Our next stop takes us east through a roundabout and eventually leads us across the city. I expand the map in my WV and find that Tower Bridge is called Topsy Bridge and the River Thames is instead the River Turvy. The Pool of London is termed the Pool of Tears, just like it was on Charlotte's old map. We've entered the Spade Quarter, and before us waits a rather anticlimactic version of the Tower of London.

On the outside it appears to be the same as always, causing me to question what lies within. My heart does a backflip, then plummets as several Spade players with their black-and-white bangles make their exit. Chess didn't ride with us, but he's a Spade. This is where he'll be from now on. Where he'll eat and sleep and laugh.

Did I really offend him to the point of being written off completely? Why would he go to all the trouble of protecting me, of trying to get me here, only to toss me out like yesterday's rubbish?

Kit. It has to be. Something has happened. Could Chess have been threatened? And where is Dinah? Shouldn't she have caught up to us by now?

My mind brews with questions and worst-case scenarios. I'm so distracted the remainder of the ride that I fail to notice we've headed west again, keeping north of the river. When we reach our final destination, it feels like no time has passed at all.

"Welcome to Heart Palace." Madi's face beams a smile. It's the kind that says she's been burning to divulge this secret.

My own expression is one of wide-eyed wonder. Which is fitting, given where I am.

Madi and I disembark along with an angular boy wearing

old-school, over-the-head earphones more ancient than my soundbuds. He sports a bangle that matches ours. When he sees me staring, he gives a single nod that looks more like a head jerk. No smiles. No mischief behind his eyes, fluid and the shade of black licorice—dark but with a tinge of purple.

My WV blinks an alert.

Add @SirKnaveTheBrave to your pack?

Madi elbows me. When I turn to face her, she wags her eyebrows. "That's Knave," she whispers. "Not your classic type of handsome, but there's something about him, wouldn't you agree?"

I don't agree, but accept the suggestion. The number one next to the card icon in my WV changes to two. He is my teammate, after all. We'll be mates sooner or later.

Emphasis on the later, it would seem.

I try not to let Knave's cold shoulder get to me and instead focus on the landscape ahead.

Buckingham Palace. It's more extraordinary than in my Reality. And yet, somehow, entirely the same.

"It pays to play for Team Heart." Madi links her arm through mine as has become her habit. "Come on," she says. "This is only the beginning."

QUEEN

At the open gate, beyond the veil of the Wonderland Reality, Queen Cordelia's Royal Guard stand erect with their bearskin hats and red coats. They don't notice our presence, nor do they flinch when we pass them and walk straight towards the palace.

Each gate to either side of me hosts a royal coat of arms. In the Normal world, it's a crowned jade lion and noble steed supporting a shield bearing symbols that include a harp and more lions. At the crest sits another crowned lion, golden and roaring.

Wonderland's coat drowns it out almost completely. Rather than fashioned from green stone and gold, this one is studded in gemstones of ruby, opal, onyx, and, of course, diamonds. Its shield at the centre is guarded by a dragon, fierce head with teeth bared peeking out one side and a horned tail curling around the other. The crest is a royal crown, the ruby heart symbol at its centre. Each quarter of the shield houses a different card suit. A heart, yes, but also the spade, the club, and the diamond. One for each house and quarter of Wonderland.

Orchestral music plays softly from someplace unseen. I turn in a full circle as we walk across the yard towards the palace entrance. I've never been beyond the gates in the Normal world, but I can still tell the difference. It's Buckingham, but it isn't, hints of common here and there but mostly new and beyond what one might expect to see at the heart of the capital city.

Inside, the contradictions continue. It's as if someone had the idea to combine modern with timeless. Victorian with contemporary. An oak cabinet to my left. A chandelier crafted from canning jars and different-sized lightbulbs above. There are nods to every century. And every ruler. Charlotte's always been the history buff, but even I can appreciate the creative touch with the architecture and decor.

The foyer is as grand as I would have anticipated. The poised and proper woman who greets us needs no introduction. She wears a WV bangle like ours on her wrist, but rather than four lit-up hearts, hers flaunts a solid ruby heart, the word Advisor engraved around it in golden script.

"Madi." Blanche nods. "I see you ave found our Vildflower." She eyes me. Everything and nothing passes between us in a single look.

Add @WhiteRabbit to your pack?

I have so many questions I'd like to ask her. Why me? Are you working with Dinah? Why have you been meeting with Charlotte? Did she give you the book to give to me?

But the questions don't come. Blanche has escaped around a corner before I can organise my thoughts or accept the suggestion.

We walk through a set of double doors that lead into the central courtyard. Wonders and Normals coexist, the latter unaware of the former's presence. My map icon jumps, and I open it. A compass rose appears in one corner of my vision, and caption bubbles pop up over various points. The Queen's Audience Chamber. The Throne Room. And there, over a high window, the bubble reads "Team Heart Suites."

"Here it is," Madi says after we cross a threshold, climb a flight of fanned, red-carpeted stairs, and reach a hall with a lift on either side. "Boys on one side and girls on the other. This lift is ours." She punches the button next to the lift on our right. "It was an addition by a player from last year's team. I plan to leave my own touch on the palace this season. In my rather un-humble opinion, the place could use a bit more colour."

At her words, the lift doors spring to life, opening and changing from silver to sapphire blue. We step inside as vines and flowers seem to grow out of the lift floor. The space becomes its own version of a mini rainforest. It even smells like rain.

"Goodness." I reach out and touch a bright orange tiger lily petal. It's one hundred percent real.

Madi gives me her signature wink. "Why don't you give it a try?"

I think of the abbey and how the ceiling opened up at the mere thought of seeing the sky. I do the same now, gazing upwards. As we rise, the ceiling does too. Expanding until it forms a glass steeple above us. The pink clouds are still there, but this time the sky has transitioned into a deep shade of plum.

"The sky changes often here," Madi says. "Everyone has a different version of what they want it to be."

I nod, still trying to wrap my mind around the idea that a mere thought could not only change the way I see the world, but how everyone else sees it too. It's like living inside my own dream. One I can control and manipulate as I please. And, it seems, I can invite others in as well.

A raw, empty ache grows stronger. I invited Chess in. And he . . . left. Just like that. No warning. Gone. The key and watch weigh heavy around my neck. I've unlocked the door to Wonderland, but so many others remain mysteries.

When the lift doors open, my breath catches before entering the suite. The foyer is bigger than my dormitory room. And the common area is double the size of Charlotte's flat, complete with a hearth and television. To either side of the common wait four doors, two on the left and two on the right. A name has been handwritten on three of the four.

Madi Hatter written in rainbow colours and swirling font.

Willow Reed in a straight and neat black serif.

Sophia Marigold in gold, the edges of each letter sharp and pointed.

The final door is blank, and I assume it's meant for me.

"We'd better get ready," Madi says. "You'll find your uniform and everything you need in your quarters. Once you're dressed I'll introduce you to the others." She slips into her room and closes the door behind her.

After all the instructions I've been given today, I feel at a loss now. But with nothing of my own aside from the rucksack on my back and the chain around my neck, I'm still curious as to what might await beyond the blank door.

Except, there's no handle. How very peculiar. I'm about to plop onto the comfy chaise lounge and wait for Madi's help, but then I remember my WV. It has everything else. Why not a way into my room? At the moment the thought occurs, a lock icon bounces into my view. My mind invites it to expand, but instead of a code or a password, a question scrolls across my vision and promptly disappears.

Who are you?

Strange. I feel utterly absurd, but I whisper to the door, "Alice."

It doesn't budge.

I try again. "I'm Alice."

Nothing.

Then I offer, "Who are *you*?" to the door, thinking perhaps this is some sort of passphrase. But still it remains stagnant.

Frustrated at yet another roadblock that makes zero sense, I rest my forehead against the door. At my touch, a little click sounds where a knob ought to be. The door slides to one side, swallowed by the wall.

The words *"Welcome, @Ace"* appear in my WV.

This day is full of surprises. Including, but not limited to, the rather bland scene before me.

White walls. No bed. No furniture at all. Not as much as a wardrobe.

"You look like you've never seen a blank canvas before."

I whirl to find a girl with exceedingly long legs and skin the richest shade of brown staring at me. She's stunning.

"Sophia," she says, holding out her hand. "I'm the team Four. Sophia's my actual name, by the way. I'm not much for nickna—er, Aliases."

Add @SophiaMarigold to your pack?

I shake her hand and allow access. "Ali . . . Ace," I say, feeling awkward at not wanting to tell her my full name. I don't know why, but Alice feels so plain here. The extra two letters feel too . . . Normal.

She smiles, making me feel considerably more comfortable than I did at her abrupt introduction. "Lovely to make your acquaintance. Do you know your Mastery yet?"

My brows scrunch. I half expect my WV to pop up a definition and allow me to cheat. It doesn't. "Mastery?" I'm forced to ask.

"You know, the unique skill you bring to the table?"

I shake my head.

"You know, like how Madi blends tea? That alone gives us

a huge advantage over the other teams. I could be wrong, but I think she's the sole Tea Master in the Trials this year."

And here I thought I was special based solely on invitation. Now I have to find my Mastery? Intimidated doesn't begin to describe how small I feel right now.

"I found out last year," Sophia says. "That I have the Gene. It was weird. My Normal parents wanted me to Register, naturally. I almost did. Walked all the way to the Registry and everything. But at the last minute, I saw it."

And, somehow, though I don't know exactly what she saw, I relate entirely.

When she continues, her eyes glisten. As confident as she looks, the emotion and insecurity they reveal connects instantly. "This flower. It was sticking up out of the ground right outside the Registry office. There were officers waiting to escort people in. People voluntarily giving up their freedoms, and the constables still treated them like dogs." A shadow passes over her already-darkened expression. Two deep wells overflowing with heartache and pain.

"I wondered if they saw it. How the flower changed colours. Red, orange, green, blue. I watched it. And when it turned into my favourite shade of purple? I knew it was this amazing gift I'd been given. The dream only a select few could see. And I couldn't throw that away, you know?"

I did know. I do.

"That's my Mastery, by the way," she adds. "I can talk to flowers."

Wow. Suddenly my ability to pick pockets seems awfully dim. "How did you end up here?"

She shrugs. "How does anyone? You ask questions. You find your people. Wonders find one another. It was Willow who found me, helped me hide in plain sight, and showed me how to find this place. She taught me how to believe in what I couldn't yet fully see."

As if she expected Sophia to say her name, the girl who must be Willow appears at her side. Curvy, with wide-set eyes that seem to stare into your soul and dark hair wrapped in a thick crown braid about her head.

"You would've found it on your own eventually, Soph," Willow says. "All real Wonders do."

Her words are for Sophia, but her glare is for me.

Add @WillReed to your pack?

I hesitate. Not quite ready to accept. This girl is anything but friendly.

"So, this is our Wildflower, huh?" Willow looks about as unimpressed as I feel. "She seems more like a common weed to me."

I feel her sizing me up. Scrutinising me in such a way that I suddenly feel as if I don't belong. I'm an imposter. A pity invite. A Normal trying to pose as a Wonder.

Willow seems to think the same. "You may have weaseled your way into my position. You may have the sympathy of my best friend." Her gaze flashes towards Sophia for an instant. "But you're not fooling anyone. Don't think for one second because I'm a Two that means I'm weak. A Two can replace an Ace any day. I'd watch your back if I were you."

She saunters away without as much as a proper greeting or introduction, turning the corner I assume must lead to a kitchen or the loo.

I ignore the Card suggestion.

Sophia glances at me. "Don't mind Will. She's just a little guarded, you know? Not so easily trusting. She was supposed to be the Team Heart Ace. When she got bumped to a Two . . ." She laughs awkwardly. "I'm sure you can understand how she must feel. Her Normal family disowned her when she was young, and she was homeless for years until she found her way in without any help or guidance. We're the only family she's got. She'll warm up to you after we all kick some Spade tail in the First Trial."

At the mention of the First Trial, my ears perk. With all the worry about Charlotte and the missing players, I'd nearly forgotten about the one thing I've always wanted—needed. To play.

"What are you two standing around for?" Madi leans against her doorframe dressed in a knee-length red tutu and short black jacket that cuts her waist just right. "Do you want the boys to beat us to supper? They'll eat everything before we've had our first roll."

The boys. How could I forget? Teams are made up of seven players, which means there must be three boys on our team. I've already met Knave—sort of. Who could the others be? Wonder-born, or from the Normal world, like me?

"They'll regret it if they do." Willow reenters the sitting room, sporting the same colours as Madi, but her outfit is a bit simpler—flowy black trousers that could almost pass for a skirt and a red blouse with cold-shoulder sleeves. "You can decorate your room later, new girl. Get dressed. If someone eats my roll, it will be your fault."

Sophia gives an apologetic smile then disappears into the much more colourful room beside mine. I enter my own blank space, and the door automatically shuts behind me. Nothing happens. I feel ridiculous.

A message icon pops up. It's from Madi.

Team colours are a must.

Thanks for the tip, I think. The words become a message that I assume she receives in her own WV. Are none of my thoughts my own?

I drop my rucksack and sigh. Charlotte's always been the more fashionable of us two. Years of being forced to wear a school uniform have stifled my creativity. I stare down at the striped leggings Charlotte gave me. An image of myself in a looking glass pops into my mind. I'm a little girl in a bright red dress.

Whoa. Another forgotten memory?

Whatever it is, my clothes begin to change colour. Blue is exchanged for black, and white is replaced with red. My leggings remain unchanged, and I'm perfectly fine with that. I close my eyes and keep picturing that little girl. For whatever reason, the image of myself as a child seems to spark my imagination.

When my eyes open, I find my ensemble completely transformed, aside from the leggings. The red dress with a sweetheart neckline and puffy skirt that stops just below my knees is fancier than anything I've ever owned. It swishes and rustles when I move. For the first time since arriving, I feel almost pretty. Special.

And, best of all, I feel like a Wonder.

I could get used to this.

When I exit my room, the other girls are waiting. Though each of our outfits is unique, we look uniform in our red-and-black Team Heart colours. The boys are waiting for us at the palace entrance, but I'm surprised to see there are only two. Knave and another boy who immediately greets us with a wave and a grin.

"You ladies look sensational," he says.

Add @JackBNimble to your pack?

The boy hasn't introduced himself yet, but I immediately accept the suggestion. There's just something about him that says I want him on my team.

But, where's the third boy that will make up our seven?

I don't have time to ask. It takes my short legs extra work to keep up as we head past the gates. Blanche de Lapin stands at the kerb in her white high heels and laced everything. She winks at me but says nothing about our previous encounters or her mysterious invite. Instead she waves towards an old-fashioned limousine. "Ve must travel een style. I prefer zee classics to zee more modern forms ov transport. Hurry now, or ve shall all be very late."

I can't keep up with how upside down it is here. One minute I'm travelling along in a futuristic hover bus, and the next I'm back in time, being transported around town in a decades-old vehicle.

Topsy-turvy doesn't begin to describe this place.

Oyster and Pearl Hall isn't far, located just west of Heart Palace. When we arrive, both Team Diamond and Team Club make their entrances too, all dressed to match in their team colours—the Diamonds in silver and black and the Clubs in black and green.

We're ushered in over a red carpet and into the grandest version of a cafeteria I've ever seen. This must be Royal Albert Hall beneath the Wonderland layer. The concert venue would undoubtedly stand on its own in grandeur, though I've never seen it myself. This version needs no additions, yet there are clearly details only Wonders would be able to imagine. Tables in the shape of each team's symbol on a rotating floor at the centre. Chandeliers that appear to dance above. Floating compartments in the place of spectator seats that rise up, up, up into the dome, hundreds upon thousands of members in the audience looking down at one thing and one thing alone.

At the centre of the rotating tables, a dais where Blanche and several other officials congregate on either side of a throne.

And there, at the heart of it all, is Lady Scarlet.

Queen of Wonderland.

RIDDLES

My jaw drops. I close my eyes. Blink. Then blink again. This has to be an illusion.

I've come across portraits of Scarlet from years long past. As a child. A young woman. From before the Divide and the falling out with Queen Cordelia when Scarlet went into hiding. I knew they were fraternal twins and looked about as different as night and day.

Cordelia is blonde. Scarlet has dark locks.

Cordelia's eyes are light blue. Scarlet's are rich and dark.

But now that I've seen Scarlet up close? This is something else entirely. Because the Queen of Wonderland bears a striking resemblance to someone I know very well, indeed. Could this be a side effect of missing her?

Charlotte.

The pieces come together one by one.

Charlotte was born into the House of Spade. Her father is a minister, her mother a lady. Except . . . Charlotte played for Team Heart. Why wouldn't she play for her own quarter? Her family? Apparently she's close with Blanche, or at the very least has been in communication with the queen's closest advisor. Could that have something to do with it?

Then there's her desire to keep her Wonder identity a secret, not just from society, but from me. From herself. Because if Charlotte is somehow related to *this* queen, that means she's connected to the one in the Normal Reality as well.

And she's in more danger than I ever could have fathomed.

Her Majesty, the Queen of England, would not want it known she has Unregistered Wonder relations running about.

"Velcome vun and all." Blanche steps up onto the centre dais, drawing our attention as we find our seats. She doesn't speak into a microphone, but her voice projects all the same. "Zis year marks our twenty-fifth annual Vonder Trials. Our silver year, ladeez and gentlemen. A time ven our youth come together to compete for zee fun and entertainment ov all. Players go on to lead lives ov opportunity, fame, and fortune. Ov course, no vun has completed zee Trials een zeir entirety since zee Queen ov Hearts herself."

Blanche pauses a moment. She looks at Scarlet with a rather dramatic expression of awe and reverence.

Hushed whispers sound and knowing glances are given among teammates. No doubt circulating more speculation that anyone who actually managed to finish the Fourth Trial would be named heir to the throne.

"I think it's all one big show," Madi whispers to me. When I give her a quizzical look she adds, "The Trials can get dangerous, even deadly. Plus there's that fact that players keep turning up missing."

"You know about the missing—?"

"Everyone does. But that's the thing, isn't it?"

"What do you mean?"

"Well," she says, "If I were in Scarlet's position, and I

wanted to keep kids competing for my own entertainment, I might start a rumour to make them think there is some bigger prize worth playing for. Wouldn't you?"

Her observation is a dark one, causing me to question Scarlet's motives. Could she have something to do with—?

I shake off the notion before it forms into a proper thought. The queen founded Wonderland to save Wonders. What purpose could she possibly have in taking them?

It isn't until Her Majesty humbly acknowledges Blanche's adoration that @*WhiteRabbit* continues. I open her profile in my WV, scanning her bio as she speaks. There's nothing of consequence. She's been involved with the Trials from the beginning, enjoys sleeping in, gardening, and hopping from one party to the next on weekends.

I close out Blanche's profile and try to focus on the here and now. This should be exciting. No, more than exciting, this is *epic*. But I can't stop letting my attention wander to the queen. Rigid. Serious. Expression full of intimidation and power. If anyone fits the bill of villain, she does.

I sink lower in my chair, letting the floral centrepiece on our table block my view. It's my first night, and already I'm playing detective. Dinah's still absent and Chess is no help. How am I supposed to do this on my own? I don't know where to begin.

"Foxgloves," Sophia informs our table. She reaches out but stops shy of touching the bell-like, violet-pink blossoms. "Poisonous when in contact with bare skin. An interesting choice for a table decoration."

The bloke to my right—Jack—must notice my damper mood. He offers me a roll. "You'll feel better once you eat something, mate."

I turn my head to find a genuine smile greeting me. Nothing like Willow's aggressive tone or Mouse's haughty air.

"I heard you're the team Ace," he remarks, buttering a roll for me and setting it on my plate. "I play Jack, if you haven't already guessed. Looks like we have something in common." His accent is warm and inviting, soothing my nerves and helping me ease up in my chair. "Using your position as an Alias? Glad it's not just me who enjoys the obvious. Of course, Jack is actually my name, so there's that. Jack B. Nimble II. My dad—also Jack—played Jack in the Trials way back, if you haven't already guessed. Do you know your Mastery yet?"

I shake my head as I tear off a piece of my roll. It flakes on my tongue, practically melting before I have the chance to chew. Smelling of yeast and salt with a hint of honey, I don't know what the first course is, but I don't care.

The wide grin on Jack's face and the way he starts buttering another roll tells me he doesn't either. "Don't let not knowing get you down," he says. "You'll figure it out in time."

"What's yours, if you don't mind me asking?"

"Not at all." His smile broadens, as if he was hoping I'd pose this very question. "Puzzles are my specialty. It's pretty common among Wonders, honestly. Each team has at least one Puzzle Master. Who knows?" He shrugs. "Maybe our team has two." His look says he hopes this is true, and that we'll have more in common than our appreciation for keeping things simple.

I nod. With a full mouth and my stomach happier than it's ever been, I say, "Maybe."

"Ve ave a roster ov splendid players zis year," Blanche goes on. "Our Trainers are prepared. Zee locations are set." She twists from side to side, arms wide, indicating this is not only the dining hall, it's the playing field as well. "You vill compete een four Trials, vun to represent each quarter and house." Four fingers in the air, Blanche's glittery white manicure twinkles under the spotlight. "Points are given for completing each Trial and vut position you finish een, but also for teamwork and, as alvays, creativity. You each ave four Fates, represented by your suit's symbol. Four chances to survive. Lose all ov

zem, and you are benched. Zis veakens your numbers, giving
an advantage to zee ozer teams."

I glance at my four pulsing hearts in the corner of my WV,
then at the matching lights on my bangle. What would it take
to lose one?

"Vichever team captures zeir clue card at zee end of each
Trial first eez pronounced zee vinner."

Across the table, Knave snorts. Then he dons his
headphones.

Perfect. One of our team members thinks he's too good for
the rules. This ought to go smoothly.

"Zis year's Trials are bigger and better zan ever," Blanche
says. "Ve expect you all to do your best, and play like zee
Vonders you are."

Cheers and applause ripple over the crowd, followed by the
rise of instrumental music. But the jovial blend of strings and
flutes does nothing to ease my disquiet. I'm definitely in over
my head here. My thoughts drift back to Clash of the Cards.
When Blanche named Black Hearts her game of choice.

In all the rules she's mentioned, I know that which remains
unspoken. The Trials involve risks. Just as in Black Hearts,
rules are expected to be bent, maybe even broken.

A plate prepared with the most beautiful presentation of a
roast dinner I have ever seen is set before me. But my appetite
has vanished.

"Eat vell, players." Why do I feel as if Blanche is speaking—
and looking—directly at me? "You ave a long night ahead ov
you. Our First Trial—representing zee Spade Quarter—begins
at sundown tomorrow. And now, for zee moment you ave all
been vaiting for . . . zee first clues."

The buzz that filled the dome moments ago falls silent. As
if everyone is leaning in, frozen in time, straining to hear what
Blanche is about to say.

But it isn't Blanche who speaks. She steps aside, making

way for one of the officials on the dais, a man with slick black hair and sunken, deep-set eyes shadowed by thick eyebrows. From this distance I can still spot the tattoo on his right hand.

He clears his throat. "What grows stronger the longer it rests?"

The Minister of Spades is shorter than I expected. And he looks less like his daughter Charlotte than the queen does. In fact, he doesn't appear to belong in Wonderland at all. Amidst the colour and whimsy, he's more Normal than anything I've seen since arriving.

Madi nudges me. "That's too easy."

Attempting to mirror her emotion, I force a half smile. She's here to play, not investigate, even if she did speculate about the queen's motives.

"Tea," she finishes. "The answer is tea." The odd look she offers suggests she expected me to know the answer and play along.

Maybe it's the fact that I've spent far too many years in the Normal Reality. Or maybe I'm cynical. But it can't be that easy. That's not the entire riddle.

"How can you stand if not on your feet?" The minister gives the next riddle, and the teams at the other tables speak in hushed tones, as does the crowd above.

This time it's Sophia who whispers to our group. "Your head, right?"

Every member of Team Heart nods. Aside from Knave, who seems as if he couldn't care less.

"What disagrees but never argues," the minister adds, "and always wins but never fights?"

We all stare at one another.

I think on the third riddle, wanting to contribute something to our team and at least be useful. But nothing rings a bell aside from the knowledge that I ate far too many rolls and they are certainly disagreeing with my worried stomach. It was bound to happen sooner or later.

"And lastly . . ." The minister steps closer to the edge of the dais, looks at each team table in turn before finishing. "Why is a raven like a writing desk?"

I nearly choke on the sip of water I just took.

Madi pats me on the back hard. "You okay?"

I nod and squeeze my eyes. My throat burns and water drips out my nose onto my plate. Jack hands me his serviette, and I dab at my face, taking a careful drink to help calm myself.

"Solve these riddles, four," the minister adds, "and you will find the door. Look through and you will see. Right there they will be." The minister returns to his seat at the left hand of the queen.

The rhyme is reminiscent of the poems in Charlotte's book.

Blanche steps forwards again. There's a pause before she speaks this time. Like the minister moments ago, she looks at each table in turn, resting her attention on us last.

On me.

She's helping me cheat. Again. Why? Did the queen ask her to secure Team Heart's victory by giving me a head start on one of the clues? What interest could Scarlet possibly have in me?

With a clap of her lace-gloved hands, Blanche says, "Come dressed een your best and ready to test everything een you zat eez Vonder!"

The other officials on the dais commence their meals.

The minister twitches his nose so that his mustache looks like a creeping caterpillar.

Another man, with a muffin-top and pudge at every joint and bend, digs into the potatoes on his plate like they're roasted nuggets of gold.

"Minister Mocktur Telle," Jack says, pointing with a fork that has a sizable piece of roast lamb at its tines. He takes a bite before he continues speaking. "Oversees Club Quarter and funds his team. It'll be interesting to see what sort of Trial he's cooked up this year. It never fails to be . . . interesting."

I watch the chubby little man eat his fill. He flags down a server, asking for a second helping no doubt.

"He's a Trainer?"

Jack nearly spits out his food. He shakes his head then wipes his mouth with a serviette, a mannerism I wouldn't expect from someone who talks with their mouth full.

Oddly enough, I like him more now.

"Old Quincy up there"—he glances over to the Minister of Spades—"likes to train because it keeps him in control of things on his team. Classic narcissist. But most quarter heads don't train their own teams. They pay Trainers who've had a good run in prior years' Trials, sit back, and reap the rewards."

I nod, starting to understand how some things work around here. "Who's that?" I gesture towards an ethereal looking woman who's decked out in more frills and jewels than the queen herself.

"Duchess of Diamonds. And no, those long, pointed dragon nails of hers do not allow her to train her team either." After a polite pause, Jack asks, "Are you going to eat that?" He's pointing at my now-cold roast with his fork.

Her Majesty leans to her right and whispers something to Blanche.

The queen's closest confidante pops up and hurries off the twirling platform and out of view.

I shake my head, my appetite still absent, but my curiosity in full swing. Where is Blanche running off to in the middle of dinner?

A few of the players mingle with the members at other tables, and I can't help but glance in the direction of Team Spade. Chess appears to be having a grand time. Leaning close to the Wonder goddess beside him, living up to every expectation I ever had of him.

He's exactly who I thought he was.

I swallow hard. As Queen Scarlet rises to speak, I watch how her long bell skirts swish and sway, the border of hearts at her skirt hem almost seeming to pulse alive.

"Welcome, Wonders, one and all." Her voice is firm but kind. "I am delighted to see how Wonderland has advanced year after year. When I first discovered our dreams could become our Reality, Wonderland was merely a blank canvas. A place I could hide. Where my Gene was not the oddity everyone said. I was not a danger here. Never a threat. Here, I could be anything. Here, I could be who I was meant to be."

A long pause ensues, as if she wants her words to sink in. And they do. Taking root inside me. Coiling around my soul and latching on for dear life. Is this what it feels like to finally belong?

"Many of you sitting in this room today followed me." She takes her time, making eye contact with her audience. "And you discovered that by simply believing in the impossible and dreaming what you wanted this world to be, it could bloom beyond anything we ever imagined."

At her words, vines begin to climb the walls, stretching towards the domed ceiling. Like Madi's garden in the lift, but on a much grander scale. Tulips. Daisies. Violets. And hybrids of flowers. Ones I've never seen or thought existed.

Sophia's expression in particular emits pure awe.

"I wish you all the best in the Trials this year, and I look forward to getting to know each and every team player." Now she nods in turn to each of our four team tables, beginning with Clubs and ending on ours. "Play well. Choose wisely. And, no matter which team comes out on top this year, you are all winners in my book."

A round of applause follows and our dinner plates

disappear, replaced by the most delicious Yorkshire pudding. One bite is heaven, and I know I'm going to be sick from how rich it is. But I can't help it. I ignore how Jack eyes my portion after he's had his fill.

The Trials can wait for tomorrow.

This dessert is mine.

TRAINING

It's the first decent sleep I've had since . . . last week? Since before Charlotte helped me escape Bill, and Chess decided to invade—and abruptly disappear from—my life.

More than that, it's the first dreamless night I've had in years. Perhaps it's due to the fact that I am quite literally living inside a dream world. Who needs subconscious imaginings when you have anything you could possibly wish for at your fingertips?

When I wake, my glasses are askew and I have no idea what time it is. The hazard of sleeping in a room without windows, which I'll need to rectify soon. I was so knackered last night, I forgot to set my locket watch to wake me.

I adjust my glasses and sit up in the bed I created just before crashing into it—fully clothed, I might add—around midnight. It's nothing fancy or as remotely artistic as what the other girls no doubt have in their suites. But it's mine. Larger and softer than my dormitory bed or Charlotte's settee. Covered with a cream-coloured duvet with floral embroidery and gold stitching around the hem.

At the thought of Charlotte, I swing my legs over the side of the bed and reach for my rucksack on the floor. I haven't had a chance to go through my things since arriving. Pulling them out now and spreading them across the duvet, they seem incredibly unimportant. Plain. Normal.

A sigh escapes, followed by a rogue tear. I catch it with one finger, staring at the drop as if it can explain itself or me or anything. My eyes have been unusually dry since arriving. I don't feel much like myself at all, now that I think of it.

"Where are you, Charlotte?" I whisper to her birth certificate. More questions form as I thumb through the pages of *The Adventurer's Almanac* Blanche gave me—the book that really belongs to Charlotte. Nothing makes sense, yet everything seems connected.

I read through a few of the game sections, then a couple of poems. There doesn't appear to be anything particularly important, aside from the obvious conclusion this book was penned by a Wonder with experience in both Realities. Some of the margin notes are in Charlotte's hand. Others are in a neat print I don't recognise. Perhaps notes made by R.S.H.?

The chapter about the Trials is listed in order of the year they originated, with older games at the front of the tome and more modern games near the end. I stop at a section from several decades back, glancing over a few forms of amusement that are completely foreign to me. The titles alone sound like nonsense, in my opinion.

The Wonderful World of Minecraft.

An Imposter Is Among Us.

The Art of Escaping Escape Rooms.

Escape rooms? Why would anyone purposely put themselves in a situation they needed to escape? Absurd.

This is getting me positively nowhere. Determination and

new purpose fuelling me like a bold cup of coffee, I pull out my pocketscreen. Dead. Of course it is. I'm about to chuck it across the room when a notepad icon bounces into the top menu of my WV. I don't know if I'll ever get used to this tech reading my mind. It's proven useful, I'll give it that.

The notepad expands. A sort of digital board hovering before me, transparent yet solid. I begin thinking through everything I know thus far, making a column for facts, a second for possibilities, and a final for suspects.

> FACTS (Maybe):
> —Charlotte is a Wonder. She resembles Queen Scarlet, yet she is the daughter of the Minister and Lady of Spades.
> —Charlotte is the first missing player to be found. She was found with me. This is important, but one can only guess why.
> —Blanche knows Charlotte. They've been meeting secretly, and Charlotte gave her the book to give to me.
>
> POSSIBILITIES, CONJECTURES, & QUESTIONS:
> —Charlotte is somehow Scarlet's daughter, or at the very least, related to her.
> —The Minister of Spades is, quite possibly, the "imposter among us," pun intended.
> —Why do players go missing?
> —Why did Kit go missing?
> —Why am I important?

After that last question appears on the board, I hesitate. I almost erase it but decide to leave it for now. Although I've been told why I've come, I still feel the answer isn't quite clear. As if there's more to the story. I attempt to clear my head and move on to the suspects column. This list forms faster than the others. Several people come to mind as having ulterior motives.

SUSPECTS:
—*Blanche. (Suspicious from day one. Why did she have Charlotte's book? Why is she helping me cheat? Why is she always coming and going in a rush?)*
—*Minister of Spades, as previously noted. (Obviously. A shady-looking man with shifty eyes and zero smile. There's also the memory of his tattoo to take into consideration.)*
—*Queen Scarlet. (Isn't the leader always suspect? Her possible connection to Charlotte seems important too. She also doesn't seem the warmest sort. Must get to know her more before forming an opinion.)*
—*Chess and Dinah. (Too many reasons to name.)*
—*Knave. (He's around my age, so he's too young to have accomplished much, but he still rubs me the wrong way.)*

My thoughts pause, and I scan the notes so far, not wanting to add the final suspects who float to the forefront of my mind. But I'm here to help solve this mystery surrounding my past. Which means I have to follow every lead. Every thought. Every clue.

Slowly, with another tear forming at the corner of my right eye, I add the last suspects to my list.

—*My parents. (Who are they? What happened to them? Did they leave me, die, or is their absence from my life something more sinister?)*

I slouch back onto my solitary pillow. Whatever Charlotte did or didn't do, said or never said, she came after me. In the Cotswolds. In the middle of the night. Knowing she could have been caught. She *was* caught. She's not my blood, yet she came for me. But my parents?

They never came.

Charlotte told the truth about one thing, at least. My parents didn't want me.

Maybe they never cared about me at all.

Breakfast in the common room is a lavish spread of jam-filled pastries, treacle tarts, and cream-stuffed Danishes. It's nothing like the rather dull and plain morning meal I'm accustomed to in Oxford. By our eight o'clock training session in the palace courtyard, I feel alert and ready to take on the task ahead— not just in this evening's Trial, but in gaining ground on the investigation as well. Chess and Dinah clearly aren't going to give me further direction at this point. I'm on my own.

What else is new?

The courtyard is divided into four quaint square gardens, one in each corner. At the centre, a circular hedge twice my height conceals our destination. I follow my team beneath an ivy-covered archway. Sophia is practically giddy when we're suddenly surrounded by flowers of every genus.

"Good morning, friend," she says to a yellow daffodil.

It bows towards her in response.

Sophia notices me watching her. She winks and smiles, a secret behind her kind eyes. "You can learn a lot of things from the flowers, you know."

I nod, trying not to laugh. Blanche told me the same thing

on the train. When things were Normal. Isn't the statement truer here?

Maybe I'll discover my own Mastery before the day is through.

The hedges lead us along a spiraling path. We pass blossoms in every colour. And when we finally reach the heart of it all, there stands Blanche, waiting behind a wrought iron gate.

I've been here before. This is the garden I saw in my dream.

Beyond Blanche sits an elongated table set for tea, the tablecloth hanging to the grassy floor on all sides. Various, mismatched chairs are situated around it. At the head of a table is a chair that looks like a throne, and at the opposite end, a hologram of the four Spade clues hovers in the air.

"'Ave a seat, ladeez and gentlemen. Zee clock eez ticking."

I choose a purple Victorian parlor chair with silver trim between Madi and Jack. Sophia sits across from us on a tufted seat that looks like a toadstool, Willow by her side on an antique garden bench. Knave—surprise, surprise—separates himself from our team, finding his place at the head of the table where the throne resides. The only thing missing are his headphones. Did Blanche take them away?

"I don't think that spot is meant for you," Willow comments.

"What's it to you, Two?" Knave essentially spits the last word like it's something foul.

My hope sinks as does my posture. How am I ever going to get Willow to warm up to me if she's constantly reminded that I took her position as the Ace? I still don't know what's expected of me, or everything that my role entails. I do know it's important. Otherwise Willow wouldn't be glaring knives at me from across the table.

Once we're all seated, I expect Blanche to begin speaking and to introduce our official Trainer. (Who I realise has yet to be revealed. I make a mental note to add whoever it is to my suspect list.) Better yet, she ought to explain how to best prepare for the Spade Trial. But *@WhiteRabbit* says nothing. Almost as if she's waiting—

And then the Queen of Hearts herself strolls into the garden.

Sitting straighter, I hide my hands beneath my thighs to keep from fidgeting.

Jack removes the serviette he tucked into his shirt as a joke and places it on his lap.

Scarlet is close enough this time that her Alias becomes visible. Similar to Blanche's, the queen's bangle bears no lights to represent her Fates in the Trials. But, unlike Blanche's, there's an onyx stone in the spot where a ruby ought to be.

I narrow my eyes. Where have I seen that stone before?

The suggestion to add Scarlet as a Card startles me. As if she's just anyone and not the ruler of Wonderland.

Add @QueenOfHearts to your pack?

I accept immediately. I'm too nervous to ignore it and too petrified I won't get this chance again. How does one say no to an invitation from royalty? Besides, the closer I am to Her Majesty, the easier it will be to either confirm or eliminate her as a suspect.

Dressed more casually than the evening prior, Scarlet's locks are a chocolate waterfall over and behind her shoulders. She's wearing black trousers and a fitted, waist-length red peacoat. When she speaks, it's like listening to something oddly soothing and terrifyingly fierce at the same time.

"You're our Trainer?" Jack blurts.

Poor bloke. Didn't anyone teach him to mind his manners?

But the queen does not scold him. She inclines her head in his direction, emanating the grace, poise, and self-control of a true royal.

"No," she says, gliding around to our side of the table. When she reaches Jack, she curls her fingers over the back of his glass chair. "Of course not, young man. I am the queen, after all, and have much more pressing duties to attend to."

Gulping audibly, Jack nods.

Scarlet moves on, pausing at the place where Knave reclines. He has one leg slung over the throne's arm, foot bouncing in time to the music that is no doubt inside his head.

At first glance, Knave seems unfazed. But then I catch the smallest glimmer of fear in his eyes and question for the first time if he's not as confident and cool as he comes off.

"I am merely here to show my support for your undying efforts," Scarlet continues, expression lacking emotion. "Heart Quarter deserves the very best, you know. And I would rather not have another team claim the lead this season."

"What does it matter?" Knave says. "No one ever actually *wins* the Trials, do they, my darling aunt?"

Every single one of our jaws goes slack. *Aunt*? There's a little tidbit that might have been good to know.

"Knave Civilius Heart," Blanche scolds. "Vatch your tongue."

Scarlet holds up a palm towards Blanche. The queen pushes her nephew's chair in, forcing him to lower his leg and sit up straight at the table. "You know very well, *nephew*," the queen says, "that the Fourth and final Trial—my own Heart Trial—is always the most difficult. The most demanding."

"And, of course it's no coincidence the unbeatable Trial is always *yours*," Knave says. "Perhaps you don't want anyone to actually win the Trials. Then you'd have to name an heir, isn't that right?"

So it's true? The Trials really were designed to choose Wonderland's next ruler?

For the smallest of moments, I think Scarlet will lose her patience. Rage hides behind the cool dark chasms of her eyes. But she doesn't unleash it. Instead she answers his question. "The Trials have always been and remain a celebration of who we are as Wonders. The people look forward to them every season. Any rumours otherwise circulated are simply that— rumours. I cannot help that no team has finished the Fourth Trial since my own team won twenty-five years ago."

"You can understand why he's suspicious though, right?" Where did that come from? It's the first out-of-turn thing I've said since arriving. What is wrong with me? Why am I defending Knave?

All eyes fall to me, and there's nothing left to do but continue. I push back from the table and rise, feeling the weight of the queen's notice and Blanche's disappointment. I clear my throat. "What I mean to say is, it makes sense that Wonders have begun to talk. You can't blame them for questioning the way of things, especially with the disappearances."

"Do you always say exactly what you think, child?" Scarlet stands directly across the table from me now, and I realise for the first time she's not much taller than I am.

Confidence lifting, I correct my posture. "It depends on the occasion. Do you?"

"I am the queen, a position which condones certain behaviours. Do you understand?" Her words are more warning than question.

I don't know where my boldness is stemming from but I don't care. I curtsy. "Yes, Your Majesty."

She stares straight through me for what feels like minutes rather than seconds. At last she steps away from the table, calm demeanor returning and neutral expression falling into place. "I have faith in each of you," she says. "Do not disappoint your queen."

It isn't until she's disappeared beyond the high hedge that I collapse into my chair.

The team sits silent for a spell.

Willow is the first to break it. She raises an empty teacup, offering an almost-genuine smile just for me. "Touché, Ace. Maybe you're not such a common weed after all."

The First Trial hasn't begun, but this in itself feels like a small victory. I raise my own empty teacup towards her in acknowledgement.

I may not have gained favour with the queen, who is now more suspect than ever. But, for the first time, I feel like a part of my own team. Whatever happens tonight, I'll go in knowing we are in this together.

"Ahem." Blanche taps a spoon on the side of her water glass. "Ve are vasting precious moments, Hearts. Eet eez time for your training to begin."

"Who's going to train us?" Knave lifts a skeptical brow. "You?"

"Do not be ridiculous," she says. "Your Trainer eez merely running rather late." She checks her pocket watch, taps its face once, then slips it back into her waistcoat. "I am simply filling een until she arrives."

"Well," Madi asks. "Who is it?"

"You vill all find out een due time. All I can tell you eez she eez someone who has played een zee Trials previously."

Tick. I am most definitely adding our Trainer to the list of suspects.

"For now, eet eez important zat you vork together to solve zese riddles, and prepare for vut eez to come." Blanche waves towards the holographic screen. "Put your heads together, ladeez and gentlemen. Eet's going to be a long day."

By a quarter till one, we're no closer to solving the remainder of the riddles than we were before. In the past four hours, we've added notes to the board, but they're nothing we didn't already know.

Tea grows stronger the longer it rests.

One can stand on their head if not on their feet.

And my contribution—the fourth riddle is impossible to solve. Everyone agreed and Blanche approved. I did not, however, let on that figuring out the answer was part of my pretrial to get into Wonderland as a Wildflower in the first place.

I sip at my hot tea, which Madi explained is a mild blend of yerba mate and peppermint.

"Focus Fix," she said. "Wakes the brain and relaxes the nerves at the same time."

Pink-and-green steam swirls from liquid that's remained hot after hours sitting in open air. Lunch is served, a generous spread of charcuterie boards featuring fine meats and cheeses and breads. I twirl my spoon in my cup, watching how the steam reacts. How it dances around the spoon handle, making it spin on its own.

"Maybe the first answer isn't tea," Sophia suggests, breaking my internal musings.

"And maybe the second isn't 'stand on your head,'" Madi counters.

"Could the order they were given be a factor?" I offer, speaking again for the first time in an hour. Cards I can play. Strategy, when I know the rules of the game, no problem. But this is beyond my skillset, making me question once again why I am here in the first place.

Maybe I don't have a Mastery.

Willow nods. "Ace has a point. Perhaps we're thinking too linearly." She meets my gaze across the table.

It's such a small thing, but her acceptance of my presence makes a world of difference.

I take one more sip of tea before rising. When I'm directly in front of the screen, I take a step back. I'm so used to needing to stand close to things to see them clearly, I'm amazed how much my vision has improved here. Using my fingers, I swipe and slide, switching the riddles around in order from last to first, their answers beside them.

Why is a raven like a writing desk? It isn't. Impossible.

What disagrees, but never argues? And always wins, but never fights? ????

How can you stand if not on your feet? Stand on your head.

What grows stronger the longer it rests? Tea.

I stare at the clues. "The answers," I ponder aloud. "We've been thinking about them separately. But there's a reason four riddles were given. What if together they form one answer and the key to winning the First Trial?"

"But what's the goal?" Sophia asks. "Remember what the minister said?" Her questions tumble forth. "Right there they will be? Who? Behind what door? And how about what disagrees? It doesn't—"

"Poison," an unexpected voice behind me says.

I whirl. My cheeks grow warm. I press the backs of my hands to my face to cool them.

"Poison disagrees with one sooner or later, does it not?" Chess and his broad grin wait behind the gate. He opens it, inviting himself in, stepping closer with each new word. "And it will always win, but never fight."

He's coming around the table towards me now, so close I have to force myself not to react. I want to close the distance between us. I want him to twirl me around like he did the day back at the Oxford flat.

Instead, I back away and reach to tuck my hair behind my ears, only to remember I wore it in a plait today.

Madi leaps from her chair. "It's about time you showed up. I was beginning to think you were lying when you said you'd applied for a team transfer." She stands beside me now, expression beaming.

So she was being playful when she called him an enemy at the abbey. Why does that vex me so?

Chess shrugs. "I had some . . . unfinished business with the minister. But he finally signed off on my request. And here I am. You're welcome." A wink at Madi.

A twinge of jealousy pings my heart when she gives him a quick hug. Are these feelings of betrayal? Doubt? A bit of both?

"Awesome," Jack says. "We needed more testosterone in our midst. Now we're a complete hand of seven. I worried we were going to be a man short, but we've hit the jackpot. You're a legend, sir. That move you made in the Club Trial last year two seconds before the clock ran out? That was pure gold." Jack comes around the table and shakes Chess's hand.

Perfect. Another one of Chess's adoring fans.

"Wait, you're playing with us?" Willow asks, eyeing Chess up and down, not at all helping with the jealous green monster growing at a rapid pace inside of me. "I thought you might be our Trainer."

"Nonsense," Chess says. "Training's not my style." He winks and adds, "I'm the Team King."

PARTIES

It is not impossible to drink poisoned tea when you stand on your head.

I review the answer we all finally agreed upon once more before we arrive at the dining hall, this time travelling in a horse-drawn carriage one might expect to see in a fairy story. Knave and Jack act as our escorts, riding Clydesdales to either side of us girls. Chess leads our little brigade, pulling on the reins of the carriage steeds, then hopping down from the driver's seat to open our door when we arrive.

One by one, the girls take his hand and step excitedly onto the red carpet that leads into Oyster and Pearl Hall. First Sophia, followed by Willow, and then Madi. Did Chess hold her hand longer than he did the others? Why do I care?

At my turn, I gather the folds of my gown in my left hand, offering Chess my right. When he looks up at me, I search his turquoise eyes. His mouth parts, and I almost think he's going to say something. A word to open the gates that have closed between us.

But he says nothing. The moment passes, and my feet are flat on the ground, my gloved fingers sliding from his.

He tugs me back towards him. The horse nearest to us whinnies her approval, bucking her head and swishing her tail.

It's his turn to search my eyes. I expect an apology. Perhaps an excuse. A reason he left me behind. A purpose for his indifference.

Instead he says, "You still owe me that dance, Ace." Chess slips the glove off my right hand and presses a kiss to my knuckles. His lips are warm. Feeling right and exactly where they belong.

But this isn't right. You cannot abandon a person in the middle of London one day and toy with her emotions the next.

I pull away and snatch my glove from his hand. I almost slap him with it but use my words to issue my wrath instead. "I owe you nothing. I believe it is you who owes me something."

"A waltz?" His charming grin and lone arched eyebrow are enough to make me fall into his embrace right here.

But I stand my ground. "An explanation." Do not cry. Do not give him the satisfaction of witnessing a single tear.

He nods. Bows his head. Still, he says nothing.

"You lied to me."

"Oh?" He looks genuinely curious. So curious, in fact, maybe I should smack that grin right off his face. "And what, pray tell, did I lie about?"

I choose my next words carefully, aiming them towards their mark. "You said nothing was impossible."

He doesn't reply. Good. Let him wait on me for once.

"But you were wrong," I say. "Because nothing and no one could be more impossible than you, Chess Shire."

I can't read his expression. Is that surprise in his wide eyes? I don't stand there long enough to find out. I race up the red carpet, tripping over my dress a few times in the process. With Chess behind me and the Trial ahead, tears prick my eyes again. I swipe at them with the glove I'm still holding, recalling the invitation to tonight's affair and the final, unexpected clue we received one hour before sundown.

You are cordially invited to attend tonight's Tea Party Ball.

Do not wait to escape, or you shall run rather late.

And do not dare run until you have rescued them all.

"Rescued them all?" Madi said after the invitation arrived hand-delivered by Blanche herself. "All of what? We're only supposed to find the next clue card, right?"

Our group of girls nodded in agreement that the last-minute riddle seemed out of place.

Blanche gave nothing away. She retrieved the card from Madi, turned on her heel, and went on her merry way. I suspected she wanted to give the boys a chance to read the clue too.

We bounced ideas back and forth while scrambling to get ready for the ball. Originally we'd assumed more comfortable attire would be in order for the Spade Trial, but the new invitation suggested otherwise. When we couldn't come up with any new ideas, we spent the rest of our time imagining up our dresses instead. Madi said we ought to keep with black and red. Though I'd much rather wear blue, we all agreed team colours were expected. We even visited the WV accessory shoppe for a few finishing touches.

My crimson silk bodice and black tulle skirt are dotted with live rosebuds—compliments of Sophia. While she added the floral embellishments, the dress design is all mine. I'm rather satisfied with how quickly my own imagination has blossomed.

We took turns helping one another create the perfect hair and makeup looks. Madi imagined my hairdo, leaving my straw-coloured locks soft and curled. A few purposeful strands frame my face and the rest is tied back with a crimson ribbon to match my bodice. That piece she bought for me with a few golden petals.

"Do you like it?" she asked as I admired the simple yet elegant look in the mirror. "I thought I remembered you always liked to wear a ribbon in your hair. I know we could have imagined you one, but the things we dream up fade after a while. Our clothes return to normal. Food tastes plain. This seemed more classic and traditional. Real. Like you, Alice. It's a piece of your world brought into ours."

At a loss for words, I swallowed and nodded. How silly. Getting worked up over a hairstyle and a strip of common ribbon? Yet, in that single gift, I felt truly known by the friend I didn't realise I had.

I was shocked when Willow added her final flourish, eyeing my Mary Jane shoes with disdain.

"Those are all wrong." With one blink, she changed their colour to the same red as my bodice, adding some sparkle and shine to the worn material. "Better."

And, underneath it all, I kept my black-and-white-striped leggings. I may be facing whatever tonight holds in a gown I can hardly breathe in, but beneath the surface I will still choose comfort over fashion every time.

Maybe Willow and I have more in common than I thought, because she clearly agrees. She opted for an elegant red blouse with tuxedo ruffles on the front and black skirt bottom. Simple yet classy. And easy to move around in.

Once I'm inside the dome, I catch up to my team. They're standing at the edge of the dance floor. When I reach them, Blanche forces her way through to greet me in her usual hurried manner.

"Zere you are!" She gives me a once-over, followed by a curt nod. "Zee games vill begin een minutes. And vhere eez zat Chess Shire?"

I watch her weave through the crowd, who gradually make

their way towards the escalators that weren't here last night. With Madi on my right and Jack to my left, I inhale and take a moment to revel in the transformation that's taken place in less than a day.

The dining hall has been made over. Not that it needed any help. The hall was glorious enough as a grand cafeteria at the opening ceremony. But this is beyond what I envisioned our First Trial arena would look like. The rotating centre platform has vanished, replaced by a glorious dance floor laid out in various shades of green. It shimmers like dewed grass at sunrise and appears to be made of some sort of mirrored glass. I look up at the domed ceiling to find that it's green too, making it difficult to decipher which way is up or down. The space even smells like earth. Like a fresh-cut lawn on a Saturday morning or newly picked flowers in spring.

"Spectators, kindly find your seats," a smooth-toned, sophisticated female voice announces over the din. "This year's Wonderland Trials will begin in less than five minutes."

"Don't tell me that's our commentator?" Madi is indignant. "Doesn't she know how to get the crowd excited?"

I flash her a sympathetic smile and rise on my tiptoes to gauge a better lay of the land.

Eight doors without walls to support them border the octagonal dance floor at every edge, each one a different size or colour or shape. Rounded. Squared. Double. Single. Knobs and handles and locks.

Just like in my dream.

I take a deep breath at the same moment Madi releases one.

"This should be interesting," she comments as I say, "The doors. What did the Minister of Spades say about doors?"

"Two minutes," a voice interrupts over the speakers, this one male and much more jovial than his female counterpart. "Teams, take your places on the dance floor. You will have exactly one hour to complete the Trial. Fail to do so within the allotted time, and each member of your team will lose a Fate."

I glance at the four hearts, all alight, on my bangle. Here we go.

It isn't until we step out onto the mirrored green floor that I notice it's divided into four sections, one marked for each team. We head to our quarter space. A holographic red heart floats midair above where we're meant to wait. All around us, escalators ascend to every level. The floating boxes where the audience looks on are still there, but there are floating platforms as well. Some of the attendees already dance in time to the airy instrumental music playing in the background. Others glance in our direction. Laughing. Betting. Whispering.

0:59, 0:58, 0:57 . . . The massive analog clock second hand ticks the final countdown, a digital clock face at its centre. Digital screens pop up all around the dome, and cameras zoom in, featuring each team in turn. I'm startled when a close-up of my face suddenly appears on one of the screens. I try to give off a sense of confidence in my expression, and instead come off looking confused.

0:31, 0:30, 0:29 . . .

On the scoreboard across from the clock, each of the four team names is paired with three zeros. My heart races, beating in time with the four pulsing red hearts in my WV, the excitement of it all brimming with new possibilities.

I'm suddenly ready to compete. And win.

The final fifteen seconds tick past. I examine the other teams, all wearing their respective quarter colours as well. Spades in black and white, Clubs in black and green. Dazzling sequins cover the Team Diamond players, who are outfitted in black and silver underneath.

Our own team in its heart red and raven black stands out against them all.

"Ace, take my hand."

I blink, realising I was in a daze. Did I drift off?

"Ace," Chess says again. "Please."

The sense of urgency in his tone has me turning to face him. Except I'm not turning. I can't move. Why can't I move?

"Chess," I croak out his name. "What's happening? Where are you?"

"I'm here. Take my hand."

"Where is everyone?" I shake my head and blink again. I'm alone on the green mirrored dance floor. The ceiling has lowered to average room height. If I jump, I might be able to touch it.

If I could actually move.

"Here," Chess says again.

"Where?" Is this another one of his disappearing acts? I'm in this reality now. I ought to be able to see him. But I can't see him, or anyone else for that matter.

My WV keeps track of the diminishing time, grounding me in the present. This is a game. Meant to test us. Whatever I'm seeing is part of it.

Gone are the audience and the huge hall and the commentators and countdown. There is no scoreboard. There are no other teams. Even my own team has abandoned me. I'm left alone with eight doors and no key.

If you want to get out, you must first go in.

I twist, but I still can't budge. It's only now I notice that I'm sinking into the floor which seems to be melting into an emerald puddle around my ankles. My calves. My waist. Pulling me down. Squeezing my lungs.

"Give me your hand now!"

This time I don't question whether or not Chess is there. I reach out in the direction of his voice. The floor is up to my chest now. Soon I'll be taken under completely, and who knows what will happen then. Do players die in the Trials? We know they can disappear, but that supposedly doesn't happen until the Fourth.

Fingers grasp mine. The moment they do, Chess appears before me. Pulling me up and out and flat on my feet once more.

"Keep moving," he pants. "As long as you're moving you won't sink. At least, that's my take on it."

"The opposite of quicksand." My steps mirror his in time with the upbeat tempo that marries classical with more modern melodies. Thank goodness the academy back in Oxford insisted we learn to dance.

"For your future weddings," Headmistress O'Hare would say.

Chess twirls me around, finally getting that dance he's been pestering me about.

My expression turns sour for a moment. I hate that he always seems to get what he wants, but I'm also grateful he figured out how to keep me from drowning. Disappearing. So I follow his lead. We spin towards the door nearest to us, finding respite on a stoop that barely holds us both. I have to press against him and cling to his arms to keep from falling back onto the untrustworthy floor.

"You've been holding out on me, Ace." He's far too close.

"I said that I wouldn't dance. Not that I couldn't."

"Ah, but where is the fun in that?"

His eyes lock on mine, and the air shifts between us. He's changed from silly to serious in a thrilling yet terrifying second. I still don't trust him.

Or myself.

The only way to keep my head is to focus on the Trial and the door before us—a squat little thing fashioned from oak that sits about shoulder high. Ivy vines frame this door on all its rounded edges.

I twist the rusted brass knob. No surprise there when it

doesn't budge. "Locked." I glance over my shoulder. "Where are the others?"

"My best guess?"

I nod and kneel at the same time, attempting to peek through the keyhole.

"We've been divided up into different rooms."

Straightening, I hold onto him with one hand, while reaching for my hairpin with the other. "But there were only eight doors. With twenty-eight players, shouldn't there be other teams in this room with us?"

Chess chuckles. "This is Wonderland, Ace. Normal logic doesn't apply here. Eight doors do not equal eight rooms. There are likely dozens of rooms, maybe even hundreds." He lifts his arm, tapping the bangle on his wrist. "We see what the WV wants us to see in the Trials. I believe, in this case, the key is finding the right door that leads us to the next room, and hopefully our team."

"The Minister of Spades mentioned finding the door," I muse. "And our last-minute clue . . . It said 'Do not wait to escape, or you shall run rather late. And do not dare run until you have rescued them all.'"

"I see those wheels turning." Pride punctuates his tone. "What do you propose?"

"This is a game." It's so simple.

Chess laughs. "I thought that much was obvious, Ace."

"No. I mean it's a *game*. A specific game. We have to figure out which one, if we want to win."

"You might be on to something," Chess encourages. "Continue."

"Given the doors, and the fact that we've been separated from our teams . . ." I rack my brain. Close my eyes, mentally flipping through the pages from *The Adventurer's Almanac*. One page stands out.

The Art of Escaping Escape Rooms.

"It's an escape room."

The confused line between Chess's eyebrows says he doesn't quite follow.

I blow away the fringe that has evaded my hair ribbon and fallen into my eyes. "It's an archaic form of entertainment that involved a team, trapped in a room—or rooms, depending on how complicated the task was. Each room houses hidden clues meant to help you escape within the set amount of time."

"But we've already been given clues."

His point is valid. Hmmm. "What if each clue corresponds to a different room?"

"It's possible." He stares past me, eyes thoughtful.

I crouch again, peering through the tiny keyhole of the locked door before us. We're both quiet, and my mind travels from rooms and riddles to another destination. I want to ask him why he transferred teams. What he might have learned about the minister since I shared my memory of the spade tattoo. Instead, I keep quiet, waiting for him to voice whatever he's thinking.

"Look at the doors." He nods to each one in turn. "Do you notice anything?"

I stand. Staring through a keyhole is accomplishing nothing. "They're all different," I say.

"Yes." Chess looks at me. "What else?"

I attempt to ignore the way his nearness makes my heart run wild. "They're numbered."

Do not dare run until you have rescued them all. Maybe . . .

"Maybe we have to gather our team in order of position." I point to myself. "Ace." Then to him. "King."

"Brilliant," he says, moving closer still.

He must notice my reaction to his closeness. His ever-increasing smile grows half a size.

I have failed horribly at ignoring him by this point. At pretending he doesn't make me feel things he so clearly does. But we have a Trial to win. And team members to gather.

Distractions are not in the cards today.

With much effort I pivot away from him, taking in each door placed around the floor. They're all different. Numbered. Who on our team comes after the King?

"Jack," I say. "He'd be next." Then, "It's that one."

Chess's gaze follows my pointed finger to a door on the opposite side of the floor. "An interesting choice." He strokes his chin. "How can you tell?"

"The number eleven, for starters. In cards, a Jack comes after the ten. In a sequence, he'd be eleven. You'd be twelve, and I'm thirteen." Or one, depending on how you play it. I think of Willow—our Two. I sure hope I don't mess this up.

"What else?" Chess asks.

I survey the door, looking for another clue that might give it away as the answer. "It's the only one without a knob." Now it's my turn to give my own Chess Shire smile. "It's impossible. The answer to the fourth clue."

His eyes light up, setting my heart on fire.

And this time I lead, grabbing his hand and resuming our dance. The music picks up its pace, forcing us to do the same so we don't sink through the glass floor. Though the door we need doesn't seem far off, it takes an eternity to reach it.

"Kit would have loved this," Chess comments. "He never could resist a good party."

"Chess." I swallow. "I'm sorry. About what I said in Hyde Park. I didn't mean—"

"No." His grip on my hand and waist tightens. "Do not apologise to me. I don't deserve it. What I did was cowardly at best. I'm the one who's sorry. I shouldn't have said your parents didn't want you. That was out of line."

His abrupt apology startles. I'm about to speak again, but I'm at a loss.

He finds the words for me. "I didn't leave though." His lips are at my ear now.

"What?" I lean back, finding his eyes. Searching them.

"I followed you. To the abbey." A twirl. Four steps left.

"You . . ." I shake my head. "You . . . followed me?"

He pauses and realises the mistake he's made because we begin to sink. He picks me up by the waist and turns us in a circle. He's stronger than I expected. "Why did you think I was at the abbey when you arrived in Wonderland? Why wasn't I already long gone, at Spade Castle?"

We're nearly to the door. Just a few more turns. "But you pretended not to know me. You acted as if we'd never met." He's always been the confusing sort, but this is a new level of nonsense.

Why is nothing ever easy between us?

"I had my reasons."

"So you're sorry for leaving me behind, but not for humiliating me or acting as if there was nothing between us."

He raises a brow at that. "Is there something, Ace? Between us?"

I don't have an answer, and we've reached the next door. Safely on the stoop, I focus on the task at hand.

He does the same. "What now?"

"I thought you were a pro at this. Your team almost took the lead in the Trials last year."

"Ah, but it's much more fun to watch you figure it out." Arms folded over his chest, he waits, looking far too charming in his tux with its long black coattails, red waistcoat, and crisp bowtie, one half black, the other half red.

"After you," he says with a small bow.

I face the number eleven. Can it really be so simple? Like opening the door to my room at Heart Palace?

Raising my hand, I place my palm against the smooth surface, letting my fingers graze the knots in the wood.

The door vanishes at my touch.

One clue solved.

Three to go.

POISON

I expect to find Jack waiting on the other side of the door. That would make sense.

Instead, the first thing I hear when the door vanishes is Sophia's chilling scream.

My heart freezes, then jumps to my throat, and Chess has to hold on to my shoulders to keep me stable.

Sophia is on her knees, shaking a rather lifeless Willow, whose limp body looks eerily similar to the outline of a crime scene. Arms and legs splayed unnaturally. Head twisted to one side, dark hair covering her face. Their presence at the centre of this new space confirms we won't sink when we step off the door's stoop and join them on the floor.

"What happened?" I kneel on the opposite side of Willow, gently brushing her hair away from her face. Her eyes are closed, lips slightly parted. Liquid dribbles from the corner of her mouth. An abandoned teacup rests at her feet.

Sophia is a sobbing mess, tears streaking her cheeks—some

fresh, others dried trails. "I . . . I don't know. We were . . . t-trying t-to figure out how to get out of th-this doorless room."

At the mention of no doors, I glance around. Sure enough, the one we entered through has vanished. I make a note of it in my head. I'm inclined to think we made a mistake. That we chose the wrong door and are going about this out of order, and this is the reason for Willow's situation. But that can't be right. She was already lifeless upon our arrival.

Chess touches Sophia's arm, urging her to continue.

"We thought if we chose the r-right one, it w-would—" Sophia's words become indecipherable. Instead she keeps shaking Willow, as if the toughest of us girls is merely asleep.

But Willow's blue lips and lack of pulse say otherwise. I turn my head to catch Chess's eyes, but he's several paces away, staring at a long floating bar cluttered with teacups and mugs of all sizes.

I take in the space as a whole. No windows. No doors. Sterile white walls and floor and too-low ceiling making the impression of claustrophobia grow every second. The only colour in the entire room comes from the cups and mugs and saucers, a rainbow of hope in this peculiar place.

Or perhaps the rainbow is a ruse. Meant to invite us to meet the same fate as Willow.

I pull up Willow's profile in my WV, hoping I'll see something other than what I expect to find. My hope falters. Sure enough, it's there. Or, not there, rather. Willow now has three and a half hearts instead of four. The remaining half left of her fourth heart pulses weakly, its red light fading but still lit. A glance at the bangle on her right wrist matches the WV data. Willow is about to lose one of her Fates, but that small glow is all I need.

"She's not gone," I quickly reassure Sophia. "Not yet."

I rise and join Chess at the teacup bar, giving Sophia's

hand a squeeze before I do so. It may be a game, but to her the loss feels real.

"Tea," I comment for Chess's ears alone.

"Grows stronger the longer it rests," he finishes. He's studying each colourful cup and saucer. Hand-painted ones and china ones and giant ones and ones small enough for a mouse. Despite their diversity, the tea inside each cup looks the same as the last.

"And if it's poisoned," I say, "then the longer it sits here—"

"—the more potent the poison," he finishes for me again. "It appears the riddles are combined. And the clues we thought were so obvious were a distraction."

"Do you think we have to drink the poisoned tea for a new door to appear?"

Chess shakes his head. Then nods. "Yes and no. It seems we appeared through a door at the same time Willow drank the tea. But if we follow her lead, how does it end? We can't afford to sacrifice our Fates. There's more to it, I'm certain."

"We could really use Madi right about now," I say. "She'd know which tea is which."

He nods. "That she would. Which is precisely—most likely— why she is not here."

My thoughts attempt to gather and organise. Ace, King, Two, Four. We have our ends and our beginnings. All that's left are the players in between. We can't know for certain which tea does what without our Tea Master. Which means . . .

"One of us has to sacrifice ourselves." My matter-of-fact words surprise me. "Then another door will appear, and hopefully let Madi in."

Chess waves off my suggestion. "Perhaps you are correct. But, remember our completed answer? It is not impossible to drink poisoned tea when you stand on your head."

My mind spins so fast I'm nearly dizzy from the endless possibilities that lie before us. The answer seems obvious, of course. Literal. If you stand on your head and drink the poisoned tea, it's not impossible—it won't kill you.

But what in Wonderland—or this Trial—thus far has ever been obvious or literal?

I look towards the low ceiling. Mirrored, like the previous room. Our warped reflections stare down at us. Investigating our presence as if we are the criminals who sent Willow to her demise. I'm aware of the ticking clock. How has half an hour already passed?

Thirty minutes left.

If we don't pick up our pace, we're going to be very late indeed.

"Sophia," Chess says gently as he kneels beside her on the white stone floor.

I've never seen a photo of Kit, but in this moment I can imagine what Chess might be like with his younger brother.

"Tell us exactly what happened," he says. "From the beginning."

Sophia's sobs turn into a weak whimper. "We guessed the tea would be poisoned."

I have to move closer to make out her words.

"Based on what we deciphered from the combined riddles, we were positive the answer was a cinch."

She doesn't have to explain the rest for me to figure out what happened next.

"I poured her a cup of tea, then helped her stand on her head. I wanted to be the one to try it, but you know Willow. She's so protective. She insisted." Sophia pauses a moment, swallowing to hold back her grief so she can continue.

"We figured the faster she drank, the less the poison would affect her, and since she was upside down . . ." She composes herself again. "But the second the tea touched her lips, she collapsed. And then you came through a door that hadn't been there before." She nods towards the wall that's just a wall now.

I find myself drenched in myriad emotions. Anger at the minister for coming up with such a horrendous addition to his game. Frustration that the answer seems just out of reach. Empathy for Sophia—Willow is her best friend. How hysterical would I be if Madi or Charlotte—or Chess—were lying unmoving on the ground?

But this is a game, not a war. And obvious, logical answers have gotten us nowhere. We have to change our strategy to fit the Trial and its constantly moving pieces.

How can you stand if not on your feet?

"Together," I say suddenly. "The answer isn't 'stand on your head.' We have to stand together." I pull Chess to his feet, dragging him away from the girls. My words are hushed and fast and frantic. "The rooms are designed to separate us. Keep us divided. To turn us against one another." I gesture towards the tea. "We have to drink it. At the same time. All of us. Together. They want us to choose someone to sacrifice. A player to weaken. A Fate to cast off. But if we are all weak, we'll have to rely on one another for strength."

I half expect him to call me crazy. Or say something to stop me from carrying out this insane plan.

"That is"—he stares past me into nothing with incredulous eyes—"completely brilliant."

A glow rises within me. Perhaps I am a Puzzle Master, like Jack. It's true if I wasn't playing cards as a child, puzzles were my go-to form of entertainment. Puzzles on the floor of our room at the Foundling House. Puzzles on the coffee table at Charlotte's flat. Jigsaw and Sudoku and Rubik's cube and crosswords. Puzzles calmed me in the same way holding cards did.

This is one massive puzzle.

My idea is crazy. But I've never felt surer of anything.

Chess wastes no time in picking up three cups at random. I scan the lot again, questioning if it might matter which ones he chooses. But no. They're a distraction meant to slow us down. He hands one cup to me and another to Sophia.

"On the count of three," I say.

They both nod.

"One . . ." I raise the purple-and-green cup to my lips. "Two . . ." The unscented amber liquid with a hint of red undertone steams, warming my nose. It's familiar, and I have a guess as to which tea I hold. "Three . . ."

When the bitter tea touches my tongue, the oddest sensation occurs. One I'm acquainted with. I brace myself for what happens next. Watching Chess as he turns from bloke to bushy-tailed cat.

Beast's Blend was his drink. That much is obvious.

Next is Sophia. She shifts and sways. Her hair changes colour first. Then her eyes, followed by her skin. Periwinkle. Sage. Sapphire. Mahogany. A kaleidoscope in human form. I've no idea what blend she's consumed, but at least it hasn't led her to Willow's fate.

Meanwhile I'm shrinking. Melting into myself in an all-too-memorable way. Folding over and over until I'm compact and no higher than a bean.

Dwindler's Draught.

I never believed in coincidences. And I don't now.

Because my insane idea worked.

Madi and Jack burst through the door.

I jump and wave, shouting for them to see me. But they don't. The opposite, in fact. Jack almost steps on me, and I have to run for cover behind Willow's left shoe.

"Blimey," Jack says. "What's happened to Sophia?" It seems to take him another moment to register Willow's presence. When he does, he's on his knees like we were, attempting to revive her.

In my WV, Willow's half heart is still beating. Barely.

Madi scrutinises the scene. Keeping her wits about her.

Taking in Willow and Sophia and the cat version of Chess in turn. She doesn't lose her cool or grow emotional. "We're missing two." She seemingly stares off into space.

It takes me a second to recognise she's taking a look at the virtual screen in her WV. "According to my Card locator, Ace is in this room."

"And Knave?" Jack asks, looking around, I assume for me.

Madi shakes her head, then narrows her eyes. "Out of range."

I cup my hands around my mouth and shout as loud as my little lungs will allow.

That seems to do it because both Madi and Jack swivel their heads in my direction.

"Where is she?" Jack stares past me at the blank wall. "Invisible?"

"No." Madi steps cautiously towards him and Willow. Searching. Waiting.

I scramble to climb up the handle of the teacup on its side at Willow's feet. The task would already be a challenge, but attempting it in a ballgown?

Madi approaches the teacup, picking it up by the handle with two fingers. She sniffs once, twice. Dabs at the remaining drop of liquid inside the cup with one finger.

"Dwindler's Draught." She looks closer. The moment she sees me hanging from the cup, she smiles.

I'd wave at her if I wasn't hanging on for dear life.

Madi wastes no time in crossing to the bar overrun with more cups. It takes her seconds to find the right one. Carefully, she shakes me into her palm then lines her hand up with the rim of a new cup. "Flourisher's Fate will do the trick." Her voice is a resounding boom in my tiny ears. "Just a drop, though."

I climb from her palm onto the cup's rim. I reach down

and touch the warm brew. A lick of my finger does exactly what I expect.

In a moment, I'm just the right size.

Jack gives me an exuberant hug, but Madi's all business, taking the cup of Flourisher's Fate around to each of our teammates.

Sophia squeals. But in contrast to when we entered the room and found her in distress, this is a sound of pure bliss. A peal of laughter. Unstoppable giggles. She's literally going mad with every colour transition.

"There, there," Madi says, holding the cup to Sophia's lips. "Seems you've taken a bad batch of Rainbow Regimen. Tricky stuff to make. Whoever mixed this blend used way too many rose petals and not enough cardamom. I've seen the reaction loads of times."

Sophia keeps giggling. But then her laughter slows, and her pallor returns to her beautiful brown.

Chess is next. Madi pours some of the antidote tea into a saucer for him. When he's himself again I find that I breathe a bit easier.

Finally, Madi approaches Willow. The other half of her fourth heart has completely vanished now, leaving her with only three Fates. When the tea touches her lips, she gasps for air.

And it is, with that final fix, that a new threshold appears. But instead of an open door, it's a mirror. On the other side waits a rather annoyed-looking Knave.

"It's about time," he says, arms crossed and expression twisted into a sneer. "While you lot have been playing tea party, I've been trapped in here."

I shoot him an indignant scowl. "You think we were in here getting our jollies? Willow could have died."

His sneer accentuates his flaring nostrils. "If you expect my pity, you're mental." He eyes me up and down. Then shoots glares at the others. "Seems you were all perfectly fine to forget about me."

"We didn't forget about you," Madi informs him. "We were trying to find you."

"Yeah. Right. Sure. Okay."

Madi looks as if she might deck Knave in the jaw, but Sophia steps in.

"Now is not the time. We've got twenty minutes left and still two rooms to go."

"Can't you count, genius?" Knave scoffs.

"Watch it," Willow says, defending Sophia.

"Whatever." Knave shakes his head. "I'm saying that we were all separated, right?"

We nod in unison.

"Chess and Ace. Sophia and Willow. Madi and Jack. And me. All by my lonesome. That's four rooms. Mine is that last one that opened, so mine is the last room."

He may be on our team, but I still don't trust Knave. Something seems off about him.

"If you want to win this thing," he says, "I'd suggest you follow me."

Madi and Jack exchange a glance. Sophia and Willow don't move. But Chess joins Knave by the door, taking the lead as Team King.

"Lead the way, mate." Chess steps through the liquid looking glass and joins Knave on the opposite side.

Knave's sinister smirk sends up more red flags than I can count. With a jerk of his head he says, "Welcome to the Hall of Mirrors."

MIRRORS

The fourth room is nothing like the others.

The endless narrow hall stretches on, forcing us to walk single file. The black-and-white-checkered floor is like the one from my dream, but instead of doors, the walls are lined with mirrors. Curious. Each room in this Trial has included mirrors in one form or another. I reach out to touch one. To my utter dissatisfaction, it doesn't transform into a window.

We are not in our own imaginations here. Whatever this final room has in store for us, I'm not about to let my guard down.

Especially not where Knave is concerned.

Chess walks behind him. I follow. Madi, Jack, Sophia, and Willow pull up the rear. Our steps echo.

Why do I get the sense the mirrors are watching us?

"I had to sit behind that wretched looking glass the entire time," Knave says. If he's trying to solicit sympathy, he's doing a rather poor job of it. "I watched from the other side as you imbeciles attempted to solve the tea room puzzle. It took you long enough."

"As if you could have done better," I spout.

"Oh, I could have." He glares over his shoulder, but it doesn't faze me. "And faster, to boot."

He's not worth the energy it exerts to argue. Clearly he thinks everyone's against him. I don't know why he's on our team. He doesn't want to be here. That much is obvious.

"Let's get our clue and be done with this," Knave says. "We have our entire team. We've passed through the final door together. We might still come out of this thing with some points, if we're quick about it."

We walk on through the narrow space. Our reflections act as sentries, and the walls feel like they're closing in, again reminding me of my dream.

Something rustles behind me. A stifled gasp.

I stop and whirl.

Madi collides with me. "Ouch," she says. "What was that for?" Her tone is as vorpal as the sword in the "Jabberwocky" poem.

I'm too startled by her change in demeanor to respond.

"Well?" she demands.

"Sorry," I finally say. "I thought I heard something."

"Shh," Knave whispers.

I pick up my dress and resume my walk. Why is it so quiet? What's going on with Madi? The further we venture, the less progress I feel we make.

"This seems odd," Willow breaks the silence. "Are you sure this is the fourth room? Where's the final clue?"

I am relieved I'm not alone in my reluctance to follow Knave blindly. I'm also glad Willow seems to have recovered from being almost dead. In actuality, Madi concurred she was not dead at all. The tea Willow drank—a potent mixture of chamomile, valerian root, and passionflower—had merely slowed Willow's heart rate and put her into a temporary coma.

"Serenity's Slumber," Madi explained. "You should never take more than a sip. Only the most practiced of Tea Masters should be trusted to make it. The measurements are precise, and it must steep in cold water overnight before warming it in a kettle for consumption."

When Madi talks about tea blending, it sounds like a science. Definitely not my strong suit.

Guess I can eliminate Tea Mastery from my list of possible skillsets.

I glance back at Madi again now. When we first entered the hall, she was her normal bubbly self. Talking about tea. Now, she stares straight ahead, gaze hollow.

The urge to escape this hall as soon as possible suddenly overwhelms me. I'm about to suggest we stop and turn around. Or at the very least, discuss what we think we might be searching for.

"Look at that!" Sophia's voice echoes.

Knave shoves past Chess. He knocks me into one of the mirrors. When he reaches Sophia, he grabs her arm and shushes her. "You'll keep quiet, if you know what's good for you, Soph."

Willow gears up for a fight, fists raised and eyes bulging, but Sophia holds her back, the calm to her best friend's tempest.

I attempt to catch Madi's attention, but she's still staring off into space.

"Something's not right," I murmur to her, keeping an eye on Knave as he takes the lead again.

"Tell me about it." That dark laugh doesn't belong to her.

"Madi, are you okay?" I reach for her hand.

It's ice cold.

She flinches.

Fear creeps in, clawing and clenching.

This room . . . It's done something to her. I want to ask Sophia and Willow if they noticed anything, but they're walking arm in arm, heads bent together, speaking in hushed tones. Willow's eyes meet mine and something passes between us.

She glances at Madi.

Then back at me.

She saw something. The worry creasing her forehead and the way she keeps Sophia near says everything.

She's scared too.

I nod, forcing myself to keep my pace even, focusing on Chess a few feet in front of me. His shoulders remain relaxed, his strides steady.

"Chess," I whisper.

No response.

When at last we reach the end of the hall, a veiled looking glass awaits. Knave pulls the veil aside, and it whooshes to the floor, revealing the last person I expect to see.

My hands flies to my mouth. Because it's not my reflection moving towards the glass.

It's Charlotte's.

I trip over myself. This must be some sort of sick joke or illusion. Another trick of the mind like in the first room.

Chess tries to hold me back. His grip is firm but gentle. "What's the meaning of this?" he asks Knave.

"You think I did this?" Knave lifts his hands in mock surrender.

"Who else could have done it?" I choke.

"Did you put him in there?" Chess releases me and grabs Knave by the collar. "So help me, if you took him—"

"What do you mean, *him*? It's Charlotte!" I gesture towards the mirror.

Chess's expression is one of genuine confusion. "Charlotte? Ace, that's Kit. Don't you see him?"

I shake my head. "I see Charlotte."

"I see my mum and dad," Sophia whispers.

Willow averts her eyes. She doesn't tell us who she sees.

Madi keeps to herself.

Jack remains silent too.

My stomach churns. We're all seeing someone different. Someone we've—

"The mirror shows us someone we've lost," I guess aloud. What does this have to do with the riddles? Is this the final clue?

I watch Charlotte in the mirror. She seems so . . . real. I could almost touch her. Reach forwards and pull her out from wherever she is on the other side.

"It's not who we have lost," Willow says as she slowly lifts her head. "It's what we fear. You see your sister because you're afraid of losing her. Shire sees his brother for the same reason." She looks at Sophia who now has tears streaking her cheeks. "Sophia sees her parents, not because she's afraid to lose them, because—"

Sophia breaks into a sob. "They didn't want me to be Wonder," she says brokenly. "They would have done anything to make me Normal. Anything."

Sophia's story about almost being Registered takes on a whole new meaning. Whatever her parents did to her, it haunts her.

I whirl on Knave. "And what do you see?"

"Wouldn't you like to know?" Knave scoffs, throwing back his head in taunting amusement.

But his aggressive stance doesn't make me back down.

"If you don't tell us, maybe you're not really a part of this team." All that's left to do is what I seem to do best.

Ask the right questions.

Maybe this is my elusive Mastery after all.

Knave clenches his teeth. "I'm not the only one keeping secrets." His eyes dart with venom to Willow and Jack and Madi.

I hate that he's right. I hate that this room is dividing us. The time ticks backwards. Ten minutes to go. I don't know why the mirror shows us our fears, but I do know we have to finish this thing together.

Look through, and you will see. Right there they will be.

"Maybe it's not a door or a keyhole or a mirror that we have to look through," I say. "Maybe the answer lies in seeing through ourselves. In trusting one another."

I draw the attention of each of my teammates in turn. "We already know that everything about this entire Trial has hardly made sense at all. We've been trapped in an impossible room with a sinking dance floor. We found that we had to stand together in the tea room in order to escape it. We've witnessed distraction after distraction, deterring us from our end goal."

"Winning?" Sophia asks.

"Escape." Willow adds.

"Yes." I'm a little bemused. "Win. Escape. But also to finish together. And find the next clue."

As is his nature, Chess's smile could light up this entire hall.

I reach for his hand, and he reaches for Madi's. She reaches for Jack who reaches for Sophia who is already linked with Willow.

I'm now connected to my closest allies.

My friends.

"Well done, Ace," Chess says. "I knew you had it in you. Or, rather, that I had it in me to divulge what you inevitably had in you."

I blush. Since when did his ridiculous explanations become endearing?

"English, you two," Willow says. "If you don't mind."

"I don't mind," Chess laughs. "Do you?"

I hurry on before Willow has a chance to give Chess what he's got coming. "In the Trials you're not just dealing with a pack of cards," I explain, repeating what Chess told me back on the train. "You *are* the card. We've been so focused on these crazy riddles, on finding our way out of these rooms, we haven't realised we're the ones being played. We can't let the Trials get to us, or we'll never finish. Maybe that's why no team has ever finished the Fourth Trial. The players went at it alone."

Five minutes on the clock. We can't escape until we *all* escape. Until we've rescued each other.

"What do you say, Knave?" I offer my free hand to Knave. "Are you with us?"

He hesitates. Glances at the mirror, then back at me. I can see the anger and fear and frustration in his eyes. I think he might refuse, and we'll never get out of here.

"With you?" Knave's voice is terse. "*With* you? Let me tell you something about the way teams work. You might think we're all in this. That your teammate has your back. But it's a lie. In the end, it's every man for himself. Isn't that right, Shire?" He's shaking so hard I think he might explode.

I feel Chess's grip tighten in response.

I take his hand and tighten my grip. Attempting to calm the storm building inside. To think I once thought he was nothing more than Wonderland's poster boy. That *his* interests were his *only* interests.

But he's no different than the rest of us. We all make mistakes. We may be Wonders, given an extraordinary gift to see something not everyone can. But does that make us any less human? Any less flawed?

"Tell them, Shire." Knave's words aim straight at him. "Tell your friends who really almost led Team Spade to victory last year."

That hits the mark. Chess works his jaw and visibly swallows. "I never claimed it was me. The press assumed because I was Team King that I was to thank." He turns his eyes to Knave.

"This is not the time nor the place to discuss this. We have but a few minutes remaining. Be reasonable, mate."

"Reasonable?" The question hurls like a dart. "Was it reasonable when you took credit for the work I did in our Trials last year? Was it reasonable, Shire, when you allowed everyone to believe it was *you* who nearly killed the Jabberwock in the Fourth Trial? We nearly outplayed Stark Hatter and the Diamonds until you ran."

The Jabberwock is real? Or, at least, real in the Wonder sense of the word? I thought it was just some silly poem.

"Was it reasonable," Knave goes on, "when our entire team turned against me? They followed you and called you their hero, all while I took the brunt of their anger. 'You tried to get us killed,' they said. 'Sir Knave the Brave?' they jeered. 'More like Sir Knave will take us to our grave!'" He hangs his head for a moment. "I couldn't show my face in my own quarter. Yet, you stayed silent. We were supposed to be mates. I had to take on my aunt's name and hide out in Heart Palace to save myself from humiliation." He looks at Chess again now, a sad solemnity taking over his words and gaze. "Do you even comprehend the damage your fear caused?"

Chess looks stunned and ashamed. "I—I'm sorry," he says quietly.

Apologies aren't easy for him. I know that better than anyone. But the softness in his voice and the way his eyes close as if to blink away emotion is as genuine as I've ever seen him.

Knave doesn't buy it. "Save it for the cameras," he snaps. "That's what you do best, right? You smile on the outside, but down deep, where it really matters? You're nothing but a fraud."

Chess's withdrawn demeanor shifts in an instant. He meets Knave's glare and returns it with one of his own. "You took my brother."

I can tell that it takes every ounce of control in him not to glance at the mirror. A chill runs up my arms and neck.

Knave laughs darkly. "What are you on, Shire?"

"Did you? Answer the question, Knave, or so help me—"

"Think about it," Knave withdraws a knife from a sheath at his belt and flips it once in his hand. "Players have gone missing for years. Do you really believe any one person is behind this? It's bigger than you or me." He points the blade at the mirror and then at Chess.

Chess steps back. "Did you have something to do with Kit's disappearance?" The words are daggers.

"Didn't we all?" is Knave's sole response.

"Enough with riddles and games." In one swift move Chess shoots an arm out, grabs Knave by the wrist, and twists. Hard.

Knave curses. He drops the knife, but it does not clang when it hits the checkered floor. In fact, it does not stop but goes right through the floor as if it weren't there to begin with.

The rest of our group looks on in stunned silence at the drama unfolding before us, but I'm more concerned with how the knife disappeared.

None of this is real.

"I'm the one you have a war with," Chess says, still holding fast to Knave's twisted wrist. "Leave the others out of it. Leave *Alice* out of it, do you quite understand me?"

The way he says my Normal name unlocks something inside of me.

"Don't you see?" Knave stands firm, but his attempt to remove himself from Chess's hold is futile. "None of us is safe. It's only a matter of time before we risk our lives in the Fourth Trial—"

I don't let him finish. We don't have another moment to spare. Quickly, I grab Madi's hand and Chess's arm at once. He's still holding onto Knave.

We're all linked.

The hall disappears.

The mirrors vanish.

And suddenly we're greeted with cheers and whoops and hollers as the crowd around us roars.

"Well done," a voice hails from behind me. Though it's soft, I hear it over the din.

I whirl. I forget about Knave's determination to sabotage our chances or that we didn't find our next clue. I can't think. Logic is a stranger. All I can do is fall into Charlotte's arms.

And this time, the tears that come are ones of joy.

GRIEF

I never expected it to feel this way.

I am no stranger to victory. I almost expect it—when it comes to cards, anyway.

But this win? The crowd cheering. Chanting, "Team Heart, Team Heart, Team Heart." It feels shallow compared to the ultimate relief I experience at seeing my sister in the flesh again.

"And zee first team to escape zee final room eez Team Heart!" Blanche's voice carries throughout the grand hall. "Ah, yes, and right behind zem eez Team Spade! Vell done. Vell done, vun and all!"

The moment the Spades appear, the crowd goes wild.

Their Team Queen, a girl with a muscular build and a warm smile, punches the air, a sealed envelope in her hand.

I attempt to orient myself to my surroundings. One moment we're in a long hall of mirrors, and the next I'm clinging to Charlotte, transported back to Oyster and Pearl Hall. The immediate switch gives me whiplash. I blink and crane my neck, focusing on the giant split-screen that shows both Team Club and Team Diamond yet to escape their respective looking-glass halls. It's Team Club that manages to get their entire crew linked first, taking third place and reappearing within their quarter of the dance floor.

I make eye contact with Chess, who's now wearing a rather flat expression.

Seeing Kit in that mirror got to him. Now he's watching me reunite with my sister in the flesh. My heart hurts, and I wish I'd seen Kit too so I could at least know who we're looking for. I'll have to ask Chess if he has a photo next time we're alone.

I try to convey my empathy with a single look.

He gives a slight shrug but then holds up his right hand. A hand holding an envelope with a red wax seal pressed into the shape of a heart. I guess we did get our next clue after all.

Confetti rains, and activity lights the scoreboard above the screen, revealing not only our updated scores, but how many Fates each team lost as well.

Hearts : 1

Spades : 2

Clubs : 0

The Clubs may have taken longer, yet they came out of this Trial with all their Fates intact. That will earn them some points. When Team Diamond finally makes their entrance, just before the time runs out, the fourth and final place on the board is occupied.

Diamonds : 3

"Oh, dear." A concerned looking Blanche remarks at the sight of three lost Fates. "Eet appears zee Team Diamond King did not take zis Trial vell." She *tsks* through her teeth. "Vould someone kindly escort Mr. Cressvater to zee infirmary?"

At that, two medics help a rather green-looking boy with

a space between his front teeth out of the hall. Did all three Fates belong to him?

"Poor boy," Charlotte says, adjusting her glasses. "I do hope he's all right."

The very real sound of her voice invites another unbidden sob from my chest.

"Hush," Charlotte says into my ear. "Crying won't help."

There was a time I never wanted to hear those words from her again. Now I embrace them. I know she's right. And as valid as my emotions are, the last thing I want is for the entirety of Wonderland to witness my breakdown, let alone Chess and Madi and the rest of our team. One glance at my friends shows we're all a little worse for the wear. Spent. Confused and rattled.

Why was our final room designed to expose our deepest fears? Will it serve as a clue for the next Trial?

And why is Knave nowhere to be seen?

I release my hold around Charlotte's neck, but grasp her hand, refusing to let her out of my sight until I at least receive some sort of explanation. Where has she been? Why didn't she tell me the truth?

My internal questions will elicit no answers of course. Not until we're alone, in a quiet space where we can talk. I focus instead on the landscape before me.

"Congratulations, Team Heart," Blanche is saying. "First place, and a bonus vun-hundred points for finishing *vith* your Ace at full Fate health! Bravo!"

Our team whoops and hollers as our score updates again. I blush. While I know my position as Ace is valuable, I still don't quite understand everything it entails. It feels odd to be recognised above the others. We worked as a team and finished as a team. My Fates shouldn't matter more than theirs.

A few of the Team Spade members slide jealous looks in

Chess's direction. He abandoned them, and they suffered for it. No doubt they're feeling a tad bitter about the whole ordeal.

The announcements continue with the Spades' score followed by the Clubs' who—surprise, surprise—are awarded fifty-five bonus points for sheer brute strength when it came to clawing their way out of the sinking dance floor and finishing with all Fates intact. It's enough to put them ahead of the Spades, which invites grumbles from their team. Diamonds receive a boost to their score for leaving the least amount of mess in their wake, but their numbers remain the lowest due to the blow their Team King endured. The scoreboard blinks again, and the final tallies shine throughout the hall.

Hearts : 320

Clubs : 290

Spades : 275

Diamonds : 210

Blanche goes on, noting each team's strengths and weaknesses. From what I can gather based on the information she gives, we all faced the same rooms in some sort of virtual simulation. It felt real. The tea tasted real.

And yet it was all in our heads.

How is the world inside your mind any less real than the one outside it?

Chess's words provoke my thoughts as more cheers and applause erupt.

"Eet eez not uncommon for a team to come out on top een their own quarter's Trial," Blanche explains, nodding towards the Spades with a curt grin. "Vhile zee Spades came een second, eet eez still a noteworthy triumph. Vell done, Minister Quincy and everyone in zee Spade Quarter who vas involved een concocting zis mind-boggling first round ov clues and escapes."

Another roar from the crowd. Cymbals clash and triumphant music plays. My ears ring. Doesn't anyone notice what a tax this took on us? Though we rose above the others on the scoreboard, our group seems to be more disheveled than anyone, save the poor Diamond King. We're all sunken eyes with dark circles and slumped shoulders.

I roll mine, wishing this night would end so we could get some sleep. Then I spot Mouse just as the Minister of Spades makes his rounds in acknowledging Team Club.

He shakes Mouse's hand at the same moment her eyes meet mine. There's a hollowness there that I can't process. Even she's too tired to muster up the energy to give me a dirty look. Did she see her greatest fear in the looking glass too?

My stomach churns when the minister makes his way towards us. I want to hide behind Charlotte, but I stop myself short of reverting back to the scared little girl I once was. Because the realisation of what's about to happen hits me square between my widening eyes.

Charlotte is the minister's *daughter*. And they haven't seen one another—as far as I'm aware—in ten years. Did he know she left? Does he know why? Did he care?

I'm about to find out.

"Charlee," the minister says, his voice softer than I expect. He doesn't seem to know whether to hug her or keep his distance, so he slips his hands into his trouser pockets. The stem of the spade tattoo on his right hand peeks above the black fabric. "It's been . . . a long time."

The emotion in the minister's voice throws me. I'd thought him cold. But, standing here, so uncertain, I realise he's another person I've judged all too quickly.

"Tell me," the minister goes on when Charlotte doesn't return his greeting. "How has life in the Normal Reality treated you?" His question sounds genuine. The curiosity in his tone is undeniable. And there's something else too. Longing. Remorse. "Does Raving know you're here?"

Raving? As in Raving Hatter?

"My relationship with Raving is not your concern." Is she angry? Afraid? Would she have seen the minister or Madi's brother if faced with the final looking glass?

"Your mother and I . . ." He rocks back on his heels. Scratches the back of his head. "We have always wondered . . . What I mean to say is . . . Are you home? Have you come back . . . for good?"

There's enough hope trailing between his syllables to rip one's heart out.

It's this that seems to ignite something in my sister. I'm surprised to find, not empathy, but bitterness tainting her next words. "It was not my choice to return. Blanche has been trying to convince me for years. When I learned she would be inviting Alice to play in the Trials, I begged her to reconsider. She refused. Then Dinah tracked us down. It was either Register or accept a position as Team Heart Trainer."

"Dinah?" the minister asks, amused. "How is the old girl? I haven't spoken to her in . . . Well, it must be a solid decade since our paths have crossed."

Clearly not in the mood for small talk, Charlotte gets straight to the point. "You never came after me." She steps back, tugging me slightly behind her so there's more of a barrier between her father and myself. "You just . . . let me go. Was it easy?"

The minister's expression shifts from sorrow to shock. "Easy? Charlee, you must know—"

"I know you didn't try to contact me. Or write." My sister is the last person in any reality to shed a tear. Yet, in this moment, I know I see one well.

"We wanted to." The minister is reaching for her now. "We thought you'd rather not hear from us. We understand why you did what you did, Charlee." He glances uneasily at me, then back at her. "But we stand by what we have always believed.

Like our love for you, our only daughter, that belief has never changed. Wonderland is for Wonders. Outsiders don't belong."

Outsiders? Is he talking about me? Because I'm a Wildflower? I want to scream at him, to tell him that I'm a Wonder, too, and if I hadn't been taken, then maybe—

"I see." Charlotte's response to him derails my thought train. Her voice is terse.

This visibly flusters the minister. He lowers his arms to his sides.

"Then we are exactly where we left off. At an impasse."

"So it would seem." The minister's voice is barely audible over the jovial activity surrounding us. "Our door is open to you. You will always be our daughter, whether or not we agree with the choices you make."

Charlotte has my hand. "Then you will understand the choice I have to make now."

Why do I get the feeling she's choosing me over her own father? Even though I'm not her flesh and blood.

Smoothing a wrinkle on his dinner jacket, the minister clears his throat. His jaw twitches, and he seems to have nothing more to say. There's a tired sort of way about the manner in which he turns. A slight pause to his movement before he continues on. Then the moment passes, and he's gone over to greet one of the other quarter representatives, the chubby Club man who now has what appears to be a mustard stain on his blueberry-coloured tie.

The crowd begins to disperse and make their way towards the exit doors. Mothers and fathers carry sleeping children. Groups of juveniles chat about their favourite moments of the Trial, which were televised for all to see on the big screens throughout the hall. The queen, who looks more like my sister now than ever, remains seated on a throne at the centre of the dais. She gives a modest nod to a passerby here, a sweet smile to a young girl there. When she turns her attention in our

team's direction, I wonder if she is pleased, or simply wish
we had earned more points to take us further ahead.

But she isn't looking at our team as a whole. She's starin
Charlotte. The only girl in the room who could be the que
younger self.

I turn. "Charlotte, I—"

She shakes her head tightly to cut me off, fear and anx
surging from her gesture. When she moves, the collar of
blouse shifts and reveals reddened, puckered skin in
shape of a W.

I cover my mouth. "Did they make you drink the cordi

"They did." She keeps her eyes downcast, revea
nothing more.

"Ve vill see you all in a month's time," Blanche announ
wagging a single, white-gloved finger. She gives no ot
information about the Second Trial or which house it belc
to. Instead she kneels beside Her Majesty, who speaks beh
her hand into Blanche's ready ear.

My hopes ought to lift upon a final glance at the scorebc
as we exit the hall through the wide, arching doorway. I shc
be thrilled at the victory. But all I can think about are
questions battering my mind.

And where is Knave?

He doesn't turn up. Not as we wait by the kerb for our
back to the palace or when I open up the Cards list in my
and find he's changed his status to sleeping, a little moon
star icon appearing next to his Alias.

It isn't until two red chauffeured cars pull up that I rea
how extremely exhausted I am. The last thing I wante
do was take our sweet time in horse-drawn carriages b
to the palace. I'm grateful for the quicker transportation
smooth ride.

Chess, Jack, Willow, and Sophia climb into the rear
leaving me, Madi, and Charlotte to pile into the other. N

climbs in the front seat, somehow knowing that Charlotte and I need the space in the back alone.

But the trip is short. Not nearly long enough for anything resembling an explanation. Where would I begin? And how do I begin?

I opt for the next best thing and lean my head on Charlotte's shoulder. It's softer than I remember. Strange how my perspective of her has altered in the span of a few days between losing her, hating her, and missing her so much it hurt.

At my movement, she presses her cheek against my hair. We stay that way the twenty minutes it takes to weave through event traffic. I try to keep my eyes open. But it's no use. So I don't fight it. My lids fade on the wave of a yawn.

My questions will have to wait until tomorrow.

I don't dream. Again.

I don't even need my locket watch to pull me from sleep.

When I wake in my room back at the palace, wearing cosy plaid pyjamas and one rather splitting headache, it takes me several seconds to orient myself.

Wardrobe. Check.

Bed. Check.

Rucksack. Check.

Charlotte . . . *Charlotte.*

My sister sleeps with her back turned towards me. Despite the fact her glasses rest upside down on the nightstand, I touch her shoulder to assure myself she's real, then exhale audible relief. Charlotte is here, sharing the bed like she did when I was young. I put my own glasses on. A peek at the time in my WV says it's past noon. I know Charlotte needs the rest, so I peel off my duvet, careful not to uncover her. Then I imagine myself a robe, pull it on, and tiptoe out of the bedroom.

What I find in the common area makes me wish I had waited a few minutes more.

The boys are here. Fully dressed. Eyes glued to the television. The girls are the same. Madi notices me first. She places a finger to her lips while waving for me to sit beside her on the chaise lounge.

I suddenly feel exposed with my mussed hair, black smudged eyes, and pyjamas. But no one seems to care that I'm less than presentable. When I reach the lounge, Madi pulls me down so fast I almost sit on her.

"It's about time you woke. We've been waiting," she says to me. Then she elbows Jack on her other side. "Turn it up, will you?"

He does as she says. But I don't need the sound to understand what's happening on the big screen.

"I've seen that woman before," I say. "At the abbey. When I first arrived."

"Morning, Ace," Chess says, pulling up a chair next to where I'm sitting. He sits on it backwards and asks, "Or, should I say, good afternoon?"

Why must boys turn chairs the wrong way? His lack of seriousness isn't anything less than I'd expect from him. But, somehow, it brings a small dose of comfort I now realise I need. "What's happened?" I blink the sleep from my eyes, fixing on the scene before me.

"See for yourself," Chess says, now more solemn.

Jack turns up the volume a bit.

My heart cracks open.

"Tell us again, Viola. Tell us exactly what happened evening prior."

The mother looks as if she's seen a ghost. She worries her lower lip. Glances between her interviewer and the camera pointed at her.

"I can hardly believe it myself," she begins. "It's Dan.

He came home last night." She looks into the camera. She doesn't blink when she says, "He's only spoken one word since his return."

I'd expect the mother to be sobbing tears of joy over her long-lost son. But she looks dumbfounded when she says, "Real. That's the word he keeps repeating. Real."

Chess and I exchange a glance. The solemnity in his eyes reminds me of why I'm here. That this isn't all fun and games. To think I accused Chess of never taking anything seriously.

But I'm the one who lost sight of what I came for. Nothing is ever real until it happens to you. With Charlotte back, I know one thing for certain.

I never want to lose my sister again.

And I never want anyone else to grieve a lost loved one either.

SECRETS

When Blanche said our Trainer was someone who had played in the Trials before, I never in a hundred lifetimes would have guessed it was Charlotte.

So much for getting her alone so we could talk.

A whistle blows.

"Again," Charlotte calls from across the courtyard.

Except, it's not a courtyard any longer.

This is Charlotte's imagination taking flight—Team Heart's personal training arena. Who knew she had it in her?

Gone are the gardens and hedge maze. A professional running track has been added around the perimeter. It borders an obstacle course covering one half of the yard, with conditioning equipment scattered across the other. Between timed obstacle runs and drills and warm-ups and water breaks, I haven't had a single solitary minute to pull Charlotte aside. Seeing her like this, as an experienced Wonder, makes me feel like I've stepped into an even stranger Reality than the one I'm currently living in.

I jog around to the start of the course, which Charlotte has altered again in the short moment it took me to make my way from the finish line back to the beginning. She's added a climbing rope, a military crawl, and a balance beam to the already-daunting sequence. I ready my position. Await her signal.

"You're going about this all wrong." Charlotte shakes her head and rubs her temples, but her frustration with me is nothing new. "This isn't a Normal physical education class at school, so stop treating it like one."

I growl under my breath. Because this feels precisely like P.E. to me. Too bad the person I'd normally get an excuse note from is the one barking orders. At the sound of her whistle, I leap into action. When I ran her beginner course earlier this afternoon, I could barely stand after the ten minutes it took to struggle through the obstacles. This is the most challenging course yet. My side cramps, and I'm gulping for breaths by the time I finish the military crawl.

I'll never make it up the rope at this rate.

"You're going to have to do better than that, Alice." From this distance, I can still hear her disappointment through a tsk and click of her tongue.

Must she comment on every little thing?

I ought to call it quits right here. Obviously this training is going nowhere. I'll only embarrass myself further if I attempt the rope climb. I arch my back and stare up at it anyway. There are knots spaced every few metres, and an apple floats midair at the top where the rope ends. It isn't tied to anything, but when I yank on it, the rope remains firm.

I could use my arms, which are all bone and no brawn. Using my legs would give me a slightly better chance, though not by much. What is the point of all this? Even if we have a month to train until the next Trial, that's not enough time to transform me into a true athlete.

"Use your strength!" Charlotte calls.

She must not know me very well. I'm not strong. I look ridiculous when I run. It's hopeless. I stare at the rope. Dangling. Taunting. I'll never make it to the top. I look over at my sister.

She's watching me. One hand shades her expectant eyes. Does she really think I can pull this off?

"Hey, Ace!" It's Chess who demands my attention now. I shift my gaze to where he stands on the track. "Nothing's impossible, remember?" His encouraging smile gives me the extra push I need.

I tug on the rope again. Then I close my eyes, inhale, and grasp the rope with one hand. I picture it not as my nemesis but as an ally. "We're in this together," I tell it, feeling how nonsensical it is that I'm talking to a rope and wondering if it can hear me at the same time.

Nothing happens.

Charlotte says I'm going about this wrong. Maybe she's right. I've been tackling Wonder obstacles in Normal ways. I grip the rope tighter still. What would happen if I . . . ?

"Nice job!" Charlotte says. "You've got it!"

Some of my teammates cheer and applaud.

I feel lighter than air. When I open my eyes, I realise why.

The rope is pulling me up, drawing me towards the apple with no effort at all. I'm a feather on the breeze, weightless and free. I reach for the fruit. Almost got it . . . just a few more . . .

"Better get the stretcher." Knave's cynical voice rises above everything else. "I'd bet half my golden petals she falls."

What kind of teammate roots for their fellow player to fail? I shouldn't listen to him. But, despite my best efforts, I peek at the ground.

It comes up to meet me before my fingertips ever touch the

apple. I fall fast and hard. I can't tell if it's me crying out or someone else.

"Told you," Knave says. It's no surprise that he doesn't come to my aid.

Chess is by my side first, followed by Madi.

"That was really good," Madi says. "Can you stand up at all?"

The wind knocked my voice right out of me, but I nod. They help me rise and walk to the edge of the course. A lovely spread of sparkling rose waters and finger sandwiches calls my name. But snack time can wait. I'm more concerned with where I rank. I wave the duo off. "I'm fine," I say. "Go on."

They're hesitant, but they leave me be. I'm grateful for the moment alone to catch my breath—and my wits.

A transparent screen similar to the one we used before the Spade Trial shows our team's score at the top, then breaks down our individual stats and strengths according to player. Chess is Team King. It's no surprise he's at the top of the list as our strongest asset.

I am, however, perturbed to find Knave's name second on the list. What's he done to earn such high marks? He only managed to show up today to criticise me. Now he's gone again, not bothering to stay and train with the rest of us.

Sophia comes in third, and Jack fourth.

My name, which was at the bottom before, is now ranked equally with Madi and Willow. I may have crashed in the end, but I'm satisfied with the outcome.

I take a bottle of iced rose water and scan my WV for news updates. After the feature of the mother and her found son, I added the news application so I could stay up to speed, in case any other players return.

"Real," Dan had said.

What I wouldn't give to interview him personally. I keep

the idea in the back of my mind, bringing another thought front and centre.

What Knave said in the Hall of Mirrors keeps playing on repeat. After Chess asked him if he had something to do with Kit's disappearance.

"Didn't we all?"

What does that mean? He's the first on my list to question. After Charlotte, of course.

I finish my drink and hobble over to my sister. A silver whistle wiggles between her teeth as she watches my teammates. They practice relays around the track, adding their own Wonder flare to the task.

Chess tosses a long-stemmed red rose into the air. It transforms mid-flip into a teacup, which Madi catches on top of her curly head. Willow snatches it and starts to sprint. When she reaches Sophia, a tiny garden begins to grow from the cup. By the time she meets Jack, the garden is in full bloom. Jack takes the cup garden carefully, walks it to the finish line, and sets it on the ground. The cup and garden disappear with a snap of Charlotte's fingers.

"Perfect," she says. Then, "Again." She twirls a finger once in the air.

"Don't you think it's time for a break?" I squint into the sunlight, taking off my glasses, and wiping the sweat from my brow.

Charlotte lets the whistle drop but doesn't make eye contact.

"Do you want to win, or don't you? Do not think that just because our team is ahead we will stay ahead. Laziness will not be tolerated, Alice."

Once, I would have immediately returned her comment with a quip or smart remark. Maybe an eye roll or two. Now I think on what she's asking. Do I want to win? Why? What do I have to gain as part of Her Majesty's inner circle? Fame. Fortune. A place to call home?

I used to think I cared about being a part of the Trials. But this is bigger than that. Bigger than rumours of becoming the next heir. Players are still missing. Chess hasn't seen his brother Kit in a year—not the real version of him anyway.

"Charlotte, what happened? You show up, rescue me from Bill. Then you disappear. I see an article about you being an Unregistered Wonder. I find out you lied to me for ten years." Tears threaten, as they tend to do, but I choke them back. "Now you're here and acting as if this is all Normal."

No response.

Fine. She wants to play it that way. "You hate Wonders. Remember?"

I've said it loudly enough to get her attention, but not so loud the others hear us. At least her eyes are on me now. I realise it's the first time she's really looked at me since arriving. Myriad emotions abound. Anger. Fear. Confusion. Love.

This is my sister. This is not my sister.

I don't know who she is. Not really.

"Not here," she mouths, tugging on the hem of my sleeve. This anxiety is not like her. It's almost as if she's spooked.

Or in danger.

Or both.

If she was in danger before, what kind of danger is she in now?

After a moment, she mutters in a low voice, "Tonight. When the others have gone to bed. There's a café you and I used to walk by in London. Near the abbey. Do you recall it?"

I nod. We could never afford to eat there. I'd always wondered as a child what it might have been like to enjoy high tea like the other little girls who had wealthy parents to dote on them. Girls who weren't hand-me-downs, hand-me-offs, or forget-me-dos.

"I remember," I say.

"Fine." She purses her lips, then adds, "Now go join the

others on the relay track. You lot have your work cut out for you if you'll ever have a chance against the Clubs."

By the time every lamp is unlit, I'm still wide awake. I take the covers off my fully clothed body and get out of bed. The task is more trying than I expect. I'm spent. Every bone and muscle aches, including my brain. I can only dread how sore I'll be tomorrow.

When—as Charlotte made perfectly clear—we will do it all over again.

Sneaking out of the palace isn't too difficult. In the Normal Reality, it's probably much more of a challenge. But here no one seems to notice. My WV map guides the way. The freedom is like nothing I've ever experienced.

Unlike the leftover chill of winter that carried over to spring from a few nights prior, this May evening is unseasonably warm. The moon is a half-closed eyelid, winking me on my way along the streets of Wonderland's London. The stars are like flecks of gold in an azure sky. It's as if day and night had a rendezvous, the splendor of their union as mysterious as our next clue.

With each step, the Club Trial weighs heavy on my mind. For the Spade Trial, we had less than a day to solve the mysteries laid before us. Now we have an entire month to train. I ought to be relieved. Instead I'm anxious.

How much more difficult will the Club challenge be?

No fancy riddles to pick apart, the Clubs' clue was a solitary sentence written in silver foil on a black card shaped like their tri-leafed symbol.

All ways are her ways.

The back of the invitation only gave information on the time and place of the event.

Seven o'clock. First of June.
Tulgey Wood.
Twenty-nine days to go.

When I reach the café, I'm a bit staggered to find it alive with activity at this hour. Then again, I don't know why. Everything in Wonderland is so opposite of what I'm used to. They probably don't even have a curfew here.

Rather than a bell jingling when I open the door, a live bird caws, alerting the hostess to my arrival.

"How many in your party, miss?"

But I'm looking past her, spotting Charlotte at the back corner of the room.

The hostess notices and steps to one side. She nods towards the bangle on my wrist. "You'll find the menu in your WV," she says.

Sure enough, a little bell icon sways silently in my view as I move towards the booth in the farthest corner. When I used to imagine what it was like in here, I'd always dreamed Charlotte and I would sit at the table by the front window. Showing off our lavish spread of tea and pasties for all the world to see.

But I see why she chose the more discreet location.

My sister is not alone.

I tuck my stubborn hair behind my ears as I squeeze in between Charlotte and Chess.

Dinah's here too. She's too focused on stirring her tea to bother saying hello.

On Charlotte's opposite side sits a young man with untamed silver hair. A top hat rests on the table before him. He acknowledges me with a nod before returning his eyes to Charlotte.

Raving Hatter. He's the spitting image of Madi, if her hair was less lavender and more silver.

The most surprising attendee, however, is none of these. The last one to arrive as usual, Blanche rushes up behind me.

"Alice, dear," she says. "You must learn to slow down. I could ardly keep up vith you."

Maybe sneaking out of the palace wasn't as easy as I believed. It appears I had assistance. "I didn't know I was being followed." I'm irked that my sister spilled the beans about our meeting to . . . everyone, apparently.

Blanche titters and takes a seat beside Dinah. "I ave been following you for years," she says, as if this is common knowledge. "You're a lot faster zan you used to be."

I stare at Charlotte. Whatever secrets she's been keeping are clearly more than I could have guessed. At least now I know why Blanche seemed so familiar that day on the train.

Dinah looks up from her tea. "Alice," she says. "I imagine you had no trouble finding the place."

"Not at all. Even if I did, I suppose Blanche would have helped me eventually." The annoyance in my tone is obvious. But no one seems too bothered by it.

The waitress comes by to take our orders. I scan the menu in my WV and realise my appetite is nonexistent. Rather than food, I decide on a hot wassail with whipped cream and a cinnamon stick. Partly because it reminds me of Christmas, and that, at least, will provide some comfort and familiarity in all of this.

The others make their requests.

I fold my arms and rest my elbows on the smooth tabletop while I wait. Dark knots and highlighted grain turn the simple furniture piece into a mesmerising work of art. I glance around, taking in the distinct and subtle artistry throughout the café.

Mismatched chairs painted various colours and made to look like antiques are set at every table. Distressed frames hang from the walls, but rather than housing pictures or paintings, they serve as digital windows into what I assume to be real live scenes throughout the Wonderland Reality. A cat and a rabbit— both of whom are wearing hats and trousers—playing inside a doll's house. A dozen bluebirds sitting at a table drinking tea. A babbling brook that seems to sing its own song. One I recognise to be—if my music history lessons haven't failed me—Brahms's *Sixteen Waltzes*.

Then there are the perfectly Normal details that stand of their own accord. I'll never get over the fact that I can still see the Normal Reality underneath this one. Maybe over time it will fade. For now, in some ways, it's more apparent than many of the Wonderland features.

"Now," Dinah begins, following the waitress's leave, "as for the matter at hand. I think it's time we let Alice in—"

"No," Charlotte interrupts. "Let me. Please."

Raving takes her hand and kisses it. "I agree," he says, American accent echoing his sister's. "This is Charlee's story to tell. She should be the one to tell Alice the truth."

"The truth?" I look at her. "Charlotte, what's going on?"

She inhales. "I'd like to introduce you to the Knight Society."

I glance around. Furrow my brow.

Charlotte appears to catch my misunderstanding because she shakes her head. "No, I mean yes, we're meeting at *night*." It's the first time I've heard her laugh since her arrival. "But I mean knight with a *K*, as in a game of chess."

Her mention of the classic game has my attention. "Go on."

She shifts to face me. "Do you know how the Wonderland Trials came to be?"

"Only what I've heard on the *Common Nonsense* podcast." I glance at Raving. Does Madi know her brother is part of some secret society? "Queen Scarlet won the first Trials, the sole Wonder ever to complete the Fourth Trial, thus proving she was the best choice for queen." It sounds like the recitation it is. I cringe.

Dinah nods. "Yes, that is what we have all been told." She takes her time. "This, of course, is a lie."

I gape. "And the truth?"

"The truth is the queen stole the crown, just as she tried to take it from her Normal sister, Cordelia."

"Stole it?" I can hardly believe what I'm hearing. "Stole it from whom?"

"Who else?" Chess seems as if he's been bursting to tell me all of this for ages. "The Ivory King."

"The Ivory King?"

"Yes," Charlotte says quietly. "The Ivory King is the designer of the true Wonderland."

My mind is going topsy-turvy again. "I don't understand."

"Scarlet claims she founded Wonderland," Raving joins in. "That it was created out of her own imagination. A haven for all born with the Wonder Gene."

I give a small nod, trying to follow where this is going.

"The truth is Wonderland was always there," he explains. "Scarlet may have stumbled upon it and put herself on the throne, but she did not create it. The very things we have been led to believe about the Wonder Gene are fabrications in and of themselves."

"Fabrications?"

"Yes," Charlotte confirms. "Alice, Wonderland as we know it is a lie. The lie is all the more enhanced for those involved with the Trials." She holds up her arm, revealing a WV bangle with a ruby stone identical to Blanche's. "The queen intends to have every Wonder wear one eventually. Once her design is perfected."

I think back to that day in the chapel. Right before I passed from the Normal Reality into Wonderland. The Wonder Gene always existed.

Just like Wonderland.

"Hold on." I turn to my sister. "Charlotte, none of this makes sense. You've tried to keep me from Wonderland. You only ever wanted things to be Normal. But now you're telling me you're part of this secret society? This is . . . well, it's backwards."

"I understand this is a lot to take in." Charlotte covers my hand with hers.

"But what does this have to do with me?" I ask. "With the players who have gone missing? Haven't you seen the news?" I sit up straighter and eye them. "One of the missing boys has returned. We should talk to him. Maybe he can help us."

"We are aware of the situation." Dinah lowers her voice. "Where do you suppose he went?"

"What do you mean where he went? He went missing during the Fourth Trial, like all the others, and now he's back."

"I have something to say." Chess touches my shoulder. "If I may?"

His simple gesture provides a little comfort.

The waitress stops by and sets a pan of bread-and-butter pudding at the centre of the table, along with a stack of bowls and spoons.

Charlotte serves each of us, and when she sets the sweet, sultana-garnished dessert in front of me, I imagine little bread and butterflies taking flight in my stomach with each forthcoming bite.

Eyes earnest, Chess says, "Before I transferred from Team Spade, I had a chance to meet with Minister Quincy."

He stops to take a bite. I spoon a small portion into my mouth as well, savoring every luxurious flavour. I feel him scoot the slightest bit closer to me in the booth. We're not touching, but his nearness alone is enough to heighten my senses.

He goes on. "I've been slowly gathering information. The minister trusts me. He actually believes it was his idea that I transfer to Team Heart."

"How'd you manage that?" I ask.

Chess gives a quick grin "You underestimate my skills."

The grin disappears. "He has intentions of his own, as do all the quarter heads and their respective houses. They are of the mindset that the crown is a moving piece, and that whichever team wins the Trials each year takes control of the throne, and in turn all of Wonderland, until the next season. They want a system of checks and balances. Shared power. The queen agreed that any quarter's team who completes the Fourth Trial would, indeed, be best fit to rule until the following year."

"But," I interrupt, "no one ever finishes the Fourth Trial."

"Precisely," Raving states. "And the Diamonds came close last year too."

"As did the Spades." Chess clears his throat. "But one thing always stands in the leading team's way."

I'm quite literally on the edge of my seat.

"The Fourth Trial is the Heart Trial. While the other quarter Trials differ every year, the Heart Trial has never changed. The entrance alters, but the end result is always a run-in with the Jabberwock."

I stare at him wide-eyed. "What is it, exactly? The Jabberwock?" I think of those terrifying sounds from my dream. Of the monster I imagined behind them.

No one responds. Or wants to speak first. A tangible fear is visible on each of their faces.

After a long moment, Dinah pours hot water into her mug from a small kettle. She dunks a tea bag up and down, up and down, until the liquid in her cup turns a deep, reddish brown. "No one really knows, now do they?"

Chess takes a swig of his own hot drink—some sort of cider—and then dabs the corner of his mouth with a serviette. "The Jabberwock takes on many forms, depending on what you most fear. Sometimes it's a monster of some sort. Other times it's . . . Well, no one knows for sure, aside from those who have faced it." He shudders. "We believe Scarlet couldn't care less about a successor to the throne or sharing power with the other quarters."

"What does she care about?" I ask.

"Based on what Blanche has learned"—Charlotte nods at Scarlet's advisor—"and what we know about the Fourth Trial . . ." her voice trails off. She clears her throat. "While the queen claims to have beaten the Heart Trial, we think this isn't the truth either. If it was, Scarlet would know how to get past the Jabberwock. She wouldn't need the players to do it for her. It's the reason for the WV, you see. It collects data on the players, getting the queen closer to finding the one player who might beat the Jabberwock. It's partly why she started inviting Wildflowers to play. The Fourth Trial is a wild beast no Wonder has ever been able to tame."

Hearts are wild.

"Okay," I say slowly, picturing the queen in all her desperation and lies. What is so important that she'd risk the lives of her own people to obtain it? "Do you think that anyone who manages to pass the Fourth Trial finds the real Wonderland? And the Ivory King?"

Everyone nods, confirming what Dan must have seen.

Real.

But the same questions remain. "I still don't see what this has to do with me. What's happening to the missing players?"

"I don't think they're missing," Charlotte informs me. "That's what I've been telling Dinah since she came to get me. I think they've won. I think they managed to make it past the Jabberwock. That's why they haven't returned. They found the Ivory King."

"Dan returned," I say. "If he found the real Wonderland, and the Ivory King, why would he leave it all behind to come back here?"

"Good question," is all Chess says. "Maybe he hoped others would know about it. So they could find the king too?"

"Good luck vith zat," Blanche interjects, crossing her arms. "Zee queen vill ave zat boy silenced before zee week eez out. She doesn't vant anyvun else to know. Zee sole reason she vants zee king found een zee first place eez so she can do avay vith him for good." She makes an act of cutting her throat with one finger.

"How do I fit into this?" I ask before they go off on a rabbit trail. I look at Raving. "What did you mean about the Wonder Gene? You said the things we believe are fabrications?"

Raving leans in. "Scarlet would have us believe that there are those who are born with the Gene and those who are not," he says. "But we have learned there is a third category. It's the entire reason the Knight Society—those searching for the Ivory King and the true Wonderland—was founded. And why Charlotte hid you."

I must look as confused as I feel.

"Alice," Charlotte says gently. "You are the daughter of Catherine R. Pillar."

I take in the news, shooting a glare at Dinah. "You said back in Oxford that you didn't know who I am. You lied."

Dinah gives no apology. "It was not the proper time," is all she says.

"Did you know?" I turn to Chess now, feeling betrayed on all sides.

He frowns. It is not a good look on him. "Cross my heart, Ace." He does just that. "You knew as much as I did."

"Alice, listen," Charlotte continues. "It was Pillar's research that aided Scarlet in creating her own version of Wonderland. She also invented Wonder Vision. Its original intention was to enhance the entire Wonderland experience for everyone, but Scarlet took advantage of it. She decided to steal Pillar's idea and use it for the Trials. As a way to control and track the players. A means to her end goal."

My breath catches. I touch the bangle on my wrist, which suddenly feels more like a shackle.

"When Pillar tried to destroy her invention and stop Scarlet from carrying out her plan, the queen went after her." Raving is speaking carefully, as if his own words are a death sentence. "Scarlet managed to get a hold of the WV and its blueprints, but she did not succeed in uncovering Pillar's most valuable discovery of all. You."

"Me?" I squeak.

"You were born one hundred percent Normal."

My heart thuds. Every hope I ever had lapses. Normal? How is that possible? I've seen Wonderland with my own eyes. Or I thought I did.

It's Charlotte's smile that renews my hope. "You were *born* Normal." Her smile broadens and her eyes sparkle. "You *became* Wonder."

WAR

"It's no use going back to yesterday,
because I was a different person then."

-- Lewis Carroll, *Alice's Adventures in Wonderland*

LIES

Normal.

Wonder.

Both.

It's been one week since I learned the news, and I still can't fully wrap my mind around the idea. I twist my WV bangle around my wrist. Frown. I take it off. Put it back on. Either way, I see Wonderland.

It's Wonderland, but it isn't. Not the way it was meant to be seen, anyway.

Charlotte's words echo in my mind. I gained no sleep that night. We walked back to the palace with the others in silence. Dinah in cat form bid us farewell at the gates with a meow, revealing the tea she had at the café was, in fact, Beast's Blend. Chess bowed a goodnight when he took the lift to the boys' suites. I, however, was far from ready to sleep and spent the remainder of the night badgering Charlotte with question after question.

"How is this possible?"

"Nothing's impossible," she had replied, an echo of Chess. Turns out this is the belief at the core of what the Knight Society stands for.

"Why is it called the Knight Society?"

"In a game of chess, the knights protect the king. We thought it fit."

"How did you know Pillar—my mother?"

"She was my Trainer the year I played in the Trials. I tended you often. In many ways, I felt like I was already your older sister. When she learned she was in danger—that *you* were in danger—she asked me to look after you. I never started the Fourth Trial. I took you and left. And never looked back."

"Who was my father?"

"I don't know."

She responded with more patience and grace than I deserved at the late hour. It hurt her to admit when she was unsure or didn't know. But that didn't stop me from asking.

"Why did you try to keep me from Wonderland?"

"We're all afraid of something," she finally said, a yawn trailing her words. "I was afraid of losing you. I thought by keeping you away from all of this, you'd be safe. But of course, Blanche always checked in with us. Then Dinah tracked us down. It was a matter of time before we returned and finished what Pillar started."

What my mother started. I try not to cry each time I think of her. Not knowing what happened is almost worse. Did Queen Scarlet do something horrible to her? Is she in hiding? Did she go after the king?

A tear slips free.

The grandfather clock in the common area plays a music box melody, signaling the top of the early-morning hour. Another day of training for the Club Trial lies ahead. Charlotte is harder on us each day.

"You don't know what you're up against," she keeps saying. "Now go run another lap."

Our obstacles continue to test both muscle and mind. My entire body protests as I slip on my robe and steel myself for what's in store. I should be sleeping, relishing every closed-eye moment I'm allowed. Instead my thoughts are awhirl, refusing to settle down.

Careful not to wake the others, I enter the lift and journey down to the main floor of the palace. A short ding sounds, and the doors open to a quiet, dimly lit hall. I've passed by the research room a few times, but none of our training has called for us to actually use it.

Yet.

A chill tugs at my neck, calling me back to bed. I cinch my robe more tightly, turn the handle to the research room, and find it, thankfully, unoccupied. It's similar to the library on campus back in Oxford. Aside from all the high-tech hologram screens and loads of actual books lining the shelves. It hits me. These books must be part of the actual palace in Normal London.

I choose an empty desk before a slumbering hologram screen and sit cross-legged in the chair. All it takes is a thought to link my WV with the floating screen. It comes to life, a search box with a blinking cursor at the centre.

I pause, trying to decide how to fill in the blank. What am I really searching for?

A headache pinches my brow. I squeeze my eyes shut. Even after Charlotte divulged every detail of the day she decided to abduct—rescue—me, I still couldn't get one question out of my head.

If the Ivory King is the true ruler and creator of the real Wonderland, how has Scarlet managed to keep up this ruse for so long?

I think of my encounters with the queen since I arrived.

She's seen me at the opening ceremony and the First Trial. I've been invited to play for her team. Did she know me as a child? That I was Pillar's daughter?

I think my inquiry into the search box in my WV. It connects to the hologram screen and the words *Catherine R. Pillar* appear.

Her profile and biography are the first items up.

She's stunning.

The first photo shown reveals a woman in her mid-thirties. Her flaxen hair is cropped in a fashionable cut to her ears. The expression she wears is serious, but her grey-blue eyes relay curiosity. Her crisp white lab coat makes her look important, and her square-framed glasses like mine make her look smart.

I've never thought of myself as much to look at, but staring at a photo of my mother, I can't deny the resemblance. It's like looking in a mirror.

I scroll through a few articles about her, some from the Wonderland Reality, others from Normal London. One near the bottom of the first page looks promising, and I expand it to full view.

CATHERINE R. PILLAR,
RENOWNED GENOME RESEARCHER,
DIES IN LAB FIRE.

A few facts are listed, including her date of birth, where she went to school, and . . . the day she disappeared. The same year Charlotte took me out of Wonderland. It seems she was living a double life, both Wonder and Normal.

The fire is believed to be an accident, caused by a gas leak in the building. The damage was so severe that Pillar's remains could not be uncovered, nor could her ongoing research regarding the Wonder Gene . . .

Ongoing research? So it's true. There is more to having the Gene than what we understand. But . . .

It is widely known that Pillar was not born with the Wonder Gene herself, having tested negative when the Wonder Registry was first implemented. However, many have speculated the scientist developed a mutation of the Gene. According to her Theory of Impossibility . . .

I sit back. Is my mother's disappearance the key to uncovering what I am? Charlotte says I became Wonder. Could that be this supposed mutation? And none of it explains or mentions the Ivory King, or how the missing players have managed to find the true Wonderland. Of course not. This article's Normal.

I start a new search, holding my breath when I enter the words *Ivory King*.

Nothing of consequence turns up. I scroll for a few seconds. One entry about chess sets catches my eye. I expand it, not expecting to find anything important, and scan the page.

While the queen may be the most powerful and by far the most valuable piece on the board, it is the king that remains the most important. A king might be captured, but he is the sole piece that can never be removed.

I zoom in on that last part. Never removed? The Knight Society is based on chess. Could the Ivory King and the real Wonderland be right under our noses?

My next search is a no-brainer. *Missing Wonderland Trials Players.*

Dozens of results appear. Multiple Wonder articles focusing on the same cases. This will take forever to sift through.

I stretch my back and adjust myself in my seat before selecting the most recent news story. It's about Dan, the boy who reappeared. Details pop out here and there.

Never returned from the Fourth Trial.

Parents are being questioned by authorities.

Boy claims he never left, only that he saw what's real.

I stop at that last tidbit. Highlight three words. *Never left. Real.*

Within seconds, I'm pulling up a blank note in my WV. Collecting information. Scrolling through article after article. What if, like the king, these players are still here? Right under our noses. We just can't see them?

A knock sounds at the threshold.

I startle, closing my search as if I'm caught with one hand in the biscuit jar. When I twist in the chair, I see Madi in the doorframe, wearing bright holiday pyjamas and holding a tray of tea and crumpets. "You look like you could use this."

I force a smile. Why does it feel like I'm lying to her? I want to tell her everything. About meeting Raving and the Knight Society and the king. About being born Normal and becoming Wonder.

When she nears, I remove my glasses, rubbing the sore spot on the bridge of my nose before replacing them. Once my vision is clear I make room for the tray on the desk. "Thanks."

Madi pours the tea. When I hesitate, she says, "It's a mild blend of chamomile and lavender. Not nearly as strong as Serenity's Slumber. Enough to calm the nerves. It's my own recipe. I call it Tranquil-i-Tea."

I smile at her clever play on words and choose a buttered crumpet, tearing a little bite off and dipping it into the brew. "Thanks. I thought you were asleep. Did I wake you?" I ask before popping the bite into my mouth.

"No," she says. An awkward pause. Then, "You've been sneaking out every night this week."

I don't know what to say. Madi and I haven't really talked much since the first couple of days after my arrival. Has she been distancing herself? Or is it the other way around? She acted so strangely in the Hall of Mirrors.

"You don't have to do everything alone," she remarks,

pouring some tea for herself. "I could help you. If you let me in." The hurt in her voice is undeniable.

I sink back in the chair. Can I trust her? Will she still want to be my friend when she knows the truth?

Steam rises from the mug before her face. She pulls up a chair to sit at the desk beside me. "I know it must be hard for you to trust people. Charlotte lied to you. Chess pretended not to know you. But I'm not them. You can trust me."

Maybe she's right. I want her to be. "Did you know my sister took me?" I tuck a foot under my thigh, and settle in more. The mug is hot between my palms, but it feels nice. The palace is always cold.

"I was six too," Madi laughs, but the sound has a hint of emotion to it that makes me think the memory isn't so fond. "I knew what Raving told me."

"Your older brother?" Again, I feel like I'm lying to her.

She nods and says in a voice I assume is meant to sound masculine but comes off more like a throaty female, "Alice had to go away, but she'll come back another day." She grins faintly. "As I got older, I never stopped asking questions about you. Where you went and why. Raving never would tell me the full story. But he also never lied to me."

I take a sip to keep calm. Why does that feel like an accusation?

"About a year ago," Madi continues, "Raving finally caved and helped me make contact with Charlotte. I messaged her every day for updates about you. She promised me she would keep you safe."

I hang my head.

"Alice." She grabs my hand. "Whatever it is. You can tell me. When you're ready."

She seems so genuine. And I want to trust her. But I don't know if I trust myself. I'm Normal. I'm Wonder. I don't fit into any category I can place or name.

So I keep silent, staring into the specks of leaves at the bottom of the caramel-coloured liquid in my mug.

Madi is quiet for a while, too, before she speaks again. "Raving told me once that our memories are the ingredients to the recipes that are our personalities. Maybe the key to opening up about your past is discovering who you are in the present."

I let that thought simmer. My tea has cooled to lukewarm. I finish the last third in one gulp, then set the empty mug in my lap. Who am I? "I guess I really don't know the answer to that. I like to play cards."

"That's what you do." She shakes her head. "It's not who you are. You want to know what I think?"

"Do I?"

"I'll tell you anyway. I think you're a good friend and a great teammate. You're smart, and you care about others. You don't trust easily, but you're forgiving."

"You can see all of that?"

"You called Charlotte your sister, which means, despite everything, you still see her as one."

"I guess that's true, but how does that help me with the past?"

"If you can forgive Charlotte, and let go this life-changing thing she did, I think you can give others more credit to accept you as you are too. And all the flaws and broken parts that come with you."

Madi rises. She gathers our mugs and lifts the tray. "I'll leave you be for tonight. But you really ought to get some sleep. There's a mock trial in the morning. Charlotte's going to be on us to gain some extra points before the Club Trial in June."

I'd nearly forgotten about the last-minute change to our training schedule. My days and nights have blurred together lately. A yawn escapes. "I'll be ready."

She eyes me.

"I will. I promise. I'm fine. Just knackered." The lie comes out so easily. Rolling off my tongue. Guilt pricks my chest, and a new swirl of empathy for Charlotte rises.

"Good night, friend."

I wave as she disappears around the bend of the doorframe and into the hall. When I hear the far-off ding of the lift, I turn in my chair again, expanding my screen once more.

The next article I open quickens my pulse.

HATTER FAMILY MOURNS
DISAPPEARANCE OF BELOVED SON.

Stark Hatter. Seventeen years old. Missing since the Fourth Trial last June.

The photo shows a boy who could almost be Madi's male double. Eggplant-purple hair. Overconfident grin. Madi spoke of her victorious brother and his team with such pride on her latest podcast. Not once has she mentioned this to me personally.

If Stark has been missing for a year, and Madi's been hiding it . . .

What else is she not telling me?

RUN

The mock trial is mock *everything*.

A trick. A farce. A facade.

Happiness. Joy. Excitement. They're present. In the faces of our audience. In the sounds of the trumpets. In the laughter of a little girl as she skips along to catch up with her mother. In the flashing, digitized letters on a giant screen that read:

WELCOME TO THE MOCK TRIAL

Welcome, indeed.

The sun is blinding today. The light reflects off my glasses, and I have to shade my eyes to see where I'm treading. This is not the lavish fanfare which welcomed us at Oyster and Pearl Hall at the onset of May. This is London Stadium at what used to be Queen Elizabeth Olympic Park. The place was shut down years ago, of course. Locked up. Key tossed. No need for a stadium after the Divide. Borders closed. Sports teams became obsolete. Most of the best players—as it turns out—were the very Wonders who Queen Cordelia forced to Register and serve the crown in the lowliest of occupations.

And everyone knows that Registered Wonders have no fun whatsoever.

The screams of our buoyant fans make it near impossible to hear my own thoughts. The field before us is such an inauthentic, vibrant green it looks painted. Every emotion I don't and cannot feel or express as I steal a glance at the notes in my WV once again seems to rain upon me as we make our entrance into the abandoned stadium turned Wonder masterpiece—the crown and glory of Diamond Quarter.

I review my notes as we walk. I had little time to sift through the dozens upon dozens of articles that came up in my search for missing players. Since Charlotte never actually entered the Fourth Trial and Dan is really the only one to have returned from wherever he's been, there's no way to know what to expect.

Or how to get past the Jabberwock.

Or what the Jabberwock actually is.

I focus my attention on the extravagant stage at the opposite end of the field, where a goal might normally stand. The quarter heads and Her Majesty greet one another before taking their places—the heads in high-backed chairs on either side of an elevated red throne. Scarlet is dressed in a white gown today, embellished with blood-red lace at the hem. Her collar is reminiscent of something from centuries ago, but her hairstyle is modern, swept up on one side, the other side loose and cascading over one shoulder. If she knew my mother, certainly she must have some clue as to who I am. I wait for her to notice me as we approach the stage. For a glint of recognition to appear in her brown eyes.

There is none. Only the royal glow of satisfaction in her cheeks as she surveys our winning team. If the pressure isn't bad enough, the scoreboard above the stage lights up, revealing our current scores.

We're first, as expected, follow by the Clubs, then the Spades, with Diamonds in dead last. There's a sense of foreboding. Despite our victory, we could lose it all in a blink. None of the others, however, seem to worry at the notion.

Jack fist-pumps the air while Madi does a victory dance. I watch, unsure anymore if anyone is really who they seem.

Scarlet rises and lifts her hands in a gesture to settle the crowd. It takes but a few moments for the boiling-over excitement to lower to a soft simmer.

I turn 360 degrees, taking it all in. The audience is outfitted in colourful displays representative of each quarter. Unlike the night of the Spade Trial, which was all ballgowns and glitter and glam, today carries the feeling of a true sporting event. Though I've only attended a few tennis matches here and there back at school, the atmosphere holds a sort of magic the Normal Reality lacks.

Banners fly. Foam hands wave excitedly. Painted faces filled with awe fix their gazes upon us. It's a medley of red, black, green, white, and silver. Each team is dressed in identical fitted jumpsuits, the lone difference the quarter colours. Unlike our previous attire, these suits were designed especially for this Trial, syncing with the information our WV has already learned about each of us.

Our regular body temperature.

How fast we run.

Perspiration. Dehydration. Exhaustion. The suit tracks it all and then some, sending the data directly to our WV and adjusting accordingly. It's kind of cool.

Also kind of creepy.

I don't know if the drills Charlotte had us run will be anything like what we will see today, but I do know I'm ready for them if and when they arrive. I may not be the fastest on our team—my WV knows that much—or the most practiced in using the Gene, but I am clever enough to find creative ways to get around obstacles. Which has become my forte, though I wouldn't call it my Mastery.

That remains unidentified. At least I'm not alone in that area. Willow, Chess, and Knave have yet to reveal their special skill sets either.

Though the queen settled the crowd, it is Blanche—the appointed emcee—who takes her place at the glass podium now.

She waves a white-gloved hand. Boosts her hairdo with the heel of her palm. "Velcome, Vonders, vun and all."

A wave of cheers ensues.

Blanche laughs and a rosy blush blossoms, but something tells me she's not embarrassed by the extra attention. She revels in it. It's hard to believe she's part of a secret society who aims to put another ruler back on the throne. If Queen Scarlet discovered Blanche's secret, what would happen? Charges of treason? Imprisonment?

Execution?

"Vun sing you all know very vell about zee Trials eez zat zey can change at any moment. You came here under zee pretence zis eez a mock trial."

Pretence? Oh, no.

"Surprise, surprise, today eez actually zee official Second Trial of zee season."

A collective gasp ripples throughout the teams. Some in the crowd shout "boo" or "bad form," while others cheer louder, rejoicing in the excitement and constantly moving pieces the Trials produce.

"You ave Madame Sevine of zee House of Diamonds to sank for zee quick change."

As if on cue, the head of Diamond Quarter waves her hand in a practiced motion "Rule Forty-Two, you know," is all she says.

"Indeed," Blanche replies curtly. Then to us she adds, "Let's all give her a round ov applause for adding zis creative twist into zee mix."

While there's certainly the overarching prelude of praise from the stands, the more prominent sound can be heard in the silent glares of Team Club, Team Spade, and our Team Heart, all directed at the Diamonds.

But they seem as upset and confused about this sudden switch as the rest of us. At least that means they didn't have any special training for today's sudden Diamond Trial.

We can hope so, anyway. Out of curiosity, I do a quick search in my WV for Rule Forty-Two. There isn't one, of course. Madame Sevine made it up. Apparently, some in positions of power have no problem lying to the rest of us if it suits their agenda.

"Remember," Blanche continues, "every Trial eez about fun, cooperation, and teamvork. Your goal: finish zee game and gain your clue."

Except we didn't have a clue to prepare us for today. How are we supposed to win if we don't know what's in store?

"Points vill be allotted. And, as a bonus, today's vinning team vill receive an extra clue before zee Club Trial een three veek's time." She lifts a gloved hand, wiggling three fingers in the same way she always does. "Lagging teams, zis eez your chance at redemption." She claps three times, signaling what follows.

An unseen gathering of instruments proclaims something significant is about to unfold. The sound is orchestral and ominous and riveting all at once. The stage rises, floating ten, twenty, thirty metres off the grass. And there, perhaps twenty metres off, a gate made of iron bars in twisted, thorny vines comes into view.

The vines light on fire.

The heat radiates, fanning my face, and I step back. The

blaze causes more strain on my eyesight than the sun. I shield my eyes again to get a better view.

The crowd lets out a unified "ooh" followed by an ominous "ahh."

I hear them before I see them. Birds. They squawk wildly. The sound quakes the ground beneath our feet.

Something like the crack of a whip sounds, trailed by a *pop, pop, pop.*

They're free. From the mouth of flaming thorns they fly. Four giant flamingoes in as many colours—green, red, silver, and white. They look more closely related to dragons than birds, reminding me of the guardian on Wonderland's coat of arms. Their curved beaks snap. I cover my ears and duck my head. They circle the enclosed stadium like vultures waiting to feast upon helpless prey. The way they speed past one another in the air, it's almost as if they're racing.

Another horn blasts. I turn in time to witness a new gate open at the opposite end of the field. A horde of hedgehogs the size of actual hogs rolls out, their quills sharp as blades glinting in the white light reflecting from the massive dome.

For the love of cards, can it get much worse?

The hedgehogs circle us, racing like the birds above them, acting as sharp, moving barriers between us and the crowd, most of whom are still *oohing* and *ahhing* and gasping at the sight.

That's when a holographic croquet court appears, the quadruple-diamond course twice the size of a Normal one.

I shouldn't be surprised. This is Wonderland. I count the wickets. Eighteen in all, along with two stakes. Every few seconds, the course rearranges. The wickets move as if in a dance, repositioning too quickly for anything to pass through. I shoot a side-glance at Chess. From the expression on his face, he's seen nothing like this before.

"Your objective," Blanche's voice tells us, "eez to complete zee game een zee time specified." She waves a hand towards the clock at the same moment fifty-two minutes appear. "Save vun, and you save zem all."

Save one and save them all? What is that supposed to mean? Could that be a last-moment clue just in time for the Trial to begin?

I glance at Chess again. His eyes are closed, pure concentration evident in the creases on his forehead. In contrast, our teammate beside him appears bored.

I do a double take. When did Knave show up? He's got some nerve, having skipped all our training sessions since we won the First Trial.

My glare is more than obvious, but he gives no indication he notices my fury. In fact, despite no training, Knave looks more tired than ever with eyes that are sunken into purple skin and hollow cheeks. When I think he's going to keep on ignoring me, he mouths two words that send shivers up my spine.

Knight So-ci-et-y.

It takes all my nerve and a dose of healthy fear to keep my panic contained. I glance at our teammates. Did anyone else notice? My thoughts flap about. How does he know about the secret meeting? Queen Scarlet is his aunt. It's only a matter of time before he divulges the secret that I am the daughter of Catherine R. Pillar. Both Wonder and Normal.

The others don't appear to pay Knave any mind. I join them in staring at the circling flamingo-dragons above. One does a flip and snaps its beak. Another breathes a stream of fire.

The fact that we believed this was a mock trial is laughable. This is as real as it gets.

The final horn blasts. The clock begins its countdown.

And Blanche gives her final bidding, "Best ov luck to all."

"You've got this," Charlotte says in my ear.

I jerk my head to one side. But she's not there. "Charlotte?"

"In your WV," comes her voice. "You'll have one opportunity to call a timeout if you need me."

"Why aren't you in Chess's WV? He's the Team King. You should be helping him."

Though I can't see her, I know without a doubt there's a smile crossing her lips right now. "There's one true King, Alice. In this case, you'll need to sacrifice yours to get you out of this mess."

"What?"

But the sound cuts out, and I'm standing on the field alone surrounded by deadly looking creatures and a team of Wonders I'm not sure I can trust.

The teams gather into huddles. Ours follows suit, and I try not to flinch when Madi wraps her arm around my shoulder.

"You okay?" she asks.

"Fine," I say with too much attitude and zero eye contact.

She releases me. A tangible chasm deepens in the crevice between us.

Chess directs us towards the task at hand. "Croquet is simple enough." He chuckles as he glances skywards. "As long as we keep from catching fire, we ought to be good."

Sophia scoffs. Willow has rubbed off on her. "Yeah, if we had mallets, maybe. And fireproof suits. But did you see that course? The spines on those hedgehogs? It's imposs—"

"Nothing is—"

"—impossible," I finish.

Chess grins.

"Who says we can't have fireproof suits?" I ask, all the while keeping one eye on our diminishing time.

"Now you're talking, Ace," Chess encourages me. "Anyone have some ideas?"

"Ice plant roses might work." Sophia suddenly grins in a mischievous way that says she has a trick up her sleeve. She closes her eyes. A subtle touch of glittering red eyeshadow lines her lids, contrasting with her midnight lashes, and our suit material begins to transform, turning from boring red and black to floral. Outlines of metallic rose patterns blossom across the fabric, disappearing then reappearing when they catch the light.

My skin feels suddenly cool, but not uncomfortably so, as if I've taken a refreshing drink of water in the middle of July. I feel lighter. And the heat from the dragon birds is no more.

"That ought to do the trick," Sophia says.

I guess she and Blanche were right. You can learn a lot of things from the flowers.

"Sophia, you are a genius." Willow applauds. "Her Majesty would count her lucky golden stars to have you as her gardener *and* wardrobe designer."

From the expression of newfound confidence Sophia carries, there's no doubt she is hoping for precisely that.

"Let's get this fireproof fashion show on the course," Madi declares. "Puzzle Master, what's your analysis?"

From the way he's focusing, it's clear Jack has already been running a course analysis through his WV. "The pattern alters every twenty-six seconds exactly, giving us a very small window to get a ball through the wickets in the proper order. The four-diamond course is arduous enough, the other three seem to follow no logic."

Twenty-six seconds. Four-diamond course. Why do these details set off silent alarms?

"Did you notice any pattern to them?" Chess presses. "Anything at all that could give us some sort of clue?"

Jack lifts a hand. "Hold on. It looks like . . . Well, I'll be a caterpillar's cousin." He shakes his head in disbelief. He blinks and widens his stare. "The other patterns are the team symbols. Four Diamonds. Three Spades. Two Clubs. And a Heart."

My fingers tingle.

"Could it be another riddle?" Willow wonders. "A puzzle we need to solve?"

Something that's been sleeping, dormant inside, awakens.

"That's too obvious." Knave rolls his eyes. "Is it any wonder you're a Two?"

Knave's jab at Willow is cruel. I ought to defend her. To remind him that a Two's role is just as important, since she fills in for me—the Ace—should something happen. But I can't stop seeing flashes of numbers and royal suits dancing before my eyes.

"You take that back," Sophia snaps. "Or I'll take back your fireproof suit."

Spades. Diamonds. Hearts. Clubs.

"Oh, you mean you want to take away a bunch of flowers?" Knave pinches his suit near the collar. "Please, be my guest."

"Come on, mates," Chess attempts to break the battle before it turns into an all-out war. "Arguing won't solve—"

"Cards!" I blurt out.

My entire team turns their focus on me.

My face grows hot, and I try to organise my thoughts. It's no use. They come too fast. The time on the game clock says we now have forty-five minutes to complete the Diamond Trial.

The seconds tick backwards. Fifty-nine, fifty-eight, fifty-seven . . .

But all I see is twenty-six. Half of fifty-two. *Go.*

"This isn't croquet." I point at the course, where some of our opponents have already gathered. Time is wasting, and they're not wasting it. They imagine balls and wickets, attempting to play the game as it was originally intended.

I lower my voice. We might have a fighting chance at this thing as long as no one else catches on. "It's a ruse. A distraction. Blanche didn't say we needed to complete the course. She said our goal is to complete the *game*. And this is nothing more than a common game of cards."

I almost expect them to find this ridiculous, but even Knave's eyes gleam, and he fails to conceal a smile.

"She's right." Jack's eyes dart rapidly back and forth, and it's clear he's running the four patterns through his WV again. "Four suits, just like our four teams. The courses change every twenty-six seconds, which is half of fifty-two—a full pack and the total time we were given to finish."

"So?" Willow asks. "How do we win?"

Chess gives me a knowing look and grin.

A memory from not too long ago rises to mind. Something he said to me the night we arrived in London.

You are *the card.*

"It's so simple." Almost too simple. We overlook the things that seem too easy, but it's been right here in front of us. "We are the cards. We don't need mallets or balls. We have to work our way through it ourselves." I'm suddenly grateful for Charlotte's drills, though I'll never admit it.

"But that still doesn't tell us which game it is," Willow says. "A croquet obstacle course?"

I gaze out over the field where the others are failing miserably. With each attempt to knock a ball through a wicket, a hedgehog eats it or a flamingo-dragon lights everything on fire, forcing the teams to start over. The Fours like Sophia attempt to invent new ways to keep their team members safe, while the Tens attempt to use speed or strength to overcome the obstacles.

Mouse kicks one of the hologram wickets, only to slip in the grass and fall backwards. Another Club player helps her up, but she pushes him away as soon as she's standing.

She and Knave would be a perfect match.

No matter what strategy each team tries, it's clear this game is not designed to be fair. And there's one way to win a game that's meant to be unfair from the start.

I look at Chess as dread slithers in, the unwanted serpent that it is. "No."

As is typical, he doesn't show any sign of worry or fear. But from the way he stares at me, his turquoise gaze lingering longer than normal, I know he's trying to tell me what he can't say.

"Save your Queens, Ace." He pulls me away from the others. "Discard your Kings. There's only one way to win at Black Hearts. You know this. I have to sit this one out."

"We can't do this without you." I'm not crying this time because I'm mad. It's completely underhanded.

Just like what Scarlet did to the Ivory King.

"You can and you will." Chess takes my hand in a gesture so unlike him, I startle.

Of course he would make it that much harder to let him go.

"C'mon Ace." He draws me in for a quick hug. "With me gone, you know what you have to do." He gently releases me. "You found your Mastery. Now use it, oh Master of Games."

Master of Games. It has a nice ring to it. I gather my breath as I watch him dissolve into nothing. One of his Fates along with him, leaving this Reality so he has no way of helping us.

Forty minutes left on the clock. I pivot on my heel and step into my new position.

Scratch that. I don't step. I run.

Make way, ladies and gentlemen, and say hello to the new Team Heart Queen.

♤IDE

"Where's Shire?"

Every nerve short-circuits. Madi would be the first to ask.

"Gone." I hate being irritated with her.

"Gone?" Jack asks. "Gone where?"

From the course, a Spade player screams. A pair of medics run out onto the field, a stretcher between them.

Taking effort to force control into my voice and expression, I ask my team, "Ever played Black Hearts?"

Realisation dawns on their faces.

And, just as swiftly, they come to terms.

Chess is gone, and he won't be returning. Not for this Trial, anyway.

"Well then, *Queen* Alice." Madi curtsies. If her tone wasn't borderline mocking, I might actually believe she respected the sudden change in order. "Tell us what you would have us do."

I cringe a little but whether they see me as Team Queen or

not doesn't matter. What matters is that we finish and come out on top.

A tiny voice inside scolds me. *What does it matter if we win or lose when there are bigger things at play?*

I shove it aside. There's nothing else I can do.

"This isn't about mallets or balls or finishing any of the four alternating courses." My voice shakes as I speak. I'm certainly no Chess when it comes to leadership. "Our focus should be getting me through the course—preferably alive—from the first stake to the other and back." I'm reluctant at what I have to say next. I turn towards my least favourite teammate. "Knave, how skilled are you at blocking?" I still don't know his Mastery, but I do know he's the Ten, which means he ranks high when it comes to physical abilities.

He stiffens, and one eyebrow arches. He's either surprised I've addressed him or annoyed. "I'm not *good.*" He crosses his arms. "I'm superb. A dragon couldn't get past me, let alone a bird pretending to be one." His body language conveys I'm in perfectly capable hands.

So long as those hands protect before they strangle me.

"Great. Now you can prove it. You've just been promoted to the new royal guard."

I half expect him to jeer at me and turn the assignment down. But I am pleasantly surprised as he takes off at a sprint around the perimeter. He avoids the deadly hedgehogs with ease, hurdling over them and dodging fiery blows from the sky at the same time.

Impressive. Maybe we can win this thing after all. Whatever Knave had against me and the rest of our team during the First Trial, he seems to be on board now.

I turn to Sophia next. "That leaves distractions to you, Soph. Think your flower speaking skills can help?" I explain my plans to her, continuing to keep my tone low.

Sophia's wink says it all. "No problem. Leave it to me."

Then she heads towards the course, which is currently in the shape of a heart. I've seen what she's capable of. I trust her.

"Jack." I pause. I'm getting closer to my part in all of this. "I need you to set up a signal that alerts me ten seconds before the course switches again and boots me back to the starting stake. Do you think you can create a sequence that maps my moves to follow the changes in the course?"

His laugh says such a task is child's play. "Absolutely," he says. Then he goes to work.

Within seconds, the data begins uploading to my WV. It's all complicated and jumbled and coded. Once it's finished, the code converts to a 3D map that I can view from any desired angle with a thought. He's highlighted my steps in bright red. I don't have a lot of time to memorise them. But I'll have to try.

"What do you need from us?" Madi and Willow say at almost the exact same time.

Thirty-five minutes left on the clock.

"Two words," I say to Madi, doing my best to see her as the girl who greeted me with open arms. "Dwindler's Draught." She's running towards the water station on the sidelines before I say anything more.

Which leaves Willow. Who I thought hated me but somehow became my friend when I wasn't paying attention. The girl who should have been an Ace in my place. The girl who couldn't stand me—the Wildflower—who swooped in and took what should have been hers. Yet, one look in her eyes now tells me she's all in.

I take her by the hand at the same moment Madi returns with two cups of tea. Strange to think I once believed I was allergic to anything that contained as much as a teaspoon of leaves, when really it was just Charlotte's way of keeping my true identity a secret. I take a whiff of the cup's contents. Sure enough, the relaxing scent of lavender mixed with a hint of black currant greets me.

"Bottom's up," Madi declares. "You'll both be the size of mice in no time. Goes down smooth, I promise."

Willow glances at me.

"Together?" I ask.

She nods. "Together."

Why do I feel as if I'm about to consume poison? I hesitate. Madi gave me tea last night, and it did exactly what she said it would. Am I being paranoid? When I met Raving, there was no mention of his brother missing. And Chess knows their family. Surely he would have mentioned if Stark had gone missing the same as Kit.

Right?

I shake the dread away and lift the cup to my lips. Willow mirrors me, and we down our brews in one swallow.

The strange sensation of dissolving into myself takes place almost instantly. Only this time, nausea accompanies it. And dizziness. I feel faint and as if the world is spinning up over my head and rushing beneath my feet. I study Madi's face as she watches us. Did she put something else in the tea? The wrong measurements can have dire consequences. There's no way she would have made a mistake. This is her Mastery.

Which means, if there is something wrong with the tea, it was intentional.

I want to kick myself. However we come out of this—*if* we come out—I'm going to do everything in my power to find out what happened to Kit Shire, Stark Hatter, and anyone else who hasn't returned.

And if Madi had something to do with it.

Blades of grass tower a mile above us and specks of dirt look like boulders. I've lost all sense of direction, but before I have time to grow anxious, Willow pulls up navigation in her WV and links it to mine.

"This way," she says, pulling me with her towards the course.

Together we sprint as fast as our puny legs can carry us. It takes far too long to reach the starting stake. The grass is thick as tree trunks, and I can't see the countdown clock. Still, I know our time runs shorter every second we waste.

"All right." I'm panting, gulping. With the courses mapped out for us by Jack, all we have to do is follow the steps in time. "Our biggest obstacles are lack of height—"

"And not getting stepped on," Willow adds, also attempting to gain control of her breathing.

"That too," I pant through a half-crazed laugh. "Knave is tracking us, so he'll be our eyes and ears above." I hope. "With the help Sophia provides, getting through the course shouldn't be too difficult."

Jack's signal pings in my WV, letting me know the croquet course loop has reached its beginning again. Four diamonds. Twenty-six seconds. *"Now!"*

I tag the first stake as if I were a croquet ball whacked by a mallet. Then I take off at a run, Willow close by at my heels.

This is a game, I tell myself. *No different from the obstacles you've been running for Charlotte.*

But twenty-six seconds are shorter than they seem. The course alters and so does our footwork. I almost miss the change in shape from diamond to spade. It's only thanks to Willow that I make it through the next wicket before being catapulted back to start.

"Thanks," I say, rubbing my sore neck.

"No problem," Willow says.

Sixteen seconds remain before the course shifts.

One, two, three wickets over the first spade hump. Then we're onto a new path, navigating the curved club shapes. We dodge someone's boot. Catapult ourselves several centimetres ahead to avoid a rolling hedgehog. Fall to our knees when we accidentally dash right through a path of grass blades ablaze.

"Remind me to thank Sophia for her ingenious ice plant roses if we get out of this," I pant.

"*When* we get out of this, she'll never let you forget it."

I can only hope she's right.

When the course shifts into a heart, I rotate the map in my WV, moving and talking and planning all at the same time. "We're almost to the next stake," I tell Willow. Then I send a quick message to Jack.

He responds almost immediately, the text a silent reminder that we still have so far to go.

Twelve minutes and counting.

If this was a Normal course on a Normal playing field in a Normal game, I might consider the feat of reaching our goal impossible. But I picture Chess's smile and remember that Charlotte is one call away.

Three more wickets.

The course returns to diamonds just as we reach the halfway mark.

Willow and I grab onto the second stake as if it makes the difference between life and death.

Ten minutes.

If we can make it through four more wickets instead of two before the course alters, we might actually win this thing.

Reaching for Willow's hand, I tell her, "Let's go."

But Willow does not respond.

Several things happen in succession. I twist, my hair whipping around my face as if it, like so much of the chaos around us, is ablaze. Did she get smaller?

"Ace." Her voice is so faint and weak. She doesn't sound like herself at all. "I feel rather . . . strange."

I don't like this.

"Ace," she utters again. "Tell Soph she was like the sister I never had."

"No," I state, scooping her up into my arms. I am dismayed at how easy the task is. Like picking up a toothpick. "You can tell her yourself. Madi must have put too much lavender in the tea. A sip of Flourisher's Fate and you will be your right size again. You'll see."

But I don't believe my own assurances.

We make it through one wicket before Jack sends another reminder.

Five minutes.

We'll never finish.

I stop, setting an ever-shrinking Willow down gently. I nearly collapse as I use the timeout I didn't think I'd need.

"Charlotte?" I whisper, my voice hoarse. "Charlotte, I need you."

"I'm here," she says in my ear. "The countdown and all teams will be paused until the timeout ends."

I nod, though she can't see me. I swallow. "Something's happened to Willow. I think"—I can hardly get the words out—"the Dwindler's Draught we drank was . . . something was wrong with it."

"Have *you* stopped shrinking?" Charlotte asks, concerned.

I consider my arms. My legs. The small sound of my voice. "I think so." My heart sinks a little. "Could it be . . . maybe because I'm part Normal, it doesn't affect me as quickly?"

"It's possible," she says. "Your Normalcy may just be your lifeline right now."

"We're not going to make it," I tell her. "We're going to lose the Diamond Trial. I shouldn't have trusted Madi. I shouldn't have—"

"What do you mean?" Charlotte interrupts. "What's wrong with Madi?"

"I think"—my voice is hushed though I don't know how anyone could hear me from all the way down here—"I think Madi has . . ." How do I say this? "I think she's betrayed us. I saw this article last night," my words come faster. "It said Stark went missing last year, but she never mentioned it. Charlotte, I don't feel so well—"

"Alice, listen to me," Charlotte says abruptly. "I want you to take Willow. Forget about the Trial. Forget about making it back to the starting stake. You take Willow and you wait. Understand?"

"But what about the others? And Chess? He's in the Normal Reality. I can't contact him."

"I'll take care of it."

"But, Char—"

"*Wait.*" Her fear, anger, and frustration are all clear in that one word.

I don't know how much longer the timeout will last. I don't even have to hide Willow. She fits into the palm of my hand now. Her tiny eyes are closed, and I can barely make out the whisper of her breathing against my skin.

There's nowhere to go or hide or wait, and then it's there, a single tiger lily growing from the ground before me. It bends low, scooping us up with its curling petals like a mother cradling her child.

Or a sister protecting her sister. Or Sophia growing this flower to protect her best friend. Sometimes family isn't the one you're born with.

It's the one you find. Or the ones who find you.

All I can do now is curl into a ball at the lily's heart, hold Willow against my own, and sob under the canopy of orange.

I have failed her.

I have failed us all.

TRUTH

When I open my eyes, I don't know how long I've been out. Hours? Days?

Weeks? Oh no, what if I've been out for *weeks*?

My throat burns. I reach towards my face and feel for my glasses, already knowing I won't find them where they belong.

"Will—" I smack my lips and swallow and attempt to call out for her again. "Willow." It's a rasp, but it's there. Small and weak and helpless.

Just like me. I couldn't help her before she shrank into nothing.

"She's stirring," a whispering male voice says from somewhere in the room, though it sounds miles away.

"Let her sleep," another voice—distinctly Dinah's soulful tone—replies. "The Diamond Trial took quite the toll."

"You can say that again," another male voice says, familiar but not enough to name him.

I despise being talked about rather than talked to. My effort to move is futile. Instead I reach out, hoping to find a nightstand or a stool with my glasses resting on top. My clammy palm glides over smooth, cool wood and knocks the side of what must be a lamp, then finds what feels like an analog alarm clock.

No glasses.

The world around me is a halo of light and shadow. I haven't had this much trouble with my vision since entering Wonderland. The headaches. The waves of nausea. The dizziness. All have been absent. I hardly knew my glasses were on. Now I feel as if I've stepped behind a gossamer veil, unable to see things as they truly are.

Or as Queen Scarlet wants me to see them. It's hard to know what's real and what isn't these days.

Channeling every ounce of energy I have, I sit upright. I try opening my eyes wider, but it does nothing to stop the blurred canvas of colour before me. Red mingles with orange. Blue bounces off purple. Black swirls around spots of white.

"Dinah," I croak. My legs are tangled in a mess of sheets and covers, and I can't get them free. The back of my head hits something hard. A wall? A headboard? The disorientation stings, making me want to cry. I feel the familiar sensation in my chest, creeping its way up the path of my throat.

Then a warm hand covers mine.

My almost-sob turns into a relieved gulp—I recognise the touch immediately.

"Chess." His name is oxygen. I hold fast to his hand. "Chess, where is Willow? Where are we?"

He responds by placing my glasses gently over my eyes.

I allow a tear to fall as everything shifts into focus. A shabby room with maroon carpet and yellowed walls. The curtains are drawn, and only harsh lamplight illuminates the space, shadows waging war against its ailing glow. No vibrance. No life. Plain and predictable. And all too commonplace.

"We're in the Normal Reality." My voice is hollow. "Aren't we?"

Chess's flatline expression speaks volumes. He doesn't explain, allowing me a moment to collect what I mean to say.

I stare at our entwined hands. So much has changed. So much left unspoken. "And . . . Charlotte?" Do I want to know?

"Still in Wonderland . . ." He retrieves a glass of water from the nightstand and offers it to me. "Considering what happened with the tea Madi gave you, we thought this would be the safest place for now."

"What about Charlotte?" I persist. "And the others? Jack and Sophia and Knave."

"Oh, they will be fine." Dinah appears from around the corner of the doorway, paint chipping at the edges of the forest-green frame. She carries a small tray holding a steaming cup of hot something or other on top. "Don't you worry your head about them."

That's the trouble. It's not my head that's worried. I try to suppress the dull ache inside. I watch guardedly as Dinah nears, hating that I'm suspicious of everyone, but deeming it a necessary evil all the same. "What aren't you telling me, Dinah? I want the truth."

She sets the tray on the bed beside me, her orange-and-white hair more unkempt than I've ever seen it. When she sits on the bed's edge, it's not difficult to imagine her as a cat. Graceful. Nose turned up high. A constant air of superiority about her.

I take a long drink of cold water, wincing against the burn.

"We have never lied to you," Dinah informs me. "However . . ."

Of course there is a *however.*

". . . we may have withheld certain details that were not pertinent until now."

I glance at Chess, but his expression gives nothing away. Either he was in on the withholding, or this is news to him too.

"We?" he asks his grandmother. "Try again. And, please, do not involve me unless I am, as it were, involved."

There's something about his familiar and confusing sentence that sends a sense of calm and comfort through me. Ordinary in its own unordinary way.

"Fine, fine." Dinah sighs, tugging at her high-necked lace collar. "The Knights withheld certain details." She fidgets with the broach pinned to her dress, the onyx stone at the centre absorbing any light that hits it.

That's why Scarlet's bangle stone was familiar. The stone is a part of Wonderland's coat of arms as well. Could there be a connection? Does it matter? I make a mental note at the same moment Chess responds.

"Better." He folds his arms across his chest and waits.

But I'm getting more bewildered. "I thought you were part of the Knight Society too?"

"He is." Raving Hatter has appeared at the doorway. "But he's new." The way he glares at Chess, something tells me they're not too chummy. "And still underage."

The steam from the soup cup warms my face, a welcome distraction. I inhale its warmth, the scent of bacon and peas and black pepper. It's just like the London Particular soup Charlotte and I used to eat at the Foundling House. In a small, strange way, it smells like home.

I guess Normal isn't always so bad.

"The Society had hoped by getting you into the Trials as a Wildflower," Dinah says, "that everything would fall into place on its own. Charlotte was against it at first. We took matters into our own hands, and she didn't have a choice."

I glance between her and Raving, then over at Chess. Clearly, not everyone here is on the same page.

Chess's eyes flash. "You told me Charlotte had agreed to

Ace's invite. You said it only aided in our cause to find Kit and Stark and the others." The pain jading his voice is clear.

She fooled him too. Yet his knowledge of Stark's status stings. Am I the only one who didn't know he's been missing?

"She did agree." Dinah moves a shoulder, and the lace at her collar tickles her jaw. "After some convincing. We had her removed from the picture for a time so we could put our plan into place."

Even Raving seems startled by this news. His body tenses. Now his glare is aimed at Dinah. "You reported Charlee to the Normal authorities, didn't you?"

"Don't give me that look, Mr. Hatter. Blanche agreed that, while the decision was a risky one, it was the only way to ensure Alice made it into Wonderland and the Trials."

"Risky?" Raving's voice rises an octave. "Charlotte was Registered. You know what they do to Registered Wonders. They mess with their minds, making it so they can't enter Wonderland at all."

"Charlotte knew the dangers of joining the Knight Society, young man. We all did."

"And yet those dangers and risks have brought us no closer to finding my brother." Chess's anger at being lied to by his own grandmother manifests in his furious tones.

"Or mine," Raving adds.

"Do you think I do not wish to find them as well?" Dinah asks. She's the only one remaining calm.

"I don't know what I think anymore," is Chess's sharp reply.

I stir my soup with a spoon as they argue, watching the broth swirl around and around. The broth is cooling, but I am boiling. "Let me get this straight."

Three sets of eyes turn to me.

"Charlotte didn't want me to know about Wonderland or enter the Trials. You decided to go over her head and get me there anyway, giving her no choice but to accept a position as Team Heart Trainer. Am I on track so far?"

Dinah is silent but gives no indication that she rebuts my claims.

So I continue.

"Chess didn't know about this, and, apparently, neither did you." I give Raving a pointed look. "So it would appear the Knight Society is less society and more Dinah acting of her own volition. Do I have that in order?"

Dinah rises and crosses to the covered window, hands clasped behind her back. "Let's not forget about Blanche," she remarks. "She agreed it was the best option to further our cause, which has always been and remains to be finding the Ivory King and the real Wonderland. The Wonderland no Gene could concoct. That no mind, aside from the king's, could fathom." She turns back towards us. "In any strategy, sometimes you have to make a move that leaves your other pieces vulnerable for the good of your end goal—take down the queen and save the king."

Sounds like the opposite of Black Hearts, really.

"Except that end goal could have taken Charlee from us for good," Raving says. "I've already had to live the last ten years hardly seeing her at all."

"Calm down," Dinah says, unsympathetic. "There was no harm done in the end. Charlotte is fine. Team Heart is ahead in the Trials. We've made excellent progress."

Frustration overtakes me again. "You still haven't explained why I had to be the one to enter the Trials. So what if I'm part Normal and part Wonder. Why does that matter?"

Chess's expression says he'd like that answer too. "You told me Alice was the key. To finding Kit."

"That part was true," Dinah says. "She is the key." She pivots towards the mirror opposite the foot of my bed. Her eyes meet mine in the reflection.

"I assume there is another 'however'?"

"There is. However." She rubs a hand down the side of her face. "Remember that Charlotte never actually entered the Fourth Trial? She was given a task by Pillar. The task was to hide you."

Raving could be a statue for how still he stands.

"Charlotte took Alice to hide her identity from Scarlet. Which means who she is . . . is everything." Dinah sounds as if this is a mere transaction of words and not a situation that involves actual lives. "Someone Normal oughtn't be able to see Wonderland. There is no becoming a Wonder. But Alice has. Because she believed. Perhaps that has been the key to finding the Ivory King all along."

A spoonful of broth burns my tongue as I take in this news.

I swallow and catch my reflection in the mirror across from the bed. It sparks a memory. "The Hall of Mirrors," I say slowly. "Madi acted so strangely the night of the First Trial, in the final room. We were all a bit shaken, honestly. The mirrors showed us what we all feared most. But . . . Madi never said." I look at Raving.

He's staring off into the distance. His exhale preludes his heartbreaking tale. "Last June, Stark's disappearance shook us all. Madi took it the hardest. She became obsessed with entering the Trials herself so she could learn what happened to him."

I think back on the episodes I've listened to on Madi's podcast. How she always talked about the Trials with such reverence.

"She knew about the Knight Society," Raving says. "She wanted to join when she was old enough."

That sounds like the Madi I thought I knew. Always taking charge. A force to be reckoned with.

"But . . ." Raving hesitates. "When Stark didn't return . . ." There's no mistaking the heaviness in his voice. "It's like I lost my sister too. All she cared about was finding him—no matter the cost."

This still doesn't explain her motive for trying to poison Willow and me. It doesn't fit. If she wanted to finish the Trials and find Stark, she would not have sabotaged our chances.

I think back to that day on the train. When I met Blanche and my world turned on its end. Something Madi said on her podcast seemed like it didn't quite fit. She'd mentioned giving up Normalcy and talked about how returning to this Reality would most likely lead to being Registered and alone.

But she mentioned something else too.

I like to believe there's always a way home, if you wish to find it.

"A way home." I can hardly contain my excitement. "What if Madi was talking to Stark? Communicating with him somehow through her podcast?" I repeat what Madi said. They look at one another.

"Interesting theory," Dinah muses.

"How does that explain what happened during the Diamond Trial, though?" Raving's question is a valid one. One for which I don't have an answer.

I set my soup aside and swing my legs over the edge of the bed. I'm still in my Team Heart suit, though it seems rather plain without the ice plant rose pattern or the cool effects created by the WV.

"What if Madi found a way to contact Stark?" I say again, the wheels in my mind at full speed ahead. "And he was able to contact her as well?"

Chess runs a hand through his hair. "Are you saying Stark told her to sabotage the Trials?"

I try to stand, but dizziness overtakes me. Instead I sit on the bed and take another sip of water. "Maybe he knows something we don't. I mean, we know the Fourth Trial is dangerous, but if Stark found the real Wonderland and the Ivory King, maybe it's not what we think. And maybe he's trying to communicate that somehow."

Raving's face reveals conflicting emotions.

I don't blame him. If it's true, Madi kept this from him.

"Well done, Alice," Dinah pronounces. She peeks through the curtains, and a blade of light breaks through the window, piercing the blood-orange carpet.

The small illumination produces a newfound epiphany. "We know the Heart Trial is always the same—facing the Jabberwock. It takes on different forms, based on one's fears. It's a reflection of the deepest, darkest parts of one's soul. Same as the mirrors."

Chess pounces on this. "I saw Kit in the mirror. You saw Charlotte. We saw what we feared losing most. What do you think Queen Scarlet sees? What is she afraid of losing?"

I think for a moment. "The crown," I realise. "But even more, she's afraid Wonders will find out the truth."

"Truth is a formidable weapon." Dinah places one hand on her grandson's shoulder. "Fear causes people to act in the oddest of ways. And hunger for power sends one to a breaking point. Given enough of the two, a person is likely to go mad."

"Is that what's happened to Scarlet? She's gone mad?" My emotions are in turmoil. It's her fault my mother was forced to flee and leave me behind. How could the Queen of Hearts be so . . . heartless?

"Possibly . . ." Dinah peers through the curtain once more. "There's only one way to find out the truth for sure."

I know what it is before she can say it. "We have to get back to the Wonderland Reality. If we can make it to the Fourth Trial, since we know what to expect, maybe we can face our fears, even overcome them."

And if so?

Maybe we can find Kit and Stark and the Ivory King himself.

Perhaps we can, at long last, go home.

DARE

It takes a few days to get back on my feet. Dinah comes and goes from the rundown Victorian-terraced house on London's East End. She brings food. Newspapers. Supplies.

Chess waits on me hand and foot. It would be almost annoying if he wasn't so endearing about the whole thing.

Raving has returned to Wonderland to report to Charlotte and keep an eye on his sister. He isn't sure what to believe about the poisoned tea, but he's promised to keep an open mind.

I ask about Willow. The answer is forever the same.

"It's like we said," Dinah sighs, setting down a tray of bangers and mash by my bed. "She didn't arrive with you when you fell back into this reality. We don't know where she is."

Although Charlotte gave me specific instructions to hide and wait, I don't remember anything between holding an ever-shrinking Willow during the timeout and arriving here.

"I'm trying to find out, Ace," Chess tells me one evening as we play a card game of Palace. "But no one knows where she is. Charlotte returned with you and went back to Wonderland immediately. Willow is either still in Wonderland or . . ." He plays a two, resetting the discard pile.

He doesn't finish. We both know the answer. If Willow isn't in Wonderland, she might be nowhere at all. I stare at the two of hearts card between us. I can't decide which is worse. The reminder of what we've lost or the broken expression on Chess's face.

Neither brings back Willow.

Once I'm strong enough to walk around outside, Dinah lets me know she has an alternative theory. One we'll have to test upon our return to Wonderland.

"It's a theory, of course," she says, offering her elbow as we stroll up the lane during late afternoon. "With every theory comes a gamble."

"It's a gamble I'm willing to take, if it helps us right a wrong," I say, determination to walk on my own fuelling every weak step.

After a week has passed, I'm fully recovered. Physically, anyway. I'm glad to at last be out of that drafty old house for more than an hour. Ready to return to Wonderland. Our team needs us. We can't abandon them now.

I've decided to convince both Chess and Dinah that hiding isn't the answer. Right after Chess returns to our booth with some ice-cold drinks.

"Think of it like this." Dinah begins to draw on a paper serviette as we sit at the local café.

It's the same place we met the night Charlotte returned to Wonderland, yet so completely different. It's smaller, for one. Worse for the wear. The subtle scents of burned coffee and sanitiser attempt to overpower one another. A dish drops. A hunched man in one corner grumbles at his waitress for spilling water. It isn't exactly the type of establishment you'd choose if you had another option.

And, while I could see hints of this version while in the Wonderland Reality, I get no sense of Wonder anything now. Funny how you don't miss something until it's gone. I took my glitching for granted. Popping in and out of the Reality I came from without knowing it for ten years. I long for a whiff of that world. The smallest headache or dizzy spell to remind me it's not totally lost.

Dinah turns the serviette towards me on the table. She's separated the white square into three sections with two vertical lines. "This is us." She points to the leftmost section with the tip of her pen, writing an N for Normal at the centre. "Think of this line here as a two-way looking glass. We see a reflection of the world around us. But on the other side"—she moves her pen tip to the middle section, writing a W—"we can see both worlds—Scarlet's Wonderland and the Normal Reality."

Chess joins us, balancing three clear cups in his hands.

I slide over on the booth seat. When he sits beside me, our arms brush.

Neither of us moves away from the other.

"What did I miss?" Chess asks, either not at all affected by the arm-brushing situation or rather skilled at hiding it. He produces three straws from his waistcoat pocket, dropping them on the table like confetti, giving me a glimpse of the fun and fancy-free boy I fell in—

I stop the thought before it forms fully. So not the time or place for that upside-down conundrum.

"Everything." I take a cup in my hands. Condensation beads drip down the sides, and the dark liquid within is anything but appetizing. Iced coffee has never been my favourite, though I know it will be the pick-me-up I need. Who'd have ever thought I would miss the topsy-turvy effects of tea?

"Well," Chess says, raising his cup, "start at the beginning." He taps his cup to mine and then Dinah's across the table. In the last few days, he's softened towards her again. It's good to see him smile. "And when you get to the end," he adds, "stop." He sits back.

His arm is now pressed firmly against mine. There's no mistaking it for an accident this time.

Hopefully the chill from my coffee will work as an antidote to my increasing warmth.

Dinah quickly reviews the two-way looking-glass scenario.

"What's this third section?" Chess taps the rightmost area of the serviette.

Dinah draws a question mark inside the final space. "Given what we know, we can guess that this would be the true Wonderland. Another world on the opposite side of a two-way looking glass."

I'm trying to wrap my mind around the idea. "So those in this third Reality can see us, but we can't see them?" Weeks ago I would have said such a thing was impossible. Now I know better.

"Precisely my speculation." Dinah pauses to take her own sip of iced coffee.

I trace back through my own research, recalling the faces of those who've gone missing.

Dinah flips the serviette over and marks the square in half this time, a single horizontal line from one corner to another. "We have been told since the Divide that there are only those with the Wonder Gene and the Normals without it." In the top triangle she writes a *W*, and in the bottom one she writes an *N*. "But what about Alice?"

"She's both." Chess pulls the serviette towards him.

"We've been over this," I say. "We've let fear rule us—divide us—for so long we've forgotten we are all part of the same team. Wonders. Normals. Everyone." I think of Charlotte. How she was so desperate to remove me from Wonderland and hide me from a power-hungry queen. "We think Scarlet is afraid of the truth. But what if it's the opposite? What if Scarlet just wants to go home too?"

"Now that's an interesting theory." Dinah cuts through my spiral like a dealer with a pack of cards. "It's a possibility."

"Maybe she's afraid of being alone," I offer.

"She never did have children of her own," Dinah ponders. "She never let anyone get close. There's an old tale . . . no . . . never mind. It's just a children's story."

"What?" I say, not willing to let anything pass at this point. "Tell us."

Dinah clears her throat and begins. Her voice is singsong and like a calming purr. "Once upon a time, there was a king who longed for a bride to call his own. He searched far and wide for the perfect companion. At last he came upon the girl he had been waiting for, one loyal, fair, and true. He asked her to come away with him and be his bride. She agreed, and the two lived quite happily for some time."

I'm on the edge of my seat, hanging on Dinah's every word.

"But, eventually, the bride became jealous of the king. She wanted what he had. His creation. His power. He told her that everything he had was hers to share and enjoy. But it wasn't enough for her. She turned on him, rejecting his love."

It's just a story. I shouldn't be emotional. Why, then, does my throat feel so tight?

"Her rejection broke the king," Dinah continues. "Soon his perfect love for her became what she most feared. The bride's fear grew into an untamable monster. One that nearly destroyed her."

There's no doubt Dinah is talking about Scarlet. The red Queen of Hearts and the Ivory King, the true creator of Wonderland.

"The bride left to find her own way. Eventually she regretted her decision. She tried to find her way back to the king."

Our Club Trial clue comes to mind. *All ways are her ways.*

"But she never could," Dinah explains. "Thus she remained forever lost in a world of her own. Legend has it she cried so hard and so long that day, the flood of her broken heart flowed into what we now call the Pool of Tears. Once a year, on the first day of summer, it's a tradition for Wonders to visit the Pool and leave a flower in memory of a loved one lost."

The story ends, and an extended silence passes among us as we sit there. When our drinks are nothing but melting ice and the morning crowd has cleared out, making way for the lunch crew, I offer a simple solution.

"So we find what she couldn't."

Both Dinah and Chess dart me a questioning look.

"If Stark and Dan and Kit and the other players could do it," I say, "so can we. We find the way. But not Scarlet's way. We find the way of the king. We can make it through the Fourth Trial. But not for fame or glory or for hope of claiming the crown. We do it for the sole purpose of revealing the truth for every Wonder or Normal who wishes to hear it."

Chess sits straight.

Dinah purses her lips together. "You know," she says thoughtfully. "It might work."

"You're forgetting one vital detail," Chess counters. "We have no idea how to do it. Last year, the Fourth Trial was a nightmare beyond anything I can describe. I got out just before . . ." He doesn't elaborate. "We still have the Third Trial to finish before we get there."

"That's more than one detail," I say lightly, giving him a playful wink.

I know Chess is only trying to reason. He'd do anything to get his brother back, even if it means entering the unknown. He rests both elbows on the table and nods. "I'm in." There's resolve in his tone. And something else too.

Hope.

He moves to stand, then offers to help me up.

Placing my hand in his, I rise.

Dinah beams at us both. "I guess there's only one thing left to do."

I keep my hand in Chess's as I turn to face Dinah.

"We have to get you two back to Wonderland. But, Alice, I must warn you. Being faced with your greatest fear changes you. And to overcome it? There's a reason Scarlet hasn't been able to find her way back."

I know there are risks. I know facing my own nightmares is dangerous. But I also know this has to work. For Kit. And Stark.

And every player who has braved the dangers before us.

Besides, unlike Scarlet, I won't be alone. I smile at them both.

Chess's eyes twinkle, and he pulls our clasped hands to his lips and plants a kiss on my knuckles that dissolves every doubt.

Love has a way of driving out fear.

Maybe the king's love is powerful enough to save us all.

TOGETHER

We've still another riddle yet to solve—what happened to Willow?

We know she didn't enter the Normal Reality with me. Dinah has a hunch she may have been taken to the Wonderland hospital.

"It's a hunch of course," Dinah said, "but I've learned over the years to never leave any lead unturned."

It's a small spark of hope, but I'll take it.

Our trio turns one corner then another. And another. It's said one good turn deserves another, but this is ridiculous.

"Right here will do," Dinah says, bringing our undercover midnight walk to an abrupt halt.

On a first look, our surroundings make me want to run all the way back to the sad little house where I awoke. "What part of London is this?" We've taken so many turns down dodgy alleyways and dark avenues, I can hardly tell south from north, let alone east from west from Wonderland. This street is neither warm nor welcoming.

"Whitechapel. Or it was." Dinah pauses. "It's a discreet area where we are unlikely to be noticed. And, if my theory is correct, where Willow is likely to be found on the other side." Moving once again, Dinah seems to decide this is indeed the correct location.

Just ahead, an enormous, ramshackle building practically forbids us to enter. The ancient brown bricks look as if they might crumble at any moment. Near the A-frame roof, what must have once been a clock watches us. Frozen in time, the only parts that remain are the minute hand and the Roman numerals III and IX. Boards imprison every arching window. Rusted letters with their innards missing add to the anti-ambiance of this place.

T E RO L L N ON H PIT L

My attempt to unscramble them proves futile. If we were in Wonderland, my WV would do the unscrambling for me.

Chess leans in and whispers, "The Royal London Hospital." His tone matches the mood perfectly and sends shivers up my spine.

Dinah leads us up a set of cracked steps and through an archway.

This is—was—a hospital? It feels more like a prison. I rub my bare arms, wishing I'd worn another layer over my short sleeves.

"We'll enter here, and no one will be any wiser as to where you two have been or why," Dinah says. "Charlotte's been covering for you."

Chess quickens his pace to get ahead of us both and opens a door scarcely hanging on its hinges. The door whines in protest, but Chess ignores its complaints. "After you." He dips in a little bow.

I commit to memory this image of him in the cool moonlight that accentuates his contrasting features. Sharp jaw. Soft, shaggy hair tinged with pink. Angled sideburns. Crooked nose. I don't need Wonder Vision to store this moment away. It's all mine. Saved. Downloaded. Locked.

Dinah clears her throat.

The rough, out-of-place sound alerts me that I've just been standing here on the threshold, staring at Chess like a silly dodo bird.

"Alright, Ace?"

I skirt past him, embarrassed. "Alright."

"As for me," Dinah remarks, "I'll be leaving you here. I need to meet with Blanche and fill her in. The Club Trial is two weeks away. We all need to be prepared."

Now that we're inside the abandoned and forgotten building, the urge to turn back is near overwhelming. This is all rather strange and perhaps even a bit dodgier than those dark alleyways, which seem perfectly safe now.

I internally scold myself for the notion.

Chess slides his hand into mine, and I regain the assurance I felt this morning at the café.

We're all a part of the same team.

"This will do." Taking a few strides ahead of us, Dinah pauses, pivots, and perks both cheeks. "I'll see you on the other side." In less time than it takes to blink, she disappears.

I suppose years of practice make the impossible as commonplace to her as a rainbow after the rain.

And, like that rainbow—which really isn't commonplace at all—Wonderland waits on the other side of the cloud of doubt fogging my mind.

I attempt to create space between myself and this boy I haven't been alone with—not like this, anyway—since I realised

I no longer see him as merely a friend. A familiar feeling takes root, begging to sprout. But, rather than shove it down like all the other times, I allow it to bud. Its vines curl around the walls of my heart.

"Remember, Ace." Chess draws me in. Not a command. An invitation.

I accept it. Our entwined hands are trapped between us, and I can just make out the outline of his face in the shadows.

"Nothing is impossible." Our synced heartbeats pulse through our joined hands. He looks into my eyes. "Are you ready?"

Why do I get the feeling this question could have more than one answer?

As if he knows I need to hear it, Chess says, "I'm not leaving without you this time." His face is centimetres away. Is he moving closer? Or am I? "Whenever you're ready," he adds.

Now I'm certain he's asking something else entirely.

And for this, I am ready too.

I lean into him. Soak in his warmth as he startles. We share a laugh in the same breath.

Then he draws me into a full embrace. He smells like home and Christmas holiday, and I don't want him to let go.

I tilt my head back. His eyes are trained on me. Even in the dim light, their colour is striking. Our noses touch, exploring this new space where I never thought I'd find myself and am quite glad to have stumbled into. My one regret is that I didn't find the key to this door sooner.

With the greatest care, he kisses me. Or maybe I kiss him. Whoever started it, neither of us objects. It's not long or particularly grand. It is simple and straightforward and honest and ours. And when the moment is over, I wish there was a way to turn back time and have that first kiss again.

And again.

And again.

"I knew you'd warm up to me eventually," Chess says, brushing my cheekbone with his thumb.

I give a whole-heart smile. "You're a right know-it-all," I tease, though somehow I don't mind that as much as I used to.

"And you're as stubborn as they come." He kisses my hand, then twirls me around in the shortest dance ever choreographed. "As much as I'd like to stay," Chess sighs, "we really ought to go."

"Which way?" I ask.

"That depends."

"On what?"

"On where you want to get to."

At that I close my eyes and picture where with every fibre. "Wonderland."

And, together, we're gone.

The first sense that registers the change is my sense of smell. And the aroma that reaches me is not at all what I expect. In my experience, Wonderland is sweet and sticky and warm. Like melted butter. Cinnamon rolls in winter. Or a rice bag warming my toes.

Not this, though. This is . . . sterile. Plastic. Manufactured.

Charlotte once tended my scraped knee as a child. With a glass eye dropper I could have sworn was a weapon, she put this awful orange stuff on the wound to clean it. I didn't know what it was, but I knew I never wanted it near me again.

This is like that, but stronger. My nose wrinkles, and I breathe through my mouth. This only serves to put a taste of all unpleasant things on my tongue.

The next thing I take in are the sounds. Phones ringing and wheels squeaking and the faint *beep, beep, beep* that signals life. Someone clicks a pen nearby. The nervous tick sends a shot of irked nerves up my spine.

This is a hospital. Have I been in a hospital before? Yes. Once. Though I've tried to erase the painful memory from my mind. Opening my eyes confirms the location. Gone are the dilapidated walls and unfortunate state of an iffy old building long forgotten. In its place climb high ceilings with skylights and walls painted with colourful stripes and shapes and polka dots.

"A children's hospital?"

As soon as the words leave my mouth, the words *Wonderland Children's Hospital* scroll across my WV. The sight isn't jarring like the first time it happened. Still, the band on my wrist feels less welcome. Information uploads and a map option blinks in the top left corner.

"We're on the fourth floor," I say. But rather than Cancer Wing or Intensive Care Unit, this floor appears to specialise in . . . "Common Creature Bites?"

"Bloodhounds, Mock Turtles, Twinkle Bats, Borogroves, Caterpillars . . ." Chess says, as if this is a list of completely common creatures.

"But," I argue in a hushed tone, feeling an unexplainable need to keep quiet, "caterpillars don't bite." I half laugh the sentence. I know he's going to say something to refute the idea. He can't help himself.

"Don't they?" he replies with a smirk. He squeezes my hand. "Follow my lead."

He seems to have the same floorplan that I do in his WV. He doesn't hesitate as he makes each turn through the brightly coloured halls. Left, right, left again. Down a flight of stairs. Up another. When we find ourselves in a quiet hall of doors, my stomach drops. I plant my feet. Refuse to budge when Chess tugs gently on my hand.

"It's just a hallway, Ace," he says.

Just. There's that word. If I've learned anything recently it's that our dreams—and nightmares alike—are *just* as real as anything else. Perhaps even more so. Anything we imagine is possible, true. But not every imagination has good intentions.

Exhibit A—Queen Scarlet.

I take a deep breath as we step forwards. Each door we pass hosts a small, round window nestled about shoulder height. A peek through the frosted glass reveals exactly nothing. If it weren't for my WV, I'd never know these doors lead to closets, storage rooms, and empty spaces yet to be discovered or decorated by curious little minds. My WV tells me this area is simply called *Extra*. I wonder what it might look like with more colour, and immediately the door nearest to us changes from plain white to a vibrant coral.

Despite the added flare, the place feels eerie. Too much like the hall of doors in my nightmare. I rub my arms to ward off a chill.

"This one." Chess points to one of the doors.

None of them have knobs.

That is, until Chess touches it. At the tips of his fingers, a brass handle appears. He opens the door easily. "After you."

When I step inside, I'm a bit disgruntled to find absolutely—

"Nothing," I say. "There's nothing in here."

"I'm disappointed, Ace. Seems your bout with near nonexistence has turned you into a skeptic." He snaps his fingers, ever the dramatic one, and a coatrack appears. On it, two crisp white doctor's coats hang.

"Come on then." Chess shrugs into one and offers me the other. "Let's get this duet on the road. We have to stop wasting time before it has the chance to waste us."

"Right."

He pretends to straighten a tie that isn't there. "Doctor S. Chessterton at your service." His voice has dropped an octave, and he actually sounds serious for a change.

"Chessterton?" I give him a furrowed look as I slip my arms into the too-big sleeves. I feel oddly older in this moment. Confident too. "And, Dr. Chessterton, what exactly is the point of this little game of pretend? Shouldn't we be looking for Willow?"

"You read my mind. That's exactly what we are doing. The others have believed you've been in hospital this entire week recovering. Charlotte's been keeping an eye on Hatter. So far, she hasn't made any other moves that would lead Charlotte to believe she's dangerous."

His abrupt assertion jars me, to say the least. "She tried to shrink us into oblivion," I protest, waving my arms around like a petulant child. "Of *course* she's dangerous."

He sighs. Begins again. "It could have been an honest mistake. Willow is smaller than you. Hatter could have calculated the measurements wrong."

"Or she could have calculated it exactly as she intended," I point out. "We've already talked about this. She's an imposter."

"*Or*"—Chess is fixing my upturned collar—"someone wanted you to believe she intended to harm you and Willow. Remember how Knave behaved during the First Trial? Something was odd about him. He was almost—"

"—mad," I finish for him. Is it really possible that someone didn't want me to trust my teammates? My friends? My family?

When I discovered Charlotte had lied to me, devastation, hurt, and anger took root. Thankfully, our bond was too strong to be severed for long.

I didn't trust Chess from the moment we met. Only time bridged that chasm.

Willow's position on the team was taken from her and given to me, so we started out as enemies.

Knave was suspicious from the outset. His poor attitude and piercing glare were not to be trifled with. Then there was his outlash during the First Trial.

And Madi. We'd been getting to know one another again when I found that article and learned Stark had been missing. Then she up and ruins everything with her poisonous tea.

My trust has been sabotaged at every single solitary turn. It's downright infuriating.

Someone either wants me exhausted. Or they want me to feel isolated. Alone.

Just like the queen.

"You in there, Ace?" Chess waves a hand in front of my eyes.

"Dinah." Her name creeps out, tasting of lies. "She orchestrated all of this. She—and you—" I look at Chess and take a step backwards. "You helped her." The words nearly strangle me. I touch my lips. Betrayal lingers there in his kiss.

"Ace." His voice sounds shaken. "Alice, you're not thinking straight. You know you can trust me. You know—"

"Do I?" Another step back. Away from him. "Because it seems to me that all of this started the minute you stepped into my life. Charlotte is taken, and then what? You honestly want me to believe you didn't know Dinah reported her? After Charlotte told her no. Really, I was never supposed to be here at all."

"You were always supposed to be here." He's trying hard to be convincing but doesn't attempt to come near. "You were always supposed to be with me."

"That's a line if I've ever heard one." I hate my words and my doubt and my traitor tears. "Dinah reported Charlotte to the authorities. She admitted it."

His jaw is tight. "Yes, but we've been through this. I had no idea that was her or Blanche's plan. If I'd known, I would have tried to suggest an alternative. You know this. You know *me*."

"No," I shoot back. "I don't. Not really." The realisation dawns like a dreary winter morning. Cold and bleak and lacking light. "I've seen the parts you want me to see."

Chess's expression is disconcerted. "Ace, you're afraid. We both are. But don't shut me out again."

I sniff and wipe at my nose. "Thinking logically and shutting you out are not the same thing."

"Your head has always been the problem."

"What's that supposed to mean?"

"It means you're so busy thinking everyone is against you, you've forgotten who is for you. We're a team, remember? However we come out of this, we will do it together."

I lift my eyes to meet Chess's intense turquoise ones. "Did you know Willow was alive? When I asked? Because I did ask you and Dinah and neither of you seemed to have an answer. How is it Dinah happens to decide today that she might know where Willow is?"

"Why would I lie to you?" Chess jams both hands in his pockets, never breaking eye contact.

"Seems to run in the family."

"That's low, Ace."

"Why would you lie to me? Maybe you're an imposter too."

"And maybe you are," he counters. "If you refuse to trust anyone, you'll never get the chance to find out."

His words bite. Probably because they're true. Or maybe because he wants me to believe they are. "Leave me alone, Shire. I can find Willow on my own."

He jerks as if he's been stung. Darkness coats his next question. "It's Shire now, is it? Same as everyone else?"

"That's your name, isn't it?"

"Yeah," he says bitterly. "I guess so."

Unsaid apologies and too many hurt feelings hang in the air between us.

So I open the door.

Not bothering to glance back.

And leave Chess behind.

APART

Despite the guidance my WV provides, my abhorrent sense of direction does me in. What's the use of having the Wonder Gene if I can't find my way around an imaginary building?

Willow is here somewhere. I need only find the right floor.

Darn you, Chess. Just when I was certain you were one of the last few I could trust. Whatever. Who needs him, anyway?

Apparently, I do. With every stair flight or corridor, a new one seems to pop up on the floor plan in my view.

"That can't be right," I tell my WV as if it can hear me. "I could have sworn that hallway wasn't there a moment ago."

But, as my clear Wonder eyesight reveals, the map alters again. New rooms appear and old ones vanish. Now I'm sure these walls are mocking me. Pointing their brightly painted petals and curvy stems and laughing. I can almost hear the flowers in that garden mural straight ahead of me now.

"What do you think of that Wildflower?" the dandelion titters.

"Wildflower?" the tiger lily scoffs. "She looks more like a weed to me."

Weed. That's what Willow called me the first time we met. Now I really am losing it. Where's Sophia when I need her? At least she wouldn't think my flower hallucinations are crazy. Or maybe she would.

Frustrated, I stop, turn, and lean against the garden mural, knocking my head back against a rather large daisy.

Someone clears her throat nearby.

I nearly jump out of my skin. But when I open my eyes, my heart rate slows to semi-normal. It's not the daisy talking to me, but a woman dressed in white scrubs. Her oval glasses remind me of eggs, as does the cracked alabaster foundation covering her face. At least three shades lighter than the skin on her neck, I might add.

"Tut, tut. Don't you have someplace to be, young lady?" She clicks a pen, and I immediately recognise her as the person with the irritable tick from earlier.

"Pardon?" I push off from the wall, straightening my lab coat. Doing my best to look official.

"You're expected any moment now, are you not?" Her impatience is penetrating. Seeing right through my dress-up facade.

I squirm where I stand. My doctor's coat now appears to be a beacon, drawing her scrutiny. "Uh . . . I don't understand what you mean?"

"I mean exactly what I choose, neither more nor less. And the moral of that is, be what you would seem to be. If I say you are expected at any moment, you are. Do I make myself clear?"

Not even a sly trick, it seems, will get me out of this one.

"Well, get on with it." Clicking her pen yet again, then tapping it once on her sharp chin, she eyes me until I move one foot in front of the other. "Time is of the essence. Don't doddle now. Forever is only as long as a second, you know."

I must look like I have no idea which way I ought to go because she gives such an exhaustive sigh that I'm sure it can be heard from another floor. Maybe even another Reality.

"Didn't anyone explain it to you?"

She must be referring to the map. I shake my head.

"It's perfectly simple. There are ten floors. Each floor has five levels. The stairwells take you up or down by floor." She uses her pen to point this way or that. With each new gesture there's another *click, click, click.* "When you reach a new floor, taking the hall on your right will keep you on that level." *Click.* "Choosing the hall on your left will take you to the next level on that floor." *Clickety click.* "Understand?"

Not really. If anything, I am more confused than when I first began. But I nod. Then I force myself to find the words to the question I really need answered. "Can you tell me, please, if there is a patient named Willow Reed here?"

The woman appears to search something in her WV. With a curt nod and click of her tongue she says, "Floor Nine. Level Two," she says. "Hall of Intense Allergies and Impossible Ailments."

If my exhale doesn't exclaim my relief, my attempt to hug her does. "Thank you . . ." I pull back and glance at her name badge. "Nurse Humpty."

"Now off you go." Stiff beneath my embrace, she acts like my hug might break her fragile frame. Once she's free of me, she brushes off my invisible germs. "And please, try not to lose any more time, Mary Ann."

A peek at my own name badge reveals my temporary Alias. Mary Ann it is, at least until I find Willow and get out of here. I salute the nurse and immediately wish I hadn't because of the funny look she gives me. Then she's gone, *click clacking* down the hall with her heels and *click clicking* her pen with each step.

Checking the floor plan, I see that this is Floor Five. I sprint for the stairwell and climb four flights, being sure to turn left when I exit so I can go up another level. I keep walking straight, rather than turning again, and find the nurse was right. As soon as I reach the end of level one, it vanishes from my view, and a new level appears. My senses tell me this is the exact same stairwell as before and that somehow I've gone in a circle, though I haven't turned at all.

What I see in my WV, however, tells me a different story.

Floor Nine. Level Two.

Bingo.

Now all that's left to do is to check the rooms. Like the hall of closets and empty spaces where Chess and I donned our coats, these doors have no knobs, and each one is decorated with a small, frosted window. I touch each door, inviting a knob to appear. Some greet my hand readily, allowing me to peer inside. Others are more stubborn, refusing to give me the entrance I need.

"Why can't you cooperate?" I say to one of the doors. "I need to find Willow."

The door on the opposite side of the hallway creaks open of its own accord. Was it listening to me? Or did a draft from the vents make it give in? Either way, it doesn't matter. Because the person inside is the only thing I care about.

I almost don't recognise her. The room she's being kept in is much like an infant's nursery. A rocking chair in one corner. A little teddy bear on a shelf. Lullaby music plays softly from some hidden speaker.

And there's Willow, cradled in a bassinet at the room's centre. No larger than a turnip, the toughest girl on our team looks to be fighting for her life with every tiny bone in her body. Her breathing is labored, her muscles soft. Yet despite this drastic sight, my heart soars. She's bigger than she was when I left her. Whatever treatment they're giving her must be working.

Right?

"Willow," I whisper. My fingers find her tiny foot beneath the crocheted blanket covering her. "Willow," I say again, this time a decibel louder.

Her eyes open. She blinks. Stirs. When her miniature eyes meet mine, tears brim. In hers, and in mine.

I feel a special kind of connection with her that we didn't share before. The Ace and the Two. Interchangeable and each as vital as the other.

"Ace?"

Is she surprised to see me? Angry I left her behind?

Then, with all the Willow she still has left in her tiny little body, she says, "Get me the blazes out of here. *Now.*"

At the panic in her voice, fear floods my veins, followed by urgency. I don't question her. Instead I pick her up and cradle her under one arm, doing my best to conceal her with the extra fabric of my coat.

"I don't know what's going on," Willow squeaks, "but this place is creep city. Like sitting in one long timeout forever with no end."

What did the nurse say? Forever is only as long as a second?

More fear. And the need to get back to the rest of our team sends a firestorm of adrenaline through me. Head held high, I march out into the hall as if I own the place.

"Where is everyone?" I ask under my breath.

"There's just one that I've ever seen," she says. "And she's not to be messed with. Calls herself The Ref."

"What about the staff? The doctors? The nurses?"

Willow shakes her little head. "I've been in that room for ages. Nurse Humpty a.k.a. The Ref is the only person who has ever come in or out. I'm too weak to walk. I thought I was going to die in there. She keeps giving me shots that burn like the dickens. I think she's stunting my regrowth."

Whatever Chess did or didn't tell me, I'm beginning to

regret ditching him. As for Nurse Humpty, if she's a bad egg, why would she tell me exactly where Willow was?

Something smells rotten. We have to get out of here.

Every step feels heavy. The closer I get to the stairwell, the farther away it seems. For whatever reason, this highly complicated building has zero lifts. I try to imagine one. Fail. The place is a labyrinth. My WV is no help. I think it into sleep mode, then adjust my glasses to focus my vision. Without the map of the floor plan obstructing my view, everything alters, suddenly becoming painfully clear.

No wonder the WV wasn't helping. It must have been hacked, because clearly it was putting blinders on me. Where there were no doors, now there are dozens. Where there were no lifts, a handful now wait to give us a ride. Abandoned halls transform, lined with hospital beds and doctors and nurses and visitors.

What in Wonderland is going on?

"Alice?" Willow tugs on the lapel of my coat.

"Put your WV to sleep, Will. Then tell me what you see."

She does as I ask, her bangle the size of a small ring with only one Fate light left. At that moment, she says a choice word or two, followed by, "Hackers. Now we have really got to go."

"I'm on it." Choosing the closest lift, I push the down button, and it lights up. When the doors open, I can't move. I let them slide closed in my face.

"What are you doing?" Willow's tone is frantic but an octave lower than it was moments before.

If I didn't know any better, I'd say she's grown a few centimetres since I rescued her.

"Chess," I tell her. "He was with me. I can't leave him."

"Fine." Willow crosses her little arms. "Do you know where he is?"

I think back through the steps I took to get to this floor. According to my actual vision of this Reality, we are on the fifth floor. So strange the WV was making me see something else. Just like—

"Oh my . . . *Willow*, this . . . I think this is part of the Trials."

"Come again?"

"It's something Chess once told me. In the Trials we are the cards. We're the ones being played. So what if not every Trial is one we know about? What if every move we make is all a part of it?"

"Makes sense," she replies slowly. "And it would explain a lot. The question is, what kind of game are we playing?"

I think back to the escape rooms of the Spade Trial. And the unknown that lies ahead in the Club Trial. The Diamond Trial felt never-ending.

Maybe because it never did.

"We never finished," I say, backing away from the lift. "We never made it back to the first stake in the course."

"You're saying we're still playing?"

I nod and swallow. "We must be. It's the only explanation."

"So, what? This was some sort of long timeout?" she asks. "Like the Diamond Trial was waiting for us to finish it?"

"Yes." I consider my sleeping WV bangle. "Which means it's you and me. If we can finish this, together, the rest of our team will be waiting for us on the other side." I look down at her. She feels considerably heavier in my arms. It's a good sign.

I know this will work. It has to.

Willow takes a deep breath. "Ready?" She prepares to wake her WV.

"Ready," I say. Together we turn our Wonder Vision back on.

"We're still in the hospital," Willow observes. "Does that mean we're still in timeout?"

"Maybe." I shrug, not sure where to go from here.

"How do we start the clock again? Do you remember how much time was left?"

Time. Clock. "Jack!"

His name is like a password. The space around us transforms.

"Five minutes, girls," Jack says in my ear, picking up right where we left off.

It feels like we've been apart from the others forever. In the Normal Reality, seven days passed. In the Wonderland Reality, it's only been one second.

The hospital—or holding place for the longest timeout in history—has vanished. We're back on the croquet course, dragon-flamingoes circling overhead. I'm small again, and Willow's height is slowly catching up to mine. A killer hedgehog barrels towards us. When I think it might run us over, Knave dives, serving as the barrier between us and the beast.

"Run!" he bellows. If there's such a thing as Beast Master, Knave is that and then some.

I don't think or question or attempt to reorient myself to these surroundings I was so ready to leave behind. I thought I'd failed when really I was prolonging the inevitable.

"Let me run," Willow says. "I think I can manage."

I don't hinder her. Even on her worst day I won't deny Willow is still more physically capable than I ever will be. She's half my height now, but her legs and heart are strong. She doesn't wait for me, beginning her sprint through the remaining wickets towards the finish line.

The course alters. I follow Willow just in time to catch a wicket before it moves too far left.

"Three minutes," Jack says in my ear.

Willow's faster than I expected. But we have to reach the final stake together, or it doesn't count. With every ounce of determination and energy and whatever else I have left in me, I dodge a hedgehog's hind legs and narrowly escape Knave's foot as I make a last-ditch effort to win this thing.

I'm centimetres from the end, but they stretch on for miles. Willow is waving me towards her, shouting something through cupped hands. When I reach her, we join hands and touch the starting stake together. We wrap ourselves around it, holding on for life and the fact we actually made it.

The course disappears.

Confetti falls.

A buzzer sounds.

Our clutch is broken apart, and Willow and I are separated as our cheering team lifts us onto their shoulders. Our eyes meet, and we nod at each other, then grin.

Raised above the other teams, I search for him. He's standing to one side, smiling in congratulations. But it doesn't reach his eyes. When he turns his back on me, I feel like a downright git.

Everything around us screams victory.

So why does it suddenly feel like we've lost?

DEFEAT

The tune of Jack and Madi's nonsensical victory song does little to brighten my sour mood.

> *"Will you, won't you, will you, won't you,*
> *   will you join the dance?*
> *Will you, won't you, will you, won't you,*
> *   will you join the dance?"*

It sounds like something from the in-between pages of *The Adventurer's Almanac*. I haven't had a chance to flip through it lately between training sessions and nearly shrinking into nothing.

My teammates—my Cards—have moved the coffee table and pushed the chaise and chairs against the walls in the common area of our girls' dormitory. A fire has been lit in the hearth. They dance in circles around one another, arms linked and voices raised.

Sophia and Willow relax beside the fire together, back-to-back. Sophia claps along with Jack and Madi's song, while

Willow leans against her friend, eyes closed, content to be home, her right size once more.

Even Knave joins in on the fun, tapping one knee as he sits and looks on. It's hard to tell, but I'd wager some of our team points that's a smile about to appear on his usually snide lips. My WV registers the thought, reminding me exactly where we stand among our competitors. We remain in the lead at 490 points, despite losing three of Willow's Fates, leaving her with only one before she's off the team.

I stare at my four pulsing hearts. All I can think is that it should have been me.

We've won the Diamond Trial, giving us a substantial, ninety-point lead ahead of the Clubs and a bonus clue. I should be dancing on the table tops right now. Celebrating with my friends. Willow is well. We're all alive. Anyone else would be toasting to the win.

Yet, here I am, sulking in the overstuffed armchair in the corner, keeping one eye and ear on the lift at all times. Charlotte has yet to make her appearance. I understand that she's our Trainer and probably has important business to attend to. But shouldn't she be here? Congratulating us or something? The bonus clue is another that doesn't seem like much benefit at all. If Charlotte were here, maybe she could help make sense of it.

Don't step on the mome raths.

The mome raths? Is that some sort of Wonderland creature? Why does it sound familiar? Combined with the original Club clue—*all ways are her ways*—it seems more like nonsense than anything.

What else is new?

I pull my knees up to my chest, tucking my feet underneath me and resting my chin on one fist. How is it possible to feel so alone in a room full of people?

Unbidden, my kiss with Chess enters my mind. I touch my

cold lips at the thought. I miss his warmth, though I wish I didn't. Chess claimed exhaustion and turned in early, though I know he left to give me space. Or maybe he's the one who needed to be away from me. After my accusations towards him earlier today, I wouldn't want to be around me either.

But something about Dinah is irking me. She only divulges information when it's convenient. Seems rather . . . well, *convenient,* if you ask me.

Which leaves me with countless doubts as to whom I can trust. Aside from Willow, my suspicions towards the others flourish. I watch each of them, wondering how Madi acts as if she did nothing to harm us. Peering at Knave, trying to understand why no one seems to suspect him or question what happened during the First Trial.

Am I the only one who sees a problem with the inconsistencies here?

Madi trips on the rug and collapses, taking Jack down with her.

I jerk upright.

But they start laughing hysterically. The sound is so infectious, Sophia, Willow, and Knave join in.

My knee-jerk tension dissipates, and I sink back into the chair.

"You're going to pay for that one," Jack says, shoving Madi playfully on the shoulder.

She crab-walks away from him and jumps to her feet, fists up and at the ready. "Is that a challenge?"

"Don't do it, Jack," Knave says, tossing a fistful of caramel corn at him. "She'll take you down."

Everyone laughs at the comment, but my mood darkens. Willow and I both know how true Knave's statement is. Is she as guarded with Madi as I am? Or has she somehow let it go?

I'm about to drop a snarky remark when the lift doors open. The moment I see it's Charlotte, I bolt from my chair, tripping over the dangling belt of my bathrobe as I move to greet her.

The horseplay stops. My teammates go still. They notice the same thing I've noticed.

The sealed green-and-black envelope in Charlotte's hands.

Another clue? Based on her worried expression, my guess is whatever's in that envelope is not meant to help us.

"Change of plans." Charlotte opens the envelope with all of us watching, perusing it quickly, her eyes jetting back and forth. Then, "Due to the time lapse during the Diamond Trial—and the second victory in a row for Team Heart, it would seem—the Clubs have decided to move up the date of their Trial on account of Rule Forty-Two."

I speak first. "What is it with this Rule Forty-Two business?"

"It's an idiom," Madi says, as if I should know this. "Not an actual rule."

"My mum used it with me all the time as a lad," Jack chimes in now. "It's a Wonder way of saying, 'Because I said so.'"

"Basically," Madi adds, "it's their Trial, so the Clubs can do what they want. Rule Forty-Two."

Well, that is unfair. "What date did they choose?" I ask Charlotte. I know the answer can't be good.

My sister eyes me through black rectangular frames. "Tomorrow."

Knave jumps to his feet, the fire in his eyes rivaling the one in the hearth. "But that gives us no time to recover from—"

"Exactly," Charlotte cuts him off. "We're well ahead of the other teams. They see our advantage and will do anything they can to thwart it."

"I don't blame them," Madi says. Whose team is she on, anyway?

"Neither do I." Charlotte hands the letter to me first.

We pass it around. It reaches Willow last. She stares at the words as if they will alter the longer she looks at them.

"Part of what makes the Wonderland Trials what they are," Charlotte says, "is the ability for them to change things at the drop of a hat. We have to be sharp. Ready for anything that comes our way. You all have had your fun." She motions to the boys. They take a moment to catch on before they join her by the lift. "I trust you two will wake Shire and fill him in. The celebration is over now. It's time to put our game faces on. We don't know what lies ahead. But we do know one thing."

We're all thinking it, but I'm the one to ask, "And what's that?"

"This will be the trickiest Trial by far. Get through this, and you're almost to the end. Get through this, and you might have a chance at winning."

Winning is subjective.

While the others are nervous and excited at the prospect of dominating another Trial, I'm dwelling on what's to come. On the possibility that we may not make it to the Fourth Trial or get the chance to save anyone at all.

I wish I could talk to Chess.

Morning ushers in hunger, but I don't eat any breakfast. Nothing sounds appetizing. Especially not the crumpets and orange marmalade Madi made for everyone.

"You really should have eaten," she says quietly as we gather our wits and wait on the kerb outside the palace.

"Not hungry," is all I say. I still wouldn't touch another creation of hers with a jousting pole.

When we board Champ, the other teams are already here. Despite the contrast in our jumpsuit colours, we all have one thing in common this morning as we hover along the streets of Wonderland—the Club Trial location is our shared destination.

Utter and complete silence.

Even Team Club doesn't seem pleased that they lost out on the extra practice and preparation that we were supposed to have over the next two weeks. I feel like I might explode from the nerves building inside of me. Nothing's been resolved with Madi or Chess. Charlotte appears to be avoiding me . . . again. Last night she gave me a very short, "We'll talk tomorrow, Alice," before heading off to bed. This morning, she left before the sun rose, leaving only a note on my nightstand.

See you on the other side of the finish line. No timeouts this round. Take your things with you this time, as a return to the palace is unlikely. Don't be afraid. I am always with you.

The note is inside the almanac in my rucksack on my lap, but right now it provides little consolation.

When we pull up at our destination, two very different sides of one lane greet us. One side houses Wonderland buildings like many we've passed over the course of the ride here. A bank with glittering gold columns. A pub called Drink Me. A museum that boasts Wonderland's rich history.

Rich history, indeed. Another lie of Scarlet's, no doubt.

The other side of the lane doesn't look like it belongs in this Reality. I let out a low whistle as I step off the hover bus, sling my rucksack over one shoulder, and plant both feet firmly on an overgrown, grassy kerb. I can barely make out Hyde Park under the Wonderland layer of leafless trees with branches that look like claws. In between them, mushrooms as tall as skyscrapers bow and bend, forming an arching canopy over a winding path.

My WV tells me our location before my attention lands on the sign.

Tulgey Wood.

I guess things really do come full circle. In the Normal Reality, this is where Chess left me behind. And here in Wonderland we enter together, on the same team but kingdoms apart.

The teams gather in clusters, walking up the path into the darkness since no one instructs us otherwise. The moment we find ourselves beneath the ominous awning of spotted fungi and tangled branches, the day seems to vanish, transforming into twilight with a faint full moon peeking through each tree's talons.

"Brillig," Jack comments as he sidles up beside me. "The Clubs really know how to set the tone."

"Brillig?" I ask. "What's that?"

"The time of day between sunset and dusk," he says matter-of-factly, but the underlying tone he carries lets on there's a hidden meaning as well. "It's said to be the time of day the Jabberwock wakes."

My nervous laugh is anything but reassuring.

Jack gives an exaggerated shiver but keeps his focus on the ground. "But it's only the Third Trial," he adds. "No Jabberwock here."

There's no doubt in my mind he's just as anxious about what's to come in the Heart Trial as the rest of us. I want to tell him about the Knight Society and what we're really hoping to accomplish. But I can't quite bring myself to spill the beans, so I ask, "Is the Tulgey Wood always like this?"

He kicks at air. His shoelace is untied, but he does nothing to fix it. "They use this space for the Trials each year." He looks skywards. "And every year it's completely different. My favourite was a couple seasons back, when the forest floor was a pool of lava, and the only way from beginning to end was through the tree tops."

My eyes go wide. Attempting to avoid being burned alive doesn't sound at all like a game. We walk on in silence. Jack seems to pick up that I'm avoiding Chess and Madi. He's not usually this quiet.

Now I feel all the more dimwitted. Jack has been nothing but kind and welcoming. I ought to try being a better mate. I ought to be honest. But . . . what if telling the truth puts him in more danger?

The air around us is damp, the sudden onslaught of night doing nothing to ward off the almost-summer humidity. The path splits four ways ahead, marked by arrows pointing in all directions as they climb up the tall pole they're nailed to. At the pole's base, beds of minuscule mushrooms in every shade imaginable grow. They look more like candy than an unappetizing, most likely poisonous species.

As we near the quadruple fork in the road, I adjust my glasses, waiting for my WV to offer direction. Any indication or instruction or notice the Trial has begun. A map. An announcement. A clue.

For the first time, it remains idle.

Maybe we don't get a signal in here.

"Looks like we have a traffic jam." Jack cranes his neck, attempting to see what the holdup is.

I search for the rest of our team. Sophia's chatting with a pair of Diamond girls, Willow looking rather bored by her side, since she's not much for small talk. I like that about her.

Chess is as elusive as ever.

And Madi . . . is talking to Mouse? The rude Club girl from my first day seemed to have it out for my fake best friend. To look at them now, you'd never know they were enemies. Mouse's shoulders shake from a chuckle as Madi talks animatedly with her hands.

A touch of jealousy turns my gut.

Once again, I feel utterly alone while surrounded by people.

Maybe that's my greatest fear—being alone. And perhaps that's my own fault. I turn to Jack. "Hey, Jack, listen. There's something I need to tell—"

A winged creature with black feathers and an orange beak swoops low over the crowd, *caw, caw, cawing* through the air. Too many shadows cling to wherever they may, rendering it impossible to tell if the thing is a bird, a bat, or another hybrid beast like the dragon-flamingoes.

I shudder at the thought of what else might be creeping behind the knots in the trees. Like the ones mentioned in our clue. The mome raths . . .

. . . outgrabe.

That's where I've heard the mome raths mentioned. In the Jabberwocky poem in *The Adventurer's Almanac*.

Something like claustrophobia wraps itself around me, and, after a moment, I find it difficult to breathe. The Jabberwock isn't supposed to appear until the Fourth and final Trial. But the connection between our bonus clue and the poem is too strong. I look at the signs pointing in every direction. If all ways are the queen's ways, what does it matter which path we take?

Separating myself, I step off the paved main path. It's immediately quieter here in the grass by myself. I inhale deeply, taking in the surroundings that don't seem to notice me one bit.

I smile. Is this really the first time our teams haven't been separated by tables or quarters? What a sight. Spades mixed in with Clubs. Diamonds chatting with Spades. A part of me wishes I'd gotten to know members of the other teams. It's a competition, but that doesn't mean we can't be mates, right? Add more Cards to our hand? Then again, if I can't trust members of my own team, can I trust my rivals?

Minutes pass. No one chooses a path.

I snatch the chance to try and make sense of our two clues. Withdrawing the almanac from my rucksack, I flip to the "Jabberwocky" poem. With each new stanza, my pulse quickens and my head spins.

   . . . *And, as in uffish thought he stood,*
    The Jabberwock, with eyes of flame,
   Came whiffling through the Tulgey Wood,
    And burbled as it came!

The Tulgey Wood? How can that be? The Jabberwock is not supposed to appear until the Fourth Trial.

I'm attempting to understand the connection when someone says, "I'm not going first. You go first."

A Club boy gives a frustrated shout. "We must have taken a wrong turn!"

"Are you daft?" asks a Spade girl. "There haven't been any turns. There are four paths and twice as many directions. I say we start over."

"What good will starting over do? Clearly we have to choose one of the four."

I don't happen to see who says that, but inside I'm pondering on their point.

In the Normal Reality, direction is a concrete, almost tangible thing. There's left, right, east, west, north, south, and so on.

I use my WV to zoom in on the signs. Perhaps whatever they say could clue us in. I thought maybe my poor eyesight was to blame for not being able to read them. On the contrary. Now I see the problem is that the signs don't say anything at all.

They're completely blank.

It doesn't matter. It appears we've been duped. What sort of Trial never begins?

A message pops up on my WV.

"Where are you?"

I stare at the words. What game is Chess playing?

Searching the various players, I spot him off to the south side.

He appears to be looking right at me.

I wave a hand.

He doesn't acknowledge it.

Another message flashes. *"This isn't funny, Ace. It's one thing to ignore me because you're angry. It's another to pretend you're lost or to go off on your own without telling anyone. We're in this together. Remember?"*

My gaze finds him again. Now he's weaving through the others—who are all still standing around waiting for the signs to sprout words. He turns one girl around by her shoulders, then frowns when he realises it's not me. I have to admit, her hair colour is similar to mine. But c'mon, Shire. She's far too tall to be my double.

I really shouldn't be laughing at him. He does look genuinely worried. Then again, I'm right here.

"Alice, I mean it. Show yourself, or I'm choosing a path to look for you."

Something about the urgency in his message says he's one hundred percent serious. Or maybe it's the way he tugs at the ends of his hair that draws me from the shadows.

Gingerly, I step back onto the main path.

The moment he sees me, his posture relaxes, and his breathing slows. The expression on his face says he wants to run towards me. But he controls himself, taking easy, controlled strides until we're closer than we've been in twenty-four hours.

Close enough to remember what it was like to be even closer than this.

"Why did you do that?"

"I needed a minute," I say. "What do you care?" The last part slips out before I can capture it. Too late to regret my defensiveness now. Besides, he's the one who told me to say what I mean.

"You know I care, Ace." His fingers graze my chin. His touch is a brush I can barely feel and yet feel completely. "And, despite all of my flaws, I think you care too." He smiles a sizable grin that reminds me of the first time we met. "With you, I don't care if I win. With you, I'd gladly find myself defeated every time."

I think he might give me my second kiss. And I think I

might forgive him and allow it. But a commotion in the crowd pulls us apart.

A gasp. A curse. A scream.

"What happened?" someone near the fork in the paths asks.

"Isn't it obvious?" a hushed voice replies. "She's stepped on a mome rath."

VICTORY

I wasn't allowed to get lost.

When I was little, Charlotte packed more anxiety than I knew how to carry. Wherever we ventured, she always held a firm grip on my hand or wrist. If I left her sight for a second, she'd spin around and call for me, panic saturating her tone.

"Where *were* you?" she'd scold, making me sometimes wish I really was lost.

Even now her note is near, reminding me that she's never too far.

I'm watching Team Club carry Mouse back up the path the way we came. She's whimpering, and her left shoe has a sizable gouge taken out.

So mome raths, whatever they are, bite. Good to know.

The moment the Clubs are out of sight, a single, stricken word appears on the uppermost sign.

~~Clubs~~.

"You think they've been disqualified?" Chess asks. Our

arms hang at our sides, but his little finger is linked with mine. "From their own Trial?"

"It looks that way. Or maybe they have to start over? I wonder how many Fates they'll lose for this one."

A strange thing occurs then. So quick and so faint, I'm sure I must be seeing things.

There it is again. I blink, trying to clear away the blur. I'm overtired. Overwhelmed. Perhaps my astigmatism is finally breaking through the rose-coloured WV, so to speak.

But no. There. *That.* I'm sure I saw it this time. We're standing near the path's edge, close to the place where the shadows hid me moments ago.

Chess shifts. His entire left arm disappears.

My half gasp, half hiccup comes out sounding like a squeak.

"Watch it, Ace," Chess says. "You don't want to invite more wrath from the mome raths, if you know what I mean." He gestures towards the entrance.

The Clubs are long gone. If the Clubs had our bonus clue, could this have been avoided?

"What exactly is a mome rath?"

Chess shrugs. "Don't know. Never seen one. Neither has anyone else, as far as I know. But their bites are nasty things. Not deadly, but nasty." His voice is sober. "I don't envy Mouse. She'll spend the next few days in excruciating pain until the venom's out of her system."

I frown. The image of the girl who was so unkind upon my arrival into this Reality haunts me. Someone once said what goes around comes around. But I wouldn't wish the pain Chess describes on my worst enemy.

I glance at Madi. Is she my worst enemy or my childhood best friend? Perhaps she is both. Or is there something worse waiting for us in the woods? Either way . . . "I'll be right back," I tell Chess.

Her lavender hair is a light in the crowd. We haven't spoken two words to one another in over a week. So it's awkward when I clear my throat and tap her on the shoulder.

When she faces me, surprise widens her eyes.

"Hey," Madi says, voice guarded.

"Hey," I reply. I take a breath. "You alright?"

Her expression mostly relaxes, but the lines around her mouth remain tight. "A little stunned, to be honest. Seeing Mouse like that?" She shakes her head. "It's sobering. This stuff is real."

I nod, because I don't know what to say. And also because I do. I do know what's real, and if I can't tell Madi, who can I tell?

"Listen," Madi says suddenly. "About the Diamond Trial. I cross my heart, I never intended for Willow to get hurt. I thought if I could make it so you didn't continue in the Trials, you'd be better off. Safe. It was meant to be temporary." Her words sprint and stammer, but in that moment, our misunderstanding dissolves.

"I believe you," I tell her just as she says, "I told Charlotte it wouldn't work."

"Wait." I put my hand up. "What did you say?"

"I told Charlotte it wouldn't work," Madi repeats. "She assured me if we could keep you from reaching the Fourth Trial, then you'd be safe. She promised."

You were supposed to keep her safe . . . you promised.

"Charlotte." My mind whirls. I think back to every encounter I've had with her since Clash of the Cards.

It was Charlotte who left me the clues in the almanac.

Charlotte who has been avoiding me.

Charlotte who didn't want me to ever find out Wonderland existed. Or about the Knight Society. Or that I am the daughter of Catherine R. Pillar.

"Madi." I place my hand on her arm. "What did you see in the mirror? During the First Trial?"

She almost looks ashamed. I expect her to say she saw Stark and that never finding him again is what she fears most.

But she doesn't. With tears in her eyes she says, "You, Alice. My greatest fear is and has always been losing my best friend. Because I lived it. And I don't want to go through that again."

Her words shock my core. Because that's exactly what Charlotte is afraid of too—of losing me. Except Madi hasn't let her fear rule her, not in the same way.

"I love my brother," Madi goes on. "But Stark can take care of himself." When I knit my brow, she swipes at her tears and rushes on. "I saw you trying to hide the article. I know I should have told you, but I didn't want you trying to help me. I didn't want you risking everything to save him. I knew if I told you . . . you would."

I throw my arms around her. Sorry doesn't begin to cover what I'm feeling. It shouldn't have been so easy to doubt her. "I'm a wretched friend," I say.

"So am I," Madi replies. We're a mess hugging each other. Both cry-laughing. Probably inviting stares from the other players. But who cares?

Nothing's going to separate us this time.

When we pull apart, newfound resolve takes hold. I grab her hand. "Let's go."

"Where?" she says, stumbling after me.

"None of those paths are the right ones." I wave towards the ridiculous sign. "Any of those ways will lead us astray." Like Queen Scarlet. The clue was right—all ways in the Trials are her ways. But her way is not the right one. Maybe that's what Stark and Dan and the other missing players discovered. Perhaps they too found a different path to follow.

We find the others and pull them away from the crowd. Once we're together, standing with Chess at the edge of the pavement, I smile. "Remember what you said?"

"I've told you many things, Ace," Chess says. "All of which I'm quite sure are brilliant."

"Not you," I tell him. "Madi. You said on a podcast once that you have to be willing to step off the obvious path."

"But this isn't Black Hearts," Madi counters. "We already played that in the last Trial."

"True. But the concept applies to more than one game." I think about the games in *The Adventurer's Almanac*.

"Oh yeah, Ace?" Chess looks at me. "And what game is that?"

With a sly smile I reply, "Labyrinth."

Taking the road less travelled has its benefits.

It also has its curses.

The other teams don't seem to notice as we walk past them, remaining unseen as long as we stay off the paved way. The deeper we tread into the Tulgey Wood, the more uncertainty grips me. Weeping trees with their depressed branches hang low over us. Any light we had on the main path dims. Soon the other teams are no longer in sight, and I begin to question whether I've led my entire team astray.

In the corner of my WV, four hearts beat, reminding me there's more at stake than winning or losing.

"Stop." I halt and pivot, facing my team. "If we're going to do this, we need to level the playing field." I pull up Willow's profile. When I choose the option I want from a menu, a little bubble appears.

Are you sure you want to transfer two Fates to Willow Reed?

I select "Yes," and immediately two of my pulsing hearts vanish, both from my WV and my bangle, leaving me with just a pair.

"I can't accept these." Willow steps forwards, shaking her

head. Her bangle lights up, giving her three hearts in total. "The Ace is more important than—"

I cut her off. "You are the Ace now." My next words are directed towards Chess. "I hope you don't mind sharing your position."

"You earned Team Queen." He bows. "And it is my honor to be the humble King by your side."

"There's only one King," I reply without thinking. But it is this that has me releasing a long exhale. It's time.

Chess nods his encouragement. I don't know if Charlotte would approve, and I don't care. My teammates. My Cards. My friends. They have a right to know.

So I tell them. I tell them about the Knight Society and the Ivory King and the legend of the King and his bride. I share Dinah's theory regarding a third Reality, though I'm still not sure if she can be trusted. I talk about Dan and Kit and Stark.

"So," Knave says, when I'm done, "you're asking us to follow you? Even though we have no idea what we're really facing? Even if we could die or never return or who knows what else?"

"No," I say, offering him a small smile. Hoping that will be enough. "I am asking you to believe in what's real. And to go after it. To step off the obvious path."

Knave frowns but doesn't protest or retreat either. He's in.

And, it would appear, we all are.

When no one runs or speaks, I nod a silent thank-you to each of them in turn. And then I see it. The start of a new path. Just past Chess and to the right. Where grass transitions into pavement that wasn't there a moment ago.

"Well, I'll be." Excitement pushes me to investigate.

"What?" Jack asks.

"Right there, don't you see it?"

"See what?" Sophia is looking all around.

"The path," I point ahead. "It's right there."

"Ace," Chess says. "We stepped off the path, remember?"

Strange. Why am I the only one who can see it?

"There it is!" Madi declares. "I see a new path."

I start to exhale my relief at her words. Except she's moving away from us, walking deeper into the darkness.

She's going the wrong way.

"Where are you going?" Willow calls after her. "The new path is clearly over here." She, too, separates from us, moving in the exact opposite direction of Madi.

This can't be happening. "Stop." My voice echoes through the trees, returning to me in ominous *caws* from the winged creatures above. "This is a labyrinth, remember? It's trying to divide us. It's showing us different ways on purpose."

"But," Knave demands, "which way is the right one?"

There's no way of knowing. "We have to pick one," I say uncertainly.

"You choose," Chess urges. "You're Queen, after all."

It doesn't seem fair to make such an important decision on my own. I have no idea what paths the others are seeing, but it all may be part of the answer. Are the paths the same? Different? I'll have to trust them and find out.

"Madi, what do you see?"

"The path is bright pink. There's music. Laughter, like a party waits at the end." She meanders towards it, as if whatever she hears and sees is drawing her in. Inviting her to play.

"And Jack?"

"Bricks," he says. "They zigzag along a low stone wall. It looks narrow. And dark."

Each player tells me what they see, one after the other. From Chess's striped road to Sophia's flowered hedges, it's almost as if each path was designed with the individual in mind. Each one is the obvious way we'd take. A path we're drawn to.

The one I see is less elaborate. The pavement is cracked

and reminds me of a road back in Oxford. The one that leads me home.

"I think," I realise aloud, "I think we have to split up." It's the opposite of what I thought before. That we needed to stay together. But maybe this *is* our way of staying together. And we have to trust that these paths will all lead us home—and back to one another.

Chess takes my hand and kisses it. "See you soon, then." He flashes a grin as he meets my eyes.

I nod. Let my hand slowly drift to my side. I'm not ready to say goodbye. "See you soon," I manage.

Our team of seven stands apart, scattered in a sort-of circle, each at the helm of a path none of the others can see.

"To find the Ivory King," I say.

"And the real Wonderland," Sophia and Willow say together.

"And Kit," Chess adds.

"And Stark," Madi chimes in.

"For answers." Knave flexes his hands, then clenches his fists. His eyes flash towards Madi for a split second, then he's stomping off into the darkness.

"For truth." It's Jack who has the final word. Then he and everyone, aside from me and Chess, begin their journeys.

"Alright, Ace?"

I glance between Chess and the path before me. "I don't know," is my honest reply.

"None of us knows," he says simply.

"I feel like I'm someone else lately." I take one step towards him, then two. The closer I get, the less clear my path becomes. "The Trials were supposed to be fun. Being Wonder was supposed to be fun. Now I don't know who or what I am."

"I'm not all there myself." He grins a sad sort of incomplete smile. "But it is when we are not ourselves that believing in the impossible—in the unseen—becomes most vital. We must believe in something beyond you or I."

I expect him to move away from his path as well, and perhaps embrace me in one last goodbye. But he doesn't. Chess steps backwards, retreating into the shadows. The scarce light hits his face just right, so only his smile and eyes are visible.

It takes every bit of courage in me to pivot on my heel and take the path laid out for me alone. The moment I step onto it and begin my trek, what's behind me disappears from view. Chess. The dark trees and overgrown grass. Any sense that I was in the Tulgey Wood has evaporated, replaced with walls of hedges on all sides. I was right.

This is a labyrinth.

With each step around another corner, a new extension of the path appears. Turning back isn't an option. Even if I wanted to, the hedges move, closing what came before off from what lies ahead. The maze has suddenly become my guide. I'm careful where I tread, afraid that the wrong move could earn me a nasty mome rath bite.

But though I encounter strange sights here and there—a stork wearing glasses or a violin-shaped tree—I get the feeling I'm being watched more than anything. And the further I walk, the more the hedge walls feel as if they're closing in. Like in my nightmare, I war against them, though here they do not budge.

There are no crossroads. No decisions to be made. When the path shifts, the hedges guide me around another corner. It's clearly a labyrinth, yet I have no difficulty in finding my way. In fact, this is almost too easy. As if I've stumbled upon a back door or shortcut rather than what ought to be a network of confusion.

Just when I think the path will never cease, I turn another corner and stop abruptly at a dead end where a wide tree trunk blocks my way completely.

Now what? I attempt to turn back but am once again forced to stay precisely where I am. The hedges have formed a small circle around me and the tree, leaving me with no choice and nowhere to go.

Unless . . .

Do you suppose . . . ?

What if the tree is the door?

If you want to get out, you must first go in.

I place my palm against the tree trunk. In a blink, the trunk hollows. A window appears—or no, not a window, a looking glass, like the last one in the Hall of Mirrors. On the other side I see Wonderland, but it's dark and covered in shadows. A dream transformed into a nightmare. I'm startled when I notice a girl walking towards me. When she reaches her side of the looking glass, she frowns.

I mirror her expression. That girl . . . she's Charlotte. When she was my age. She's alone and looking more like Queen Scarlet than ever.

When she promised she'd be waiting for me on the other side, I didn't know she meant this. What's happened to her? And why is she walking away? Is she leaving me behind once again to figure things out on my own?

I tug on the chain around my neck, pulling out the locket watch that's been hiding beneath my jumpsuit. The tick of the secondhand steadies my pulse.

Tick, tock, tick.

Bom, bom, bom.

I feel like I might suffocate. I'm not ready for this.

This is truly the cruelest game of all. There's no other way. And so, I step through. Into the glass. And the nightmare that waits beyond.

There will be no time to prepare. No clues or training sessions.

My greatest fear has manifested.

The Fourth and final Trial has begun.

CHESS

She's gone.

Just like Kit.

And there is nothing I could do to stop it, prevent it, or otherwise reverse what would inevitably occur.

I'd kick myself if I thought it would help. Or at the very least, follow her down whatever path she ventured upon. But there is no use in attempting to return to what was. There is only now.

And now I must prepare to battle my own fears. To sacrifice my Fates, if I must.

To find Kit. And Ace.

"Alice," I breathe when I do see her.

She's on the other side of the looking glass.

Where the Jabberwock awaits.

AUTHOR'S NOTE

"I give myself very good advice, but I very seldom follow it."

Of all the sayings I could have selected as my senior yearbook quote, this is how I chose to be remembered. I thought it was rather clever and fitting at the time, since several people in my class referred to me as "Disney Girl." While my fellow classmates dreamed of college to pursue this career or that one, I chose a university close to Disneyland so I could work at the "Happiest Place on Earth" and live out my favourite stories.

I went on to "hang out" with real-life Disney characters. Eventually, the Disney College Program led me to Walt Disney World, where my job training involved learning to speak in a British accent and memorising lines such as, "If I had a world of my own, everything would be nonsense . . ."

There was a time I lamented ever leaving that job and world behind. Those were some of the most fun and memorable days of my life. But, as I've grown older (perhaps wiser), I've realised one thing remains true—"It's no use going back to yesterday, because I was a different person then."

This book is a nod to my past. It is my love letter to *Alice* and fairy tales and children's literature and games. But, most importantly, it is a "thank-you," of sorts, for the present I am blessed to live in.

This story is for my family, who loves games just as much as I do.

It's for anyone who believes in the impossible or unseen.

It's for you if you're searching for what's real. I'll let you in on a secret—the King is real, friend. The true Wonderland awaits. All you have to do is believe.

Cheers!

Sincerely,

Sara Ella
Hebrews 11:1

ACKNOWLEDGMENTS

With every new book that somehow manages to get published, I'm reminded of just how many hands and hearts it takes to turn my ideas into Reality. My name on the cover is only a sliver of truth. I may be the author, but the ones behind the scenes are the real MVPs. It is to you I raise my teacup!

To the three fathers in my life to whom this book is dedicated:

First, Dad—we don't share blood, but you raised me as your own. You and Mom taught me to have faith in what I couldn't see. Thank you for believing in me along every step of my winding path.

Next, for my birth father Greg—you will never read this, but I wanted to acknowledge you just the same. Thank you for loving me from a distance. I only wish I'd understood what your silence meant sooner.

Third (but really first), for my Father in Heaven—somehow, despite my constant mistakes and shortcomings, you show me grace upon grace. Thank you for allowing me to write another book. Soli Deo gloria.

To my husband, Caiden—you are the real-life Chess Shire. You make me laugh, even when I don't want to. Without your support, this book would never have been finished. Thank you for reminding me that I don't always have to be so darn serious.

For my children, N, M, and J—I love you, and I am so proud to have you on my team. Thank you for stepping in, stepping up, and being the best kids any mom could ask for. Thank you for singing, laughing, playing pretend, annnndddd . . . kazoo! You are my favourites, LOL. :D

To my family—Mama Jodi, Aunt Terri, Brooke Larson, Staci Talbert, Brunkes, Carringtons, Fletchers, Blasers, and the rest I haven't named—you are all constant reminders that family goes beyond shared genes. Thank you for accepting me and loving me like your own.

To Steve and Lisa Laube—you both believed in this story more than I did. Thank you for giving me the opportunity to join the Enclave family and take a swing at this classic tale.

To Nadine Brandes—you are the Madi Hatter to my Alice. I'd probably never get past chapter one of any novel without your encouragement. Thank you for being my best friend, sister, and for sticking around through every insecurity. I love you to the moon!

To Mary Weber—you have remained a constant in the storm since my crazy notion to publish a book took flight. Thank you for being a sounding board, mentor, and friend.

To Ashley Townsend—everyone needs an Ashley in their life, just sayin'. I'm so glad you're mine and that my kids get to call you Auntie. Thank you for being my sister!

To Carolyn Schanta and Janalyn Owens—miles never seem to matter with you two. Thank you for staying true, supportive, and loving friends, no matter the distance between us.

To Janelle Amundsen, fellow Hufflepuff and fierce friend—thank you for our monthly writing sessions and for teaching me to play chess. Without you, I never would have had my epiphany about the Ivory King.

To Erin McFarland—thank you for my magical headshots

but, more importantly, for becoming the friend I didn't know I was missing.

To the Phoenix Panera Ladies—Lindsay, Erin, Liz, Sarah, Tina, Ruth, Rhia (Emily), Jen, Breana, and Tari—thank you for keeping me sane and lamenting with me over all my writerly woes.

To Kirk DouPonce—wow! The cover is beyond what I ever imagined. I only hope this story lives up to your phenomenal artwork. Thank you!

To Hanna Sandvig—this map! It's my favourite yet! Thank you for helping me bring Alice's world to life.

To the Enclave team—Trissina, Jordan, Jamie, and the rest of you I haven't had the pleasure of encountering yet—your work behind the scenes makes my job so much easier. Many thanks for your invisible efforts and stealth support.

To Lindsay Franklin—your great attention to detail while editing this book brought happy tears to my eyes. Thank you for helping me keep this story as authentically British as possible, and for making me smile all the way to the very last Oxford comma.

To Megan Gerig and Katie S. Williams, proofreaders to perfection! I couldn't let this book go to print without thanking you both with a pool full of happy tears for finding those last-minute mistakes and inconsistencies. You make my job so much less stressful. For that, I salute you!

To my street team, influencers, and Bookish Belles—if I try to name any or all of you, I will inevitably leave someone out. That's how blessed I am! Your names would fill pages upon pages. Thank you!

To the authors who inspire me—once again, you are too plentiful to list by name. Thank you for crafting stories that make me want to be a better writer.

To the winners of my November 2019 #saraellamermaid challenge—I'll bet you thought I forgot about you! Thank you for your support and participation, Melanie DeJong (@avidreader19), Jessica McCarty (@jessicamccartyauthor), and Abigail McKenna (@thepurplegiraffereads)! You ladies are awesome!

To Paul J. Hale of the Cinema Story Origins Podcast—keep those podcasts coming! You're my first stop along the long road of fairy tale research. Thank you for doing the grunt work for me, even though you have no idea who I am.

To the crew at Amped Coffee—Dani, Sara, Keith, and everyone else I haven't named but who provides me with the best lattes and scones in town—thank you for keeping me fuelled and for all the flavours Starbucks doesn't have.

To my readers—with every new book, you bless my socks off. I'll never be famous, but I'm okay with that. I have the best readers around. Thank you for continuing to give my stories a chance.

GLOSSARY

BRITISH TERMS/PHRASES

Advert—Advertisement or commercial

Alright—Slang greeting, often used as a way to say "hello"

Budge up—Asking someone to move down or make room for another

Bloke—Slang for boy, guy, fellow, etc.

Brolly—Umbrella

Bugger off—Go away

Dosser—Homeless person

Fascinator—A fashion hat or headpiece, often worn by royals, and usually decorated with flowers or other embellishments; Blanche's favourite accessory

Fiver—Five-pound note (currency)

Frock—Dress

Git—Jerk

Handbag—Purse

Iffy—Slang word meaning not very good

Knackered—Tired

Lift—Elevator

Mobile—Cell phone

Notes—Paper money/currency

Not my cup of tea—Not my preference

Off your trolley–Drunk
Plait–Braid
Pullover–Hooded sweatshirt or "hoodie"
Quid–Slang term for money, interchangeable with pounds (i.e. fifty pounds/fifty quid)
Serviette–Table napkin
Settee–Sofa
Tenner–Ten-pound note (currency)

BRITISH VS. AMERICAN SPELLINGS
Apologise/Apologize
Backwards/Backward
Behaviour/Behavior
Centre/Center
Colour/Color
Cosy/Cozy
Favourite/Favorite
Fibre/Fiber
Grey/Gray
Kerb/Curb
Metre/Meter
Neighbour/Neighbor
Pyjamas/Pajamas
Recognise/Recognize
Rumour/Rumor
Towards/Toward
Travelling/Traveling

TERMS OF THE CURIOUS REALITIES
Brillig–the time between sunset and dusk when the Jabberwock appears
Burble–A murmuring noise
Callooh callay–An exclamation of joy or excitement
Cards–Friends/mates linked in Wonder Vision

Fates–The four lives/chances each player has in the Trials, coinciding with four lit team symbols (Spades, Clubs, Hearts, Diamonds) on one's WV bangle.

Frabjous–A combination of fabulous and joyous

Golden petals–Wonder Vision money/currency allotted to players

Lost–Those living in the Divided Kingdom with no papers, no job, no home, and no family

Mastery–A special skillset a Wonder player has and uses in the Trials

Mome raths–No one quite knows what a mome rath is. We do know that they live in the Tulgey Wood and bite if you step on them, but it's nearly impossible not to step on one since we don't know what they look like. How unfair is that?

Outgrabe–To emit a strange noise

Registered–A Wonder living in the Normal Reality who has been branded and chipped

Slithy–A combination of "slimy" and "lithe"

Suits/Quarters/Houses–**Suits** are the four symbols representing the four quarters/houses of Wonderland. The **quarters** divide Wonderland's geography by suit, and the **houses** are made up of quarter heads, such as the Minister of Spades or Duchess of Diamonds, and their families.

Toves–Badger-like creatures

Unregistered–Wonders living undercover in the Normal Reality

Vorpal–Sharp or deadly

Wildflower–A "wild card" Wonder raised in the Normal Reality who is invited to play in the Trials

Wonder-born–Raised to know, see, and believe in Wonderland from birth

Wonderground–The underground of the Normal Reality where Wonders hide and mingle with the Normals who don't mind their company

Wonder Gene—The anomaly in some DNA discovered by renowned genome researcher Catherine R. Pillar.

Wonder-less/Unders/Normals—All terms referring to those born without the Wonder Gene

Jabberwock(y)—The monster described by Lewis Carroll as having "jaws that bite and claws that catch." Though believed to be a dragon beast of some sort, it takes on many forms depending of what you fear most.

Wonder Vision (WV)—Invented by Catherine R. Pillar, this unique bit of Wonder tech worn as a bangle on the wrist was originally designed to enhance the Wonderland experience. It is used in the Trials as a way to gather and keep track of data on players/teams.

WONDERLAND TEA BLENDS

Dwindler's Draught—A unique blend of lavender and black currant causing one to shrink.

Flourisher's Fate—Lemongrass, ginger, and honey made from sunflower pollen. Potent stuff. Serves as an antidote for most other blends.

Beast's Blend—A mixture of cinnamon, cloves, and bergamot. Turns Wonders into animals. Every Wonder reacts differently.

Focus Fix—Yerba mate and peppermint. Wakes the brain and sets all nerves to rest.

Rainbow Regimen—Rose petals and cardamom. Meant to cause a frabjous effect of colour-changing and joy.

Serenity's Slumber—Potent mixture of chamomile, valerian root, and passionflower. Causes a deep sleep.

Tranquil-i-Tea—Madi Hatter's own blend of lavender and chamomile. Just enough to calm the nerves.

TEAMS

Team Colours
- ♥ **Hearts**—red and black
- ♠ **Spades**—white and black
- ♣ **Clubs**—green and black
- ♦ **Diamonds**—silver and black

Team Positions

Ace—Most important player; as long as the Ace is still standing at the end of each Trial, the team gets an automatic one hundred points added to their score (Alice)

King or Queen—Team captain; usually the most experienced player who has competed in the Trials previously (Chess)

Jack—Player with the highest IQ; skilled at solving riddles/puzzles/codes (Jack)

Ten—The most physically capable team member (Knave)

Nine—Support system player; can play any position aside from Ace; fills in when other teammates are down (Madi)

Four—Most creative team member; solves problems and thinks outside of the box (Sophia)

Two—Lowest position and often written off as unimportant, but the Two can also step in as an Ace if needed (Willow)

ABOUT THE AUTHOR

Once upon a time, **Sara Ella** dreamed she would marry a prince and live in a castle. Now she spends her days homeschooling her three Jedi in training, braving the Arizona summers, and reminding her superhero husband that it's almost Christmas (even if it's only January). When she's not writing, Sara might be found behind her camera lens or planning her next adventure in the great wide somewhere. She is a Hufflepuff who finds joy in the simplicity of sipping a lavender white mocha and singing Disney tunes in the car. Sara is the author of the Unblemished trilogy and *Coral*, a reimagining of *The Little Mermaid* that focuses on mental health. Her latest journey into the world of *Alice's Adventures in Wonderland* feels like coming full circle after her time spent chasing a white rabbit around Walt Disney World. Sara loves fairy tales and Jesus, and she believes "Happily Ever After is Never Far Away." Connect with her online at SaraElla.com or find her on Instagram at @saraellawrites.